The Rise of Genesis
An Ash Lawson Novel

M.R. Merrick

For Val,

When I became rooted, you were wings.

When I thought I'd fall, you taught me to fly.

And when it stormed, you showed me the beauty of rain.

Thank you for believing I could. You were right.

ACKNOWLEDGMENTS

To me there are many reasons a story is born: the urge to write, a fictional voice that refuses to be silenced, the magic of ideas coming together into something unexpected and beautiful with nothing but words. But mostly it's born from a dream, coupled with determination, hard work, love, and support.

Thank you to my wife for enduring the ups and downs this novel—and the others before it—have brought with them. Thank you for reading it repeatedly and helping me break down the self-built walls that held it back. Thank you for being a voice of reason when all I could speak was doubt. Your love and support while I've pursued this crazy and outlandish dream are beyond what a person could ask of anyone, yet you give it freely. You are a rose among thorns, and the sun that allows my stories to bloom.

Val, you are the reason this story exists. You taught—as you always do—that perseverance is key. Sometimes it's all you need. You showed me that even when I didn't believe in myself, I had people around me who did, and they believed enough for me. Thank you for your encouragement all these years. My dream grows each day because of your friendship and support, and I'm so much further along because of it. You are not just a friend or an associate, but a part of my life and I'm blessed to have you.

To Lindsay, thank you for helping keep me up when I was down. When I doubted myself, you were there to set me straight. When I needed a second set of eyes or advice, you never hesitated, always being honest and reassuring. You've been with me since shortly after my first book and I have never stopped appreciating what you bring to the table.

Thank you to Jason for always offering your expertise and opinions. Thank you for being kind yet critical when that's exactly what my stories needed. You bring new viewpoints and ideas into the picture that I could have never seen on my own, and you force me to think out of the box. You help me advance as a writer with every story I tell, and I'm grateful both for your friendship and support over the years.

Thank you, Tim for dedicating your time and effort to me when I needed it. I can always count on you to be another set of eyes for me, and you never let me down. Your support and encouragement have always been important to me, and I'm grateful to have them.

Rachel, you are the reason my books get a face. After all the words are on the page, your art allows my story to come to life in a new facet of creation. Your talent puts a dusting of magic on something close to my heart. I treasure your work and professionalism, and thank you for designing such incredible covers. On a separate note, your advice and encouragement give my stories a much-needed edge. Your expertise and opinion are always appreciated, and I'm grateful you share your time and knowledge with me.

Hollie, you polish my stories into something I could never manage on my own. Working with you, I take on a new appreciation of language and structure. You enhance my ability as a writer, and with every novel I become stronger at my chosen form. Thank you for your dedication and hard work. My stories are always the better for it.

To you the reader, whether this is your first story with me or the fifth, thank you. Thank you for taking a chance on me. Thank you for choosing the written word for your next adventure, and more so, thank you for choosing mine. This story is a collaboration of time and effort over two years. It has my smiles, my tears, my screams of pain, and my cries of joy. It's a piece of my heart and soul scrawled on paper and in digital ink. But it doesn't mean anything without you. Your time and attention are gifts to my story that I will do my best not to squander. The truth is, it's your imagination that brings this story to life, not mine, so thank you for letting me borrow it. *The Rise of Genesis* is an adventure for both you and for me, and I am thrilled that we get to take it together.

THE RISE OF GENESIS

CHAPTER 1

My stomach twisted, anxiety clinging to me like a wet sheet. I held the sheathed dagger along my back and let a deep breath fill me with the scent of salt water. I hoped one or the other would help calm my nerves. They didn't. Water splashed around the dock posts and old tires squeaked as the ship rubbed against them. Whitecaps peaked and settled, leaving the water darker than the sky. A line of people walked along the dock and up the ramp to board the ship. Excitement should have decorated each of their faces, instead they looked tense. This was the first day of the rest of their lives—we were all eager to get on with it.

With bags draped over their shoulders and squeaky suitcases rolling behind them, they offered uneasy smiles. These were the last steps they'd take on American soil. Soon they'd be free from the persecution our kind faced here. A woman, Tara, dropped the handle of her suitcase and it smacked the rotting boards of the dock. She fumbled trying to pick it up. Samantha, her four-year-old daughter, stood idle beside her, utterly confused by the unfolding events. Her blue eyes gleamed in the moonlight, but in the sun I'd seen them shimmer with an emerald green that could brighten the world. She looked scared. Tara covered her embarrassment with trembling fingers, ignoring the pawing hands of Samantha, who wondered what was wrong. She never liked Samantha to see her upset.

"Hey, it's okay. I've got it," I whispered, propping up her suitcase. A glossy film filled Tara's eyes and she turned away as Samantha's petite hand touched her shoulder.

"One second, sweetie." She cleared her throat and wiped her eyes.

Samantha looked sad and confused.

I grabbed another boy out of the line, Jasper, seven years old with shaggy hair and a smile that couldn't be stripped off his face. A wooden spaceship stuck half out of his pocket. He'd told me once it was piloted by Braven Guardlink, sent here from another world to save his family and destroy ATOM. When he learned I had found a spot for them on the boat, he told me I was like Braven Guardlink, only I didn't need a spaceship to fly.

"Hey, buddy, can you take Samantha on board and keep an eye on her for me?"

"For you, Ash, of course!" He said it with more enthusiasm than the three hundred others boarding the ship. "Come on!" He offered the young girl his hand and she hesitated. He pulled out the spaceship from his pocket and extended it to her. "Do you want me to show you how Braven Guardlink saves the galaxy?"

Samantha looked to her mother for approval and smiled when it was granted.

"Follow me!" Jasper made a whirling noise with the weathered toy. "I'll show you how he defeated the Toadmen of planet Blaxbar!"

Samantha giggled and took Jasper's hand. The pair ran up the ramp and jumped on board. The innocent laughter that followed filled the tense and eerie sky.

A tear trickled from Tara's eye. "I don't know if I can do this."

"I know you can."

I took her hand and helped her to her feet. Her knees wobbled and delicate hands trembled against my touch. She pulled herself into my chest and wrapped her arms around me. She felt thin and tremors ran through her entire body. I squeezed her tight. I hadn't spent five months putting this together to let anyone back out now. They deserved this, she deserved this, and kids like Samantha and Jasper deserved this.

"I'm so scared," she whispered through sullen breaths. "What if they find me? They already took my husband, I can't lose her too. Not Sammy!" She buried her face in my chest and gripped my back with sharp fingernails. The air escaped my lungs. She was a petite woman, but for a moment she seemed to forget how strong she could be, especially for a harpy. She pulled away and shook her head. "I can't, Ash. I can't do this. Not without him. I can't do this alone."

A strand of hair clung to the streaks of tears on her face. I pulled it away and tucked it behind her ears. "Then we'll do it together."

I picked up her duffle bag and pulled her suitcase behind me. She weaved her arm through mine and although still apprehensive, she nodded. We walked up the ramp together and found Samantha on a crate, legs dangling over the edge. Jasper's spaceship zoomed all around her, complete with sound effects. His face was animated as he weaved a tale of heroes and the monsters they defeated. Samantha's laughter was pure, unscathed by the realities of life. A gift that didn't last long in this world. It brought a smile to her mother's face. Tara ran her hand down my arm and patted my hand.

"Thank you, Ash Lawson. You are a savior."

"I appreciate that, but I'm just a guy trying to do what's right."

"The world needs more of that." Without a goodbye she scooped Samantha into her arms and followed the line of people below deck. Jasper's thick curls bounced toward me and I ruffled them before he ran off.

An hour passed and the boat was almost loaded with three hundred and five people. We were missing two. I ran down the dock to hurry along the stragglers, but the long aisle of wood was barren.

The captain shouted from the side of the ship. Time to go. I demanded he wait, and after a brief argument I threatened to withhold the other half of his payment. He offered a begrudging frown and permitted five more minutes.

I ran down the dock as a cab squealed around the corner, swerving to avoid a steel container and jerking to a stop. An old man named Harry threw open the back door, waving his hands in the air and cursing with a thick Irish brogue.

"You manky arse! You nearly killed us."

The driver replied only with the tab.

"You want money after that? I should give you a clatter!"

An elderly woman slid off the seat behind him and waved her

husband away. "Oh, stop now, you flaming brute, and pay the man."

"Dorothy, how could you even suggest—"

"All right, all right," I said, placing a hand on Harry's chest. His white beard was thick but trimmed, and it shifted when he frowned. His bright blue eyes narrowed on me and I offered the kindest smile I could. "I'll take care of it." I slid the driver his fare plus a generous tip. I knew how much of a handful Harry could be even when he wasn't aggravated, and on a night like tonight, emotions ran high for everyone.

The driver grabbed the cash and let his tires squeal, the stench of burned rubber left behind.

"I tell you, young lad, you let people take advantage of you like that and you're going nowhere in life, you hear me?"

"I know it, Harry, but you're late and you've got a boat to catch. We don't want it leaving with you."

"Without me? Ha! I'll tell you what I'd do to that captain if he left me—"

"Not the time, Harry."

I picked up his luggage and ushered him down the dock. His wife, Dorothy, a woman with more patience than any person I'd met before, smiled and thanked me, working her way up the ramp like a woman half her age.

Harry lingered below, his face still red with anger. It looked stark against his aged beard. "You know, lad, I've been around a long time. One hundred and fifty-six years to be exact, and I ain't never met one of your kind I liked. They're all filthy, treacherous beasts that would as soon stab you in the back as shake your hand. All politics and greed, no better than a typhon. If you'd asked me a year ago what I'd do to an angel if one ever crossed me, I'd have told you how the beast inside would've torn it to pieces and left nothing but ashes." He pursed his lips, swollen belly sticking out over the edge of his pants. His thumbs were tucked into suspenders and he stretched them outward. After a long moment he nodded to himself as though he'd made up his mind. "But I gotta say, for maybe the first time in my life, I was wrong. For a kid, and an angel, you're all right, young fella."

I released a nervous breath. Harry might not have looked like much more than an old, out-of-shape man, but he was a shifter like no other, and I knew better than to underestimate him.

"I appreciate that, Harry." The ship's horn rang again. "We better get you boarded."

"Hogwash!" He waved away the crew urging him upward. "We'll go when I'm damn good and ready." He stepped toward me and took my hand before I had a chance to offer it. His grip was hard and strong, fingers calloused from the axe he wielded most of his days. "I'll tell you what, you keep up what you're doing and you're going to change the world for the better. You take that foot of yours and shove it so far up ATOM's ass that they can taste the lint between your toes. And when you think you can't push any more, you give it a little extra sauce for me, you hear?"

I patted his shoulder and gripped it tight. "Yes, sir."

For the first time in the year I'd known him, I saw Harry smile. "Good man. Take care of yourself." He pulled me in for a quick hug, patting my back like he was hammering in a nail. He pulled back but still didn't let go of my hand. "And for all this, you know…" He nodded, struggling to get the words out as though he didn't know how.

"It's okay, Harry. I know."

The crew grumbled as he moved up the dock at the pace he felt suiting, and he let them know what he thought of them with a slur of curses only a man like Harry could get away with.

A pang of sadness filled me as he disappeared over the edge. I didn't think I could ever miss a man like Harry, but as gruff as he was on the outside, he was as human as any other on the inside. He didn't show it much, but when he did it was quick and bright, burning out like a young star in an old sky.

Chains and gears rattled as the anchor rose, salt water raining from rusted metal as it was pulled from the sea. The wind picked up, a breeze rolling in and blowing strands of my blond hair over my face. The ship began to drift from the dock and with it, the tension left my shoulders. They were out of ATOM's grasp. They were safe now.

I pulled my jacket around me and zipped it up. Tonight the spring air felt cold, but it carried hope, and that was enough to warm me. I breathed it in and held it deep in my chest. Water rippled around the hull of the boat, leaving fear behind and moving toward a horizon of rebirth. The ship was a phoenix that had risen from the flaming ash of persecution. It had taken me more than a year and a small fortune to put this together. It was the biggest job

I'd ever pulled. Before now, I'd only managed to help a few people here or a small family there. To be able to help so many at once was a surreal experience. The warmth of success danced alongside the hope I breathed in. I couldn't help but smile, a bit of laughter spilled from my lips. A pool of white breath dissipated in front of me, and I held back the tears of joy that wanted to fall from my eyes. ATOM had forced supernaturals into a fearful existence, and today I was able to take some of that fear away. Not me alone, but everybody involved, including the people who boarded that ship. It wasn't easy to pack up your life and venture off into the unknown, I should know. It took courage and the belief that a better life awaited them across the waters. It did. I knew in my heart it did. A sigh of relief broke the tension that had tightened my shoulders.

"We did it," I whispered to the air as if it would carry my words to all the scared people on board the ship. "We did it."

Part of me wanted to stay and watch the boat disappear, part of me wanted to leave without saying goodbye. Goodbye meant it was over, and I knew that it was—I was thrilled that it was—but a piece of me left on that ship. A piece I'd never reclaim. I had done this to help them, but the truth was it had all started as a business transaction, a way to make money and help my people at the same time. Everybody won. It didn't take long before the business part faded away. I had come to care for these people like they were my own flesh and blood. During the past year I'd watched their struggles and fears come to life. I'd seen the disbelief in their eyes when I offered them a way out, and then the hope when I told them I could take ATOM out of their lives. Saying goodbye now was saying goodbye to family. I wanted happiness for them more than I wanted it for myself. Saying goodbye meant I'd never see them again. I hoped I wouldn't. Never seeing them again would mean their lives were reborn in a place of peace, where they were free to lurk among the shadows like they did in the old world. If I never saw them again it meant I succeeded.

Goodbye. I mouthed the word, but I didn't say it. Then I lowered my head and prayed I never saw them again.

With a final breath, I prepared to leave behind this chapter of my life and the people who had filled it. I expected the page to be turned, and that made me smile, but the smile was taken from me when instead the page was torn out and burned to ash.

I saw it before I heard it. Red sparks and fire rolled in a wave of destruction, followed by a thunderous boom that rippled across the sky. Three small explosions erupted across the ship, igniting a fourth that decimated the entire portside. A succession of ATOM's signature bombs detonated. Flares of copper, silver, and iron fire splayed into the sky like a ladder climbing to the heavens. Metal flakes fluttered down and swirled around the ship. Darkness vanished, fire exposing the entire world. The black ocean reflected the flames, creating a mirror of annihilation.

The water rippled violently and a blast of heat ran across my face. My chest tightened and my knees gave out. I hit the ground and the world slowed. Fire crept around the boat and over the water, grey and black smoke devouring the moon that had emerged from the clouds. Screams filled the air and sheets of debris crashed over the dock. Massive splinters of wood collapsed into the water, and people jumped overboard, searching for the salvation they thought they'd found. My heart slowed to a near stop.

"Beautiful, ain't it?" The southern accent and poorly pronounced words came from an all-too-familiar voice. Colby Adams. "You know what that is right there? That's justice, my friend. Mmmhmmm. Served on a warm platter of loyalty to my country."

I crawled forward on hands and knees, my legs trembling when I tried to stand. I stumbled over the remains of the dock. The water grew rough, debris floating over the surface and banging into the wooden posts that managed to stay upright. The screaming didn't stop. Some were endless wails, others were cries for help, and a few were directed to me, calling my name. The sound clawed my heart like a rake dragging across dirt.

"What have you done?" I didn't recognize the voice as my own. It felt distant and cold.

"Only what was necessary."

I didn't look at him. I couldn't tear my eyes away from the disaster that had unfolded. A small boat rippled over the angry waves with two men inside it. I didn't see the guns, but I heard them as they fired into those who swam for shore.

"No!" I screamed, running forward. Colby didn't try to stop me.

I dove into the water and let its icy grip engulf me. Lifeless bodies floated past as I swam toward the wreckage. Their faces were void of color and their skin began to break, red embers devouring them from the inside out. I felt heartless pushing them away, but they were already past saving. Soon they'd be ash drifting in the sea.

The screaming quieted and smaller explosions ignited like the aftershocks of a quake. An unseen child cried, their arms splashing in the water as they struggled to stay afloat. The sound cut across my body; a slice of regret that planted an ache in my heart. I found it difficult to tread water, and I spun in a circle. My heart raced, breath spilling from my lips in panicked clouds of frosty air. I wanted to call out to the child, but I couldn't speak. I wanted it to be a dream, a nightmare, but as icy fingers gripped my wrist and nails clawed at my skin, the truth crashed all around me. This was all real.

Tara pawed at me, eyes wide with panic. An open wound on her forehead bled profusely, painting her face a shade of red. Her lips were split, one eye swollen shut and bruised. Shards of copper shrapnel were stuck in her neck, black veins bulging as infection set in. Copper was debilitating to harpies, but not to angels. I tried to pull it out but Tara screamed and jerked away before becoming still. We floated together for a moment. She tried to say her daughter's name but it wouldn't come out. Water filled her mouth and she gagged. She was weak. The world seemed to fall silent and she looked me in the eye, beaten and disheveled, whispering a single word.

"Why?"

I didn't have an answer for her. Instead I tried to pull her to shore against her will. She continued to fight against me, screaming that she couldn't let her go. Her? Samantha. Tara broke away from my hold in an attempt to find her daughter, but her body betrayed her. She'd lost too much blood. She was weak. She dropped beneath the surface of lapping waves, lunging upward with panic ripe on her features. She clung to me like a buoy, but within moments she was gone. A final breath sputtered across my neck and she fell still.

"No, stay with me," I whispered, it was more of a plea than a statement, as if I could entice death to bring her back. I couldn't.

I caught a glimpse of Samantha, her innocent face floating in the distance. Black veins rippled across her face. She must have inhaled some of the metal flakes. I swam toward her, dragging her mother's body along with me. The child's once golden locks were black with soot, half of her hair singed into tiny broken coils. Her pulse had stopped, and her skin felt cold and slick. She had draped herself over a piece of wood, but without life to help her keep hold of it, she had begun to slide into the water. I held her for a moment, running my fingers along her face with an apology that meant nothing to her now.

Flashes of red shone all around me as bodies were swallowed by embers and turned to ash. A final few gunshots rang through the night; any who'd fought for survival soon found it was wasted effort.

A blanket of icy fear and sadness prickled through me like a bed of needles. Tara's cold, dead grip clawed at the back of my neck as I unraveled her from my body. I let mother and daughter vanish into the depths of the ocean bay together. Flashes of red flickered in the darkness for a moment, and then nothing. They were gone.

I no longer felt the urge to look for survivors. There was only death, and it tugged at me like a child vying for attention. Part of me wanted to go with them and let death's icy breath welcome me into her embrace, but I was a supernatural, the water alone couldn't kill me.

I crawled onto the shore, salt water dripping from my hair. The ship's remains creaked and moaned in the background as it became one with the ocean. My eyes burned with sadness, and my body shook. I wasn't sure if I felt cold or exhausted. Maybe both.

"Look what you've done." Colby grinned at the disaster behind me.

Any exhaustion I felt was suspended at the sound of his voice. Anger came like a rogue wave and carried everything with it. I jumped up and hit him under the chin with a sharp uppercut. He stumbled back and fell to the ground. I reached for the blade at my back to find the sheath empty and waterlogged. I wouldn't let that stop me. Colby stumbled to his feet and I kicked his side with the force of a jackhammer. He rolled way, using the momentum to his advantage, and with surprising fluidity he came up to his feet with his pistol drawn.

"Don't make me do this, Ash." He cocked back the hammer and kept his aim steady.

I couldn't see him. Not really. He was a streak of red in a world that had lost color, and I charged it like a bull. He fired the gun and a bullet zipped by my head. A warning shot. I didn't take it. I moved with unnatural speed and collided with his torso. I threw him off his feet and thrust him against a metal cargo trailer. The metal crumpled with the force but it wasn't enough. The butt of his gun came down on the side of my face, metal and wood hitting quick and hard. Anger and magic spooled inside me but I wouldn't let it out. I couldn't. I gripped the collar of his jacket and head-butted him. His nose exploded with blood and he covered it with his hands, red spilling between his fingertips. If he had expected me to hesitate or let up like I had in the past, tonight he was wrong. My fists rained over him like the fire and debris of the wreckage. I unleashed an assault of rage, knees and knuckles rapping against his face.

Colby summoned his beast, power rising with a low growl from his throat. Clawed hands plunged into my chest, tearing at the skin. I stumbled back and skidded across the pavement. Colby plowed into me and threw me to the ground, gun drawn and pressed against my face. His human hands were back, but it became apparent he didn't plan on taking it easy either.

My breath was ragged, and blood trickled down my face from where his gun had hit me. Colby's eyes were wild and angry, like a wolf on the verge of making his kill. I lifted my head and pushed my cheek against his gun.

"Do it," I said through gritted teeth.

For a moment I thought he would. His yellow teeth clenched and he screamed through them, easing back on the gun.

"Hell no, that's no way for a bounty hunter to get paid, but if it were, by god I'd let this copper bullet drill right through you."

"Screw the money. Eight years you've waited for this moment. Eight years of failure and now you've got me. Do it!" I screamed. When he didn't react, I fought against him, struggling to get my arms out from beneath his knees. He kept me pinned to the ground, hardly reacting when I smashed my knees into his back. I shifted his weight enough to slip my arm out, but I wasn't getting away. Not this time.

He raised the gun above his head and smashed it against my face. Once. Twice. Pain lanced my skull as dots filled my vision. The third blow merged the dots together like a velvet sheet. Then there was nothing.

CHAPTER 2

C igar smoke wafted through the air and stung my nostrils, a rude awakening that came with a pulsing headache. The world warbled through a haze of heat, and a harsh beam of sunlight scorched my eyes. I tried to turn away but the burn of metal against my wrists forced me back. Rusted iron clasps were tight around my arms and legs, securing me to a chair and leaving little margin for movement without consequence.

To my right, the world rushed by through a glass pane. Wheels chugged, metal on metal squealed, and smoke billowed outside the window. A horn screeched and added to the agony dwelling in my head. It forced me to dry heave and almost puke. I was on a train. How did I get here? The details were murky, fluttering at the edges of my mind. I had been on the docks. There was the ship, it was—I gagged as it all came back. Faces flooded my vision: Tara, Harry, Jasper, Samantha. I shook them away but they were replaced by a hundred others. Icy flares of panic and sadness swelled in my chest. It felt surreal. When I closed my eyes I could hear the lapping of waves and voices crying out my name.

The door separating my car from the next opened and supernatural bounty hunter Colby Adams walked through. He was a brick house of a man, dwarfing my six-one stature by five inches. He hovered over me with a saliva-soaked cigar stub between his teeth. Blood and sweat stained his shirt, chest hair curling over the collar. His square jaw was thick like a boxer, decorated with salt-

and-pepper stubble. When he took his cowboy hat off and ran a hand through sweaty hair, he revealed a few strips of silver among the black. He grinned, satisfaction owning his swollen and bruised face. I got him good. I glanced down at the chains. Not good enough.

"We're not like humans, Ash." The twang of his voice irritated me. "We're different: stronger, faster, more powerful, and because of that, we've got a responsibility to our country."

Colby thrived on regurgitating ATOM's own words. I tuned him out. I didn't want to hear any of it. ATOM was the American Terrorist Opposition Military, and they were designed to recoup America's lost position in the world. What was once a world power had fallen to a third world nation, and they thought we were the ladder to take them back to the top. We'd either join them and build an army of supernaturals that could never be rivaled, or we'd deny them and become lab rats, destined for a life of testing. And all the while nobody had a clue what was happening. To the rest of the world, we were myths, creatures fictionalized by books and television. To the American government, we were the golden goose.

"Save me the lecture," I interrupted him. He didn't look pleased about it. "I won't volunteer to be cattle on the butcher's block, and I won't live my life locked in a cage. I'll be free or I'll die."

"There ain't many of you flyers left. You sure you don't want to reconsider? There's always a place for you with ATOM. And being free is better than being on the run, ain't it?"

"News flash, Colby. Just because you can't see the shackles doesn't mean they're not there. You're nothing more than a whipping horse with a retractable leash."

Yellow, crooked teeth disappeared behind tar-stained lips. "You watch your mouth, boy. I'm here trying to converse with you and offer you a better way of life, and you go on insulting me?"

"Sorry, I thought by now you'd realize I'll fight ATOM's cause until the end. There isn't anything you can say to change my mind."

"That's downright un-American."

"No, that's the reality of what ATOM has done to this country."

Colby gritted his teeth and clenched his fists. "I'll have you know that before your time, this was the best damn country on the planet: freedom, truth, liberty, patriotism. You could take it all in with a single breath. War and economic collapse brought us down, and the world took advantage of that. It's up to our kind to build it back up. We're the keys to returning it to its former glory, maybe even one better. We aren't slaves, we're saviors. Our kind can save this country and dammit, it's our duty to do so. Why can't you see that?"

The eye roll had been unintentional but unavoidable. His idea of freedom and mine were two very different trains that found themselves on the same track.

"Where are you taking me?" I asked.

"Come now, after all these years of fighting you don't even want to try talking? I've gone and laid down the god-honest truth for us to converse about and you're going to change the subject?"

"You want to know why? Because it isn't right," I said. "It isn't right to force people to fix what the government destroyed. It isn't right to imprison men, women, and children and subject them to a lifetime of tests so power-hungry politicians can try and replicate whatever it is that makes them different."

"Now hold on there a second! I'm offended you would—"

"Of course you are," I roared. "This whole damn world is offended. What the hell did you expect, Colby? Did you think I'd sit here chained to a chair and talk politics with you? You killed three hundred and seven people on that ship, plus the crew. There were children on that boat! All that for some force-fed philosophy about how great this damn country is? This country is a disaster, and you're part of the problem."

The impact of a truck collided with my jaw before my head snapped to the side. I swallowed the blood that seeped into my mouth. It was a quick reminder of Colby's force.

"You're a little pissant, Ash, you know that?" Colby drew out. "All those people you think are so damn innocent? They betrayed their country. Did they have to die? No. But they chose that path when they lined your pockets with cash and got on that boat. So don't go thinking you're better than me. You're no savior. You're as much a politician as the men you love to hate."

"I'm *nothing* like them. I *help* people."

"You abandoned your country. You weren't helping no one but yourself." He took a long haul of his cigar and let smoke billow from his mouth. For a moment his lips moved but he didn't speak, as though he were having a conversation with himself. "You want to know whose responsibility it is to fix this country? All of ours. You do your duty and contribute and you earn yourself a future in these damaged times and help your country recover. You helping other supernaturals escape their duty as Americans is a goddamn sin. If you're not contributing to the cause, you're hindering it. If you hinder it, you're a risk to our future. We can't have that. This country has seen enough war for a hundred lifetimes. No need for any more bloodshed."

"Is that a joke?" I asked in disbelief. "After what you did to those people?"

"I did my job to make this country better," Colby attempted to reason. "You ruin it with false promise and greed. ATOM ain't the enemy here. They force Americans to uphold their duty. Ain't nothing immoral about that."

"Look at you, an amarok; a werewolf with no pack who bows to no alpha, neutered to the point he's become an augmented snitch," I said. "You're a running advertisement for the worst agency on the planet."

This time when he hit me blood spilled from my lips. My skull screamed in response, and I couldn't hold it down. Vomit poured from my lips and splattered against the tattered red carpet that lined the floor.

"Eight years I've been chasing you. This should be a good day, but now you've gone and put me in crooked mood. Damn you for that." Colby sighed. "It seems our story has come to an end and the rightful cause won. Mine. It cost me all the feeling in my left hand, a few new scars, and my favorite pistol handed down from my great granddaddy. You think I feel good about what happened on the ship? I don't, but you made bad choices, mistakes, and I had to clean them up. I did my job and now I sit here victorious. And to think I was naïve enough to believe I could set you on a good foot forward for what's coming next."

Next? There was no next. I'd be taken to a facility a dozen feet beneath the earth where they pumped oxygen in from above. White coats would swarm my tile-and-steel room. I'd be given water and vitamins in between tests. Needles, scanners, scalpels. That's what would become of my life. I wouldn't let that happen. I'd die first.

"The only mistake I ever made was letting you live," I said. "I should've killed you the day I took that pistol out of your hand. If I had, nobody would've died on that boat and ATOM would be without their prized horse."

He drew his gun and pointed it toward me. "Damn straight you should've. Then, or any of the other times you had the chance. God knows you've got it in you."

"Do it," I said.

Rage filled his eyes and his hand shook. His thumb hesitated on the hammer, threatening to pull it back. He lowered his gun with a heavy sigh and shook his head.

"I wish I could, but the job doesn't call for it," Colby said.

Disappointment filled me as I cursed at him. "You're what's wrong with this country, Colby. Your weakness is an accelerant in burning it to the ground."

Colby's breath became still. His eyes panned my face until he sheathed the gun and smiled. "You think I'm dumb 'cause I talk a little funny? I won't play into your hand. I'm not going to kill you, and you ain't going to some cell. Not yet anyway. You ever heard of the Academy?"

I shook my head.

"It's a special place where kids like you come around…with the proper tutelage. Don't want to go wasting youth on a mind that can be reshaped, now do we? So you can stand your ground and you preach your sermons all you want, but we'll see how you feel with the Academy's hands gripping your nuts." He chuckled. "But first things first." Colby walked across the train car and pulled a syringe and a vial of clear fluid from a wooden box.

"What the hell are you doing?"

I grew uneasy as Colby studied me. "I'm getting old, Ash, and I ain't got eternity like some of you," he finally said. "I've put in my time and I'm going out with a perfect record. I'm tired of chasing you around like a dog after a hawk. So not only am I going to make sure you can't ever get away again, you're going to bankroll my retirement while I'm at it." He walked toward me and my pulse broke into a panicked sprint. "You know, I ain't as whipped as you might think, Ash, and ATOM isn't the only one that knows about us. Supernaturals have always had an underground following of sorts. Admirers, you could say. They're the quiet type, not much for hunting, but they do love their souvenirs. And they pay top dollar and then some. So why don't you make it easy on everyone and cooperate? Show me those beautiful flappers."

I tugged at the chains, ignoring the burn and the closer he came, the more I flailed. Steam rose and my skin blistered, filling the cabin with the scent of burned flesh. Colby called for help and a man came to restrain me. I screamed and smashed my head into him. Adrenaline surged through me. I swung my fist and tore the chain from the wall, making impact with the next man through the door. I used the chain like a whip and hit the needle from Colby's hand, crushing the glass beneath my foot.

One of Colby's lackeys stumbled to his feet and drew an iron blade. He struck out toward me but I grabbed his wrist, twisting until I felt the joint pop. He dropped the weapon and I caught it midair, plunging the blade between his ribs. An inhuman growl lurched in his throat as his beast responded. If only it had been silver.

Fear and adrenaline danced alongside one another and I jerked the chains out of the wall one by one. The lackeys blocked the door. They were all that stood between me and freedom. I would let them.

I let loose the very thing they wanted to steal from me. The skin over my shoulders split. Fluid leaked down my back, the break expanding down either side of my spine until two white arms unfolded. With a stretch and a snap, my wings expanded with a gust of authority. Thick, soft white feathers fluttered through the air and filled the cabin, knocking all three men to the floor. The muscles in my shoulders flexed and the wings retracted, falling neatly along my back and down to my ankles.

One of the men lunged toward me. I sidestepped and let his head fall into a loop I'd made with the chains. I pulled it tight, the iron links coiling around his neck. With a forceful tug I smashed his head into the window. Once. Twice. On the third collision the window shattered. Glass exploded and the wind vacuumed away the debris. His screams were lost in the rushing wind. I threw him to the floor and lunged for the open window, prepared to make my escape, but Colby's massive arms wrapped around me and shoved me against the wall. My wings flexed in response, sending his body across the car, but the other man was already up and attacking. An iron blade cut across my wings. I bit back a shriek and deflected the next attack, thrusting the man across the car. He almost fell out of the window, and I escaped through the door to the other cabin.

The next car was larger than the first with a long and narrow aisle of seats. I moved in a blur toward a door at the end. Freedom. I reached for the handle. Locked. It didn't matter, I'd go through. I stepped back and charged forward, ready to smash my way to the outside. The clasps around my ankles tightened and the chain went taut. My legs flew out behind me before I could make impact and I hit the floor hard. Colby dragged me back inch by inch, all the while screaming at his lackey to bring another syringe. I scrambled, hands flailing about. Carpet tore in my grip, unable to slow me down. I gripped the bottom of the seats using the bars as a last-ditch effort. It was no use. Colby was too strong. My heart hammered against my ribs, breaths quick and sharp, mind scrambling for a way out. Too late.

The other man's knee hit my back and with the help of Colby, they pinned me to the ground. Their beasts hummed beneath the surface, primal and strong. I couldn't overpower both of them.

The iron needle burned as it entered my neck, hot and slick. Then something cold moved alongside the heat as liquid plunged into my veins. The world blurred and the pain vanished. I felt the urge to give in. There were no problems or struggles anymore, only cool warmth that overtook me. The pressure on my back lifted. It was no longer needed. I couldn't move. I didn't want to.

"That's about enough of that," Colby said. "It's time to say goodbye to the gift of flight, Ash. You're about to get clipped."

CHAPTER 3

A fog encased my body and electricity snapped in the air. Pressure pushed against my spine. My mind screamed for control, but whatever Colby had injected me with wouldn't allow it. Voices came and went, sometimes muffled, sometimes I heard bits and pieces: wings, extractor, unfold, retract. They came from all directions. My mind swam as my body was jerked left and right. Each moment stretched an eternity. A dream. That's all it was. My wings were a part of me as much as my head or arms. He couldn't take them. He wouldn't.

The room seemed quiet. No footsteps, no voices, and nothing pressing against me. My fingers twitched, the movement jump-starting my mind with fright. A tingle moved through my arms as if the circulation had been cut off and then released. Feeling returned limb by limb. My eyes fluttered open and I started to push myself up, shaky and uncertain in my movements. The tile floor was stained with red and brown. My arms trembled, the muscles weak and unsteady. I pushed anyway, pulling my knees beneath me. Paralysis released its hold an inch at a time. At first I felt grateful for the ability to move, but then came the ability to feel.

Heat lanced my back, agony beyond what I had ever known. It revealed the truth of what had happened. My arms went weak and I collapsed in disbelief. I fell off the edge of the table and hit the floor. I remained hunched on my hands and knees; it seemed impossible to sit upright. I attempted to reach over my shoulder and feel the damage. The wounds screamed in revolt as I pushed them farther than they wanted to go. The stitches' thread felt rough beneath my fingers. I gasped for air with lungs that seemed to forget how to breathe. No.

Doubt and horror moved up and down like an equalizer. Each took their turn snapping inside me like a string of rubber bands. I reached for the table and the metal groaned and curled beneath my grip. My eyes filled with tears either from sadness or fear or shock or rage. I didn't know. The remnants of sedative faded. My wounds seethed like a farmer's broad fork had trenched its way across my shoulders. Heavy breaths came through a clenched jaw. My teeth squealed as they ground together. My knuckles popped one after another, the heat scorching my back like a torch against bubbling metal. When it reached a peak I could no longer restrain, I screamed. The sound was inhuman, almost primordial, and it didn't stop until I ran out of air. My muscles had forgotten how to work. They twitched beneath the surface, each pulse causing more distress than the last. I tried to summon my wings, hoping to see feathered limbs fill the room. They would carry me to safety, they always did. The response was blinding; the room went black.

When I came to, I didn't try to move again. I traced a maze of patterns along the wall from splattered blood. Emptiness swirled inside. Everything I was had been stripped away, everything I'd worked for deconstructed. I pondered the fate of my allies; those who had helped me build the pipeline to freedom. They were probably dead, like the people I'd put on that boat. I wished for the same fate, but it never came.

Colby's entrance was quiet. He moved around the table, not looking remorseful but disappointed. I skittered back across the floor when he moved toward me, but I tried not to let him see me cringe.

"Meds wore off, huh? Can't say I'm sad about it," he said. "After the choice words you had for me, I'd rather like to sit here and watch you squirm all day, but I need you mobile. Take this." He leaned in with a syringe, but I smacked his hands away. The movement was sharp, causing white and black dots to flicker in my vision. My heart was a jackhammer chiseling at my ribs, and my breath seemed caught in my throat.

"What have you done?" My voice sounded raspy and dark, but the words trembled. I felt violated, yet an ethereal rage boiled beneath my frightened voice.

Colby held a single white feather in his fingers. He dragged it across the palm of his hand. His smile made bile rise in my throat.

"I've been doing this job more than half my life," he began. "Been damn good at it too. It's 'bout time I had a break. Thanks to you and those fancy flappers, I'm gonna get it. I got a rogue off the streets and earned myself a long vacation."

I pressed my back against the wall. It hurt, but it felt safer. I wouldn't turn my back on him again.

"Where are they?" I whispered.

"What's that there?" he asked, leaning forward. "Couldn't quite hear ya."

"Where are they?" I screamed.

Colby grinned. "Gone. We made a stop while you were having your siesta. Perfect timing if you ask me."

"Where?" I smashed my fist into the floor. The tile cracked and broke away with a blast of gold energy rippling around my hand. Magic. The table screeched across the floor, and spiderwebs cracked along the window. Seeing the power glimmer around my hand scared me, so I retracted the rage.

Colby cringed, stumbling back. A smudge of soot stained his cheek and a trickle of blood ran from his ear. He slid his fingers through it and smeared it across his face. The sight of it stiffened his lips.

"They're gone," he growled. "Get over it, you little shit. You've got an opportunity coming your way—one you've refused to seize in the past. Look where it's gotten you. Let your wings and all those people be reminders of the consequences your actions have. Use it as motivation to change your ways."

The fire inside me was eternal. The idea of being without my wings brought such wrath to my soul it hurt in an entirely new way. It was worse than death. Maybe that was the point. Maybe that's what I had earned myself.

"I will destroy every piece of your life." My words were soft and crisp, but my lips trembled. My threat hadn't resonated with him at all. How could it? I sat huddled on the floor, quivering against the wall.

Colby winked, pulling his cowboy hat low over his right eye. "Whatever you say, Ash. Look, you don't want this? That's fine by me." He kicked the syringe toward me. "But you better get your walking legs together. We've got a hike after we get off this train, and you can be damn sure I won't carry you." The door slid shut as he left me to bathe in my new cruel reality.

The clock ticked, each second an eternity that intensified the torment. I stared at the needle. It sat in crusted blood that had filled the crevices between tiles, rocking with the train's movements. The iron tip glinted in the sunlight, enticing me. I rejected its advances. A drop of medicine clung to the metal point, threatening to fall. The train jerked, forcing my back to hit the wall. Hot coals raked over my skin. I cursed, grabbing the needle and jamming it into my thigh. Fluid hit my bloodstream; ice water bathed the flames, then relief coiled through me, numbing everything.

My insides faded from anger and panic to quiet reflection and indifference. The feeling was temporary but I didn't care. My wings were gone and everybody I cared for was dead. My spirit had been broken and *any* reprieve from this reality was welcome. I toyed with the small needle in my hand. I wondered what damage a small, sharp object like it might do. I pressed my thumb against the tip and it broke the skin, a tiny drop of blood rising to the surface. Not enough to take reality from me. I craved death and she desired me. I felt her lips above mine, threatening to suck away what remained of my life. I longed for it, begged her to, but she teased me with the flick of her icy tongue, and I drowned myself in disappointment.

Metal on metal squealed as the train stopped. My body rocked against the floor. I felt nothing. A part of me hoped it was all a dream, but no matter how hard you wished, there would always be a part of you that remained in reality. We were all sewn to the fabric of the world as it is, not the world we wanted it to be. Reality was a cruel, unrelenting mistress. You couldn't escape her. Her command was deafening and patience endless. My wings were gone, the blood of innocence stained my hands, and it could never be washed. It was etched into my skin, stuck in the crevices of my soul for eternity, or until an iron blade met my neck. I wished for the latter. Instead I got Colby.

The medicine had worked too well. Even with Colby's hand helping me balance, I fell off the edge of the train car. He laughed and dragged me to my feet, jerking my arms behind my back and cuffing them together. He latched a chain to them that acted like a leash and ushered me forward. We were off the grid, he'd said, and the farther we walked, the more I realized he wasn't kidding.

The train tracks ended at the bottom of a hill and we started climbing. The air had cooled and leaves dripped moisture, pine and sap licking the air. The gravel path became a dirt trail that ascended two aisles of trees. With the meds fading, each step hurt more than the last. Blood trickled down my spine, both shoulders moving in awkward ways as I tried to traverse the incline with both hands behind my back. I cringed at the sharp volts that snapped across my shoulders. I stumbled on more than one occasion, but I fought through it all. Colby had taken enough from me; I wouldn't give him the satisfaction of my struggle too.

Colby's lackey cut through the final wall of brush with a machete. Soft green leaves fluttered to the ground, pieces of broken flower petals decorating the spaces between them. We had arrived at the Academy.

Twenty-foot brick walls stood before us, topped with another six feet of rolling barbed wire. Colby snapped the chain and pushed me along the wall, my arm sliding against the stone. Surprisingly, the rock cut into me, and a strange irritation rippled over my skin. Red dots sprouted up like a tiny mountain range. The skin became raw and marred. Next came the itching, but being unable to scratch, it became a new form of torture. I was a supernatural. An angel. Iron was the only thing that should've been able to hurt me. What was this place?

We stopped outside a set of gates. Each bar lined with tiny barbs of iron, silver, and copper. The metal sparkled like a precious gem that reflected the light. Through the bars lay a series of circular stones embedded in the earth. Each had a symbol stamped into it that represented a different breed of supernatural. I recognized them as glyphs designed to keep unwanted visitors out. In this case the opposite was true. They weren't here to stop supernaturals from getting in, but keep them from getting out.

Colby grinned. "There's one for every breed that lives inside these walls, but we had a new one put in special for you. Nobody ever expected an angel at the Academy. Most of 'em thought your kind extinct in these parts." He slapped his hand against my back; the blow dropped me to my knees. "Not that you're going anywhere, are ya?"

CHAPTER 4

Three guards dressed in camouflage met us at the gates. They searched and seized all the weapons (much to Colby's dismay), never once taking their guns off me. We were guided up a cobblestone road to a mansion-style structure. Everything was red and grey stone. Seven floors were lined with large windows and thick metal bars that matched the gate. Massive columns reached from the base of the stairs to the awning that hung over the front door. Patches of moss grew on sections of the walls, but even they looked trimmed, and dark stone gargoyles guarded the base of the staircase and the edge of the roof; deformed creatures that watched over the Academy grounds. On either edge of the path stretched miles of landscaped grass, well-manicured bushes, and an assortment of small buildings. A glimpse of movement from the roof and I spotted two more guards watching us through the scope of dark rifles. The guards were everywhere.

At the top of an intimidating staircase were two large wooden doors with thick brass knockers. The faces of two toothy gargoyles stared back at us with round handles hanging from their mouths. They weren't needed. As if on cue, the doors opened and a breath of rustic air rushed to escape, carrying the musk of stale incense and a smell that could only be described as old.

Inside, a long and winding stairway encased with dark wood added to the aroma with a fresh coat of polish. At the base stood a man in a pressed suit, his face shadowed. The grey handkerchief in his pocket stood erect, folded with two peaks protruding above the edge. His thin torso was covered with a grey dress shirt and buttoned vest that disappeared beneath the blue jacket of his suit. His tie and polished shoes matched the jacket. He looked far too proper for me to feel comfortable. An old chandelier dangled above him, hanging from a long chain that reached the peak of the vaulted ceiling. It offered little light. Only enough to reveal the pale tone of the man's creased skin.

He looked human, but the thrum of something beneath the surface told me otherwise. Colby shoved me forward and we stood on a large red-and-cream carpet with ruffled edges. The tension felt immediate when the man didn't move. He gave off a statuelike illusion, but unlike the gargoyles outside, the blue eyes that studied me were far too alive.

"Welcome to the Academy, Mr. Lawson." His voice was quiet, sounding as aged as he looked, which was probably close to sixty, but his words were perfectly articulated. He was a man who had studied language. The creases around his mouth became more defined when he spoke, the crow's feet around his eyes twitching. He stood with excellent posture, a faint nod given to acknowledge each of us. "Forgive the ominous nature of your arrival. When new recruits arrive, our facility becomes locked down. We take no chances here at the Academy."

"You must be Hendrik," Colby snorted. "Well, I ain't one to like being disarmed, but I understand the need for precautions. Especially with this one."

Colby's elbow hit me hard in the back, causing me to stumble forward. With scarcely a movement, Hendrik crossed the foyer in a blur to steady me. When I was confident in my footing, I nodded. He looked at his hand and grimaced, wiping it on the edge of his jacket.

"How you handle your business outside of the Academy, Mr. Adams, is not of my concern," said Hendrik. "However, you are *not* outside of the Academy, are you?"

"I beg your pardon?" Colby questioned.

The man adjusted his tie, eyes twitching. "While on my property, you will behave in a manner befitting a man in your position," the man ordered. "You will respect your captive, refrain from unnecessary violence, and refer to me not as Hendrik, but as your superior. You may call me sir or Mr. Powell. Now, although your speech leaves much to be desired, I've read your portfolio and know you're a somewhat educated man, so I don't need to ask you if you understand."

Colby raised a brow while letting out a gruff noise that sounded almost like laughter. "As you wish, *Mr. Powell.*" He gave a dramatic bow and grinned.

Hendrik frowned. "You can start by taking that filthy, germ-ridden butt out of your mouth and discarding it. Your associate can wait here, and you may follow me to my office."

Colby pulled the unlit cigar from between his teeth, eyed it, and jammed it into his pocket with a mumble.

Each door in the narrow hall was closed, and every lamp dimmed. Old-fashioned fixtures clung to the wood paneling with a brass finish that matched the doorknobs. The building's smell remained consistent, although everything looked clean and polished, the scent of age couldn't be scrubbed away.

Bookcases lined Hendrik's office with the exception of a large bay window that overlooked a section of land. The same manicured grass stretched onward toward the wall that surrounded the property.

"I asked you to discard your cigar butt, Mr. Adams. I find the stench emanating from your pocket irritating," Hendrik said.

Colby looked offended and grumbled under his breath. He closed the button on his pocket as if that could eliminate the smell.

"We are adults, Mr. Adams. We speak the words we want to say. We do not mutter like insolent children." Hendrik sighed. "Please sit."

"I'll stand." Colby's forehead creased as he crossed both arms.

I stepped away, relishing the chance to put distance between us, but that meant getting closer to Hendrik. At the moment I didn't know who was the lesser evil.

One of Hendrik's eyes twitched. "As you wish. Please remove your hat."

"I'm fine," Colby said. "In fact, I haven't got all day, so if we could move this along."

I expected a movement, a facial tick, something from Hendrik, but he remained still. He became statuesque once again, as if that alone was enough to frighten Colby. He sat in his high-back leather chair and pulled himself toward the desk. Everything sat in neat order: no loose papers, no pens or pencils outside of their holder, and nothing but a thick manila folder in front of him. He adjusted his stapler a quarter of an inch to the left and tilted the lamp to the right. When he seemed prepared, he studied my face in a way that made me deeply uncomfortable. He didn't open the folder, instead he ran his fingers over it several times before clasping his hands on top.

"Acquisition form 2789-576e. Detain one Ash Lawson. Age: nineteen. Breed: Angel. Known affiliates: Hector Romans (Shifter), now deceased; Sophia Hardy (Clairvoyant), now deceased; and Fredrick Alscoe (Vampire), deceased."

If it hadn't been decimated enough, my heart broke a little bit more hearing those words. The answer to my question had been fulfilled. Friends, trusted allies, people who had helped me...dead.

"Such a mess, Mr. Adams," Hendrik said.

"Unfortunate, yes, but part of the job," Colby responded.

Hendrik continued. "Destination: The Academy. Means of transport: Private Rail. Detain Status: Alive. Detainment Condition: A.G.A.P. Bounty: $750,000 if received as per request. Deductions as per receiving officer." Hendrik shook his head. "It seems we've found ourselves in a predicament, Mr. Adams."

"How do you figure that?" Colby feigned confidence. I'd known him long enough to tell he was nervous. He slid his hands into his pockets, then took them back out. He adjusted his cowboy hat and fixed his hands on his hips. "Far as I can see, I delivered quality goods. Goods ain't nobody been able to deliver before and goods my government sought to have bad enough to offer a fat paycheck. I'd say the only predicament we have is that you haven't cut me my check yet."

Hendrik studied the bounty hunter. I expected a well-articulated response. Instead, Hendrik rose from his chair without a trace of sound. He looked old, almost frail, but an eerie command stemmed out around him. Before I could form a thought, he vanished. My hair wafted as a breeze moved past. The black cowboy hat rolled across the floor and Hendrik stood behind him, both of Colby's arms bound behind his back with a single hand. The hunter looked uncomfortable, sweat beading off his face.

Hendrik's face showed no sign of strain. He didn't seem to notice Colby's crushing discomfort. Colby was an amarok; a supremacy among werewolves. He was a beast that could not be tamed by any alpha. No supernatural should've been able to manhandle him like that.

"Do you know what A.G.A.P. stands for, Mr. Adams?" Hendrik asked.

"As good as possible." Colby's voice was strained, words coming through gritted teeth.

"That is correct!" Hendrik jerked Colby's arm to the side and forced him to face me. "Now take a good look at the condition your detainee has arrived in."

"He's fine. If anything he's even better than when I found him," Colby maintained. "Those traps out there, that wall, they wouldn't have been enough to hold him. You don't know what he's like. He'd find a way out."

Hendrik adjusted his grip and Colby cried a monstrous growl. Colby's eyes shifted from human to wolf, olive green spiraling outward to consume his entire eye. The amarok's presence amplified. His shoulders cracked, loosening Hendrik's grip. The growl became primal, teeth elongating into fangs. His elbows snapped, tufts of black fur fanning outward. He nipped at the air, teeth smashing against one another while bones shifted beneath his skin.

A mystic energy I'd never felt crept over Colby. Strong and swift, it cut through the air and sucked the oxygen from my lungs. The taste of sulfur bit my tongue and burned my nose. Fear ripened in my loins, unpredictable and intense. My breath caught in my throat, heart palpitating. It was like a nightmare; uncontrolled fear forcing its way into me.

"No!" Hendrik shouted, and an electric snap of influence ricocheted through the room.

Colby's growl turned into a yelp. His beast retracted, suffocated beneath Hendrik's guidance. The headmaster released him and Colby fell to his knees, breath hoarse and wheezy as if recovering from a cold. I tried to close my mouth but my jaw hung open. Hendrik smoothed his jacket and adjusted his tie. He returned to his desk and placed both hands back on the folder.

Colby struggled to stand, hesitating on all fours to catch his breath. "Do you have any idea who I am? Who I know? What I'm capable of?"

"I certainly know what you are *not* capable of: following simple directions, keeping your own abilities in check, respecting your superiors, doing your job, valuing your position as a part of our rehabilitation team. I can go on. Shall I continue?"

"Don't you dare for one second tell me—"

"As it stands, I am your superior. I will be submitting a grievance with your direct senior officer. Perhaps if you had been trained at the Academy, a *man* such as you would not be marring the name of ATOM. Should you step out of order one more time in this office, I shall see to it that you yourself are detained for betrayal to your country."

"Betray my…I have never—"

"You are excused, Mr. Adams. Let us hope the next time we meet you have taken the time to better yourself," Hendrik said, dismissing Colby.

Colby looked as though he would respond, but he bit back whatever words he wanted to spew. He picked up his hat and brushed it off, placing it back on his head.

"I need to collect payment, *Mr. Powell.*"

"Of course." Hendrik's eye twitched again and he retrieved a leather book from the desk. Withdrawing the feathered quill that sat upright in its glass container, he wrote a receipt and slid it across the desk.

"A detainee who's arrived with preventable damage is subject to a chargeback or deduction, if you will, as per section eight of the Bounty Endeavor," Hendrik advised. "I'm certain I don't need to tell you what percentage that is."

Colby bit his lip. "Forty-three percent. No problem, *sir.*"

"Excellent. You're making progress already. Now you'll be on your way. Good day."

Colby's eyes were on fire and fixated on me when he pulled the receipt off the desk. He glared at it, mumbling under his breath. "Good day."

The tension in the office collapsed when the door closed, and without a word Hendrik opened the folder and read through several pages. I scanned the room for an escape, but this place seemed a fortress. Even Hendrik's windows were barred, and guards walked passed them every few minutes. If I'd had my wings—the thought made the muscles in my back tense, bringing forth a crippling sting. I cringed and keeled over.

Hendrik released an annoyed sigh. "Your discomfort is making me uncomfortable, Mr. Lawson."

I didn't know how to respond. I tried to neutralize my expression and hide the discomfort, but it dug deep. He appeared unimpressed, and although offered condolences, his voice was cold.

"I should apologize on behalf of the Academy, bounty hunters everywhere, and more to the point, ATOM, although I fear that will offer little solace," Hendrik said. "Still, I can understand how you may feel."

"You can understand?" I didn't mean to laugh. I didn't know if it was his words, or if it was the only way to deal with the distress. Either way, it slipped through my lips. "No, *sir*, I don't think you can."

"Please, call me Hendrik. And believe it or not, I know more about it than you might think, but for now let's broaden the scope. You're hesitant to cooperate. You wish to be free to do as you will. Alas, what you want and need are two different parallels that do not align. As supernaturals, we have a responsibility to use our abilities to better ourselves and the world around us. This country is what is around us and it is hurting; therefore it is our job to better it. Now, you've been through quite an ordeal; I can see that. After your detainment with Colby, I imagine you've little patience for formalities. However, as a guest, they are a necessity and I will do my best to be prompt as we move through things."

"Guest?" I glanced to the window. "Is that what I am?"

Hendrik frowned. "Your stay here is not permanent, and I care little for terms like detainee. My preference is toward more welcoming language."

"Detainee. Prisoner. It doesn't matter what you call it, that's what I am.

Hendrik leaned back, folding his hands over his stomach. "Mr. Lawson—"

"Call me, Ash. Mr. Lawson died a long time ago."

"As you wish, Ash. In life, we have choices. They may not be choices we want or even like, but they are choices nonetheless. Given the option of life and death, or easy and difficult, one commonly will choose the former in both cases. It's human and supernatural nature alike. Here at the Academy we believe—quite simply—in teaching the value of said life."

"You mean doing whatever ATOM wants: living under a microscope and spending my life being poke and prodded, or perhaps being microchipped and having all my movement tracked and recorded while kidnapping and/or killing whomever they deem fit, supernatural and human alike," I countered.

He shrugged ever so slightly. "There are many positions in ATOM's repertoire; a place for everything and everything in its place."

"My place does not fall into any of their categories," I argued. "I don't kill innocent people. I don't kill people at all."

"Don't you though?"

He didn't mean the boat and I didn't need him to elaborate; we both knew the person he referred to. The thought of him stung, and the quiet ache that always existed within me awakened with vibrant force. I closed my eyes, wishing this place away, but the faces of the people I'd lost appeared. Faces that had offered me kindness, laughter, friendship. Faces that had given me their trust. The guilt flourished and turned to anger.

"If you want to blame someone for their deaths, blame yourself," I said. "It's people like you—people who've conformed and dedicated their lives to stealing their own brethren's freedom—who are responsible. Without you, they don't have shackles to hold us."

I should've been careful how I spoke to him. After seeing what he did to Colby, I should've been afraid. I wasn't. Survival was an instinct we all had but I no longer wanted. Colby wouldn't finish it, maybe he would.

Hendrik's face remained still and even more unnerving, he smiled. "Your legend precedes you. Defiant until the end, as your kind often was."

I hadn't earned even a facial tick of emotion. That ripened my anger even more. My wings were gone, my cause dismantled, and I sat in the center of a fortress in shackles that burned my skin. What did I have to lose?

"I will *not* join your cause," I insisted. "I'll fight it every step of the way. If you keep me here, I'll unleash a hell on you and everyone here who serves ATOM, in a way you'll only find deeply disturbing. You think you know what an angel can do? You have no idea. There is *nothing* you can do that will change that. Nothing. Do you understand me?"

"I see." Hendrik leaned forward in his chair and closed the folder. "Perhaps you misunderstand what this place is. I cannot blame you for that. Few do when they arrive. Before we kill, we try, Mr. Lawson. So until then, the formalities can wait. You see, few believed there were any angels left in our country. To know there is one as young as you is encouraging. Youth, however, is both a gift and a curse. It is narrow minded and lacks perspective. Both are lessons not easily taught to inexperienced souls, but ones which I have become proficient at educating. It is why I am here in this chair and running this facility. You are not presently open to receive that lesson. I respect that. One cannot put treasure inside a chest without first lifting the lid, now can they?" He let out a soft laugh and pressed a button on his phone. "It's my experience that the Tank can open that chest for us, and allow you to see the possibilities your judgments blind you to."

"The Tank?"

"You are a mountain, Mr. Lawson: an enormous rock that will not be re-formed by rain. Rather, you must be dipped into the ocean and surrendered to the waves. The Tank will be your ocean."

"I don't know what that means," I said. His ease made me uncomfortable. Where was the anger, the frustration? He should've been upset. The rage I'd felt drained from my face. I felt nervous. Magic nipped at me from within, begging to be unleashed. I ignored it. I wouldn't use it. Not even now. "Never," I whispered, a reminder of the promise I'd made to myself.

"It means in order for you to become who I believe you can be, first we must break away everything that you are. Erosion can wash away even the strongest embankment, Mr. Lawson. It's for your own good, and if I'm not mistaken, what's best for both of us," Hendrik said. "Perhaps all of us."

CHAPTER 5

Far from anything else on the property stood a rectangular building covered in moss and vines. The guards carried me, each holding a limb while others surrounded them with drawn rifles. I struggled and fought to break free, but each jolt stung my back and the guards' grips were relentless.

The building was dilapidated with loose bricks and mortar decorating the ground. A rusted steel door housed a single staircase that led underground. Thirty-seven squeaky steps put us in the pit of the building. The Tank. The air felt moist, tasting of stagnant mold over softened fruit. It lingered, ripening with each passing second. Four iron cages stood in each corner, none of them occupied.

With the cuffs removed along with my shoes, I was tossed in a cell. The dirt floor was as hard as concrete and cold as ice. The guards shuffled up the steps and the brief glimpse of light from outside vanished. Steel ground against steel and locks slid into place. Silence.

Darkness hung pure and even, leaving me to crawl on the floor and search with my hands. Bits of dirt clung to my fingers as I felt along the ground. Two of the walls were made up of iron bars littered with spurs of silver, copper, and iron. They cut into me and the wounds burned, injecting flares into the bone. Singed flesh was added to the list of rank smells that indulged me. The wound was superficial at best; I expected it to heal in an instant. I was mistaken. The other two walls were concrete. I huddled against them as if they offered shelter. They didn't. The stone burned and I slid away, forced to center myself in the cell. Minutes passed and the blood continued to trickle from my hands, while a searing pain settled along my arm where I'd leaned against the wall. I didn't understand. I chalked it up to the damage done from Colby taking my wings. My body didn't have time for the little things, it was busy trying to repair major damage. Damage it didn't realize could not be repaired.

A breeze rolled across my skin that came from every direction. I stood in an enclosed room. It wasn't possible. It came again. A draft? A way out? Excitement built at the thought, but the longer the air blew, the more I realized it couldn't be. It didn't carry a scent of fresh outdoor air, but more burned skin and spoilage. I rubbed my hands along my arms and pulled my knees to my chest.

The floor grew colder the longer I remained still. I trembled, feeling around until I found a small straw sack. After folding it several times I had a small pad to sit on. Silence lingered, and the shadows pressed against me. I shivered as another breeze came and tiny bumps spiraled down my arms. It felt colder than before, reminding me of the wind at altitudes high above the clouds, but without the sensation of sailing through them. The memory of flight brought a foreign ache to my soul. In the cloud of silence I realized for the first time that flying was an experience I'd never have again. It was a difficult thought to manage. This was real. It was all real. I sat in a dank, dilapidated basement, shivering beneath the wrath of a mysterious breeze, and reality had crept in and found a home inside my chest. I felt a loss for my wings; as though life had betrayed me, but I couldn't wallow in self-pity. There was something larger and darker here with me. I felt it coaxing its way into my cell, coiling around me like a black serpent that had already struck and would now devour its meal. Its venom filled me with dread and doubt. It felt heavy, like slick oil that trudged through my veins and slowed my movements. If I could have seen anything but darkness, I imagined the world had greyed.

Remorse rose in my throat like hot acid, scalding my insides, and the weight of three hundred innocent souls bore over me. I'd become the anchor to the ship they'd perished on. Pieces of my past terrorized me, faces that swam in the darkness. Eyes open or closed, it didn't matter. They haunted me. What a life I'd made.

From runaway to murderer, to living in seclusion like a monk, to seeking redemption and rescuing families in need of a new life, to murderer again. This time on an enormous scale, and now, imprisonment.

I smashed my fist into the wall. It didn't crack nor did it ease the inner-lashings I gave myself. Instead it burned and broke the skin. Blood trickled between my knuckles, warm at first, then cold before drying on my hand like a week-old scab. An hour passed and bruising formed beneath the skin. My bones ached. They shouldn't have. Not for this long. Not from something like this. I tried to shake it away, but the skin burned as if someone had sprinkled my arm with iron dust. Heat seared my fingers and I cringed. Finally, the faces I saw in the darkness faded and the cold breeze became still. I was left alone.

A trembling breath rolled from my lips. What would Father have thought of me now? What would the man who raised me to be loyal have to say? Would he frown? And Mother? Would her eyes hold the disappointed rage I had so often seen in my uncle's after my parents were gone?

"Father?" I whispered to the darkness. "Mother? Are you there?"

I hadn't said their names in eleven years, yet somehow it didn't seem strange to call out to them now.

"What do you have to say? What do you say to the boy who abandoned his people and cowers at his own magic? What do you say to a boy who killed for a simple meal? For pride? To a boy who wishes for death?"

I waited as if a response was imminent. I expected a lecture. Perhaps one of Father's taglines. *A Lawson never breaks his bond.* I felt their eyes from the other side of the cage, floating in the blanket of black that surrounded me. I knew it was impossible for them to be there, yet I sensed their presence and begged them to answer me, even if it was to scold me for breaking my word. They didn't.

"You say nothing! You think I do not deserve death. You think I am a taker of lives who is unworthy of the reaper's kiss." I traced my fingers in the dirt, and the cold returned, working its way deep into my bones. "You are right."

There was no method to track time. Sleep eluded me. Sweat ran across my body and burned my skin like the acid rains that fell from poisoned heavens. The Tank became so hot that I could not touch the floor without scalding my feet. The straw sack became my saving grace, giving me a small square of reprieve. But without notice, the temperature shifted, dropping below freezing. The broiling floor became a veiled sheet of ice, and the wind bit at my skin like razors.

I'd been in the Tank an eternity, or days. It could've been hours. Exhaustion tugged at my eyelids but they refused sleep. The open wounds my wings once occupied were no longer the bane of my existence; every part of me suffered in unison. Wounds festered and refused to heal, some of which I didn't remember getting at all. My parents' heavy eyes had left me long ago, replaced by whispers. When bearable, I paced my cage. I'd memorized its square footage, avoiding the iron bars like the plague. My finger still bled and if possible, I thought the wound had deepened. Hunger clawed at me, twisting like a feral beast, and thirst tempted me with the sounds of running water beyond reach. My mouth became sandpaper, shaving away a layer from my lips each time I licked them.

My eyes adjusted to the darkness and figures scurried from cell to cell. Children's laughter danced around me, playful at first, but soon muted by a gurgling sound. The floor had turned to water and sucked them in. They struggled to stay afloat and gasped for air. I felt penitence for their lives and it cut my chest like an iron blade. Hot blood ran over my stomach, but as I wiped it away, I felt nothing. Whispers became voices that shared their darkest secrets, flashes of haunting memories. My memories. They burned my eyes and when I closed them, my mind became a canvas for fear.

The dirt floor had become an ocean, and hands reached from the black waters in a plea for help. I could offer them nothing. I was here to watch them drown. Silence was a fantasy; dark skies filled will shrill cries screaming my name.

"Shut up! Leave me alone."

My shoulders pulsed, wings begging to be released. For a moment I'd forgotten they were gone, but the reminder came as I flexed the muscles that once unveiled them. Molten fire rippled down my back and I fell to my knees. Frost crawled along the weathered dock, devouring the wood and covering my legs.

"This isn't real. This is *not* real." Lies I told myself to keep from going mad. It didn't work.

Whatever sorcery clutched my throat would not be deterred by will. I had forgotten I was at the Academy. It no longer existed, nor did the Tank. The walls had melted and the night sky sucked the darkness away, showering me with stars and a moon so full its dimpled craters smiled upon me. Explosions rang in the air. I didn't need to look. I knew what I would see. I'd already lived this nightmare once. Still, it would not be daunted, and as if I stood on a turntable, the world moved around me, forcing me to face the ship. I suffered through that horrid day again and again, until everything was a blur through teary eyes. Colby's voice replayed through my mind, and the chills it gave me caused an ache in my back. I tried to run, but I was surrounded by water. It rose up from my ankles, climbing like the devil's cold hands scaling my legs. I shivered, no longer capable of movement. The cold seized my muscles and I lay paralyzed, sinking in a black sea of rough waters. It splashed over my face, salt water burning my eyes, and then I saw nothing. A dark pool of despair swelled within and acted like a concrete block pulling me deeper. I didn't struggle. My mind didn't scream for help. I gave in to it. I had no fight left in me. I closed my eyes, ready to surrender to the ocean's call, and released a final bubble of air; the last ounce of hope I'd retained. I prepared myself for death, but I would not be rewarded with that gift.

A hand cut through the water like a light in the dark, gripping my arm and jerking me upward with unnatural ease. I sailed through the air, landing on the floor of my cell. The ground was ice and the cold sent a shock through my body. I gasped for air, failing miserably and choking. Violent coughing led to the rise of bile, and I vomited salt water across the floor. My hair stuck to my face, drenched, with water dripping off the ends. Violent shakes ruptured my body, searching for the straw sack. When I found it, it did little to insulate me. I fell onto my side. The energy to sit up evaded me. The cold felt relentless, and I forgot what it might be like to feel warmth. Even the Tank's hold wasn't enough to keep me awake now. The cold, the exhaustion, it all won me over, and my eyes fluttered shut for what felt like the first time in a millennia.

When I came to, my hair was still wet. Sweat pooled on the floor around me, dirt stuck to my skin. The smell of sulfur and salt water filled the air, the aroma of rotted fruit and vomit not far behind. The peace was short lived as a force stabbed through my stomach. I curled into the fetal position, grinding my teeth as an invisible blade drove into me. A raised scar to the left of my stomach burst open and blood spilled over my hands. The once-healed wound from five years previous felt as though it had just happened. Memories of distant wounds flashed through my mind from battles won and lost. One by one they became reality. Blisters on the balls of my feet split, my left eye swelled shut, and a throbbing at the back of my head split my scalp clear open. My breaths came in sharp, short wisps and I cried out. I called for help and begged forgiveness for my wrongdoings, and when nothing happened, I wept for death. I longed for her release.

I struggled to my feet, open sores sticking to the dirt and making it hard to walk. I had nothing left to say or think. Tears spilled down my face as I placed both arms against the iron bars. My skin burned. I didn't pull away. I found the tiny iron spikes that protruded from the bars and placed them against my wrists.

"I'm sorry," I whispered. My head fell forward and pressed against the bars. "I'm sorry you died. I'm sorry I did not become the man you taught me to be. I'm sorry for what I have to do."

I took a breath and prepared myself. ATOM could not have me. I wouldn't let them. I told myself to pull my arms back as hard and fast as I could. My hands trembled, struggling against the heat. I took a breath, biting my lip hard, and mouthed the word goodbye.

"Wait!" a voice shouted.

I jumped and pulled back from the bars. The blisters on my feet screamed in revolt as I stumbled onto my back.

"No! No more tricks!" I covered both ears.

The staircase squeaked, each step a gunshot next to my ear that sent coils of electricity flowing through my skull. I scurried to the center of the cell and curled into a ball. I buried my face into my knees, hiding from the surrounding darkness. Eyes watched me. Anxiety rampaged through my chest like a stampede of lions toward fallen prey. I couldn't breathe, panicked by thoughts of what the Tank might deliver next. What torture lies in wait? I imagined a rotted corpse lingered beyond the iron bars, waiting to devour what remained of my soul. I welcomed it. He would know only disappointment. I squeezed my eyes shut and braced for pain, but nothing came to gnaw at my flesh. Instead, a flame flickered to life. I turned away and covered my eyes. The voice came again, although I couldn't make out the words. I had expected a beast to tear into me and rip meat from my bones, or a waterlogged carcass to crawl across the ground, wet skin slithering toward me. It would rake dead nails across my skin and pull me back into the undertow. Nothing came. The voice that lingered outside my cell sounded warm and inviting. It offered a hope so real that I longed for it to come closer. A trick. The Tank had been devious thus far, and I wouldn't be fooled. I refused to open my eyes. I waited for the Tank's cruelty to come and take it all away. Instead, the voice came again. Not a cruel, punishing voice, but something soft and gentle and enticing.

"Hey, it's okay," a woman whispered. "Don't hurt yourself. Don't let the Tank win. Take this and it will all be over for a little while." Her voice was the melody to a song I craved to hear. It was sanity, safety, and everything this place wasn't. I wanted it close but feared what might be lurking behind it. I didn't move or respond. It was a trap. Whatever apparition the Tank had fabricated was taunting me. "I've been where you are; I know what it's like. This can make it go away." No matter how hard I fought it, her voice grew more inviting with each word. I couldn't bear it. It didn't matter if I ignored it. It didn't matter if it were real or fake. The Tank's patience was endless, one way or another it would draw me in.

I gave in and looked at her, but what I saw was not expected. No corpse or beast or face from my past lingered. It was a girl; one I didn't seem to know.

"Drink this. I promise you'll feel better."

The lantern hurt my eyes, forcing me to squint. "I can't. No...this place...it knows the things I've done. It uses them against me. I can't...this world is no longer a place I want to be. It cannot be changed. The darkness...ATOM, they cannot have me."

"It's everywhere." Her voice was firm. "It's everywhere and you fight it. You don't stop. If you stop, they win. Is that what you want? Do you want to give up?"

I tried to seek an alternative, but more than anything that's what I wanted. "Yes."

"Then take this first. If you still want to give up after that, fine." She reached through the bars, unfazed by the iron, and pointed to a vial on the floor.

"What are you?" I asked, expecting her to morph into a cruel memory.

"Maybe a friend," she said. "For now, I'm someone trying to save your life. Drink."

I unfurled my body. The joints creaked and ached, fighting the movement. The neutral warmth of the room faded and the cold breeze began again. Ice scraped my skin, frost creeping across my cell. I shivered. Whatever that vial was, it couldn't be worse than this, could it? I crawled toward it, and the lantern revealed blistered arms and cuts along my hand. Deep bruises had formed over my knuckles, the skin taking on shades of purple. My fingers were wrinkled and cracked, fingernails missing and green scabs oozing pus.

"What if I don't want it?" I whispered. "What if I don't want to be saved? I can't be here. I don't deserve to be alive. Not after what I've done."

"You don't earn redemption by giving up," she countered. "You can't fight once you've turned to ash. You're a symbol of hope, or at least you used to be. One bump in the road and you're ready to throw in the towel? Some champion."

"You weren't there." I shook my head. "You didn't see what happened. The water, their faces, their screams. So much screaming." I could almost feel the shrill of their voices rippling against my skin. It wasn't just the Tank. It was reality too. My time here had been the first moments I'd had to let things sink in, and sink they had.

"Then do it for them. *Fight* for them."

Something in the way she spoke made me reach for the vial. I felt a hope that lingered in her words. Hope I thought the Tank had obliterated. The purple liquid swirled inside the glass and I looked up at her. Her face was masked by shadows.

"Keep fighting," she whispered.

The cork popped, but not without a struggle. It shouldn't have been hard, but I was weak. My arms trembled when I tilted it back, and cold liquid hit my tongue, dousing it in flavor; raspberries first, then apples with a hint of caramel. As quick as it had come, the flavor vanished and the distinct copper aftertaste of blood lined my mouth. A flare of heat formed at the back of my throat as I gasped for air. My fingers went numb. I dropped the vial and it smashed into diamond shards that glistened across the floor. When the liquid hit my stomach a bomb exploded inside me. I fell to the ground. Ice and fire filled my veins. I wanted to scream but I couldn't move my lips. Tears ran from my eyes and my muscles shuddered. A sharp lance split my skull like an axe and the world collapsed around me. I was left with a single word from the girl. A whisper among the shadows.

"Fight."

CHAPTER 6

An unwelcome state of nothingness devoured me. When delirium faded, dread flooded in. A light flickered outside my cell, bringing a reprieve to the nightmare I'd been squandering in. The blisters that covered my feet, the wound along my stomach, and the lacerations across my arms were gone, but the cut on my finger and the gashes on my back remained. A thrumming ricocheted across my shoulders, reminding me that the unique gift my kind carried remained absent. I'd never have the rush of diving through the clouds at an earth-rattling speed again. I'd never fall from great heights knowing I could catch myself. I would never fly. I would never be what I was, and although it hurt, it seemed selfish to feel it when the void in my heart remained; a black hole of unseen depth that carried the agony and unrelenting guilt of having sent a small village to their grave. My stomach twisted into a knot, a mixture of remorse and hunger colliding together.

I shivered. Not because the air was cold, but because the feelings that roamed through me were foreign and sickening, amplified by everything I'd endured in the Tank. Hendrik had sent me here to break me down, and break me he had. I realized now I was not the angel I thought. I was not a beacon of justice against an evil force, if anything, I was like them: a danger to supernaturals across the country.

"That's the worst I've ever seen it." Her voice was back, sliding through the shallow depression I'd wrapped myself in.

"It gets better, does it? Or maybe I'm not handling it as well as most." I didn't mean for it to sound as condescending as it did, but I didn't make an attempt to apologize.

"It never gets better in the Tank. The longer you're here the worse it becomes, and nobody handles it well," she responded. "Although judging by the looks of you, I'd say you're haunted by more than most. All I meant was that this is the worst sentence I've ever seen someone get fresh through the gate. Hendrik must have had a point to hammer home with you."

I pushed past shaking arms, the scabs over my shoulders cracking and breaking with the movement. A cold drop ran down my back. I shuddered.

"Well, he's made it."

"I would hope so. Nobody should be stupid enough to challenge Hendrik again after this. You're not stupid, are you?"

"What? No."

"What did you do?"

"Nothing. It doesn't matter."

"That's right, it doesn't. Nothing does. If you want to get by here, you play along. It doesn't matter what you stand for or what you believe in, it's not worth dying for. Not in here."

"So I should go against everything I believe?" I asked. "No, that means they win."

"You're going to do this over pride? Don't you realize how pathetic that is?"

"It's not pride, it's moral…it's ethics," I argued. "It's fighting for what's right."

"Is that what you were doing while you crawled along the floor begging for it to stop? Were you crying tears of ethics? Is whimpering in the dark fighting the system?"

"You don't even know what you're saying. You don't know me, you don't—"

"Everybody knows you," she said. "The infamous Ash Lawson, rogue angel and enemy of the state. You've run an underground movement for five years, smuggling supernaturals to other countries. Until a few days ago, you were both a myth and a legend. One of the last remaining angels in the country fighting the people that put us in this godforsaken place. And then the hero who couldn't be captured was…and you came limping up our little cobblestone road in handcuffs. Tell me, Ash Lawson, are you worth saving?"

I struggled to provide an answer. I had always said I'd die before I worked with ATOM, I still felt that way, but having experienced the horrors of the Tank, a part of me was afraid to stay here. The other part was afraid of what might await me on the other side.

"I don't know."

"That's a strange answer."

"Is it? I'm responsible for the deaths of a lot of people. Does that sound like someone worth saving to you?"

"I don't know what to make of you. Either you're brave or stupid. Maybe a bit of both. You should've used the two free tickets you were born with to fly the hell out of this country when you had the chance."

"I did," I said. "I did leave once, but then I came back."

"Okay, now I know you're in the stupid category."

"What if I am? I thought we deserved a chance. All of us. Maybe we don't. Maybe we're all doomed, like them..."

"Like who?" she asked.

"Like the ship full of people I sent to their graves. Surely you've heard by now."

"Is that why you're acting like a petty fool? You feel guilty?"

"Do you even hear what you're saying?" I asked.

"You've helped hundreds of people over the past few years. You lost one. It was bound to happen at some point. Is that all it takes to defeat you? Things don't go your way one time and that's it?" she questioned. "Some legend. You sound more like a toddler."

"I didn't lose one," I snapped. "I lost three hundred and seven." I shook my head. Saying the number out loud was like striking the nail that had already been hammered in. It didn't help; if anything it damaged everything around it. "If you were expecting a legend, sorry to disappoint. I'm a lot of things, but legendary isn't one of them."

"And dying in here proves what?" she asked.

"It proves I'm not willing to succumb to what they want. It proves I'm willing to take a stand to the end."

She laughed, though it was anything but humorous. "You think you're being a martyr? You're not. All you're doing is giving up.

That's weak. Nothing sticks it to them better than surviving."

"What do you even care?" I asked. "Or better yet, how did you get in here? Who are you?"

Silence filled the space between us before I heard a shuffle in the shadows. She stepped into the lantern's reach, revealing bright violet eyes and a pale complexion. Her hair was parted in the center. Warm golden locks hung past her shoulders, layered with strands of light and dark blonde mixed together. Her lips looked soft, arching with a visible scar that marred her bottom lip. She was five ten, shorter than me by a few inches, but she looked strong, firm definition sculpting her arms. Curves defined her hips. Blue jeans ran along her legs and black runners tapped along the floor. White lines traced her knuckles, scars that matched a larger version along her neck.

"Tryst Rivera, and I got in here with this." She held up a weathered string with a skeleton-like key dangling from it. "I'm here to give you a chance to reconsider your position. As for why I care? I don't. If you get out of this place I'll care, but until then I'm off the hook."

"What does that mean?"

"Don't worry about it. The truth is I hate to see a newbie get taken down the first week, especially one that comes with a reputation like yours."

"Some reputation," I whispered. "And the drink?"

"Soliloquy. It's all that can balance you out in here."

I looked at the spiky bars between us and at the concrete throughout. Cracks in the walls and ceilings had sprouts of moss stretching across them.

"And this is the Tank," I said. "What is this place?"

"Magic, enchantment, witchcraft, voodoo, an ancient charm? There is no one answer. It's different for everybody. It's alive in a way. It feeds off memories and fears and life force. Nightmares are fabricated in ways you can't imagine until you've been here. It almost makes you human and then some. That's why those gashes on you back are infected and the cuts on your hands haven't healed. This place makes an oubliette of your mind and body, twisting you into something different from when you entered. You either give in or you die. There is no in between. Some say its Hendrik's creation; others think it's some concoction ATOM has drummed up. It doesn't matter. When you've been here once, you'll do anything to keep yourself from coming back. Most of us, anyway." She raised an eyebrow and crossed her arms.

"I get it. Once is enough. And I've been here a week?"

Tryst laughed. "You wouldn't survive a week. Four days is bad enough, isn't it? Before you, the longest anybody ever saw was two. Hendrik must think you're special or something."

"Or something is more like it."

We stared at one another for a few moments before Tryst turned away. "Well, now that the Soliloquy has kicked in, I need to report back. The last thing I want to do is end up locked in the cage next to you."

"You've done time here before?"

"Not my proudest moment." She paused, a violent shiver running through her. I saw the hint of a past horror in her eyes, but she quickly masked it. "Listen, once I report in, Hendrik will be around to check on you. If you want to die, do it in here. Don't walk up these steps unless you're serious about survival. You'll be putting someone else in danger otherwise, and based on what you've said, that's not something you're keen on doing again. If you want to live and get out of here, keep your mouth shut and do what he says."

I scoffed at the idea. Now that the torment was over my pride had time to try and rear its head. It failed. I couldn't be determined or defiant. I was too weak. Four days in here had been a nightmare. I couldn't lie to myself. I'd give almost anything to get out.

"I mean it, Ash. You want to help people? Live. But don't you dare walk out that door if you're not serious about playing along."

"Okay, I got it."

"Do you?" She seemed irritated, almost worried.

"Yes."

"Good, then play along. Hendrik talks a lot about self-preservation. You may not agree with everything he has to say, but he's not wrong about that. You do what you have to in order to survive. You can trust me on that one." She fidgeted with her fingers, eyes avoiding mine.

"Can I?" I studied her face. "That's asking an awful lot considering we just met, isn't it?"

Tryst picked up the lantern and stopped at the base of the staircase. She shrugged. "Or don't, it's not my ass in the fryer. Not yet. If you want to stay down here and suffer until your last breath, that's your choice, but is that the way you want to go? I'd never seen an angel before now, but I'd heard things. I'd heard how prideful, defiant, and reckless they were; yet once upon a time they were forces to be reckoned with. Which is it?"

"Both? Neither? I don't know."

She shrugged. "Well, you better figure it out, because if it's the latter, that seems like a pretty lousy end to your story, doesn't it?"

CHAPTER 7

I rocked back and forth, hugging my knees against my chest. Blond hair dangled in my eyes and I watched it like a hypnotist's pocket watch swinging back and forth. It distracted me from the coming whispers. Soliloquy had been my saving grace, but it seemed like days since Tryst had been here and it had vacated my system. The cold breeze came and went, lining my arms in goose bumps. My heart palpitated, hammering inside as nervous dread ripened for the coming torture. I needed out of this place. Tryst had made a point and I took it to heart; dying in the Tank wouldn't prove anything. Once upon a time I felt the need to prove there could be a better life for supernaturals. Now I didn't know what I had to prove, but I couldn't help feeling it was more than this.

"The Tank has power." Hendrik's voice cracked like a whip. I hadn't heard him come in, and my heart paused, fear rupturing within and sputtering into my chest. It was hard to breathe. I gasped for air and searched the darkness. Only the shadows stared back at me. "It's a strange power. It's almost...alive, isn't it? To conquer the Tank, one must have mastered himself. He cannot be affected by trivialities like warmth, comfort, or sanity. He must not be a slave to his emotions. Few possess the discipline it takes to achieve such growth. If you want to know the truth about what is wrong with this world, it is that."

"How does one reach such a plateau?" I asked.

"It is not something that can be taught; it is a realization discovered with sheer will. One must find harmony amidst his flaws and have the vision to realize they are not flaws at all."

"How did you find yours?"

"An interesting question." His shoes echoed, a soft tap that made the room seem larger than it was. The strike of a match bit the air and a flicker of flame came to life. Hendrik's face lingered in the orange glow and the flame wrapped around the waxy stem of a candle. "Anger showed me mine. A pure rage that boiled my blood. It would've killed me if I let it. When I developed the ability to let it go and gain control over my emotions, my awakening began. Control of the inner workings of your soul and you control the world—an ability that will forever need to be honed in order to maintain the equilibrium."

"Even after mastering the skill you struggle?"

Hendrik offered a halfhearted smile. "To master something is to understand you are never finished. Even the master becomes the student on occasion. To some you were an outlaw, but to others, a savior. You were a master of your craft. Smuggling became not a crime, but a work of art. By all accounts you are still a child, yet supernaturals entrusted you with their lives based on reputation alone. Why is that?"

I hesitated with a response. Was he actually asking, or was he expecting a certain answer?

"Because the chance at a free life was worth it to them. To live without fear of ATOM was a freedom they'd lost."

"Was it?" He arched a brow, peering in through the bars. "Supernaturals have always been hunted. From those who didn't know we existed and wanted to prove otherwise, to those who knew us all too well and felt us a threat to humanity. ATOM is simply those people working together. The truth is, there is no life for us in this world that does not involve fear in some part."

"I suppose you're right," I surmised. "Although until ATOM, the hunters were a small group, self-funded and with limitations. Now it's a government unit with endless reach, supplies, and manpower."

"Staying here means dealing with ATOM, leaving means dealing with those small, self-funded groups," he said. "There is no land in which we are free. Such is the world we find ourselves in, and in that world, you went against the grain and chose the latter and became a master of your craft. Deceiving ATOM for nearly a decade is impressive, and you brought your definition of freedom to many."

"Not master enough," I whispered. Or hardly at all. If I'd truly known what I was doing—if I'd been as smart as I thought I was—I wouldn't be here, and those people would still be alive.

"Can you think of another as accomplished as you?" he asked. "There was a seven-hundred-and-fifty-thousand-dollar bounty on your head. That is not a small number given the state of our country. Consider your encounter with Colby your learning moment. You became the student. What was it you learned?" His bright blue gaze looked intense, but his expression soft.

What did I learn? I learned to never get cocky. Never stop being careful. Always prepare for the worst-case scenario. But I wouldn't tell him that. He wanted to hear something different.

"I learned we all have to play our part and contribute in our own way. Nothing is free, not even freedom. Especially not freedom. "

Hendrik gave what I assumed was a smile, though it looked more like a grimace. "Indeed. Unfortunately, sometimes we don't realize the cost until it's too late." Hendrik tapped the bars, running his fingers over the iron, copper, and silver barbs, unaffected by the metals. "Sometimes one cannot fight the battle head-on. He must tunnel up from within. Isn't that right?"

He watched me carefully. Too carefully. My chest tightened and I questioned my response. I didn't think he wanted me to pretend my stance on everything had changed, but he wanted to hear I was open to playing nice. I nodded, even though I wasn't entirely sure the point he was trying to make.

"You have potential for great things, Mr. Lawson, but your defiance and pride is... well, to put it plainly, intrusive," he continued. "You want freedom, but you insist on breaking down the door to attain it. That will not do. Youth is your drawback. You have yet to learn the art of patience, and frankly you are brash and irresponsible. Bringing you into the Academy is a risk. I question its worth."

I felt the Tank rising up around me. The floor became ice beneath my feet and something cut across my stomach, the sensation of blood trickling down my waist. I cringed, but I didn't look down. It wasn't real. The Soliloquy had faded entirely and the

Tank took control of my consciousness. I clenched my fists and kept eye contact with Hendrik, fighting to stay on my feet. My freedom had always been worth fighting for, but maybe Tryst was right—and in some way so was Hendrik—I had to fight in a different way.

"I...I can change. I can contribute."

"I'm not certain you can." His icy stare narrowed and a sharpness pierced my back like the fangs of a serpent. "I am in a difficult position. Many challenge and question my methods. As such, I must make examples where I can. You are a fine example to prove my reach is merciless. If you die in here, it reinstates the fear of my rule as a trusted source running this facility. Additionally, it enhances credibility to the Tank; a mystic place that can break the most defiant angel's will. That would do nicely on my resume. On the other side, however, if you change and cooperate, it returns confidence in my ability to rehabilitate. Also a fine example. To which camp you fall into I am unsure."

The temperature spiked. Sweat beaded on my brow. Hendrik remained unfazed, standing tall and confident in his finely pressed blue suit. He adjusted his silver tie, studying my face. My knees buckled, blisters bubbling and splitting on my feet. Voices from the ship called my name; broad strokes of guilt rippled inside me. Nausea circled my head and I grabbed the iron bars for balance. It seared my already injured palms and I bit back a scream. I had to get out of here. I wouldn't give up or concede. I'd adapt. I wouldn't leave this world like this. Not on my hands and knees, begging for it to end. I had to make amends for the things I'd done.

"It's a win for you either way." My words trembled, lips quivering as I spoke, struggling to keep the hurt from my voice. "Let me out. If I step out of line you can let this place deconstruct me then." The temperature became too much. There was no such thing as confidence. I'd been beaten down and consumed by the Tank. I cried out as a shadowy whip clawed across my back. "Please."

The world warbled, color and light coming and going from my vision. Hendrik stood outside the cell, his face completely still and both hands clasped behind his back. His shoulders rose and fell with a heavy sigh.

"Redemption is not a task easily achieved. There could be a

future here for you. A great one, should you claim it. One that will leave us both remembered, if only you can acquire the qualities you currently lack. Or perhaps your fate is to be the angel that never made it." His fingers pinched the wick, snuffing out the flame. "An awakening will come, Mr. Lawson. I do hope you don't disappoint."

CHAPTER 8

I had forgotten daylight. Even with scattered clouds to block the sun, the blue skies burned my eyes. I welcomed it. Sap and moist bark lingered in the cold morning air. I drew it in with the deepest breath I could manage. Four days in the Tank and I'd forgotten the world, and it seemed the world had forgotten me. Without me, it still turned. I had left it untouched. Another lesson in my defeat. What change could one man make in a world made of walls?

Hues of green spread across the property. Long grass tickled my marred feet, causing spurs of pain to burst between traces of happiness. After being in the Tank I found exhilaration in the dewy grass. The earth was hope; the sky future. It kept my body—which had surpassed exhaustion—moving forward.

My senses were overloaded with reality and I breathed it in between broken and scabbed lips. Thick concrete walls and barbed wire encased the property. The guards were on constant patrol and from above they studied the grounds. Through all the security, however, there seemed to be an odd section of the land that remained unguarded. A stretch of woods that lined the north side had been left exposed. Shadows loomed inside the first row of trees, making it impossible to see within.

"Eyes forward," one guard said.

I responded immediately. I'd been granted a ticket out of the Tank, and I was never going back.

Paths of golden cobblestone wound from the Academy toward flourishing gardens and fountains that trickled symphonies of rain. A steel door, a long corridor, and several winding halls took me from the air outside to Hendrik's office. I stood on the area rug that emitted a musty smell of dust and age. Spiral patterns and weathered edges danced around me. My toes curled into rough fabric.

"Sit down, Mr. Lawson," Hendrik said. He didn't look up from his notebook, feathered quill scrawling over ivory parchment. I took the only available chair, the other occupied by a girl. Both hands in her lap and one leg crossed over the other. Strands of blonde mingled with darker streaks, barely touching her shoulders. "Tryst will be giving you the tour and going through the basics, but first you need to get cleaned up. We have an image to uphold and sloppiness will not do. You've missed dinner. We make no exceptions for tardiness, therefore your next meal will be breakfast, which is served at six a.m. sharp. Let's go over a few of the ground rules, yes?"

"Yeah, sure." I felt out of place. Hendrik's eyes were serious and Tryst didn't acknowledge me.

"Wake-up is five in the morning, lights out is ten at night. Meals are served three times a day. You will be in the mess hall during these allotments and nowhere else. When you are not working, you will be in your room. Additionally, guests are prohibited from speaking to the guards. You will answer when spoken to and nothing further. If you have concerns, bring them to your advisor, whom will bring them to me. If action is necessary it will be taken as I see fit. Everybody at the Academy is worthy of your respect. Whether or not you feel that way is negated. You will offer it to them. Lastly, your abilities, whatever they may be, are not permitted. Period. These rules are nonnegotiable. No exceptions will be made. I do not feel the need to explain what happens should you disobey these rules."

"No," I responded.

"You will start at the bottom like all guests," Hendrik continued. "You will work at whatever task is given, and you will work hard. Based on your advisor's evaluations, the opportunity to move up in status may be bestowed. Such advancement comes with perks to be discussed should the situation arrive. The Academy is a fine institution, Mr. Lawson, but the quality of your life here will be entirely in your hands."

"I understand."

"Do you?"

I thought it had been a rhetorical question, but Hendrik leaned forward and clasped creased fingers into one another.

"Yes?" A question or an answer, even I wasn't sure.

Without a thought I began squeezing my knuckles. A pop sounded as the knuckle cracked, and one of Hendrik's eyes twitched. Tryst shifted with unease, her violet eyes cringed.

"A disgusting habit," Hendrik said. "May I continue?"

"Yes. Sorry." I rubbed sweaty palms along my tattered pants and tried to remain still. I fought the urge to pop the remaining knuckles. The more I resisted, the more they yearned for it.

"You will see things that you will not like here. Things a person of your background may feel the need to change," Hendrik said. "It is in your best interest to do the opposite of what your instincts tell you. Focus on self-improvement and nothing more. I will not go to the trouble of explaining our methods. You'll learn soon enough. Or you won't. For both yours and Ms. Rivera's sake, I hope it's the former."

Both our sakes? I didn't understand what he'd meant, but he didn't give me a chance to ask. We were excused, leaving the words to creep through me and sink into the pit of my stomach like a viper beneath the sand lying in wait.

Tryst and a guard led us through the building. Guards fortified each entrance with weapons in hand. Those who had nothing to safeguard wandered the empty halls like spirits trapped between wood paneling. They didn't look at us. We didn't exist. They simply passed by, aware of everything yet acknowledging nothing.

The halls were a web of polished wood and brass fixtures. Dim lamps led the way. Tryst waited at the base of the stairs while the guard pressed his earpiece, speaking to someone on the other end. After a moment he nodded to himself and ushered us up with flat and commanding words, while he stayed behind to stand post at the bottom of the stairs.

The upper level stretched as a single hallway with closed doors on either side. At either end stood a Plexiglas booth with a guard behind it. Almost every closed door led to a separate room—the guests' living quarters—with the exception of one, a single bathroom for all to share.

We hovered outside a door that looked like any other and Tryst pointed at it. "Hendrik wasn't kidding. You need to get cleaned up. I'll wait here, so don't take long."

"I might need a bit of time. I haven't showered in—"

"A long time, I can tell. Let me give you a brief rundown of how your days will look here: up before dawn, breakfast, work, lunch, work, dinner, and then lockdown. That's it. This isn't a school; it's a government-run facility. You don't have the freedom to wander the halls or ask questions. The only reason we're out right now is because you were released from the Tank and I'm responsible for you. Get clean and get out or there'll be room in the Tank for both of us."

Her words echoed Hendrik's and the viper struck from the sand. A drop of venom rose in my throat like hot acid. The thought of going back made the vomit thick and hard to swallow. I wasn't going back. Not ever.

The water burned like gasoline over wounds. Black and red ran over my body, slithering around the drain long after the first wash of soap. My hair felt gritty, caked with dirt and blood and who knew what else. By the time I'd finished the second shampoo, it felt like hair with layers of sandpaper intertwined. My skin had split along the crevices of my neck and inside my elbows, while the scabbed-over wounds on my shoulders softened and peeled back in the pressure. The muscles that once controlled my wings throbbed, reminding me of what Colby had taken. Clouds of anger and guilt blinked inside me. There wasn't one without the other, they worked together to wreak havoc. Perhaps my wings had been karma. A down payment on what I'd taken from the people aboard that ship.

I thought the shower would soothe me, but the water's burn had only been the beginning to a crescendo of heartache. It broke down the anger and washed it away, leaving only sadness and guilt. I saw Samantha's eyes shimmer in the sunlight, and the whir of

Jasper's lips as he flew his wooden ship through the air. Harry cursed at me to stand up straight, and Tara reached out to me with a hesitant touch. A dozen others smiled or laughed. Some of them even thanked me for all I'd done. Tears ran from my eyes, bile rose in my throat, and my knees weakened. I couldn't hold it back this time. Vomit spilled from my lips and splattered the floor. I dropped, unable to stand, and it swirled around me in a stench that burned my nostrils and urged me to vomit again. I coughed and gagged, wishing the water could wash it all away. It took the mess I'd made on the floor, but it couldn't wash away everything.

I thumped my fist weakly against the wall. I should've been strong and held it all together—I couldn't. The Tank had reduced me to a man I didn't recognize; not a man at all. Being strong seemed impossible right now. Maybe I never was. Pangs of sorrow and guilt crashed against me while tears danced clumsily along my eyes. The tranquility of the shower was gone, replaced by the sloshing waves that swallowed the ship and everyone left inside. The truth had settled and it was hard to face. Reality often was. I hated myself for what had happened and even more for the sadness I felt over my wings. They'd been a small price to pay compared to what the others had suffered, but a price I regretted having to pay nonetheless. I had preferred flying over running, over everything. Taking my wings was like taking my heart. My heart would've been better. Then I could have joined the souls whose lives I squandered.

The bathroom door squeaked open and my chest tightened. I clenched my jaw and bit back the sobs and frustrated screams I wanted to release.

"Did you get lost?" Tryst's voice snapped. "This isn't a spa."

I cleared my throat and wiped my face, shakily rising to my feet. Water splashed over my skin to erase any trace of what had happened and I masked my shaky voice with a deeper-than-usual tone.

"Sorry, there was a lot of blood and dirt."

"I received a warning," Tryst said. "Do you know how rare that is? You've been in here twenty minutes. I don't know where you're from, but where I come from that isn't a quick shower. Get your ass out before the guard comes back."

I tried to shake the remnants of despair that lingered. "I'll be right out."

"You already told me that once. I'll wait here."

She seemed pushy and impatient and I wanted to scream at her to get out. In the Tank she'd seemed softer. Then again, anything would've seemed soft in the midst of that hell. Instead of yelling my frustration, I shut off the water, scared of what might happen if I didn't.

The shreds that remained of my jeans were unacceptable Academy wear. Instead, I wandered the hall with a white towel wrapped around my waist and wet footprints trailing me. The last door on the right was ours. The guard behind the Plexiglas stared with cold eyes, his face mostly covered by a black mask. A buzzer sounded and our door's latch retracted. Home sweet home.

A tiny room with a single three-drawer dresser, four beds in the form of two bunks, and a nightstand between them. The bottom bunk on the left had a pair of folded jeans, a pair of sweats, four pairs of socks, two pairs of underwear, and two black T-shirts.

"Those are for you," Tryst said. "Laundry is done Sunday evenings. Keep them clean. And for future, do us all a favor and use the allotted bathroom time before lockdown." She pointed at a red bucket that sat in the corner. Her cold violet eyes cut into me. She seemed even more irritated now than in the shower.

"Have I done something to upset you?"

Her lips hardened and a single brow arched. Her face seemed cold, eyes studying me, and then all at once she relaxed.

"No, why?"

"I spent four days in the Tank," I reminded her. "I haven't eaten or slept in longer than that. You're on my ass to wash a week of blood and filth off, and you're rushing me around like the hourglass is running out of sand. Cut me some slack, will you?"

The softening features stiffened. "Is that a joke? Was your time in the Tank not enough to hammer home the reality of where you are?" Tryst asked. "There is no slack. There is the way things are and that's it. It's my job to make sure you don't end up back in the Tank, or worse."

"Don't mind her," a male voice said. "Her panties are a little tighter these days now that you two are hitched." A boy appeared over the railing of the top bunk. Black hair parted on the left, thick and dangling past his ears. His olive complexion made him look younger than Tryst, but his eyes didn't hold the same youthfulness. He eyed me head to toe, and it somehow seemed invasive. I adjusted the towel that began to slip off my hips.

Tryst stepped between us. "Ash, this is our other roommate, Soren. Soren, Ash."

He took in a big whiff of air through his nose and contemplated it. "He smells different." His head canted to the side with a ripple of confusion on his face. He licked his lips dramatically and his eyes rolled back and forth. "The taste is not bad..."

"Good?" Tryst asked.

"Different. Definitely no sulfur, no metallic resin. He might actually be okay."

"Really?" Relief reflected in her voice.

"What does that mean?" I asked.

"Too bad he is what he is." Soren shook his head. "Sad to say, but I think seven days is a good bet."

"For my sake you better hope you're wrong," she said.

"Seven days?" I asked. "What are you two talking about?"

They both looked at me with more intensity than I could understand and I gave up trying to figure out what was going on.

The bed squeaked and sighed, springs dug into me. Getting dressed was harder than I'd expected. My body had stiffened, wounds felt crisp and tender, and the muscles ached softly. The shirt caught on the ragged edges of the scabs along my shoulders, stinging as I pulled it over. The scab tore and moistness bled into my shirt. I cursed under my breath. Why hadn't these wounds healed?

"You okay?" Tryst asked. I couldn't tell if she was genuinely concerned or asking for the sake of asking. She and Soren both watched me as if they'd never seen someone get dressed.

"Fine."

Awkwardness fell between us and Tryst sat on the bunk across from me and rubbed her hands along her legs.

"I'm sorry." She spit the words as though they burned her lips. "I'm not trying to be a bitch. I hate seeing anybody go into the Tank, and you were in there a long time. Honestly, I'm amazed you're as coherent as you are. You should be...well, it usually takes a few days for someone to get their bearings."

"And this has led you to disliking me? Great. Rooming with you will be a picnic."

"I don't dis—" She sighed. "Look, Hendrik told me to bring you Soliloquy, I did. He asked me what I thought. I told him.

That's it. I didn't ask for *this*."

"What's *this*? Me in your room?" I asked. "Sorry I'm not sleeping outside in the grass. Perhaps you'd sleep better if I were chained to a tree?"

"Hey, man, take it easy," Soren said. "There's a good chance you're in here because of what she had to say to the headmaster. Cut her a break, will you?"

"Look, Ash," she said. "Hendrik assigned you to this room and made you my responsibility. I don't want that on me. Can you blame me for that?"

"Maybe if I knew what that meant, or what any of this meant, I might understand."

Soren's brows raised and he looked serious. "You two are hitched, dude. For your entire Academy-bound lives—as long or as short as they may be—you two are one in the same."

I had become Tryst's fate and she mine. If I earned a week in the Tank, then so did she. She was entirely responsible for my actions; a method-program set in place by Hendrik to teach us how one's actions affected others in society. At least that's what he had everybody recite. As far as I could tell, it was a secondary plot to keep everybody under control when the guards or advisors weren't present. Clever. Soren explained it all to me with playful exaggerations I didn't appreciate. He flipped his head to the side, constantly trying to wave the strands of silky black hair out of his eyes. They were undeterred, but I didn't need to see his eyes to understand the severity. His tone was enough.

The Academy wasn't a facility to rehabilitate. It wasn't a place to show us the great arc of ATOM. It was a fear camp. Worse. It was a prison. A bordered landscape designed to mold supernaturals into cooperative soldiers. You obeyed or you were punished. The Tank wasn't the only option; they had many methods set to break you. All the guests were young, most under the age of twenty-one. The Academy was a retreat for youthful minds that could still be reshaped. We were the Academy's canvas, and those that could not be made into art would be studied for their failure.

"The favorites are obvious enough. They've been upgraded to white shirts," Tryst said. "If you think I'm harsh, wait until you meet them. They're often worse than the advisors, trying to prove who the most reformed is. They're going to have their sights set on you. You've broken ATOM's rules, fought back, and for a long time were a kink in the system. Everybody thinks you're some defiant, fearless angel of death, and they'll be out to see if they can be the ones to put you in your place. I hope for my sake they're wrong."

"I haven't even met anybody. How can they think anything about me?" I asked.

"You're an angel. Isn't that enough?" she answered.

I didn't need a history lesson. To most, angels were beasts, uncontrollable and insatiable in our appetite for destruction. The truth of angels had been clay in the hands of their enemies for centuries, formed and reshaped as necessary. Between typhons and ATOM, we'd become monsters. It wasn't all a lie, angels weren't exactly caring participants in supernatural history, but they weren't entirely evil either.

"Don't forget," Soren added, "that angels are to blame for ATOM's rule. If they'd have waited instead of rushing out like a pack of wild dogs, the typhons could have united supernaturals everywhere and destroyed a common enemy." Soren laughed. "At least that's the story, right?" Everything he said seemed to have that touch of playfulness to it, and I couldn't read him. Did he believe the stories or was he mocking them? I couldn't tell.

"I'm an angel, but I'm not a *monster*." I lingered on that word. I never used to be a monster. That's not what I had set out to be, but as I said it, I wondered if it wasn't true. After all, does the boogeyman look in the mirror and think himself scary? "I know where I'm from and I know what people think of my kind. I didn't choose that world, I was born into it, but I'm not ashamed of it either. You have your history and I have mine."

"Relax, man, it was a joke. I don't judge," Soren said, rolling onto his back and looking at me upside down. "Besides, everybody knows typhons are psychotic. If it wasn't for them, angels might have been our saving grace. Once upon a time I suppose, but that time has passed. The point is, you need to be careful. You've got Tryst to worry about. I won't let you bring her down. Especially after the docks."

"What did you say?" I asked. Soren stumbled over some words, but I didn't let him get any of them out. "You don't know what happened there!" The anger was unexpected, even to me. I reeled it back, trying to curb my tone. "Nobody does."

"Okay, guys, can we relax?" Tryst asked.

Soren rolled back onto his stomach. "You don't get it. It doesn't matter what happened. It only matters what people *think* happened, and ATOM has made it clear that you killed those people to remind the underground what angels are capable of. To send a message. They want people to think you were endangering us in typical angel fashion, and because of that, everybody will have their eyes on you."

"I didn't—that's not what happened! I was trying to save those people."

"Soren, enough!" Tryst said.

"What?" He shrugged, the bounce back in his voice. "I'm just saying."

She rolled her eyes. "I know, but stop saying anything. He doesn't need to hear this."

I wanted to scream. How could anybody think I would kill those people? My breaths came fast and hard and I had to remind myself that I did. I killed those people. I kept my mouth shut and let my eyes drop to the floor. Soren was right. It didn't matter what angels were really like. It didn't matter what was true and what wasn't. All that mattered was what people believed.

"I think we broke his spirit," Soren said.

They hadn't. My spirit broke with the hull of the ship and the clip of my wings. This place was no different than the rest of the country, a prison like any other.

Tryst lowered herself to look me in the eye. "I don't want to bring you down, Ash; I want to prepare you. No matter how bad this place might seem. You do not want to go back to the Tank and neither do I."

Soren's face appeared over the edge of the top bunk again. "Or worse, they'll give you a lashing worth a thousand nightmares, or worse than that, they'll literally string you up in the yard and make a festival out of killing you."

"Soren!" Tryst cringed and rubbed both sides of her temples. "Easing in, remember?"

He cringed. "Sorry, forget about me. I'm not even here."

"You and I are connected now. Your life is mine and mine is yours," Tryst said. "It's important to me that you understand that. You don't know me, you don't owe me anything, and as far as you're concerned, I'm some girl whose been snapping at you since you escaped hell. I get it, but I don't want to die in this place."

Soren peeked over the edge of the bed again. "So we're clear, when I said they'd kill you, that was serious. I mean, like, dead. Tryst is in charge of you, so whatever you get, she gets. So—"

"I get it, man! I mess up, they torture—or worse—kill us," I replied. "Being responsible for someone else's life is nothing new."

Soren's eyebrows rose. "Okay, okay. Don't shoot the messenger, man. I want to make sure my friend doesn't get killed. I'm sure you can understand."

I closed my eyes and shook my head. I didn't want someone else's blood on my hands. And Tryst wasn't some girl; she'd helped me get out of the Tank and that meant something. I owed her, and I didn't take debts casually.

"I promise I won't get your friend hurt," I said. "Just give me a minute. This place is a lot to take in."

The red digits on the alarm read 10:00 and the room went black. The darkness matched the uncomfortable void inside, and I tried to find comfort in a bed to sleep on. It squeaked and sighed with every movement, springs jabbing into my back, but it was better than the cold floor of the Tank. Soren fell asleep in moments. His breaths were heavy and occasionally his lips smacked. I was exhausted, but sleep eluded me. I lay alone with thoughts I didn't want but couldn't deter. Cries for help moved around me, sloshing in the waves of defeat. They always lingered, but seemed louder in the quiet. My burden to carry. My curse to live.

A splash of moonlight fluttered from behind the curtains and voices came from outside. At first I thought them haunting memories, but soon realized they were real, and found them a welcome distraction from the barriers of my mind.

"Vampires," Tryst whispered. "As you might expect, they work the nightshift." She sounded sullen and lost with a tremble in her voice. She was scared of me. She feared I would get her hurt.

I didn't respond. Part of me felt scared she might be right. I'd spent the last few years fighting ATOM and everything they represented. Now I'd have to follow an archaic system they'd put in place to make us fall in line. I shuddered at the thought. I knew I'd have to dig deep to survive and keep myself and Tryst alive.

"We don't believe what they say, you know," she murmured.

"You've heard what a terrible creature I am all your life, no doubt," I whispered in return. "Now I'm a murderer too. Typical angel, right? What's not to believe?"

"My parents had friends who were angels. They knew they weren't all like that and they raised me not to make judgments. As for being a murderer, I don't know," she said. "I know there was an angel out there saving supernaturals and fighting back. I'd heard he once took on an entire patrol to save a young girl and her family who were supposed to become lab rats. There's even a story that once he infiltrated one of those labs to save a man he hardly knew, but who had once helped him. Then there are the stories about an outlaw smuggling people out of the country. Taking refugees and sending them to safe lands. Lands where they'd lurk in the shadows like the old days, but where ATOM wouldn't so easily find them. His bounty went up and the government issued death warrants for anybody who assisted him."

"That's quite the story," I said.

The picture she'd painted made it sound heroic, it wasn't. Like most things too good to be true, it was a path paved with good intentions that became a slippery slope, and the downfall to many who didn't deserve it.

"It was. Nobody could believe it when they caught him. A real-life angel." She released a laugh. Silence filled the air between us, rolling in the darkness. I could almost hear the thudding of her heart and the nervous shake in her voice.

"I don't have a death wish," I said. "You don't have to worry. I'm not going to let you down,"

A heavy breath, perhaps a sigh of relief, slipped into the darkness. "Goodnight, Ash," she whispered.

CHAPTER 9

Morning came to the raging drone of an alarm through the building. It wasn't a gentle wake-up, and once it stopped I was stuck somewhere between the real world and the dreamscape. I wanted to roll over and go back to sleep, but the Academy said wake up, and my life existed by what they said now. Besides, even if I had the choice, Soren's chatter wouldn't allow for any more sleep.

"He doesn't look like an angel," Soren whispered.

"What did you expect him to look like?" Tryst asked.

"Where are his wings? And isn't he supposed to have a halo or glow or be angelic looking or something?"

A pang of sadness hit me and my shoulders throbbed. I wished I could stretch out my wings in a morning yawn, giving them the reach they craved. I squeezed my eyes shut and pushed the thought away. They were gone. Being sad wouldn't change that.

"A halo? Are you serious?"

"Yeah, isn't that what they have?" Soren asked.

"Why don't you ask him? He needs to get up anyway."

"I'm not waking him up. He's big. What if he hits me?"

"Then it would be no different than how anybody else treats you, would it?" Tryst said. Quiet followed. "I shouldn't have said that."

"It's fine. It's not like it isn't true," Soren admitted.

"I'm preoccupied and frustrated," Tryst replied. "I'm sorry. I shouldn't have taken it out on you."

"Don't worry about it, or him. He'll come around. This place is an adjustment for everybody at first."

"That's what has me nervous. Do you remember how it was when we got here? I'm on edge, that's all."

"Don't be." I threw the blanket to the side. "I told you there wasn't anything to worry about." I still didn't feel confident, but I feigned it nonetheless.

"It's not only you. It's everybody else," she said.

Soren nodded. "Yeah, everybody else here sucks. Especially the advisors. Ugh! I hope he doesn't get Gareth. He's the worst."

Tryst sighed. "We're hitched, Soren. I have Gareth, which means he does too. We're one in the same now."

"Right." He looked up at me and contrived a smile. "I think a week was generous. Four days?"

"Shut up," Tryst warned. "You're not helping."

He shrugged. "I was just kidding."

"I'll be fine. This isn't my first rodeo."

Soren laughed. "Yeah, well, this is a different kind of bull. Gareth is the most low-tolerance supernatural in the building. His crew works harder than any other, and most of them are real jerks, present company excluded. You're an outlaw with a bad rep. Reason says..." Soren curled his fingers and placed his hand up to his ear as if straining to hear something. "Your outlook does not look good."

The buzzer sounded and the latch retracted, the door to each room swinging open. A line of guards awaited us. We placed our hands against the wall and received a pat down, gloved hands invading our bodies. Each room was checked one by one: first the drawers, then windows, and finally beds. I'd made mine as per Soren's instructions, immediately grateful I'd listened.

One room was met without approval, and the two boys and two girls that occupied it were pushed to their knees. Nobody moved, eyes fixated on the floor. The quartet held out their arms and the guard raised his baton, but rather than strike their hands, it cracked against their backs, one by one. They tried to remain silent, but after the second strike they could no longer hold it in. One boy cried out for them to stop. They didn't. He received three extra strikes. The first landed across his back with a solid thud, the second snapped across his knuckles, and the last struck his jaw. I heard it buckle from the far end of the hall. Blood spilled from the boy's mouth and his jaw hung awkwardly to the side. I had the thought to step forward. I couldn't stand here and watch this, could I? No sooner did the thought come that Tryst's hand gripped my wrist.

One of the guards caught the motion and stepped in front me, drawing his baton. He shoved it into my chest, pushing my back against the wall. I cringed at the pain and anger flared inside me, but I didn't move. The small man looked up, eyes burning into me. He pulled his mask down and spit on my face. Warm froth splattered my cheek.

"What the hell do you think you're doing?" His face crinkled with age, his bald head spotted with blemishes. The stench on his breath reeked of malt liquor. His nametag read Calm. Ironic, as he yelled obscenities at me. I bit down on the inside my cheek and Tryst's hand still held my wrist. Her grip tightened as the man grew more irritated. "Well, you going to be a hero, Angel Boy?" The tip of his baton poked me harder after each word. "Please do, it'll make my day sweeter to show an angel what a pissant he is in this world." I moved to wipe the spit off my mouth but he ordered me not to. More of it splattered my face.

"No," I said, trying to keep my lips closed as spit ran over them.

"What?" He struck my arm with the baton.

"No, *sir.*"

My body screamed to hit him back. He would crumple. Tryst's hand on my wrist reminded me that wasn't a good idea. Instead, I avoided eye contact, staring at the lines of black in the hardwood floor. I focused my breathing and reminded myself of the blue sky I saw when I emerged from the Tank. The grass on my feet. The dew-licked air. When the emotions settled, Calm was still staring at me with an ignorant grin that curled at the corner of his mouth.

"That's what I thought, New Fish."

I didn't look back at the foursome of guests being beaten. It made me feel like I was watching the ship sink all over again. I felt a piece of me die then. I hated feeling helpless.

The main building stood as a cylindrical behemoth. The walls curved and polished wooden columns held up an intricate ceiling of stoops and beams. At the rear of the building stood a line of steel doors with small wire-glass windows. They opened to the mess hall; a sealed room with no windows. Old-fashioned fixtures dangled from bronze chains mounted to a stipple ceiling that might have once been white, but now held a yellow hue. Old eggs and burned hash browns scented the air with a hint of copper that lingered afterward.

Breakfast was a quick-moving line toward a small counter. There were different lines for different diets. The shifters lined up and received platters of meat. Most of it was raw and spoiled. Vampires were on a liquid diet. No choice in blood type, only a single plastic bag that looked battered and old. Another line was solely for those in white shirts. Guests who'd exceeded their advisors' expectations but were not yet twenty-one, the age required to leave the Academy and be put to work directly for ATOM. The white shirts had bowed down to those who put them in chains, impressed them, and in exchange, they were given a cut above the rest. A strange agreement considering we were all prisoners here, but everybody did what they had to in order to survive. For the white shirts, a king's breakfast awaited: mountains of steaming eggs filled their plates with rows of sausage and bacon lining the edges. Fresh toast so hot the butter melted in a pool before it hit their plates. My mouth salivated and I lifted my tray absently. A wet splat left a portion of yellowed eggs in the center. Liquid leaked from the bottom and spread across the foam plate. They were cold and rubbery, flakes of black that had been scraped off the pan topping the pile. A small circle of meat came next. It resembled ham, but it was marbled and discoloured, the smell confirming its expiry had long past. Burned hash browns were last, hitting my plate with a clank and rolling across it. I grimaced and my stomach flopped.

"Take it and don't complain," Tryst said. "You eat it or you don't eat. It's that easy."

It had been too long since I'd eaten and I knew beggars couldn't be choosers, but keeping this down would be a challenge.

"Can't wait!" I said, sarcasm dripping from my words.

"That's the spirit." Soren grinned. "Hammer away at the walls of icy death closing in around us with an abundance of positivity. Eat this garbage with a smile!"

"Ignore him," Tryst said. "Soren lives off a diet of cynicism and awkward metaphors."

"That is entirely untrue," he said, sitting at an empty table. "I choose to explore the world through vocabulary and in a way that always keeps you thinking. It helps pass the time." A brief glare from Tryst and he shrugged. "Okay, it's a little true. But we all do what we must to prevent ripping out the beautiful locks of shiny raven hair that decorate our flawless features. Don't we?" He ran a hand through his hair and let it fall back around his face. "This hair is all I have left."

I laughed and it surprised even me. It felt good. Strange, but good. Or maybe feeling good is what felt strange. It was a deeper thought for another time.

"What do we have here?" A boy approached the table, silver eyes gleaming. His white shirt looked stark next to the black of mine, and the smirk fixated on his tanned skin made me dislike him instantly. He oozed arrogance and I tried to avoid eye contact. "Flower Boy and the succubus have a new friend." He laughed, and a small group of boys joined in behind him. None of them stood too close, but admiration flooded their eyes. I already knew this was exactly the situation I did not want to be in.

"As always, your lacking wit is not welcome here, Gage," Tryst said. "Nobody enjoys you except you."

"Ouch." He cringed. "Weak burn from the dirt sucker. What's the matter? Isn't Flower Boy putting out? I mean, if you're finding the mud and grass lacking, I have something you can suck on." He slapped my shoulder harder than necessary and the sting resonated over the stitched wounds. I buried the animosity that brewed within and shrugged his hand away.

"What, you don't like chicks? Flower Boy over there more your style?"

"I like women. I have an allergy to douche bags though," I replied.

His smirk faded, eyes flaming with silent rage. "What did you say?" His magic hummed beneath the surface—a torrent of heat and rage spiraling around us. It flared and pressed against my skin. A threat. I gripped the thin metal fork and rubbed my thumb against it, quelling the desire to stand up and oppose him. This wasn't my world anymore.

"Magic?" Tryst asked. "You're getting a little too comfortable in that white shirt. You've forgotten the Tank." Gage's eyes flickered with something I didn't recognize and he retracted his talent. "Good boy. Run along now."

"Uh-uh. I asked New Fish here a question. I think he needs to learn respect for his superiors and answer me." He set his foot on the edge of my chair and leaned down. "Now, what did you say?"

A chill ran across my skin. It was enough to remember the cold air that cut across my body in the Tank. He might have forgotten his time in the Tank, but I hadn't.

I took a breath and smiled. "Nothing."

We stared at one another for an uncomfortable time. His eyes squinted, knuckles turning white before he nodded.

"I didn't think so."

The cronies behind him laughed.

"You realize you're a guest here like us, right?" Tryst asked. She paid him little attention, continuing to eat her breakfast. "The white shirt doesn't change that."

"Whatever helps you sleep at night, sweetheart. I'll tell you what, you follow my lead and we'll have you squirming out of the black and into the white in no time. You think we're equals? Your first day in a white shirt—as an elite—will change your mind."

"No, thanks. White stains and always looks dirty," Tryst quipped.

"Defiant still, but you break a little more each day," Gage returned. "I can feel your temptation luring you in. Once we clean you up, you're going to be a piece worth showing off. A trophy among trophies. One to be mounted. Of course the color of your shirt isn't enough. You need a tuning like any other, but when I'm done with you, you'll play like a fine instrument."

Tryst cringed, and a hint of anger glimmered in her eyes. She let it fade and offered an insincere smile. "The only thing you're going to be tuning is yourself. And if you want to mount something, there's a lineup of sheep waiting." She acknowledged the boys standing behind him. Their smiles faded and they looked confused.

I envied Tryst in that moment. She knew how to handle Gage, and seemingly this entire place. She controlled her emotions and masked everything. It all came natural. I wasn't used to masking anything. I had stood against the system. I had learned to never back down. Not to ATOM and not to other supernaturals. If you did, they knew they had control over you. And on the outside, a lot of times that meant death. At the Academy, backing down was all you could do if you wanted to survive. A wrinkled sheet caught a beating. I could only imagine what putting a guy like Gage in his place would get me, and I wasn't about to find out. Instead, I watched Tryst as she deflected Gage's ignorance and advances as though they were petty jokes. They weren't.

"Feisty." Gage grinned. "You kids needs to relax. It's all in good fun, isn't it, New Fish?" Gage slapped me on the shoulder again and I cringed. "Oh, ouch! It's true then, you've been clipped? My mistake. I didn't realize that was something your kind could survive."

It wasn't. Major arteries ran through an Angel's wings, and Colby used an iron blade to cut through them. I should've bled out in a minute before turning to ash. He'd informed me he'd used something to cauterize the wound quickly enough, and a specialized potion from a hired witch to keep the iron from infecting my bloodstream. He'd been careful with his calculations, and I survived, and now I lived with intricate pain that hummed constantly across my shoulders and along my spine.

Gage didn't retract his hand right away. Instead he gripped my shoulder tightly. I didn't have Tryst's control and she knew it. She shook her head and lowered her eyes as two advisors moved in closer to the table. Hendrik appeared at the far end of the room, hovering on the staircase and staring at us. I took a breath and swallowed the pain.

"No problem. Accidents happen," I said.

"That they do. You know, in all honesty, this is disappointing," Gage said. "I'd heard you'd been grounded, but I didn't know it took the fight right out of you." He leaned in and whispered. "Did the bounty hunter cut off your nuts while he was at it?"

Hendrik descended the stairs, weaving between tables toward us. My stomach clenched and I pulled my cheek into my mouth, biting it. I felt nervous. I hadn't done anything wrong, but in a place like this I didn't need to. I lowered my eyes and avoided eye contact, focusing on the things I could smell in the room. It wasn't pleasant, but it was distracting enough. Still, Gage was persistent.

"I think we all looked forward to seeing what kind of fight a real-life angel had. All we really know about your kind is that arrogance has led to your near-extinction and that you can fly. Well, some of you anyway. Oh, and let's not forget how great you are at murdering people! The work you did on that boat was art, my friend. Convincing three hundred innocent people to board a ship and then taking them all out at once with a bomb? I mean, wow. That's impressive work. Cold. So cold. That's a page out of my father's book."

I closed my eyes, both an ache of regret and a surge of irritation washing through me. My knuckles popped. I didn't realize I had been clenching them. Energy burned in my hands, an icy flare that wanted to wrap around him and obliterate his soul. I wished I could unleash it on him. I wanted to show him what angels could do. I didn't. That kind of power wasn't to be used here, or anywhere for that matter. I'd sworn off it a long time ago, even though it managed to rear its ugly head and tempt me on occasion.

Tryst reached across the table as a crackle of golden energy flickered in the creases of my knuckles. She covered my hand with her own and squeezed tight. Her skin felt soft, and her grip surprisingly strong. Her eyes met mine and she gave me a nod as if to tell me I was okay. I could do this. I didn't realize until now how much I was ruled by my emotions. This would never work. I needed to have control like her.

She whispered for me to look at her and I met her gaze. Violet eyes sparkled, somehow quelling the angry breath from my lips. My body relaxed, the light withdrawn from my hands. It seemed easy when I looked at her. The sharpness I had felt from her last night was gone. Instead I saw understanding and calm. I nodded to let her know I was okay, and I reminded myself I was responsible for more than myself now. Tryst and Soren had learned to deal with this place. I could do the same.

"Uh-oh," Gage said. "It looks like you've got some competition, Flower Boy. This one is moving in on our trophy."

Another boy stepped up beside him, dirty brown hair falling in his eyes. "Yeah, right. I think the flyer's more his type." The group laughed and Soren's shoulders slumped forward. He kept his eyes on the table, stirring his food and not daring to look up.

"All right, all right," Gage said. "We're messing with you, Flapper. Testing the waters if you will. I'm Gage Daniels. Typhon."

Typhon.

Powerful, cruel, and unpredictable creatures. Once upon a time they had dethroned the angels to become rulers of the underground. It was a war that lasted nearly a decade, and in the end, we lost. The typhons condemned any who supported our cause, obliterating any obstacle that might stand in their way. They forced the underground into a world of fearful control. A century later, when ATOM became known to us, the angels emerged from hiding in hopes to unite the underground against a common enemy. The typhons cared only about keeping their throne secure. While the angels rallied forces to oppose ATOM, the typhons waged war on angel-kind once again. And once again we lost. The typhons protected their throne, and the end result left the underground weak. ATOM's rule became absolute and supernatural-kind went further into hiding.

I shuddered. A history of blood and fear, and now I looked into the eyes of the first typhon I'd ever met. Everything I knew up until now had happened before I was born, and I steered clear of them for good measure. Gage was a gleaming example of why. He represented everything I hated: arrogance, intimidation, and self-entitlement. I wanted to stand up and make an example out of him like his people had sought to do to mine. I wanted to give the world a reminder of what angels were capable of, but I couldn't. Instead, I stared at the hand he'd extended and took a breath, working to regain composure.

"Ash Lawson." I took his hand in mine. "The wingless angel."

"Wingless? Hmm, fallen perhaps?" Gage winked. "Sounds a little more badass, doesn't it?" His grip tightened, a blaze searing my palm. Hot spikes drilled into my flesh and I fought not to let him see my struggle.

"Sure." I squeezed back, struggling to maintain an even expression. I could have fought back but Hendrik told me no magic and I would abide. Besides, the wrath was a rare angelic power too dangerous to be used. I knew that all too well.

"A pleasure to meet me, isn't it?"

His strength surprised me. He was my size—six one—but heavier. I'd been starved for a week and before that, the stress of the upcoming job with the ship had taken its toll. He was a year or two younger than me, yet his strength nearly crushed my fingers. I had known typhons were strong, but this was more than I had expected. His grip tightened and the heat amplified. Perhaps I'd been naïve. There was a reason they'd overtaken my kind so long ago. Uncle had said I'd be lucky if I never met one. I started to think he was right.

The bones in my hand ached, threatening to buckle. My skin blistered and the faint smell of burned skin mixed with the rotted ham and cold eggs that lined my plate. Finally, it felt like my bones might snap, the warmth becoming too intense. I squeezed back, and let him feel that angels were strong too. His face shifted in surprise, his grip loosening and his own joints creaking against the pressure.

"What the hell is your problem?" I asked. He tried to pull away. I didn't let him. I had half a mind to twist his wrist to the side and dislocate it, but Hendrik's approach muffled any ideas I might have considered.

"Boys?" A single word full of authority. A warning. Gage's heat had been suppressed and his grip broke from mine. I let him go, considering exposing my palm enough to let the headmaster see the burns along my skin. Instead, I pulled it beneath the table, blisters lashing my hands with a fiery whip.

"Yes, sir?" Gage grimaced and covered it with a smile. His hand hurt too. Good.

Hendrik's gaze loitered on me and the smell seared flesh lingered, no doubt he could smell it.

"Things looked a little tense over here. I hope everything is all right and you're making Ash feel welcome," Hendrik said.

"Sorry, sir. Perhaps not as welcome as I should be," Gage replied. "I admit I am a victim of my own curiosity. I wanted to look into the eyes of a real-life angel and meet the man capable of sending three hundred innocent lives to die under the masquerade of freedom." His demeanor and voice changed entirely. Now it was quiet, soft, and sad. It held a tinge of innocence to it that hadn't been there a moment ago.

Hendrik smiled and placed a hand on Gage's shoulder. "A typhon eager to meet an angel? In the old days such a thing would never take place. Still, curiosity and temptation are for nought. It is weakness that must be corrected. A true contributor to the greater good does not fall victim to such persuasions."

"Of course. I should speak with my advisor and request assistance in correcting my behavior."

"See that you do."

"Yes, sir." Gage reached out and patted my shoulder. "I'm glad the old days are past, friend. We are adversaries no more. The Academy is a new beginning for each of us, Ash. You've struggled, as I once did, but you can find your place here and better yourself. We all can."

"Well said!" Hendrik's crow's feet deepened. "I continue to be impressed by your advancement as of late. Walk with me. Let us talk."

I watched them wander off, Hendrik's arm draped across Gage's shoulder. When I was certain they were out of earshot, I pulled my hand from beneath the table.

"Yikes." Soren grimaced.

The skin had blistered and parts had peeled away, leaving raw pink skin exposed. Clear fluid filled the wounds and the edges were marred with black.

I cursed under my breath. "Who the hell is he? King dick?"

"He's a typhon," Tryst said.

"Same thing. " Soren grinned. "But not king, prince. At least he thinks so. He's top of the class here. He does anything he wants and can do no wrong according to Hendrik and the advisors. Looks like you're already on his bad side. Not that anybody should be surprised. Four days might have been generous. Two?"

"Will you cut it out with that? I'm not going anywhere."

"Time will tell, grasshopper." Soren squinted and bowed to me. "I heard Gage's dad was on the council in the underground for centuries, and now he sits on the throne. I heard he has connections with the European underground, and when he finds out Gage is here, he'll unleash a wrath unlike any other, destroying ATOM and anybody who gets in his way."

"That sounds like a lot of hearsay." I'd lost my appetite. I stirred the food on my plate, watching it roll lifelessly around my fork.

"Not all of it," Tryst replied. "Gage *is* the underground king's son, and he doesn't play around. He'll step on your toes and try to get you to cross the line. And unfortunately for everyone, he can back up his mouth. Not to mention he has the advisors on his side."

"She's not kidding," Soren said. "He earned their respect. He has scars all over his back. Torture marks from when he first got here. He never gave in. Not after twenty lashes with a silver-laced whip. Twenty! The only reason they stopped was because they couldn't believe he was still standing. Once they saw that, they didn't want to lose him. The fact that he took that kind of beating put a spotlight on him. They were impressed. And once he turned it all around and became a contributor, he became practically invincible. Don't ask him about it though. Anybody who asks about it disappears."

"Disappears? Okay, now I know you're being dramatic."

"If anything I'm being generous," Soren said. "I heard his dad trained him for the family business from birth. He doesn't flinch. He kills without mercy. I heard he doesn't even feel pain."

"Enough with what you heard." Tryst rolled her eyes.

"It's true. I heard—"

"Soren, he gets it. We should all keep as much distance between him and us as possible. We don't need a bunch of embellished stories to understand he's dangerous."

"Embellished? No way! I heard from—"

"Enough!" Her voice was a harsh whisper and Soren looked appalled.

"Geez, Tryst, who borrowed your panties and left a streak? I'm only trying to help."

She grimaced. "That's disgusting."

"Well, he needs to know what he's getting into. If someone would've warned us—"

"We have enough to deal with right now without worrying that Ash is a new target for Gage. Let's make it through the first day before we jump to any conclusions."

"Isn't he a prisoner like the rest of us?" I asked.

"No, he's not." Tryst pushed her empty plate aside and leaned in. Her voice a low whisper and eyes sincere. "Gage is here as a guest but lives in a world of his own. Most of the white shirts do. If he likes you, you're safe, if he doesn't. Well, ask Soren."

He scoffed. "I'm trying to warn him, not share every detail of my life. I prefer to leave being the object of torturous obsession off my resume."

"What does that mean?" I asked.

Soren shifted uncomfortably.

Tryst patted his hand. "Soren was the focal point of Gage's wrath shortly after we arrived. Soren did well in the placement they gave him on Gareth's team and Hendrik took notice. It infuriated Gage. He became obsessed with making Soren uncomfortable. It was all verbal at first, nothing out of the ordinary, but he pushed the boundary constantly. Eventually it moved into physical abuse here and there, and then full-out beatings. That is, until Gage found a new target—a fresh arrival, a boy named Trace who'd captured the advisors' attentions also, but for entirely different reasons.

"Can we not talk about him?"

"Who is Trace?"

"I said I don't want to talk about him," Soren snapped. A few moments of awkward quiet passed before he released an irritated sigh and dropped his fork. "Fine. You want to know about Trace? He was a great guy. The best, in fact. He didn't taste metallic either, and he was my...we were close. And then—" His voice trembled and shook his head. I waited for him to continue, but he couldn't. A wall of tears had built up in his eyes. "Tell him whatever you want, but I don't want to be here when you do. I can't." He pushed his chair back and ran out of the room.

"I didn't mean to upset him," I said.

Tryst frowned. "It's not your fault. Trace is a sore spot for Soren, that's all."

"What did he mean Trace didn't taste metallic? He said that about me last night."

She pulled Soren's plate in front of her and began to finish what he'd left. "Soren's a deva; a type of nature spirit. He's tied to the earth and nature in a way you and I can't comprehend. He draws life from her, feels her sadness and her glory. It gives him a closer connection to life, so although he can't see auras exactly, he can taste them. It's his way of reading people. And Trace...well, he was one of the good ones, and now he's gone."

It was the first time I hadn't seen her reel back her emotions when they showed. Her face fell into a solemn blank stare like she'd just realized he wasn't there. She seemed lost in a different time and place. It took a few minutes before she came back to me, and when she did, she was a sadder version of who she'd been. She told me that when Trace had come to the Academy, everybody had liked him immediately. He was a caring person, and in hindsight, that made him a bad fit for the Academy. Caring could get you killed. When Trace found out what Gage had been doing to Soren, he didn't stand for it. He was a Wiccan and adept with his abilities. He confronted Gage in front of the entire Academy, laying him out in a feat of witchery before the advisors could lift a finger to stop him. But that didn't stop them from doing anything at all. He should've been hung up and slain, but he'd garnered favor with Hendrik and some of the other advisors, and instead earned himself two days in the Tank—more than anybody had ever received. The night he got out, he came back to his room beaten like everyone is after a spell in the Tank, but he had a half-dozen lashes to go along with it.

"Two days in the Tank? That's it? I'd say it was worth it to give Gage a bit of what he deserved."

"We did too, but for Trace the Tank didn't work. I don't know why, but he wasn't affected by its corrupt embrace. There was no torture for him. Instead, he had dreams of a full stomach and freedom we've never known. He had conversations with family and friends he'd lost over the years. For him it had been a retreat. But when the Tank didn't work as punishment, the guards made sure he felt it. They whipped him and beat him nearly to death. He came back looking worse than you did. We bandaged him up and fell asleep that night, happy to be reunited, but when we woke up he was gone."

"Gone? He up and vanished? What makes you think he didn't escape? If he survived the Tank the way you said, there's nothing saying he couldn't get out of this place."

"Nobody escapes this place."

"Everything has a weakness, Tryst. Everything."

"You might be right, but that's not the point. Trace could hardly walk he was hurt so badly, and even if he could, he would never have left without Soren. That's a fact."

I thought the Academy had changed their minds and killed Trace, but Tryst assured me if they were going to they'd have done it publicly. They never missed an opportunity to set an example. But the details surrounding Trace were scarce. I thought maybe she underestimated the sway of desperation. If Trace could escape the Tank's hold, he could escape this place. Maybe he did. Maybe after what the guards had done, he couldn't handle it anymore. Maybe he found a way out and didn't want anybody slowing him down. ATOM had put people in a position to do whatever necessary in order to survive. Who was to say he wouldn't leave a friend or two behind to get himself out of here? That was the world we lived in. Harsh and cruel, but reality nonetheless. As much as it made me feel bad to see Soren as upset as he was, it had me thinking. If Trace escaped this place, then so could I.

CHAPTER 10

Tryst took a deep breath outside Hendrik's office, hesitating on the lever. "You're going to meet our advisor. Be respectful and...don't speak unless spoken to. Eyes down, mouth shut. Oh, and don't look at the scar."

"What scar?"

The lever flew out of her hand and a man stood in the entrance, disapproval scrawled over his face.

"Gareth," Tryst sounded breathless. "Good morning, sir."

His gaze was cold; a single eye solid black, the other completely white with the exception of his pupil. His shaved head practically shone, but his dark skin was far from perfect. The scar started near the middle of his scalp, marring his forehead and wrapping around his colorless eye and rippling over his lips.

"Were you planning on knocking or whispering in the hall all morning? You realize I've sent some to the Tank for less?"

"Yes, Gareth. I mean, sir. Sorry, I was—"

"That's quite enough," Hendrik's voice interjected. "Come in, Ms. Rivera, Mr. Lawson."

A flash of relief flickered in Tryst's eyes but her insecurity swelled. She'd handled Gage so easily but now seemed flustered.

Gareth cringed as he stepped to the side. Out of uncertainty, I offered a smile, but it only hardened the man's face. I walked as though a creak in the floor could set off a chain of events that would be unrecoverable, and reached to pull out the chair from the front of Hendrik's desk. Gareth barked at me to stop. I froze.

"He can listen," Gareth said. "Based on his file I'd thought perhaps he were deaf."

"On the contrary," Hendrik said. "His hearing is quite competent."

Gareth circled the desk to stand beside Hendrik. He eyed me from head to toe, his face unmoving.

"Stand in the center of the room." I followed the order and moved out in front of the desk. A puppet on strings. "Huh. A few days in the Tank did him good."

"Indeed. I think you'll be pleased with this one," Hendrik replied.

"We'll see." Gareth grunted, stalking forward with a commanding presence. My shoulders tensed as he circled me. "He's a good size. Six one, about a hundred and ninety pounds. Two hundred if he ate right. He might be of use on the wall, except he's an angel." His arms were thick and muscular, the ripple of his abs and his pecks bulging through the tight fabric of a red shirt. "He'll start at the bottom, but if he's anything like the rest of his kind, he won't make it far."

"Come now, Gareth. We must have more faith in our guests than that," Hendrik interjected. "He's strong. We've yet to see what he can do. Imagine the scouts he could bring. We've lost Trace, but in his absence, look at what you've done with Gage."

Gareth's eyes darted to Hendrik, the muscle along his jaw flexing. "No. Gage is different. You only see it now because the other boy is absent. Gage is *unique*. A typhon. A creature raised on respect and discipline. He was bred for success, he *wants* rehabilitation and he works toward it. Gage Daniels is a survivor— a beast forged of fire and stone who's become a well-oiled machine."

"Be that as it may, I'm certain Ash is not beyond saving," Hendrik replied. "As certain as I am that you're up for the task." Hendrik's face softened, but his tone suggested something less friendly.

"I will do my best not to disappoint."

"I know you will. You're the greatest among your peers. A soldier and true symbol of what the Academy can do. And you are well educated on how I hate to be disappointed."

Gareth tilted his head to the side and the joints popped. One of

Hendrik's eyes twitched in response and Gareth grinned.

"On with it then. You two, follow me."

The forest stood in the distance, exposed from the stone wall that encased the property. Past the first row of trees nothing could be seen but a blanket of darkness. It was as if sunlight had no place within the growth. Guards paced the grounds and groups of guests were working hard beneath advisors' demands. Sweat beaded along the back of my neck; I couldn't tell if it was the warmth or my nerves. Maybe both.

Warm air carried a sweet scent of berries and oak and I let it wrap around me to ease my tension, though being near Gareth ensured some of it remained. His demeanor embodied wild aggression, walking with a soldier's posture and a beast's ferocity. He barked orders at any guests he saw that weren't performing as he deemed fit, and they responded promptly.

"Keep up." His voice was a dagger that sliced through the humidity; a corporeal energy that prickled along my skin.

Tryst seemed unfazed by the command. She kept her stride constant, eyes forward and face still. There was no flinching, only focus. Any nervousness she'd felt had now been buried.

We walked half a mile toward a large broken gap in the wall, and the vastness of the Academy overwhelmed me. I could unleash a primordial scream and nobody outside the wall would hear a sound. I once thought such isolation from the rest of the world a holiday. Today it sent a shudder of fear through my core.

Gareth stopped short of the broken section of wall. It had collapsed inward: sharp coils of barbed wire sagged over a pile of rubble with stains of brown and red splattered across the rocks and grass. Pieces of broken copper, silver, and iron sparkled in the debris—weapons and tools that had been obliterated to tiny shards.

Guests were already at work, some applying mortar and adding new blocks, others hauled debris outside the wall. They crossed the threshold with ease but did not seem interested in the outside and the potential freedom there. They moved back and forth like drones under the supervision of Gage who stood with arms crossed, snapping insults and barking orders.

"A cattle master!" I saw Gareth smile for the first time as he approached Gage, patting him on the shoulder like an old friend. He watched him with attentive eyes and a hint of emotion I couldn't decipher. "Progress report?"

"Very well, sir." He bowed. "We're ahead of schedule."

"Good." Gareth watched the workers for a moment. "Where do you need the extra hand?"

Gage squinted, his lips stiffened when he saw me. "The debris isn't moving out fast enough. The sooner it's gone, the sooner we have more room to rebuild."

"Smart thinking. Tryst. Work. Now." He didn't look at her when he spoke, and I got little more than a finger pointed in my direction. "You, come."

We'd been downgraded from prisoners to animals.

Gareth stepped through the rocks and boulders with ease and I tried to keep up. The wounds on my shoulders were healing slower than they should have, and movement caused ridges of pain to cut across them. I stumbled behind him, ducking beneath the sagging barbed wire. I hesitated at the threshold. Was this one of those things that I would get in trouble for? Should I wait to be given permission to cross?

The advisor stopped at the first row of trees and took a deep breath, releasing a clearly frustrated sigh. "Did I tell you to stop?"

"No, I wasn't sure if...I thought—"

A blast of air blew the hair around my face and Gareth stood an inch away from me. I hadn't even seen him move. His unsettling gaze burned into me and his forehead creased, wrinkling the scarred flesh.

"You thought, you thought. Have you forgotten how to speak, *boy*?"

"No, sir."

"Then speak!"

His voice was physical, the force shoving me back. I stumbled into a boulder, bracing myself with my hands. The stone burned and I jerked away, dots of red marring my skin. I cursed under my breath.

"I assumed I was supposed to stay on the grounds. I was *trying* to follow the rules."

"Who do you think you're talking to?"

Gareth's colorless eye dilated, nearly consuming all the white. A vein bulged along his temple and his jaw flexed. In a blur his arm shot forward and hammered into my chest. I sailed through the air and crashed into the corner of the wall they'd been rebuilding. The stone exploded over the other guests and wet mortar smeared along my arm. I caught the edge of the broken barbed wire on the way and tore a small gash into the back of my arm. I covered my face as rocks rained over me. The dust seared like gasoline after the match had been struck. I cursed and shoved the rocks away, but the burning didn't cease. The dust clung to my face and arms, burning feverishly. I brushed it away, Gage's laughter the soundtrack to my anguish.

Anger flourished, the governor I'd attempted to put on my emotions faltered and I jumped to my feet. With two quick steps toward him, Gareth's stance changed; one leg back, knees bent and braced for impact. I stopped, swallowing the anger and stripping it from my face.

"Go ahead," he said. "It'd be my pleasure to beat your ass to the Tank, or better yet, hang you up in the yard for all to see. Damn angels think you're better than everybody, don't you?" He screamed the words and the sound became visceral. Needles shot through my skull. My equilibrium collapsed and I dropped to my knees. It was like hot metal being poured into my ears while blood trickled out. Spikes ricocheted through my skull, and grenades of lava exploded behind my eyes. Gareth was a banshee. I smashed my fist into the ground as if it could offer relief. The earth cracked around my fist, dirt shooting into the air. I cursed. If I'd had my wings, I could've wrapped them around my body and protected myself. But I didn't have them. My enemies surrounded me and my strongest line of defense was gone. I was no longer an eagle, I had become a sitting duck waiting to be snatched by one of the many beasts that lurked beneath the mirror-calm waters. I couldn't be me. I couldn't think like me or act like me. I had to be someone else. I had to show them what they wanted to see in order to survive.

The sound had faded, but the effect remained. My brain pulsed, pushing against the inside of my skull as it tried to recover. Gareth towered over me like a child with a magnifying glass would hover

over an anthill. He grinned.

"I asked you a question. Need I ask it again?"

I gasped for air. The banshee's scream had taken my breath away and shook the world. I struggled to my feet. The other guests around me cowered, covering their ears. Tryst cringed, pain written across her features. Everything felt like it had turned sideways as I stumbled forward.

"No, sir."

He watched me for an uncomfortable time while I struggled to remain standing. A sly grin crossed his lips and he pointed at a cliff a few dozen feet away.

"Look over the edge."

I wanted to question his motives, but I didn't. I couldn't. Things had taken a turn and I felt the tension mounting Tryst's shoulders from behind me. I could imagine the fear that stirred in her guts. I felt it too.

I passed three rows of trees, using them as a crutch so that I didn't fall over. When I reached the edge, the ground vanished and exposed a long drop. My vision went in and out of focus; I felt like I might vomit. I gripped a low-hanging branch to stabilize myself, staring down the sharp incline of rock and dirt.

Trees had tried to grow upright, but their massive trunks sagged from the broad side of the cliff, causing huge bends in the bark. A river stormed a few hundred feet below, sharp rocks protruding from the water. White caps crashed along the sides, the current quick and uncontrolled.

"The Tank was your first strike," Gareth said. "Your attitude has now cost you your second. You take a tone with me again and you won't have to worry about wings. I'll send you flying over this cliff myself. When you hit the bottom, I'll be there with an iron blade to cut your neck through to your spine. You'll be a forgotten pile of ash drifting among the rapids. You got me?"

I'd been a fighter until now. I fought for those who couldn't fight for themselves. I stood against my adversaries not without fear, but without cowardice. Today, I was no longer that person. I couldn't be. I chewed on the inside of my cheek until blood welled into my mouth; self-inflicted injury to divert my emotions and the natural responses that swelled inside.

"I understand."

"I thought you might. Now get to work. When I am not

present, Gage is your supervisor. You disrespect him, you disrespect me."

The instructions were clear: break down the boulders, remove the debris, and rebuild the wall. Though whatever disrespect Gareth had felt I'd delivered to him did not go without punishment. He pulled the pickaxe from a stone and threw it over his shoulder, instructing all the other guests to leave. I wouldn't get the benefit of tools or help for this job. He left me with Tryst, the one who was currently destined to suffer alongside me, and Gage to supervise. Upon Gage's suggestion, Gareth allowed Tryst a pair of gloves, but he was quick to scold a small boy named Brandon when he tried to hand me his.

"No! Let's see if the metal-laced rock can help burn off the innocent blood that stains this angel's hands," Gareth said.

I didn't have a pickaxe or gloves, and although my hands looked clean, they didn't feel it. Gareth's words were a cruel reality.

Gage laughed. "You heard him, Flapper. Get hauling."

CHAPTER 11

The buzzer unlatched the door and we straggled through, the guard ushering us to move faster. We couldn't. Walking was accomplishment enough. He slammed the door shut and we found Soren's legs draped over the edge of the top bunk.

"Missed you two at dinner. Any juicy details?" His eyebrows waggled as if something pleasurable had occurred.

"Don't even start. Thanks to Ash we didn't get the pleasure of eating."

"Enough, please? I got the message." I limped in behind her. Everything from my neck down ached.

"Did you?" A single brow arched and she crossed her arms. "You might not care what happens to you, but I kind of want to stay alive. I don't—"

"I get it, okay? Even if you hadn't spent the last nine hours lecturing me, I would still get it. I see what's going on here. I understand the dangers. I'm not used to living like this. The boundaries are a little blurry. It takes some getting used to."

"You've been here five days and four of them were in the Tank. Get used to it," Tryst advised. "If you think Gareth's kidding about three strikes, you're wrong. You've already had more chances than most."

"Stop!" I took a breath, reeling the frustration inward. It wasn't her fault. I knew that, but part of me didn't care. Gareth had angered me, and Tryst's nagging had frustrated me all day. Any semblance of patience that remained was burned away by the flakes of metal dust that covered my body. My hands were raw, skin torn off the back of each finger and covered in blood. A rash had spread up my forearms and blisters decorated my skin. Breaking the boulders by hand was the alternative Gareth left me, and still he had been disappointed in our progress. That was why we missed dinner.

Tryst's face had softened somewhat, eyes following the wounds along my arms. "Ash."

"Do you want me to apologize again?" I snapped. Tryst flinched at the anger. I recoiled, taking a deep breath. "It shouldn't have come to this, I know that. I wasn't disrespecting Gareth, I was trying to be careful. I didn't realize how fine the line was."

"I don't want an apology."

"Then what *do* you want?"

"I don't want anything. I'm scared, okay?" Her eyes showed the truth in her words. The nagging I'd endured the entire day had vanished and she appeared vulnerable.

"So am I."

Soren propped himself up and cringed, ignoring the tense atmosphere. "You're looking a mess, bro. Didn't you get gloves? Never mind. I know the answer. Gareth's brutal, and his aura tastes like a penny. I heard he used to be a freedom fighter before he was captured. He's been here for almost a decade. A reformed, as they like to call it."

"You hear a lot of things."

He shrugged. "You hear a lot when people don't notice you." A look of sadness came across his face, and I realized he had a shiner.

"You don't look like you had a great day either. There's a chance you're more noticeable than you think," I said.

"It's true. Sometimes I wish I wasn't this spectacular." He joked, but his face didn't match his tone.

"Gage?" I asked.

"I guess running away from the table this morning wasn't the right move. I traded one discomfort for another."

"Is there anything I can do?" I asked. I didn't like that he'd been hurt, but part of me welcomed the break in tension with Tryst.

Soren laughed. "You come in looking like that and you want to help *me*? I hope you last more than two days. I need a good laugh once in a while." He jumped off the bunk and the smile fell from his face. "Trace tried to help once too. It's better if you stay out of it. Besides, being a deva has its perks. I'm on lawn duty tomorrow and being what I am, I'll be in tip-top shape by lunch. If you want to help anybody, help yourself. Rule number one: keep your mouth shut. That'll do more than anything in this place." He pulled out a pencil case with first-aid supplies from the inner foam of his mattress and turned to Tryst.

"No," she said. "I only have a few cuts and scrapes. He's a mess. We'll help him first."

"I'll be fine," I said. I didn't want her help. I appreciated everything she'd done, but I was used to being on the front lines helping others, not the other way around.

Determination burned in Tryst's eyes as she grabbed my blister-covered wrist. I jerked away.

"Dammit, Tryst. This isn't your problem. I am not your problem."

"Yes, you are," she yelled. Silence followed briefly before a guard banged on the door. Our one and only warning. Her voice dropped to a whisper. "If you knew what was going on inside you right now, you wouldn't be refusing. What you feel now is nothing compared to what it will become. We have to clean it up or the dust will settle beneath your skin, sink into your muscles, and there it will stay. They'll blister and burn with every movement until eventually it works its way into your bloodstream and then your heart. It'll make you wish you were back in the Tank."

"That was probably Gareth's plan all along," Soren said. "He doesn't like angels, or anyone for that matter."

"You think he's trying to kill me?"

Soren shrugged. "And why not? Gareth has a golden track record of producing aces. To him, you're a joker. But regardless, the dust won't kill you, but it'll make you wish you were dead."

"How does he get away with that?"

"How does anybody get away with anything here?" Tryst said. "There's nobody watching out for us. This place is off the radar for a reason. Now give me your hand and cooperate. I'd rather not start my day tomorrow watching you writhe in misery."

I relaxed my arm and let her go to work. She appeared focused, the frustration I'd caused receding. It gave me a moment to appreciate how soft her features were when she wasn't yelling at me. She wiped the excess dust and debris from my skin and did something that surprised me. She placed her hand over mine and closed her eyes. A tingle danced up my arm, a wash of cold unfolding with icy relief. A red glow glimmered between her fingers and she pulled away, fingers coming together as if picking something out of my palm, but she never touched me. She pulled her hand back, brushing her fingers together to wipe something unseen away. She repeated the motion until strands of black began to stretch from my palm like wisps of oil. She rubbed her fingers together and they fell, twisting in the air and dissipating on the floor. The next set was thicker and darker. I felt the pull from inside my arm like a long sliver being retracted beneath the skin. It hurt and offered relief at the same time, all the while feeling alien. My stomach flopped with unease. As more came, they gained specks of grey and brown and silver like the dust that lined the wall. Over time, the gleaming flakes covered the strands she withdrew.

She continued until what came out of my hand was no longer black or sparkling. The last strand glowed bright white, gleaming between her fingers. A piece of my life force, my soul. At the sight of it, her eyes widened and for a moment she seemed enticed. She licked her lips, leaning in toward it before disgust overcame her expression and she dropped the strand to floor.

"Too far," she whispered. "Too, too far." She shook her head, blonde strands whipping across her face. She repeated the words.

Soren watched for a moment before jumping off the bunk and grabbing her shoulders. "Hey, it's okay. Relax. Breathe. Deep breaths." He held her tight in his grip and forced her to look at him. She avoided his gaze and continued to shake her head. "Tryst, look at me. It was an accident. It doesn't have to be bigger than that. It's okay."

She opened her mouth as if to argue, but Soren wouldn't have it. He cut her off and repeated his words. There wasn't a trace of playfulness in him. He was as serious as I'd ever seen him. Tryst took a few deep breaths, eyes locked with his. When he inhaled, she inhaled. Soren nodded and smiled, exhaling slowly. After a few minutes, the calm of his voice relaxed her and she nodded. Soren pulled her into a hug, rubbing her back and hushing her. Her hands trembled when she wrapped her arms around him.

"Did I miss something?" I asked.

They ignored me.

"Trust yourself," Soren whispered. "I do."

Tears filled Tryst's eyes, but she held them back. "Okay." It had hardly been a word, more of a wisp of air slipping between breaths. Soren reassured her and Tryst nodded, forcing determination to override whatever look had occupied her eyes. She cleared her throat. "Trust. Right. Okay." They pulled away from one another and looked at me. The confusion must have been clear on my face. "Did I hurt you?"

The question shocked me. I had been more concerned for her. I did a mental check, surprised by the realization that the pain had receded. My skin remained blistered, but my muscles and joints no longer felt like someone had stuck sandpaper between them.

"I feel better, actually. What did you do?"

"She did you a solid, my man. Leave it at that," Soren said. "And what if tomorrow you return the favor by minding your P's and Q's so she can eat dinner? I heard we're having meatloaf. Or as I like to call it, road kill. But it has barbeque sauce so I'll take it." He winked, somehow cancelling the seriousness of his tone.

"I'm a succubus." Tryst stared at me as if that alone answered my question. "As much as we can steal the life from others, it can be controlled. We can take other things like poisons and infection too. And as I'm saying this, I realize this doesn't seem to bother you."

"Why would it? By the sounds of it, you saved me a whole lot of torment. Again."

"I don't know...because most hate my kind?"

"Welcome to the club. If I'm unsure about anything, it's not what you are, but why you keep helping me."

"I told you, I don't want to die."

"That's it?"

"Do I need more of a reason?" she countered. "Would you prefer specifics? Okay. I don't want to get clubbed until I'm nearly unconscious, hung in the yard by my neck and then whipped until I can't feel anything but blood rushing down my body. And then I don't want to die. Although with you that's proving to be a difficult task."

"Maybe you should've left me in that Tank after all. You could breathe a lot easier then."

"Maybe I didn't want the guilt of someone's death on my hands when I knew I could help." The look in her eyes was fierce and the words bit like hot razors, but she hadn't meant it as an attack. I could see that by the way her eyes retreated from mine. "I'm sorry, I didn't mean—"

"It's okay. I deserved that."

"No, I'm certain you don't."

"Well then, you're wrong." My words were quick and harsh. I did have death on my hands, and I felt it in every pulse of my heart and every breath from my lips. "You don't want death on your hands. Trust me. I'm sorry I've put you in a position where you might."

Soren's head popped up over the rail of his bed. "On the bright side, if you screw up and get whacked, at least the death won't be on her hands for long. If you get killed, so does she."

Soren's silver linings were rarely comforting. He wasn't wrong though. I think that bothered me more than anything. I paced the room, trying to shake the tension that mounted my shoulders and think of a way out. How the two of them had survived here for years was beyond my comprehension. Even with Tryst's help, I still hurt. A few remaining flakes constantly bit at the back of my neck, splitting the skin. Clear fluid filled the wounds and trickled over my skin, trying to repair the damage. I could hardly stand it. The entire premise of this place made me want to tear out my hair. I went stir crazy in the locked-down room, gripping the metal bars that lined the window, only to have them retaliate with a burn. Everything had flakes of metal in them. I cursed under my breath. I wanted to conjure a plan to relieve Tryst of the burden that was me, but this place was a fortress. At face value it seemed impenetrable.

"You remind me of him." Tryst interrupted the cycle of never-ending plans that ran through my mind. They all seemed a dead end. "Trace."

Soren fell still, almost statuesque at the mention of Trace's name.

"Me? Why?"

As if the pressure had melted away, she smiled. It was as though a happy memory played out in front of her that only she could see.

"Not entirely. I mean, he never almost got me killed, and he never had the advisors in a tizzy, and he never—okay, you're not like Trace at all. I don't know. He had a fire in him like you do now, but he had better control."

"You know, for a moment I thought there might be a compliment coming. My mistake."

Tryst shrugged. "I never believed what I'd heard about you, or angels in general. I thought you got the short end of the stick like my kind often does. Even still, I hadn't planned to help you. Walking to the Tank I wanted to throw the Soliloquy over the wall. I didn't want to be linked to anyone, least of all an angel."

"What changed?"

Tryst shrugged, biting her bottom lip. Either she didn't know, or she was trying to decide what to tell me. She sighed.

"I stared at the Tank for a long time before I came in. I could toss it over the wall and nobody would be the wiser. I told myself to do it, but it didn't feel right. I sat and watched you—wondering who you were, where you came from, and if the stories were true. But there was so much hurt in your eyes while you relived your losses, I knew they couldn't be. How could a person who cared that much be a monster?"

"All you saw was a pathetic creature, desperate and crawling across the dirt floor crying for help," I said. "Isn't that what the Tank is designed to do to everyone?"

She released an airy laugh. "It is, and it does. Everybody cries in the Tank. There's nothing romantic about it. You'll piss yourself, cry, beg for help, and swear you'll be good if only they'll release you, but you had a desperation that wasn't from the Tank's torment. It lingered in your voice and I saw it in your eyes. I don't know what it was. Hope, I think."

"Hope?" I laughed. "You must be mistaken. In the Tank, I was ready to die. There was no hope left."

"Maybe it wasn't something I saw. Maybe it was something I felt. It wasn't in you to give up. You were different. You *are* different. I can't explain how or why. I feel it like I did with Trace. There's hope; it moves around you and it makes *me* hopeful. For what? I don't know. A chance maybe. For life?"

I studied her for a moment, waiting for the punchline. When she didn't laugh, I realized she was serious, and it seemed strange to me. I didn't know how she could see anything positive, but somehow she did, and it made me feel good. If she—practically a stranger—could see good in me, surely I could find some in myself. Couldn't I? Hope. Who would've thought?

CHAPTER 12

The days moved in slow motion. I became a saint of good behavior. I didn't toe the line. I was nowhere near it. I broke down the boulders day after day with bare hands. I suffered through blisters and burns, and the aches of metal dustings working their way through my skin like tiny pieces of shrapnel. Each night Tryst used her foreign abilities to withdraw them bit by bit. I became accustomed to the trails of iron dust that scarred my arms in lines of red and brown. They itched and burned constantly, never given a chance to fully heal. Eventually they were nothing more than background noise.

We worked all day every day, and most days we weren't permitted lunch. Gage cursed and yelled, pushing each button he could find to try and get a reaction. I didn't give him one. Gareth waited for me each morning, plaguing me with his eyes when I stepped into the hall. After the disappointment of a room in perfect order, he'd leave, screaming at one person or another. He became the epitome of a sulking child who didn't get his way.

The other guests grew accustomed to me and I was no longer the subject of stares or whispers. I had become old news, and as such I endured the Academy with Soren and Tryst to lighten the load. Aside from Gage, who took every opportunity to get a rise out of me, I became nobody. I watched students as they were beaten and tormented from the advisors whose names I'd never bothered to learn. Tryst assured me that standing up for them wouldn't be helping at all. In fact it would only make things worse for everybody involved. I believed her, and it became my personal torture to stand idle and listen to them scream. It was the ship all over again. But regardless of the behavior I became acclimatized to, I refused to truly become a slave to ATOM. One way or another I would find my way out. I was certain of it. The only problem became Tryst and Soren.

As invisible as I had managed to be at the Academy, my roommates had become prominent fixtures in my world. They were real, honest people. That wasn't something you came across often, even on the outside.

Soren's humor got him through the days, and it brightened my own. He wasn't somebody to talk about deep feelings or emotions—he kept things simple—but the more I got to know him, the more adept I became at reading him. He buried things beneath his nervous laugh. I saw it in his eyes when he didn't think anyone was watching, and in between moments of sarcasm I found him in serious contemplation. He called out Trace's name in his sleep sometimes, and I worried for him. A hurt like his couldn't be kept down forever. That much I knew. Still, I looked forward to him every day. He made life a little more bearable.

Tryst wasn't entirely different. She kept mostly to herself, never delving too deep into anything. She was witty, smart, and impressively in control of her emotions, although she tried to dumb down all of her attributes, I paid attention. She remained quiet about her past. In fact, neither of them spoke much of life before the Academy, which meant as time went on the stories they shared were repeated. I was okay with that. They were my friends and they'd share what they wanted to. They didn't pry into my past, and I reciprocated that respect. As horrible as the Academy was, Tryst and Soren made everything a little bit easier.

I climbed the ladder and placed a final brick onto a smear of fresh mortar. My fingers lingered a moment, as though I'd forget the burn of the iron-laced stone once we were done. It hardly hurt anymore. Strange how a person could adapt to anything, even something that caused such discomfort. I adjusted the barbed wire, snapping the final metal clasp around it. The edge of the wire nicked my skin and drew a drop of blood. It tasted of concrete, salt, and copper swirled together. A hint of iron seared my tongue as I sucked at the wound. It barely bothered me.

The air felt crisper at the top of the wall. I took a deep breath. After this, the chance to use the hole as a doorway to freedom would be gone. I'd impeded it with my own hands. Tryst smiled, urging me down, and I felt a pang of guilt at the happiness on her face. I'd considered running off more than a few times throughout this project. She was the reason I'd stayed. I worried what would happen if I left, or worse, if I left and didn't quite make it. Would they really kill her because of me? It hadn't been a risk I was willing to take.

"You finally did it," Gage scoffed. "Took you two long enough. Get down so we can report to Gareth."

I rolled my eyes and descended the ladder. I felt freedom drifting away with each rung, and each step became harder than the last. When I touched the dead grass below that had been painted with blood a month prior, I knew it was the right decision.

Gareth stood over a group of young boys as they cleaned the grout in the Academy fountain with toothbrushes. It already looked clean, but he demanded some form of perfection I couldn't grasp.

"Done?" he asked. "And here I was about to bring you these." He pulled a pair of long gloves out of his pocket with a grin.

"No problem, sir. I earned punishment, and it was a well-taught lesson."

He grimaced at the retort. Even I didn't know I was that good at kissing ass.

"Save it. I've got nothing else for you today. Get back to your room."

There was something about the look on his face that gave me immense satisfaction. It was a cross between disappointment and rage that swirled in his eyes. For once I had gotten the better of him, and I reveled in it.

Soren remained outside, tending to the lawn. It was a massive undertaking, but one that he represented proudly. Each day he returned covered in grass clippings and dirt, but when Gareth wasn't watching, he smiled. Devas drew energy from the earth, and as horrible as this place was, Soren had found a way to bear it. I wasn't sure if that made me happy for him or sad. I didn't believe we should get comfortable here. This wasn't going to be home. But as I walked back to our room, seeing that gentle smile upon his face brought a little piece of happiness back into my life. Something that had been missing for far too long.

Tryst flopped onto the bed. It had only been a seven-hour day, but two hours shorter than typical felt like a holiday. My body screamed when it hit the mattress. I felt more exhausted than usual. It was in part because the work on the wall had come to an end. There hadn't been a day off since we started and from what Tryst and Soren led me to believe, they were few and far between.

"Feels good, doesn't it?" Tryst asked, a strange smile dancing on her face.

"What?"

"Accomplishment? I don't know. I feel like we did it."

"Finished putting the final wall of our jail cell back into place?" I asked. "I suppose there's an ironic sense of achievement in that." She was right. I felt it too. The Academy had brought such dissatisfaction to my life, but I felt a sense of triumph in finishing the project. And with that thought went the one small piece of happiness I'd gained. It fluttered away on the wings I no longer had, desperate to be expelled from the man who once fought the beast, but now conformed to it. I shuddered at the thought. The line between who I was and who I pretended to be blurred, and I scolded myself for it. I told myself that wasn't true. It never would be.

"Not the job. No, there'll always be another job. I mean, I feel like we're in the clear," she explained. "It's no mystery that I was worried about you. About us. I didn't know what was going to happen and to be honest, those first few days were scary, but I feel like that part is over. We made it over the hump, you're adjusting, and things are going to be okay."

"Good." I smiled, but it was forced. As much as I felt things were okay, they weren't. I didn't share her delight. I didn't want to stay here. I trucked along and endured this place because it was the right thing to do for Tryst. But she was right; now that the wall was complete we'd be given a new job. The thought of that sucked away any satisfaction I'd felt. I had been so busy trying to get through every day I hadn't thought about what would happen next. After the wall was complete there'd be another project, and after that, something else. When did it end? It didn't. It was a never-ending cycle of slave work until we turned twenty-one, then we'd be recruited directly to ATOM. Then we'd truly have conformed.

No. The thought scared me. I wanted out and I wanted out now, but I couldn't leave without her. That would put all this work to waste. I had to make her come with me, which meant Soren too. Three people. That made escaping more complex. It wasn't a matter of just getting out; with them I'd have other people to be responsible for. My stomach cramped. The thought of making them fugitives made me uneasy. Was *that* the right thing to do? The idea of freedom seemed grand, but it was far from simple. There was a cost involved. I knew that. So did the ashes of the hundreds of supernaturals I'd gotten killed. What if I got Tryst and Soren killed? Bile rose in my throat and my hands shook as a wash of adrenaline coursed through me. Panic played my insides like an out-of-tune fiddle, my heart hammering with rhythmic thuds and my breath caught in my throat. I closed my eyes and took a breath. That wouldn't happen. Before the ship, I'd brought many people to safety. I could do this, couldn't I?

Tryst grabbed the first-aid kit, which was down to scraps. Years of Soren's hard work were squandered in a month. She looked focused as she wiped the dust from my arm, each swab turning it a darker shade. She'd clean the skin, draw the poison out, and relief would come. This routine had become my life. It made me sad and reiterated what I truly wanted, but watching Tryst and having her close made me feel good. It felt right. I didn't want to lose the part of my life that had her and Soren in it. If I did, there would be a void. Soren made me smile. He was kind and unrealistic. I liked that. But there was something about Tryst that fascinated me. It wasn't her magic, or her disposition to risk her life for a stranger, it was her undeterred will. It was the way she carried herself. She was strong in a way I wished I could be.

"You always get that look when we do this."

"What look?"

She shrugged. "I don't know. Like I'm an alien. Maybe it's because I scare you with what I can do. Most people are fearful of it," she said, and her comment caught me off guard. I wasn't afraid, I was intrigued. She wasn't the first Succubus I'd met, but I'd never seen this side of their power. "It's okay if you are. We're terrible things really." She shuddered. She was disgusted with herself.

"I'm not afraid of you, and I don't think you're terrible. This is what you are, Tryst. You can't change that."

"No, but that doesn't make it any better. My father taught me it didn't matter what we had or didn't have in life, that didn't give us the right to take things. We were put here to help people, human and supernatural-kind alike. Not steal from them."

"Your father sounds like a smart guy, but it's how you nourish yourself. That doesn't make you a monster."

"Yeah, he was, but he'd disagree with you on that."

Was? A flood of guilt entered my chest.

"I'm—"

"Don't even think about apologizing." She reached up and wiped the side of my neck and face. "He went out fighting for what he believed in—that we could do good in the world. He was a great man."

"How can you help anybody if you don't feed? Don't answer that. That's your business; I shouldn't have asked." We had silent terms laid out and I'd broken them. We never asked; we only shared what we felt like sharing.

"You'll probably think it's stupid anyway."

"I wouldn't." The words fell from my lips. I wanted to know more about her. I wanted her to want to tell me. I wanted her to trust me. I realized then that I wanted a lot from her. Too much. My chest tightened when her eyes met mine and her scarred fingers slid over my neck.

"Why don't we start by you telling me what you know about my kind? What does *the* Ash Lawson know about the succubus?"

"They feed off the life source of others," I began. "In the case of supernaturals, some can temporarily absorb abilities too. I know that as long as they feed they remain strong and youthful, like a vampire. But unlike most supernaturals they're susceptible to more than one metal. Copper's the worst, but silver and iron hurt too." She nodded, looking impressed, but then disappointed when I didn't have much more to add. "The few I've met were kids, and in my line of work you don't spend a lot of time with people. You want to meet them and get rid of them in the shortest amount of time possible."

"The faster you can do it, the less chance you have of getting caught?"

"Pretty much. Not exactly a movie-worthy escape, but you have to get them out before anybody realizes they're leaving."

"Can I ask what happened? I'm not usually one for gossip, but if the rumors *are* true, you were successful for years. What changed?"

I wondered how this had been turned on me. I didn't want to talk about it. Then again, that's probably how she felt about my questions. I opened the door for this, now I had to deal with it.

"You first."

She offered a half smile. She had finished wiping the dust away, but her hand still lingered along my neck. A chill ran across my skin and when she realized I noticed, she pulled away.

"Past for past? Okay, I'll bite." She moved beside me, her arm brushing mine. "Look at every living thing as having a reservoir—a lifeline. Every injury or sickness feeds off of it, causing it to decline faster than normal. Each time a succubus feeds, it steals some or all of that. Many supernaturals have a reservoir that refills. It's how they stay youthful and strong. Vampires and succubi are similar in that they need to feed regularly. The difference is if a vampire doesn't feed and their reservoir runs dry, they enter a comatose state until they're fed again. For a succubus, once it's gone it's gone. There is no resurrection. On a full tank, we might get six months. And that's assuming we had a big meal. For children it's even less. The reservoir grows with the person. An adult has six months. A child has a few weeks. They start feeding from birth. Mostly unknowingly, but feeding nonetheless. As they grow they learn to control it the same way people learn to walk. Being a parent to a succubus infant is like walking into a lion's den. What I've been doing to you is a variation of how a succubus feeds. I've been siphoning out the poison, the tainted life force."

"I didn't know you could even do that."

Tryst shrugged. "Most don't. My father learned in his teens and taught me from a young age. He showed me that our ability could be used for good. We didn't have to be the monsters; we could be miracle workers too. We could take away disease and help people. Needless to say that drew unwanted attention and things didn't go as planned."

"But what you're doing for me *is* good. How could that upset you?" I asked.

"It was good, until it wasn't. My father believed that in order to be an asset to the world, we couldn't be a risk to it. He was childhood friends with Soren's dad, who taught him to be different. He taught my father to feed off the earth, much like devas do. They get life force from nature: trees, water, earth, even animals. They're connected. And he taught me to use the earth as my own personal reservoir because nature has a way of replenishing itself. It's great for devas, but for a succubus it's a lot harder than feeding off people and a lot less effective. It's not how we were meant to survive."

She took a break, reaching out and starting to work on my other arm. She pulled a strand of darkness from a crease in my palm and stared at it for a long moment. It wriggled in her grasp like a worm fighting for escape. Red magic sparkled between her fingers and she released it. It tumbled to the ground like a stained feather and dissipated against the floor.

"We were young when our parent's died. Soren and I were on our own, and I was emotional." Her lips trembled and her hands shook. She wouldn't look at me. I could feel the battle she fought within. I started to reach for her hand to console the shaking, but she looked up at me with a cold gaze. "I fed, Ash. I fed and I killed and not a little; I killed dozens. Even when I was full I didn't stop." The boldness in her eyes was fake, a façade to hide the tears that she fought back.

"Tryst, I didn't mean to upset you, I thought—"

"Don't be. If you're going to be here, you should know. I knew better than to think we could be close and not tell you. You *need* to know what kind of monster I am. Once you do, you might take that chance to escape you've been dreaming about."

I felt surprised. I'd never said a word about it. How did she—

"I see the way you look at the outside world. I saw you today. It was written all over your face. I told myself it wasn't, but I knew it was there. How could it not be?" She sighed. "The last thing my father did for me was bring me back from the brink. Even after I had killed—taken the only thing those people had to give—he never left. Never gave up on me. And I'm..."

She glanced down at my hand, a single strand of black lay across my palm, part hanging out and part still embedded in my skin. Tryst knelt in front of me and ran her fingers over the inside of my palm, circling it. The black wrapped around her like a snake and she pulled it out, entranced by its movements.

Hearing the waver in her voice and seeing the look in her eyes, I regretted asking about her past. But I wanted to know who she was. I wanted more than the Tryst who'd lived at the Academy, and my greed had unleashed a storm of emotions I hadn't meant to throw at her.

She shook her head. "The first time I tried to take the poison out, I was confident I could do it. I *knew* I could help you like my father taught me. I wanted to, but then I went too far. I was stupid. I hadn't attempted it in years, but I looked at you and felt that hope and…it was the hope I'd lost in my life and wanted so desperately to get back. I didn't know if I could have it, I *knew* I didn't deserve it, but still I wanted it. It made me excited to see and to feel," she admitted. "I lost focus. I wasn't paying attention, and I started to take too much. I saw that streak of life come out of you. A bright, shiny strip fresh from the reservoir and…" She dropped my palm and lowered her gaze. The fight she'd put up was lost. Tears began to drip from the corners of her eyes, streaking across her pale skin. She pulled her hands into her sleeves and wiped them away. "I'm sorry, Ash. It wasn't mine to take."

I slid off the bed and knelt in front of her, grabbing both shoulders and making her look up at me. "You didn't hurt me, Tryst. I'm fine."

"But I *wanted* to." The silence fell like a hammer through glass. She looked mortified when she said it, both hands covering her mouth. She shook her head, glossy eyes staring up at me. "I'm a monster."

"A monster? You're anything but. You saved me from the Tank, helped me survive my first month in this place, and look at the pain you've spared me."

"I wanted more," she lashed out. "I wanted to consume it. I felt the intensity and vitality and I wanted it to be mine. My mouth watered when I felt it, and when it came into the open air it felt even stronger. Your body masks the true power an angel carries." She licked her lips and then shuddered, shaking her head as if that could rid her of temptation.

I took her hands in mine and gripped them tight. "But you didn't. Being tempted by something isn't a bad thing. That's natural. It's what you do with that temptation that matters. You didn't take that life force. You stopped yourself. You have nothing to be upset about. If anything, you should be damn proud."

She let out a sound I thought was a laugh, but she didn't look amused. "It doesn't feel like I should be proud."

"Would it make you feel better if I told you it wasn't a big deal? Angels get energy from the sun. That's how *we* replenish. It's nothing I would have missed. I would get it back."

"That doesn't make it okay."

"I'm not saying it does. I'm saying I'm all right. It's hard, I can understand that."

"How can you understand? You can't, Ash. Even if you try, you can't. You don't know what it's like."

She was right. I couldn't understand, at least not on the level she felt it. Trying to would do a disservice to how she felt.

"You're right, I don't. But you don't have to be scared of me. We'll get through it."

"Oh, I'm not scared of you, Ash. I'm scared of me."

"Scared of the person who saw a total stranger and risked her life to help him? Scared of the person who faced what I can only imagine is the ultimate temptation and declined it? Scared of the person who day after day for nearly a month drew poison from my veins? You're the last person you need to fear, and if it came down to it, I owe you a lot more than a single strand of a life. That's a blink. A second. You deserve a lifetime."

"You say that, but you don't understand the magnitude of a blink," she said. "You don't know how fast it goes. At first it's a second. One blink. Then that one blink turns into another. That's an hour. Then another. That's a day. Before you know it, it really *is* a lifetime. By the time you realize it, it's too late. You're gone, and no amount of sunshine will be able to bring you back. All because of a blink. "

"When you found me in the Tank, I was on the edge," I said. "I was ready to die. It wasn't just the torture that had me on my knees begging for death. Death is what I wanted. You think I don't understand what it's like to be a monster? I killed three hundred people in an evening. That's on me. I hated myself for what happened. I still do. But it happened because I wasn't careful enough, and it happened because the people who put us in this prison have given supernaturals something to fear. You want to know what real monsters are? They're this place and the people who run it. You know what I see when I look at you?"

She stared into my eyes and I didn't need to put up a façade of sincerity. It was as genuine as anything I'd ever said. Maybe more so.

"A hero. You saved my life and brought me back from the darkest place I've ever been. When that place rears its head and tries to reel me back in, it's thinking of you that keeps it at bay. So thank you," I said. "Thank you for being there when I couldn't be there for myself. But please, don't for one second think you're the monster in this world."

For a moment, no matter how brief, the disdain she felt faded. Her shoulders no longer sagged and she propped herself up. She didn't smile, but the tears retreated. I wasn't so naïve to think I'd changed her mind—she'd have to alter the way she saw herself—but for the moment she felt better. Sometimes that was the first step to self-forgiveness. Sometimes it was a simple reprieve from the suffering. Seeing the change in her demeanor, I knew then what I had to do; I had to repay her. A life for a life. She gave me mine back. I owed her the same.

"Thanks," she whispered. "But can we talk about something else now?"

"Sure, how about getting us out of this place? You have an extraordinary gift that gets poison out of my veins; if you had a special way to get us out of here that would make my day." It was part joke, part serious, and part feeling her out. I wanted to know how she'd respond.

She laughed. "Sorry to disappoint, but nobody escapes. Plenty have died trying."

"Correction: nobody has escaped *yet*," I said. "There's always a way out; a path yet untaken. If I've learned anything in my life, it's that."

"Well, when you find it let me know. I'll gladly go with you. This place has been my personal hell for four years. I'd walk out the door in a heartbeat if I could. Sadly, I imagine I'll leave much the same way as those who tried to escape."

"Why do you say that?"

"I'm a succubus, Ash, not a warrior. And fighting is the only real chance anyone has at an escape, but it's a fight they can't win. There are too many guards, too many advisors, then there's the wall and the glyphs at the gate. It can't be done."

She was right. I'd been studying everything I could for weeks.

The glyphs at the gate were no joke. They wouldn't hurt you, but no supernatural could walk past them or break through the spell. It was set to allow movement in one direction only—in—and it was strong. The walls were as dangerous as they were tall, and the guards' routines were spot on without a chance to slip through. The Academy had it nailed down perfectly...almost.

"There's the north forest," I offered. "The one that has no wall. It's open woods. We could be lost in there in a day. They'd never find us."

The look she gave made me question my own sanity. "You're crazy. There's no wall because no wall can stand there. They've tried to build it, trust me, but the forest devours it to nothing more than grains of sand. It's a cursed forest, enchanted beyond even Hendrik's control. You can go in and get lost, sure, but you don't come out. It's a worse option than trying to fight."

"How do you know? How do you know people don't go in and come out the other side?"

"Because if there was freedom on the other side of those woods, you could be damn sure we wouldn't be able to take it. These people—ATOM—aren't stupid. So far they've managed to somehow overpower supernaturals everywhere, and now they're going to use us to regain position in the world. It's to the point people are too scared to fight back. They'll fight for ATOM or donate themselves to their whim. Do you really think ATOM is about to put they're up-and-coming talent at risk by setting up shop next to an escape outlet? I don't think so."

"What if—"

"Trust me," she said. "It's not an open door. There are no guards there because even they're afraid of it. It's a no-go zone." Her words were fast and fearful. She was afraid of it too. "And that brings us back to you. Past for past, right?"

The idea of escape had come and gone. She'd shut it down and now the spotlight was back on me. Dammit.

"You want to know what happened the night they caught me?" She hesitated before giving a nod. I didn't want to relive this moment, but I'd made her relive a nightmare of her own, it was the least I could do. "I tried to do too much. Every job prior had been small; a half dozen here, a family there. This was a full ship; three hundred and seven supernaturals. It took too long to bring together and it involved too many people. The margin for error was so small, and I got cocky. After years of success I didn't think I could be stopped. Not by Colby, the hunter who captured me, and definitely not by ATOM." I breathed a sigh of relief. Saying it out loud wasn't as hard as I'd expected, but it brought with it an epiphany. "I'd been sloppy...careless. I wasn't as clever as I thought." I bit back the truth, holding it in for a moment until it was too much to contain. "ATOM didn't sink that ship, my arrogance did." I winced. The wounds on my back had closed, but the lances of fire that seared beneath them never truly faded. Neither did the screams. They filled the void of every silence, and when I closed my eyes their faces stared at me beneath an ocean of water. Waterlogged hands raked across my chest while I slept, pulling me into the icy grip of their graves. My stomach flopped as I fought the vomit that rose.

"I killed those people. Maybe my wings were punishment for it. Maybe in the end I got what I deserved." I felt my own tears burning my eyes, but I fought them back.

Before she could respond, the door buzzed and I jumped, heart hammering into my chest. Soren stepped in, stopping a few steps into the room.

"Oooh, awkward moment." He crossed his arms and put a hand over his mouth. "Don't tell me. I know this one." He licked his lips and tasted the air. "One part fear, one part unease, and a pinch of excitement, although that part is faint. Hmm...Oh! And a tinge of regret! Got it. He tried to kiss you, didn't he, Tryst?"

"What? No!" She shouted. "Why would he—"

"Uh-huh," he said. Tryst and I looked at one another and her cheeks flushed. I was too busy trying to reel back the memories to feel embarrassed. "Then what's going on here? What's with the weird taste in the air?"

"Nothing," she said. "We were talking."

"Mmhmm." He didn't buy it. For someone who believed everything he heard, he was being oddly critical.

"I was just asking Tryst how to escape." I put it simply, trying to steer the topic away from my discomfort.

Soren's eyes opened wide but he concealed whatever he felt. "Well, good luck with that. Twenty-foot walls, an army of guards, and glyphs that keep everything inside. If you wanted out, you'd have been better off running through the opening you two repaired. Hendrik manages the glyphs and the Tank himself.

Nobody's breaking that spell."

"Hendrik doesn't seem the witchcraft type," I said.

"He's not any type. Nobody knows what he is. I've heard everything from ultra-powerful warlock to forgotten beast birthed at the dawn of supernatural-kind. Nobody has a clue."

"So I'm told, which I guess brings us back to the north forest."

"Forget it," Tryst said.

"I second that." Soren shivered.

"Don't you think you're being a bit dramatic?"

"I heard it's home to some of the foulest beasts on the planet. Things we've never even seen before. You think I want one of them sucking out my intestines while another thing gnaws on my brain? If you ask me, you're not being dramatic *enough*."

"Graphic much?" I asked.

Soren shrugged. "What you lack in imagination will be your downfall. Luckily you have me to guide you on your path to certain death, should you entertain such a foolish idea again."

"He's right, Ash, at least in here we have a chance at living," Tryst concurred. "It might be small, but it's better than nothing."

"You call this a chance?" I questioned. "Stay here until we turn twenty-one and then what? Join the army and fight their war? Or do you prefer being lab rats? I don't know about you, but I'd take my chances in the woods."

"They're not just woods," Soren said. "That's Blackwood forest."

"Wait, what? You're kidding."

"Blackwood. Forest. Need I say more?"

"Blackwood is a myth."

"Oh yeah? Tell that to the two-dozen kids who have tried to escape there in the last four years. None of them were heard from again."

"Did you ever stop to think they might've found what they were looking for?" I countered.

"Ash, we're talking about some of the oldest cursed lands in the world," Soren said. "The Curse of Blackwood? The witches of darkness? The birth of evil? Baba Yaga? Any of this ringing a bell?"

"I know the stories, but that's all they are: myths, legends, fabrications of someone's imagination."

"Ask almost any human in the world about demons and angels and vampires or werewolves and what will they say?" Soren asked.

When I didn't respond, he smiled smugly. "We're myths too, popularized in movies and television. We're monsters, then heroes, and façades among Fantasy. Blackwood might be a legend to you, but there's a reason there's no wall there. I can taste it when I get too close. Evil." He shuddered.

"I told you," Tryst said. "It isn't a free pass out of this place. Blackwood is bad news. Terrible legends surround it, the wall can't stand, it's impervious to Hendrik's magic, and the guards don't even patrol the vicinity of the woods. It's a no-go zone."

Soren nodded. "And do you know why the guards don't patrol there, Ash?"

"Terrible evil?" I asked in the most animated voice I could muster.

"Because it's a black hole of death! That's why," Soren said. "You've been doing good here the last few weeks, don't go screwing it up by getting yourself and Tryst killed. Forget about escape and forget Blackwood. The things that go in there never come back, and I sure as hell won't be one of them."

CHAPTER 13

B lackwood had been legend since I could remember. It was the supernaturals' boogeyman. Be good, or they'll ship you off the Blackwood, they'd say. Turns out they were right about that part. I just didn't know it. The real question was: could any of it be true? ATOM had a firm hold on us, and hunted supernaturals across the country. To us, they were the monsters. Blackwood was just a large group of trees. A forest was a forest was a forest. Wasn't it? A small part of me wondered if any of it could be true, the rest of me wondered if it mattered. Could there be anything inside Blackwood worse than the monsters we already faced?

I tried to forget it. I tried to heed Soren's and Tryst's warnings, but it wouldn't quell the thought from my mind. I spent a month considering it. I wasn't going to rush anything, but I wouldn't write the idea off either. I examined it from every angle while working the yard. I trusted Soren when he said he could taste the aura that emanated off it. Even I could feel a shift in the air when I moved too close, but did that matter? When it came down to it, I wanted out of this place and Blackwood was the exit. Even if the legends were true, it was better than becoming ATOM's doormat, wasn't it? Besides, even if I considered that most legends had a shred of truth to them, what shred might that be? Time had a way of shifting truths, but at the bottom of every legend was someone who had lived it. Lived. That meant if it were true, someone had made it out alive to tell the tale, and if someone survived it once, it could be done again. Of course, all that was assuming any of it was real. All I knew for certain was that I needed out of this place, and Blackwood seemed the viable outlet.

Working under Gareth was like a labor camp. Chopping and hauling wood, pulling weeds, executing repairs on the Academy, and anything treacherous he could come up with. When you thought the work was done, he found more. I spent two days cleaning the rock that lined the flower beds, and then another three cleaning slime off the inside of the fountain. I polished the sharp iron gates until I bled, then I polished some more. Gage always lingered over my shoulders barking orders, and Gareth loved pairing the two of us together. The tension was thick. Gage enjoyed the authority almost as much as our advisor.

Eventually I'd suffered both Gareth's and Gage's scorn long enough and they grew bored, setting their sights on someone else. For the unfortunate girl it fell upon, it became too much. Jaycee Crawford was a small girl with dimpled cheeks and a freckled nose. At thirteen years old, her mismatched blue-green eyes held an innocence I hadn't seen at the Academy. She reminded me of what Samantha might have looked like had she been given the chance to grow up, but I did my best not to think about it. She'd arrived a few weeks after me—a witch stolen from her coven—and she had no tolerance for abuse. She conjured a spell strong enough to leave Gareth on his knees with a hundred lacerations split open across his body, yet she never laid a finger on him. I was proud of her, but it was because of that tenacity that I learned what Tryst had said to be true: the Academy never missed an opportunity to set an example. For Jaycee Crawford they skipped the Tank and strung her up by her neck with a metal-laced cord. While the cord burned through and decapitated her little by little, the advisors took turns cutting flesh from her bones. Hendrik ordered the action and while we were forced to watch, he returned to his corner office, free from the product of his command. In my time at the Academy, I'd gotten to the point that I could watch the advisors disgrace a body in its final moments and I wouldn't flinch. Of everything I'd stood by and done nothing about in my life, I hated myself for that more than anything. It revealed how far I'd fallen from the man I was, and reminded me how terribly I needed to get out of this place.

With the help of Gage, Gareth's torment continued to move

from one guest to another in predictable fashion, but fear smothered everybody into perfect behavior. Everybody except for Tryst, that is. Under usual circumstances she was a hard worker who kept her eyes down and her mouth shut, but since the slaughter of Jaycee, her work had slowed. At first I thought it a ploy to give the others exoneration from Gareth's madness. A break in the cycle, so to speak. That didn't seem out of the realm of her kindness. As days passed, however, she began to look worse. Bags formed beneath her eyes, her steps grew ragged and sloppy, and her work became poor. Supernaturals didn't get ill in the traditional way, but it was clear to me—Tryst was sick.

I reached out to her but she shut me out. Soren tried to deflect me too, but with enough pressure he caved. Tryst's body had started to break down. It happened from time to time. A succubus was built to feed off others' lives, and she didn't do that. She drew from the earth, which was a noble cause, but it wasn't how she was built. It didn't give her the sustenance she needed.

As weeks passed, she neglected her duties more and more, spending her time in the yard, with fingers clutching the earth, knuckle deep beneath the grass. Flares of red energy would spark around her wrists and spiral upward around her arms. Gareth scolded her with all kinds of threats, but lucky for Tryst, Hendrik wasn't completely out of the picture. He acknowledged that without it she would die, and for those moments flexibility existed in the rules. Gareth wasn't pleased about it, and on occasion the end of his club still found Tryst. The bruises he caused didn't heal, and the lower part of Tryst's back had a perfect outline of the club drawn in lines of black and purple. Soren assured me she would bounce back, but I wasn't so sure. Whatever she received from the earth wasn't enough. I wanted to help. I owed her. My body would heal on its own if she fed. I could take it. With Soren there we could make sure she didn't take too much. It'd be a controlled feed. I offered it time and time again. She refused. She was afraid, but that fear was going to kill her.

My days were spent distracted and worried. My nights passed in near perfect quiet. Once in the room, we didn't speak. Soren and Tryst drifted off while I stayed awake. Sleep eluded me. Tryst didn't move in her sleep. Her breathing was almost nonexistent, coming in long, slow draws. She'd developed a wheeze, her chest squealing with each breath. I didn't have the solution, and frustration welled up inside me. I'd stare at the mattress above me, toying with one idea after another. What was the solution?

My thoughts were interrupted when one of the beds squeaked. The room was dark, but I saw the silhouette of Soren's head poked over the edge of the bed. I felt his eyes on me, but I didn't move. He crawled cautiously down the ladder and moved toward me. I shut my eyes and pretended to sleep. One minute, then two. When I opened them I found him on the edge of Tryst's bed running his hand through her hair.

"Why do you do this to yourself? Your father wasn't perfect either. But he never had a chance to tell you that, did he?" Soren murmured. "After what happened, he wasn't ready to tell you. He feared you'd lose control again. Little did he know, keeping this from you would put your life in jeopardy time and time again. I guess he always thought he'd be around." A heavy, guilt-ridden sigh and Soren leaned over her, kissing the side of her head. "I love you, Tryst. You're my best friend and I hate keeping this from you, but I promised I'd take care of you."

He hovered over her and magic filled the room. Green flickers of light sparkled between his lips and drifted down toward her. I didn't know what was happening. I swung my legs over the bed and pulled him away. He hit the floor harder than I'd intended, but I didn't let up. I held him there, refusing to let him move even as fear burst in his eyes.

"What the hell are you doing?" I asked.

His hands flew up as if I might hit him, but the swelling around his right eye showed he'd had enough of that. When he realized it was me and I'd seen him, a scowl of determination fell over his face and vanquished the fear. He shoved my hand away with surprising vigor and scrambled to his feet.

"Go back to bed and forget this." His voice rushed out in a harsh whisper, lacking any of his usual humor. He was dead serious.

"Not a chance. I felt that. What were you doing?" I demanded.

"I'm doing what needs to be done. It doesn't concern you."

"She's my friend; it does concern me."

"And she's mine too. Has been since the day I was born," Soren said. "No offense, Ash, I like you, but what I have to do trumps whatever it is you're feeling. I can help her. I *will* help her. I won't ask your permission to do it." He shoved his way past me and leaned over her. "What you're about to see here is something you'll never talk about again. You won't mention it. Not ever." It wasn't a question. He stared at me with unbreakable resolve and a confidence I didn't think he could manifest. "She can't do it on her own. I have to do it for her."

Without a second glance the magic came back to life. It had startled me the first time I felt it, but now, focused and attentive, I realized it wasn't harmful. Not from him. It was warm and nurturing like a blanket on an winter day. A green strand spiraled from Soren's mouth like a ghost in the darkness. Tryst licked her lips and as it neared, she drew in a breath. Soren offered vitality—his life force—and she devoured the emerald mist.

In a few breaths, she looked more revitalized: color returned to her skin, the bags beneath her eyes smoothed, and the cuts and bruises along her hands were in repair. Soren offered her a form of energy the earth couldn't, and she devoured it. After a few more breaths it was over and Soren collapsed to the floor. His breaths were ragged, veins bulging on his arms and along his temples. His eyes shimmered a bright and fantastical green until the magic faded and returned them to brown. He shoulders shuddered and his arms trembled. He sounded breathless. It took him a few moments to regain his bearings, but even then he wasn't quite there.

"Are you okay?"

His arms trembled and he stumbled forward in an attempt to stand, legs almost giving out. He grabbed the edge of my bed and the entire frame squealed as loose screws moved against his weight.

"Fine." He gasped for air.

"You don't look fine."

"Energy is not easily given." His words were raspy and short and I wrapped my arm around him to keep him balanced. Exhaustion pulling at his face and dark circles formed beneath his eyes. "She can't live off the land like us, not completely. She needs true life from others, but she'll never take it for herself. Not after..."

"I know."

Soren questioned me with his eyes. "What do you know?"

"I know enough," I said. "You're a good friend. Let me help you."

He wavered back and forth, holding the bedframe for support. His feet moved absently around him as if he were drunk. I guided him back toward his bunk and helped him climb the ladder. He fell onto the mattress and the bed shifted.

"You can't say anything," he whispered.

"I won't," I assured.

"I mean it. Trace is gone, Ash. Gone. Tryst is all I've got left."

CHAPTER 14

Once the sun crested the trees, sleep fell over me. The alarm buzzed shortly thereafter and I found Tryst already awake and dressed. She'd become revitalized, and her eyes were bright. Soren, on the other hand, looked worse. His lips were dry and cracked and exhaustion dripped from his features. He ignored my concern and assured me he'd be fine. He could draw from the earth all day while he worked. I hoped he was right. I didn't want to trade one sick friend for another.

I worked hard through the day, but it didn't keep Gareth's watchful eyes away. With Tryst back on her feet, the routine started again and I was at the top of his list.

I sanded the outside of a rustic shed and prepped it for repaint. It was close to the Tank, leaving me a view of Blackwood. I tried not to think about it, but for a moment, curiosity got the best of me and my gaze lingered. It was brief, but enough time for Gareth to close the distance.

"Admiring the view?" he whispered over my shoulder.

I jumped, startled by his silent approach.

"No, sir, sorry." I pushed the sanding block against the plywood, flakes of broken paint fluttering to the ground in a blue-and-gold heap.

"No, go ahead. Take a good look. Blackwood Forest. A place of legends. It's perfect for an escape, don't you think?"

"No, sir. The Academy is my home."

Gareth's smile unnerved me. I didn't need to see it. I could feel it.

"No wall, no guards, just open space and room to run. It's tempting. You're not above temptation. You don't think you're better than us, do you?"

There was no good answer. I cursed myself, scrambling for something to say. When I didn't respond, he repeated the question.

"No, sir, I'm not. I admit the temptation to leave existed when I first arrived, but with your guidance I've seen what a real life can be if I'm willing to work toward something better," I replied.

I maintained a still face, trying not to show the panic ricocheting through me. My hands were clammy and I fumbled the sander. Gareth's hand shot out in a blur and caught it. I couldn't avoid him any longer.

"Sorry. Hot out today." I kept my eyes down, but when he didn't respond I felt his gaze burning into me.

"You're full of it, aren't you, Lawson?" he asked. "You think you can fool me?"

Gareth didn't like it when people shied away. He found it insulting. So when I looked up, I made sure to meet his eyes, as discomforting as it was.

"No, sir. I imagine you are a man not easily fooled."

"That's right, I'm not! You've been here a few months, but nobody turns over a new leaf that fast. You're up to something."

"With all due respect, my time in the Tank and a quick lesson with you thereafter was more than enough to realize I wasn't on the right path. I'm trying to fix that now."

Gareth didn't buy it. He grew angrier with each word I spoke. The vein in his scarred forehead swelled and his jaw tightened.

"That so?"

"Yes, sir." The title grew old. I hated it more each time I said it. Gareth didn't deserve my respect, but I bit my tongue and forced the word out. It was in my best interest for the moment.

He studied me. I wasn't sure what he was looking for. A nervous tick or something he could use against me? I gave him nothing.

"Hendrik's been watching you. He thinks you're going to be a star," Gareth admitted. "Thinks the boys upstairs are going to come down to see you, a possible recruit for some higher position within the system. Bounty hunter perhaps." Gareth laughed.

"Ironic. But you know what I think? I think you're a slimy little cockroach, weaseling your way through the cracks. You're a con man. Nothing more. Taking supernaturals' hard-earned money and sending them on a ship to their death while your pockets were lined with green."

"That's not—" I bit back my words and recoiled the aggression.

Gareth leaned in close. "Go ahead, say it. You're getting in other people's way here. You're complicating things. Please give me a reason to strike you down. One little thing and I'll show you for the fraud you are." I clenched my knuckles until they popped. The past few months had been a different kind of torture than the Tank, but torture nonetheless. I practically bowed down to a man I despised to avoid a beating and to spare Tryst. It didn't feel like self-preservation or biding my time. I felt like a coward. "An angel who can hold his tongue? Who would've thought that was possible?" He grumbled and cursed at me. "Get your ass back to work and keep those wandering eyes focused."

It wasn't without animosity, but I lowered my gaze and returned to work. Cowering once again. Paint peeled back from the wood while the sun beat down on me and Gareth shouted words of encouragement to Gage as he smacked a boy who stopped for a drink. I'd made a point of paying attention and learning what I could about the typhon, but he didn't have many faults. He was as good as he was cocky, demonstrating his strength at every possible opportunity, most times to the misfortune of another guest. Gareth watched in glee, and it unsettled me how much he seemed to enjoy it.

Work ended for the day, and the sun had already begun to set. I cleaned up the tools and anticipated the rubbery dinner I'd have on my plate within the hour when a commotion started. Soren had been mowing the grass around the Tank for most of the day and tending to the nearby flower beds. He looked better than he had this morning, but now he'd garnered an audience of Gage and some fellow white shirts. It started as jokes and name-calling, the norm for Gage, and as usual, Soren stomached it with refined patience. There was nothing easy about keeping your head down and working while somebody tormented you, but somehow he managed it week after week. Today, however, something seemed different. Gage seemed different. Aggression oozed off him, and his insults grew in vulgarity between breaths. The work day had wound down, but Gage seemed revved up. The slurs and name-calling turned into cruelty as he stomped through the flower beds and kicked dirt in Soren's face. He demanded Soren do it better, but that was impossible. Soren's work was flawless. No garden sprouted a weed and no plant wilted. He was a deva through and through, taking care of the living things around him. Soren didn't respond with anything but action. He filled the holes Gage's foot had dug in the beds and leveled the dirt. Once he turned his back, Gage leaped into the air and began trampling the flowers Soren had spent the entire day planting.

"This looks like garbage. Fix it!" Gage tore the next row of flowers out and threw them to the ground. "We have expectations to uphold, faggot."

Soren's face broke and he fell to his knees. He looked distraught, running his fingers over damaged flower petals. His gentle hands picked up the stems of each plant and cradled the roots. He set one back into the flower bed where pink and blue petals had been torn apart and lay broken along the dirt. I couldn't replicate the sadness he felt for the flower, but it wasn't just a flower. Not to Soren. To him it was a life; a wasted life destroyed by ignorance. He felt it the way we couldn't, and the tear that fell from his eye confirmed that. A revelation that would work against him as Gage plucked another from the dirt and snapped it.

Anger flared through my chest, and sharpness slashed across my shoulders as the muscles tensed. I wanted to stop him. I wanted to stretch my wings and tear him off the ground and into the sky. I'd pull him above the clouds and watch the fear ripen on his face when I let go. I wanted to, but I couldn't. I didn't have my wings anymore and any effort I would make would get us beaten, or worse. Instead, I simmered in fury and wrapped myself in helplessness.

Soren didn't let another tear fall. He reclaimed his emotions and picked up the rose as Gage threw it at him with a laugh. Soren shuffled quietly around the stone-lined flower bed picking up the pieces of broken life, and Gage rushed forward and kicked him from behind. Soren hit his face on the edge of the stone border and blood spilled in an instant as metal-laced rock cut into his skin. He scrambled to his hands and knees, blood flowing onto broken petals as he continued cleaning up the flowers he'd dropped.

"No!" Gage slapped them out of his hand and grinded them

beneath his shoe. "Those are garbage now. Wasted. Start again."

Gareth stood in the distance with an evil glare. He smirked and gave me a nod, mouthing the words "give me a reason."

It was all I needed. Screw this place.

I stepped into the shed and grabbed the first thing my hand found—a rake, but Tryst met me in the doorway and pushed me back inside.

"Don't," she commanded.

"You don't get to say that right now. Look at what they're doing!"

"I know, okay? I know, but you're not going to do anything about it. It won't do any good. It'll land you back in the Tank, or worse," she said.

"Worse? What could be worse than standing idle and watching this? Do we need to see another Jaycee die before somebody stands up?"

"She died because she stood up!"

I wanted to scream at Tryst. She didn't know the truth. She didn't know what Soren did for her, but I did. I knew the kind of person Soren was. I saw the kindness, the love, the generosity. I wouldn't watch this.

I pushed past her but I didn't get more than a few steps. Soren wiped the blood off his face, though it flowed steadily, staining his jeans. Gage towered over him with crossed arms and a grin. Soren didn't say a word. He didn't pick up the petals or scoop another handful of dirt off the grass. He grabbed the shovel beside him and swung it upward, cracking it against Gage's chin.

Gage didn't have time to be surprised, the impact rang across the yard and he fell on his back. Flakes of dirt rained over him and a smear of black tarnished his chin.

"For four and half years you've plagued me!" The shovel rang out again as it hit Gage across the jaw. The boy's head snapped to the side and back again with ferocity. "No more."

Soren swung a third time but Gage caught it in his hand and with a single tug Soren had been disarmed. Gage jumped to his feet and hammered the metal end upside Soren's head. Before Soren could fall, Gage had his shirt in his grip. He jerked Soren forward and smashed the shovel against his face. Once, twice, then came the snap of his nose with an explosion of blood. Soren's eyes rolled back and he hit the pile of broken flowers like a dead log, head bouncing off the stone edging.

I moved in a blur, and grass tore beneath my feet. Rage had consumed Gage's face and his eyes glowed red like lava. He lifted his foot and prepared to stomp Soren's head into the ground. I wouldn't let him. Both my hands hit his chest at full speed and with the force of a freight train he tumbled thirty feet backward in the air. He hit the ground and rolled to Gareth's feet.

The advisor tore the shovel from his hand and held Gage back while he cursed me out with threats and vulgarities. I tended to Soren, his face cut deep and the back of his head even worse. Red stained his raven hair and a wide gash trickled blood onto the grass. His lips quivered and hands trembled as they dug into the earth. A quiet buzz reverberated around him, sparks of green igniting between his fingers. The redness across his face and deep black circles beneath his eyes faded, and although the bleeding nose stopped, it remained crooked.

"Beat that little roach!" a boy in a white shirt yelled.

"He deserves the Tank!" another shouted. The group expanded like a wall of angry youth that closed in around us.

"The Tank? Idiot! He assaulted me," Gage demanded, offended by the suggestion. "He struck his superior. He needs to be strung up."

"That's bullshit!" I shouted. "Every one of you are cowards."

Everybody fell quiet and Gage tried to break away from Gareth's grip, but the advisor restrained him.

"What did you say?"

"Soren stood up for himself," I said. "We should all be so fearless. Instead we stand back, cowering, thankful it wasn't us this time. You all stood there and watched, smug looks painted on your faces. Gage didn't get half of what he deserved and you all know it."

"Shut it, punk!" Gage said. "Or I'll shut it for you."

"That's enough!" Gareth warned as other advisors began to move toward the group. Guards closed in around us. "You were assigned the shed, Ash. What are you doing off your post?"

"What?"

"I don't repeat myself."

"They were harassing and abusing him. You can't let them get away with that."

Gareth shook his head. "He hit Gage with a shovel. Violence is *never* tolerated by guests at the Academy."

"Soren has a right to protect himself. We all do," I argued. "Gage is lucky that's all he got."

"Are you threatening one of my guests?" Gareth stepped forward, twirling the shovel in hand. "You have *no* rights within these walls. None. You're lucky you weren't killed on sight."

"You can't be serious."

"I knew you were putting on a show," Gareth said. "You're too far gone to be rehabilitated. All it took was a nudge." The smile that crossed his lips was evil, and the malice was replicated in his eyes.

"You did this," I said. It wasn't a question, it was statement. He hadn't been able to draw out the behavior he wanted from me, so he had Gage do it indirectly.

"What did you say?"

"This isn't about me. It's about you," I said. "You sicced your lapdog on Soren and he got bit. You can't punish Soren for defending himself."

"I can punish whoever the hell I want," Gareth barked. "I'll start with you for leaving your post without permission. Two days in the Tank. I'll add on the display of assault and disobedience you displayed and when you're done in there we'll string you up."

Gage and the others cheered.

"This place is a joke. We're all supernaturals, yet you suckle at ATOM's tit like you'll starve without it," I declared. "You're an embarrassment, Gareth."

A fiery rage consumed his face and the banshee's supremacy wavered through the air. Gareth's eyes became void of color as he struck me. My jaw popped from the force, a spear shooting through my temples. Magic swelled inside me, a wrath unlike any other. I clenched my fist and prepared to retaliate. I had nothing left to loose.

"What is going on?" Hendrik's voice boomed across the yard. Silence sharp enough to cut the air followed. Hendrik stood between us and the force that emanated around Gareth dissipated.

"Nothing to worry yourself with, Headmaster."

"You hand out two days in the Tank and a death sentence for nothing?" Hendrik asked. "That doesn't sound like nothing. And what has happened to this boy?" Soren's bloodstained lips were swollen, his teeth caked with dirt and his nose crooked.

"A revolt. Led by none other than your star pony," Gareth claimed.

"It wasn't a revolt," I said. "Gage destroyed half of Soren's work for the day, and hit him when he tried to clean it up. All Soren did was stand up for himself after taking a beating."

"Silence!" Gareth said. "That boy struck another with a weapon! No matter what preceded it, that is unacceptable behavior."

Hendrik stood emotionless, helping Soren to his feet. "Is this true? Did you strike Gage with a shovel?"

Soren leaned over and spit out a splotch of blood on the grass. "He deserved it."

"The severity of what you've done comes with a steep penalty. You are aware of that?"

"I'll take my time in the Tank."

"Oh no, Mr. Kye. Assault with a weapon is not time in the Tank." Soren's eyes opened wide and he no longer looked calm, he looked scared. "It is death."

"Like I said, hang him up!" Gage shouted. The boys behind cheered.

"I said silence!" The yard fell quiet like the stillness that preceded a storm. "Are you still sure it was worth it, Mr. Kye?"

Soren didn't speak. He stared at Hendrik and his skin paled.

"That's not fair," I said.

"The rules are the rules, Mr. Lawson."

"I don't care. Soren has the right to protect himself," I argued. "If defending yourself against attack isn't allowed, then Gage is just as guilty. He hit Soren with the shovel. Does that mean you're going to kill Gage too?"

"You insolent little—" Gareth rushed forward, club out and ready to strike.

"Leave him!" Hendrik shoved him back with surprising force, and Gareth stumbled. "Is this true, Gage, did you strike him first and then again in retaliation to his attack?"

"Of course not, sir. I'm a supervising guest; I'm not permitted to take action." He shook his head, fake sincerity dripping off his words.

I moved to argue but Hendrik raised his hand to silence me. I looked around at the other guests, waiting for one of them to speak up and oppose Gage's claim. Silence. My eyes pleaded with the other advisors. I didn't know their names but I knew they'd seen it too. They stared at the ground as if they'd been scolded for misbehaving. Cowards.

"I saw it, Headmaster." Tryst joined the group, having lingered by the shed. The quake in her voice revealed how nervous she felt rivaling Gareth. "What Ash said is true."

A few smaller boys nodded, but none spoke. As Gareth's eyes fell upon them, they took a step back and became still.

"How ironic," Gareth said. "They're all roommates; of course they'll defend one another."

"The same could be said to you, Gareth," I said. "You encourage Gage to treat us like this. I've seen it and heard it myself. Then you cover for him and someone else has to take the blame. Like Jaycee."

Gareth's ethereal shriek was on the brim. It primed the air and I half expected his voice to lacerate my body, but Hendrik's voice silenced any reaction he might have.

"Enough. I have ways in which to get the truth," Hendrik announced. "Do not make me resort to them. Speak it to me. Now."

I'd never seen as much hate in a person's eyes as I did in Gareth's. He stared with an animosity so pure I could taste the sulfur spilling from his pores.

"It's true they were playing with Soren. Tomfoolery, nothing more. I saw it from a distance and I didn't correct them," Gareth said. "My team had been working hard as of late and I made the judgment that a little fun could be had. It was my mistake. If I'd known it was upsetting him I'd have stepped in myself. As for kicking him, I can't be sure. Like I said, I was across the yard."

"And you, Mr. Daniels? Do you care to revise your statement?"

Gage bit his lip and glanced at Gareth. Gareth gave him a nod—almost unnoticeable—and Gage rolled his eyes. Hendrik approached him and whispered something I could not hear, but Gage's eyes flickered with an unexpected emotion. Fear.

"I pushed him with my foot, but it wasn't hard. We were just playing."

"And the truth will set you free," Hendrik said. He studied Gage's face a moment and then sighed. "This is most disappointing."

"Punishment must be had," Gareth said. "A little push for a

shovel? That is not how we deal with things here, Hendrik."

"Do not begin to tell me how things are dealt with," Hendrik advised. "I have been a part of the Academy since its inception. I think I know how things are done."

"Then perhaps you've been here *too* long," Gareth retorted.

"I beg your pardon?" Hendrik's movements were quick and full of grace. Two strides and he stood before the advisor, towering several inches over him.

Gareth conceded and the defiance vanished. "Nothing, sir, but I ask that we remain consistent."

"Consistency? This is what you wish?"

"Yes, Headmaster."

"Then this behavior will not go unpunished. Soren, you have attacked a guest and of all things, with a weapon," Hendrik said. "That is grounds for death. Due to the unique circumstances, I will permit a lesser sentence: fifteen lashes."

Tryst sighed and her eyes filled with tears. Her head hit my chest and I wrapped my arms around her. Gareth and Gage smirked with delight, but Hendrik wasn't finished.

"As for you, Gage. Your exceptional performance does not excuse your behavior, and extravagant protection from your advisor will not shelter you. Not today. Five lashes."

"Five? That's nothing. I'll take it."

"Ten then."

Gage cursed and Gareth shrugged. "You can handle ten lashes. Be a man." Gareth nodded to Hendrik. "That sounds fair, sir."

"With an additional five for lying to your headmaster," Hendrik continued. "It's almost as if you're going for a record, but what good is breaking your personal best?"

Gage didn't respond but Gareth looked furious. "This is ridiculous!"

"You will keep yourself and your guests in check. You are lucky I let you walk away unpunished from this, Gareth."

"And what would you punish me with, *sir*?"

"Gage is under your advisement. Your position demands you oversee him and all the guests in your charge. This entire event falls under negligence on your part, and as such will be put in your review."

The scars along his face scrunched and he bit back whatever he wanted to say. "Thank you for your generosity, *sir*. It's too kind."

"And perhaps next time I won't be. Remember that in your future endeavors."

CHAPTER 15

Lashes broke the air, biting skin with sharp wet snaps. The sound of breaking skin haunted me. It happened fast, screams resounding before the whip cracked. Pain before sound. Gage remained near silent, but Soren's cries were like a tide; each one larger and more uncontrollable than the previous. Gareth gave the lashings. He was an artist, swishing the long black tail all around. It swirled above him like a dancer's ribbon before blood splashed into the air. Soren's face distorted, red accented the blue sky and stained the grass in a lopsided battle.

As it were with Jaycee, we didn't have the option to look away. Hendrik had set an example and we'd all be there to witness it or take a lashing ourselves. After a few minutes it ended and the air smelled of copper and burned flesh. As the restraints were loosened around his wrists, Soren's body collapsed with blood, sweat, tears, and piss puddled beneath him. As his knees hit the ground, the puddle rippled around his body like a stone thrown into a tranquil pond. I ran to him, lifting him from the mess and holding him in my arms. He'd passed out after the ninth lash. Instead of earning cries of torment with the final strikes, they succeeded only in mutilating him further. I carried him to our room where lockdown was in effect. No more work and no dinner, but at this point we didn't care. There was no room for food, sadness filled us.

Soren lay unconscious on Tryst's bunk. His bruised and swollen face—compliments of Gage—nothing but mere decorations compared to the rest of him. Tryst had depleted the first-aid kit with me when we worked on the wall, and now we had little with which to dress the wounds. She draped a damp towel over his back, and waiting was all that remained.

Tension suffocated the room. Tryst and I sat in silence for hours, partly in disbelief at what Soren had done, partly because of the result. A copper-laced whip was no minor thing, yet somehow he was to be grateful for it; a lashing instead of death. What a lucky guy.

I found it hard to remain still. Frustration and rage swirled inside me while I stared at the empty bed above. I wanted to hurt Gage. A part of me wanted to kill him. At this point there was nothing to lose. Life? It was nonexistent here. I had always told myself I would rather die than be a slave to ATOM. When the Academy claimed me, I thought I'd find a new way to fight them. In my search, I became the slave I swore I'd never be. I had watched students beaten for wrinkles in their sheets and leftover dinner they'd slipped into their pockets. I let guards spit thick wads of pasty saliva on my face without flinching in fear of repercussions. Now I lay across from my friend who received a near-death lashing for standing up against those who plagued him. Life? What life?

Tryst tried to comfort her friend, running her fingers through his hair. He had done the same when she fell ill; a friendship unbroken by hell.

"This was supposed to be better than death," she said. "Gage will be sore for a day; typhons heal fast, but Soren won't be so lucky. The copper festers in the wounds. After all this he might still—"

"Don't say that." I sounded determined but felt terrified. "This place is a nightmare. Lashings? It's prehistoric and twisted. This isn't living, Tryst."

She ignored me, eyes focused on Soren. "He's been with me since we were kids. He's the only family I've got. You think this is bad? This isn't even the worst of it. Even if he survives—"

"Soren's tough. He's a survivor. This *won't* kill him."

"But Gage and Gareth might. They're going to have it out for him now more than ever. Both of you."

"Then we leave."

"We've been here for four years, Ash. Believe me, I've looked for a way out. If there was one, I would've found it.

"Blackwood."

"This again? I don't want to trade one death sentence for another, and even if I was willing to, Soren would never agree to that."

"Then we convince him. Tryst, it's a chance at freedom. Think about it."

"It doesn't matter what I think. I'm not going anywhere without Soren. You underestimate his belief in the curse."

"What if it's not cursed? What if the people who go in there never come back because they made it? Have either of you stopped to think about that?" She turned away from me and I grabbed her hand. "Tryst."

"What?" She pulled away, a sharp look crossing her face. "What do you want from me?"

"I want you to choose life. It's *your* turn to trust me now. Blackwood isn't ideal, I know that, but it's our only option. I can keep you safe. Both of you."

"Can you?" Anger flickered in her eyes. "There's a few hundred people from that boat who would say otherwise, isn't there?" Her eyes were blades that cut across me.

The world warbled around me moving in and out of focus. I stumbled back and caught the bed, using it as a crutch to lower me to the mattress.

"Wow."

My chest ached, hundreds of tortured souls screeching through my mind. It was always there in the background, but as of late I'd managed to stifle it. Now it came full frontal, pressing against my heart.

"I shouldn't have said that. I didn't mean it."

She grabbed my hand, but her touch wasn't the soft and warm one I so often craved. Instead I felt the cold, dead grip of a drowning woman. Hair clung to her face, her skin a sickly green that felt like seaweed against my arm. Her grip was remarkable, nails digging into my skin in a frantic attempt at salvation. I shuddered, a spine-tingling cold rippling through me.

"Ash..."

I pulled my hand away and shook it as if that could rid me of the feeling. "Don't apologize. Please. It's the truth and the least of what I deserve."

"That's not true."

"It is. I can admit that." I didn't look at her. My eyes were lost in the dots of blood that had stained the floor from Soren's back. Another casualty. "My mistake cost a lot of lives and somehow I survived. It isn't fair. It isn't fair that they died while I lived. I know that. But I survived for a reason. It wasn't meant to end for me there, and it isn't meant to end here. Not like this. I'll never make up for what happened, but I can try and leave the world a better place before my time comes."

Soren groaned and started to move. We rushed toward him, encouraging him to remain still. He didn't produce words, but murmurs of suffering reverberated from his lips. His face twisted as he thrashed against the sheets.

"He's hot," I said, touching his forehead. "He shouldn't be."

Sweat glimmered on his face, his skin ignited in fever. Tryst lifted the towel that clung to his back and revealed gnarled flesh rippling between deep wounds. The bottom of the towel clung to his skin, requiring more force to pull away. Soren whimpered as she plied it back. His back looked like a cadaver that had been put through a meat grinder.

"The copper," she said. Strips of it glimmered between trickles of blood, embedded in the wounds. They weaved through the crevices, inflaming the skin around them. "We have to get them out otherwise the metal will infect his blood. Help me, please?"

It was a game of operation without proper tools. I slid a pair of flimsy plastic tweezers into each wound and Soren cried out. Blood trickled steadily, making finding the wires difficult. Eventually it became too much and Soren passed out. Tears streaked Tryst's face, but she didn't speak. Her eyes pleaded with me to help him, and although I caused more damage in the process, one by one I withdrew the wires.

When it was done, any exposed skin on his back had turned a deep purple with lines of black rippling through it. Soren's skin had grown hotter. Beads of sweat ran across his body and he shivered as though he had a chill. I fell back onto the floor, blood staining my trembling hands. It had taken more than an hour to get them all out and exhaustion pulsed through my muscles. The plastic tweezers were clumped with chunks of flesh and blood. I dropped them to the floor and released a shaky breath. It was done. Without bandages, we were forced to use our sheets and pillowcases to stop the bleeding. I stared at the stained fabric all around us, certain we'd get a clubbing for it tomorrow, but if Soren survived, it was worth it.

My muscles vibrated with fatigue and I stared at him, wishing him a quick recovery. I knew better; devas were not adept healers. The copper was out, but repairing the damage that had been done wouldn't be easy.

The moon cast a misty glow through the room and Tryst's head rested against my shoulder. After Soren's fever broke, the tension between us collapsed with it. I think we both felt the need to be close to someone. The night passed us in minutes that felt like hours. Neither of us could sleep. Not tonight. Worry rode the air like a static charge, and each time Soren shifted or groaned electricity snapped through us. We'd rush to his side as if we could help. We couldn't. Once again we were forced to sit idle and watch.

"Can you help him?" I asked. "Like he helped—" I cut off my words. In my stupor of exhaustion I almost revealed his secret. "Like you helped me with the dust?"

She didn't lift her head or make an effort to move. Her words sounded as tired as I felt. "No. I didn't *give* you anything. I took away the bad, siphoning it out. We pulled out the embedded metals, but what he needs is sustenance. Something only the earth can give to him. Believe me, if there was anything else I could do, I'd have done it."

"That doesn't surprise me. It seems like ever since I arrived all I've seen you do is take care of people."

"People I care about." She reached out and touched my leg, and pushed herself up. Her fingers were caked with blood, and a smear of it marred her face where she'd brushed hair away from her eyes in the midst of everything. "Soren has done his share of taking care of me too and after today, I've no doubt you would've done the same for me."

She had no idea how much Soren did for her. She checked his breathing again, lines of worry creasing around her eyes. Although Soren was in terrible shape, watching the two of them made me realize that although they'd been prisoners here for so long, and I'd lived on the outside until a few months ago, my life was the one that had been incomplete. I'd been involved in an underground movement attempting to help others, but I hadn't been a part of a family. I'd left mine behind in hopes for a better future. In reality, I'd spent so much time looking for it that I didn't realize what I'd been missing. What was freedom without people to share it with?

"This place has a way of seeping into your soul and tearing you apart bit by bit," I said. "But you can't let it. Always keep fighting, right?" She looked tired, hopelessness filling her eyes. I took both her blood-crusted hands in mine and squeezed. "We *will* get through this, Tryst. All of us."

She squeezed back, but it felt weak. "I know. I hope."

She leaned in and rested her forehead against my chest. She was exhausted, but it wasn't the kind of tired sleep could fix. It was a weight that bore down over her. It was life in this place. One thing after another crashed into you, and some days you didn't feel like you could hold your breath any longer. You expected the water to close in and swallow you. Part of you wished it would. It was watching your friends get torn apart for refusing abuse and knowing you could do nothing about it. It was hoping you could live to see another day, but in reality that day was a repeat of the one before it. There was no future. Not here.

I knew she felt it then. We all felt it. Hopelessness. It reminded me of the look I saw on families' faces across the country knowing ATOM was closing in on them. I hated that look, and regardless of the failures I'd made, it reinvigorated my determination. On the outside I had wanted to fight for hope when others couldn't. I wanted to be the light at the end of their tunnel. This was no different. The circumstances had changed, but what I wanted remained the same.

"Did you mean what you said about getting us out of here? You, me, and Soren," Tryst murmured.

"Of course." Her question startled me. She'd been so against it, I wondered what changed, but as Soren writhed on the bed and whimpered, I knew the answer.

"Even if I could convince Soren, we don't know what's in there. Maybe it isn't cursed and the stories are made up. That doesn't make it safe."

"I know, but unless we go in we'll never find out," I said.

"Soren is a deva, Ash. It's true he tells a lot of stories and he *hears* a lot more, but don't forget he can taste auras. I'm a succubus and I can feel them. Energy is what we do, and Blackwood doesn't *feel* good. It's dark and if you get close enough, you can feel its misery. Have you ever looked at it? I mean *really* looked. It doesn't matter what time of day it is, there's a sheet of darkness inside. That's not shadow play; it's dark energy. I don't say this to deter you, but if we go in there and something happens to Soren, I could never forgive myself."

I stepped back and lifted her chin so she could look into my eyes. Words wouldn't be enough, she had to see it. "I can't promise success. I've made that mistake before and it's haunted every moment of quiet I've had since. But I can promise you I'll die before I let anything happen to either of you."

She stared at the blood that covered the floor and stained both our hands. Soren groaned in the background and a trickle of fresh blood rolled out from beneath the sheet we'd draped over him.

Tryst sighed and leaned against me. "We can't stay here anymore."

CHAPTER 16

Nervousness clenched my chest and I wondered what lay within the woods. The decision had been made, and it brought with it a level of uncertainty. I sat on the floor and bathed in the morning heat that shone through the window, stuck somewhere between awake and asleep. Now that Tryst was on board, I worried I might be wrong. What if Blackwood was a worse evil than this? Was it possible? Was there another option I missed? The thought of escaping had excited me, but as I dwelled on it the feeling pacified. Reality had a way of doing that. Blackwood could be the way out, but we weren't close enough to see it yet. And if it were the only option, first we had to get out of our locked room, escape to the outside with guards monitoring every hall, and then run across the Academy's endless property undetected. All this so we could jump into another world of mystery and legend and hope we made it to the other side. Confidence eluded me as my stomach knotted. It had been easy to talk about escaping and the freedom that awaited us, but the act of doing it and risking others' lives again was something different. Before the boat I wouldn't have thought twice about it, but previous failure had a way of inflicting doubt.

The door buzzed and unlatched. Tryst and I stepped into the hall, but Soren remained in bed. He wasn't awake and any attempt to rouse him failed. My nerves twisted as guards filed up the stairs. Mr. Calm stood in front of me with an insidious smile. We'd never failed inspection, but today it seemed he anticipated we would.

As the final guard ascended the stairs, I was surprised by Gareth's absence. Most days he'd be waiting with a grin, and today of all days I expected him to look as eager as the sloppy guard before me. Instead, Hendrik stood at the top of the stairs, his presence emanated down the hall. Shoulders stiffened and tension mounted the line of guests.

Guards searched each room, and every feeling I had intensified as they neared ours. Mr. Calm made an offhanded comment about our missing guest and a pit formed in my throat. My hands grew clammy and as my fingers brushed Trysts, I noticed hers were too. At one point her hand lingered against mine. Neither of us pulled away. I felt reassurance in her touch. Not that everything would be fine, but that I wasn't alone. If nothing else, I had comfort in that.

The guards completed the room next to us. My breath became staggered. My mind raced. My heart jackhammered against my rib cage. If they tried to strike Soren or Tryst, would I stand there and watch? Was this the man the Academy had turned me into? I knew the answer and it made me feel weak. As Mr. Calm walked toward me, I felt the urge to shove him back and take a stand, but Tryst gripped my wrist and I kept my feet planted.

Mr. Calm's lips twisted into a sneer I'd come to hate. "I can't wait to get you on your knees at the mercy of my club."

"Stop," Hendrik said.

Calm's face warped into confusion. "What? Why?"

Hendrik instructed he would inspect the room himself. When Calm tried to object, a single glance silenced him. Breath caught in my throat and my chest tightened. If I hadn't been so nervous, I'd have smiled at the shock on Calm's face.

The headmaster hesitated on the threshold. Each moment seemed a lifetime. Then his still face vanished and a brief frown covered his lips. Disappointment? I couldn't tell. Perhaps he didn't gain the same joy from watching the guests disciplined as Gareth and Calm. Perhaps he'd hoped we'd be better prepared, but how could he? He'd sent a beaten and bloody boy into a locked room with no means of care. Was it the remnants of bandages that littered the floor? We weren't supposed to have them. If not that, was it the soiled bedsheets and puddle of blood that stained the weathered floorboards? Had that broken his vacant expression? If nothing else the smell of urine that ripened Soren's clothes could have been enough.

Hendrik stepped back from the room and whispered to Calm. The look of disgust that crossed the guard's face was almost humorous.

"What? You've got to be kidding me. He's—"

Hendrik raised his hand and the guard fell silent. Without another word, the headmaster descended the stairs, leaving Calm to mutter under his breath.

"There will be no work today," Calm said. "Meals will be delivered to your rooms and shower time distributed." He looked at Tryst and me as he said the last. "Rooms are on lockdown otherwise."

The action startled everyone, but the commotion was quieted by the threat of withdrawing the offered meals. Calm's eyes were alight with hate and focused on me. I moved to return to my room and his baton stabbed me in the back.

"Next time, Angel. That's a promise."

The door closed and the buzzer sounded, locking down the latch. I felt his rage lingering through the heavy door. A loud tap hit the wood, rhythmically beating, slow at first and then quicker. After each thump, Calm's voice spoke. "Soon." It muffled its way from the other side, faster and faster until silence descended upon us. I stared at the door, half expecting him to barge through. Instead, the quiet remained, leaving me unsettled. I hated this place.

"That guy has it out for me," I said.

"Not for any reason except what you are," Tryst said. "He hates angels."

"How do you know that?"

"Because he uses it as a derogatory term for the guests he hates the most, which is pretty much everybody except Gage and a few other white shirts. If I were you, I'd spend less time worried about him and more time concerned with Hendrik's reaction. Something isn't right. There are lashings all the time. Nobody gets a break because of it."

"Maybe this time he realized how bad things are."

Tryst laughed. "No, that's not how things work. You haven't been here long enough to see. He works *for* ATOM. There's no such thing as mercy. Not at the Academy. Something's wrong."

She feared the worst. Perhaps Hendrik had changed his mind

and decided to execute Soren after all. I tried to talk her down but she wasn't having it. Instead, she spent the day hovering over her injured friend, willing him back to health. It didn't work.

Sometime in the middle of the afternoon, Soren woke from his stupor. It was difficult for him to move and his attempts to mask his suffering were weak. Throughout the day, doors had buzzed to allow each guest a brief stint in the bathroom. When Soren's turn came, he refused our help. He walked keeled over, hobbling and wincing with each movement. At one point I saw the glimmer of tears but he turned away and struggled alone. When he returned, fresh sheets had appeared outside our door. Soren refused to talk and curled back into the lower bunk. Maybe he felt embarrassed or angry or sad. Maybe a little of everything. To be struck down time and time again in front of everybody you knew could be crushing in many ways that weren't physical. Instead of pressing him, I sat in silence and pretended I didn't hear his stifled sobs. He needed time to decompress. I respected that.

The door buzzed and Tryst came back with an armful of towels, some sopping with cold water, others dry. Her hair had a curl to it when it was wet, soft ringlets framing her face. She looked almost radiant, and I'd forgotten how violet her eyes were set against her pale skin. It was amazing how much filth one accumulated over a week and how quick we grew accustomed to it.

Mr. Calm waited in the hall, curling his fingers for me to follow. With his baton out, my eagerness to shower faded. I swallowed the lump in my throat and let him escort me to the bathroom, baton clanking against the keys that dangled from his waist. He unlocked the door and stepped back, an unsettling grin upon his face. He urged me forward with the tilt of his head and I braced for impact. The anticipated beating never came, and the door locked behind me. I breathed a sigh of relief.

Steam thickened the air, so much so it was hard to breath and almost impossible to see. The smell of soap lingered, but the blood didn't wash away with the ease I'd hoped. I scrubbed until I wore the skin raw and the hot water stung. The comfort of the shower was short lived. Once I'd washed away all the blood, anxiety and tension gripped my shoulders. Doubts of Blackwood crept in. I wouldn't run away from this place with foolish beliefs that the grass to be instantly greener on the other side. Nothing worthwhile ever came free. I'd learned that much. But it left me questioning the cost of our potential freedom. I didn't want any more blood on my hands.

The faucet squeaked and the water ran dry, a fresh white towel scratchy and warm against my skin. I lingered in the steam-filled stall, towel tied around my waist. A part of me dreaded going back. The shower had been a welcome escape. To return to Soren's distress and Tryst's grief wasn't something I looked forward to. They were my friends and I cared for them, but in this moment there was a part of me that wanted to stay hidden in the mist of warmth.

"Feel better?" Gage's voice cut through the steam. It came from every direction, but I couldn't see more than a few inches in front of me. My pulse quickened, a rush of adrenaline flooded my veins. My feet slapped against the wet floor as I ran to the door, but it didn't budge. It remained locked. "It's impolite to ignore someone speaking to you." His voice came from behind me. He was close. I swiped at the air but felt nothing.

"I have nothing to say to you."

"No? It seemed you had plenty to say yesterday before helping deliver my lashes." His voice was deep, reverberating through the room like an intercom. I cursed the hotness of my shower now that I had no line of sight.

"You earned every one of those strikes yourself. If you can't see that, you're delusional."

Steps rushed in front of me then behind. I spun in a circle, losing my place in the room. Then something hit me, sharp and hard like a stone. Gage's face cut through the steam, his arm against my throat pressed me against the wall. Shards of rock rubbed back and forth along my skin, butting into it. I struggled, but he was stronger than I'd expected. I pushed hard, his feet sliding against the damp floor, but he came back with incredible force and my head bounced off the wall. Tile broke around my skull, flakes of it falling over my shoulders. His silver eyes flickered in the steam like a train's headlights through morning mist.

"Exactly how delusional am I?" His arm had no skin, it was covered in brown jagged rock like the face of a mountain. Red lines formed like lava sliding through the crevices. With the glow came the heat of a typhon; liquid fire over stone that scorched my neck. Gage was a volcano waiting to erupt.

The air wouldn't come or go. It clung in my throat and I

couldn't breathe. My heart had long since broken into a sprint and I heard my pulse in my ears. My other senses amplified with the lack of air, and the echo of water dripping from a faucet crashed through the room. Moisture collected on my brow, humidity clinging to my skin. Salt and sulfur stung the air. Black dots swam in my vision as he pushed harder. Panic roared through me like a fire through dead brush. Over the past few months I'd succumbed to the guards' discipline and rules. I'd been clubbed, poked and prodded by anything within reach, and the entire time I'd stood helpless. Don't fight back. That was rule number one at the Academy. Keep your eyes down and your mouth shut. Rule number two. I was done with rules. In my struggle for air, all that faded and the fight inside me re-emerged. Fight or flight. Those were my choices, and I was an angel without wings.

My hand moved fast, fingers curled and knuckles sharp. I hit his solar-plex hard and quick, his eyes shot open and he gagged. I swung forward and let my elbow crack against his temple. It hit with a solid thud, but when I came back around with a clenched fist, he was gone. The steam hadn't thinned and the room remained mostly lost to me. I followed the wall, keeping my eyes on the area in front of me.

"You're faster than I expected." His silhouette stood in the fog like a shadow. "But I didn't come here to fight."

I touched my throat; the brush of rock and fire against my skin had been rough and irritating. "Could've fooled me."

"I misjudge my strength at times. It's been a long while since I've had to use it."

I walked toward him, his figure becoming clear.

"That's unfortunate for you, because I *know* what I'm capable of." I moved with angelic speed, fists hammering into his chest. He flailed back but I didn't lose sight of him. I charged forward and when his back bounced off the wall, my fist met his jaw. The impact was loud like rock being struck together, and he ducked into a cloud of fog.

"You're upset. That's understandable. As am I. You've become somewhat of a pet to Hendrik. Untouchable, it seems. You've taken a position that was to be mine. You're interfering with my business."

"What are you talking about?"

"I see the way he avoids giving you punishment. It obscures

145

certain goal I've worked to attain."

"You think this is my fault?" I couldn't help but laugh. "You got what you deserved."

"Of course you see it that way, Soren is your friend," Gage said. "But your vision is narrow and I find it lacking. I suppose that's why you got caught in the first place."

My anger flared. "You know nothing about me. I, on the other hand, have been watching you."

"And what have you seen?"

"I watched what you did to Soren in the yard," I said. "It wasn't the first time, but it was the worst I'd seen. The black eyes, the broken lip, the abuse you scar him with that doesn't leave a mark. I see it all. I know what you are, and you're lucky all you got was a shovel to the face and a few lashes. If it was me—"

"You see what you want." Gage stepped through the steam, both hands tucked into the front pocket of his sweater, silver eyes flickering. "I cannot blame you. The outside world, ATOM, even the Academy—they have all contributed to your shortsightedness. You are focused and loyal, that's commendable, but you are weak and without scope. It's difficult to work with, but not impossible."

I'd heard enough. Anger swirled like a twister across desolate prairie, tearing up earth and building ferocity. I swung and Gage dodged my first strike, ducking my second and shoving me back with intense force. I skidded along the floor, my towel almost slipping off. I hesitated, waiting for him to attack, but he stood like a mountain in a valley, tall and unmoving.

"You look at me and you see a monster," he surmised. "I accept that, but you've no idea who I really am."

"Spoken like a true typhon. Before ATOM, your kind ruled the outside, and here you are stuck inside, a prisoner, trying to continue the legacy."

"Enough with your suggestive banter. I'm not here to threaten you or fight, although after all this I have half a mind to pummel you into the floor."

"Have you ever met an angel?" I asked. He responded with a faint shake of his head. "Then you have no idea what I'm capable of. If you think I'll be taken out by you and you alone, you better get creative. If I'm going down in this place because of you, you can be damn sure I'll take you with me."

"Brash and arrogant. I don't hate it," he responded. "In fact I like the latter part, but the former could use some finesse. But I say again, I'm not here to hurt you. Although perhaps I should be." He paced in front of me, eyes gleaming. "You've obstructed my path in a way I find irritating, but you're not the first to do so. However, rather than approach this with my usual flare, I feel disposed to do the opposite. After all, my usual approach has not gotten me where I need to be, so as an intelligent man, I'm inclined to try something new. That something leaves me here not to hurt you, but to help."

"If you don't want to fight, what do you want?" I asked.

Gage sighed. "You stood up for something in the yard. Friendship, hope, whatever it is it doesn't matter. You lived to tell the tale and that piques my interest. It seems to have captured Hendrik's forgiving side; a side I've seen but once in my time here. He has his sights set on you, and that creates opportunity for both of us. I think if we were to align ourselves we could accomplish what we both desire."

"You want me to work *with* you? I was wrong, you're not delusional, you're insane."

"You see and hear what I've allowed. You learn only that which I've permitted to be shared. Of course you feel that way. It means my people have done their job. What I've created here is a work of art to be studied for the ages, but I digress. You need help, and we need allies."

"We?"

"A single instrument does not make an orchestra, Flapper."

"I don't want anything to do with you. Let me out of here."

"You demand it as though it has something to do with me," he said

"Doesn't it?"

Gage smirked. "Smart boy. You see, I have control where you have none, but you are the answer to the question I've asked. We need one another, Ash." He inched closer and my fists clenched, ready to strike. "Work with me and we can escape this place together."

My chest tightened. He couldn't know what Tryst and I had talked about. Could he? His words struck a chord and I reacted. My knuckles stung, cracking hard against his chin. His head snapped back, but he shook it off. Anger splayed across his face and his fist turned to stone. He was faster than I'd anticipated and I felt it, hard and sharp as the rock cut into me.

"Guards!" he shouted.

I stumbled back, trying to regain my footing, but I slipped on the tile and crashed to the floor. Making use of an awkward situation, I kicked his legs out from under him and brought him down to my level. Before he could scramble to his feet, I pounced, pinning him to the floor and cocking back my fist. Golden light coiled within my palm. I felt the bite of the wrath nipping through my arm. My soul ached for the release I'd kept bottled for so long.

"You're a fool, Ash. A typical angel," Gage said. The words crawled beneath my skin more than they should've, and my magic faltered. Realizing the position I had put myself in, a stroke of fear moved through me. The wrath recoiled and I took the opportunity to draw it back, grateful I hadn't allowed it to emerge fully. Then I'd really be in trouble.

"Stay away from me," I whispered.

"You cannot see the larger picture and the intricacies that surround you. Instead you see what you believe to be true. That is exactly the fault that dethroned your kind in the first place, making it easy for my people to take control so many centuries ago. A pity for you."

The lock snapped and two guards stepped in with clubs drawn. They charged toward me, knees bent and ready to strike. This was it. This was the moment my life would change.

I tucked my towel in at my waist. They could take me down, but not without a fight. I wouldn't become another soul lost to this place. I jumped up and faced them head-on. The magic still burned inside, and although I held it in, it filled the room with a static charge. Electricity bit at the air and I felt it flickering in my eyes. The world turned a shade of grey for me, but to them, a glowing white would emanate from my eyes. Heat filled my chest and nervousness claimed me as the wrath rose. I fought to pull it back, trying to find a medium between rage and fear. It was out of control. Once it had been beckoned, it wasn't so easily sated.

I dug my nails into my palms, using the pain to level me out. I'd sworn I would never use it. I wouldn't break that oath. Not even now. It receded again, but not without a fight. It burned every inch as I pushed back down into my soul. A ball of fire formed in my chest, scalding from the inside out. I gritted my teeth and clenched my jaw, holding it there like a pool of acid threatening to rise. As Gage crawled to his feet, I expected the guards to order him out.

Instead, he held up his hand and they stopped.

"No," he said. Shock fell over me and vanquished what remained of the rage. "He is an ally to us. He just doesn't know it yet."

CHAPTER 17

Gage had gotten to the Academy before Tryst or Soren, and he'd always been the bully; the dog with as much bite as he had bark. I didn't know what to make of the encounter, and neither did Tryst. Soren wasn't conscious enough for anything. That was Gage's fault. He was a monster and everybody knew it. He bullied Soren and Trace, threatened Tryst, and had countless other guests hurt. It wasn't difficult to see how the rest of the Academy felt about him. Guests rarely spoke in his presence. They were zombies, wandering the halls and doing work as instructed. There was no individuality, no voices of opinion, only bees tending to the hive. When he appeared, shoulders stiffened, eyes diverted, and mouths remained shut. He enticed fear like the cold attracted frost, and bees didn't like the cold.

"How did he know you wanted to escape?" Tryst asked.

I shook my head. "He couldn't. It had to be a guess. I can't imagine there are many people here that don't want out. All I know for sure is that I hit him hard and he barely fought back. His lack of reaction bothers me more than anything. It wasn't the Gage we know. He spoke like he wasn't a complete idiot. He used words I wasn't sure he could define. He was calm, almost peaceful. He wasn't there to fight. That or he's much better at head games than I gave him credit for."

"I'd vote for the latter."

The buzzer sounded and a knock came at the door. Tryst and I both looked puzzled, but after the bathroom incident, fear erupted in my chest. Hendrik stood in the doorway. His dark blue suit looked almost black, his skin stark against the fabric. An icy gaze panned the room, a frown forming as he eyed Soren. I expected him to deliver terrible news in some form. Was he there to collect Soren for the punishment he regretted not giving in the first place? Or was something about to fall on me? I felt sick, regretting everything I'd done. All the rage and confidence drained away and left me standing vulnerable before the headmaster.

Hendrik sighed, running creased fingers over his silver tie. "Ms. Rivera. Mr. Lawson." Both hands stretched outward toward Tryst, a small first-aid kit in hand. "I thought perhaps they were needed. Your supplies seem to be running low." He pointed to the empty container on the floor.

"That's not what it looks like. I mean—"

"Save it for another time. I realize it's after curfew and lockdown is in effect, though I hoped I might have a word with Mr. Lawson."

My stomach flopped. Did he have to be this polite and ask? He was the headmaster; he could order anybody to do anything. Why was he being cryptic?

He stayed silent as I followed him through the building. We traversed winding halls I'd never seen, and guards stood their ground as we passed. Were they Gage's guards? Would they tell him what was happening?

The Academy held an eerie quiet. I focused on the sound of our feet as we stepped along polished floorboards. My racing thoughts were drowned out by cool air as we walked through a steel door and into a garden. High brick walls gave off a secluded feel, while colored flowers and green vegetation decorated the space. Golden bricks lined the flower beds, not a weed amongst the dirt. I had no doubt in my mind that Soren had made this place as tranquil as it was, and I took a deep breath of cool evening air and let it calm my nerves.

I saw the remnants of sun fading behind the trees as we left the garden. The grass felt wet with dew, and guards walked their predetermined paths. A shiver ruptured through me. I hadn't been outside after sunset since before Colby captured me. The days had been warm, but the cold air revealed how close fall had crept. The leaves had started to change, greens to orange, oranges to red, reds to yellow.

"Do you smell that?"

Sap, dew, and bark mingled together as I drew a breath. Somehow, the fallen leaves carried a very distinct smell, but not one I could place. It coaxed through me and I reveled in the moment, realizing that Hendrik had led me closer to Blackwood than I'd ever been.

I cleared my throat. "Fresh air?"

"Air, yes. Fresh? Not so much. That air you smell is the air of confinement, isn't it?"

He studied me as I plotted my response.

"I'm not sure I follow, sir."

"This place, the Academy, it's a prison of sorts. Wouldn't you agree?"

Of sorts? This was a penitentiary of death and fear; somehow prison didn't seem a fitting word.

"Being as you're all about rehabilitation here, I'm inclined to disagree."

Hendrik smirked. "Clever boy, but let's be honest, shall we?"

I felt another shiver, but it had nothing to do with the weather. A flash of Soren's twisted face moved through my mind, tears dripping onto jeans stained from the inside out. The crack of a whip echoed through my mind. This was one of those times I wasn't sure honesty was the best policy.

"I'm not sure what you're looking for me to say, sir. I'm sorry."

"Don't be," he said, but his smile faltered. "After the things you've seen here, I would be cautious too." He nodded to himself as though he'd answered a question. "If your answer had been yes, I'd have been inclined to agree as well." Was he testing me? I studied his face, searching for answers. He gave away nothing. "You know, I've served at this facility for sixty-five years. That's a long time, wouldn't you say?"

"I would, but that timeline doesn't match up with things."

"Oh, how so?"

"It was fifty years ago that supernaturals were discovered and ATOM was formed. It would take another decade after that for them to develop weapons that aided in the takeover of supernatural-kind. Sixty-five years ago ATOM didn't exist, sir."

"So if I've been at this school for sixty-five years, but ATOM as you know them has only been here for fifty, what does that tell you?"

"That ATOM knew about us long before we knew about them."

"And that makes sense, doesn't it? The government often keeps secrets from the rest. They do this in part to maintain control, part for their own devices, and part to avoid widespread panic. I think it's safe to assume it was for all these reasons that they kept things under wraps. After all, it's easier to hunt the prey when the prey doesn't know it is being hunted."

A prickle slipped down my spine and goose bumps scurried across my neck. "So you're saying you've been trying to rehabilitate supernaturals since before ATOM existed?"

"Oh, my boy, ATOM has always existed. At first as a small group; humans who'd discovered the world of shadows and survived it. Hunters. It became a lifestyle, a following of men and women across the globe. As they expanded and became stronger and more intelligent, their secrets deepened. Secrets breed enigmas, Mr. Lawson, and curiosity births inquisitiveness that at times cannot be sated. The hunters evolved beyond simple predators. They became a pack of cunning beasts, our own boogeymen, at first set to kill but then to capture. They'd study us, abuse us, test our limits and attempt to recreate it in their vision."

Hendrik sighed, his expression shifting for the first time. He stared into the air as though reliving a dream—a nightmare.

"Such knowledge does not come with ease nor all at once. It needs funding, stronger weapons, more adequate research facilities. Hunters sought to better understand what we were so that they could use it," he continued. "What began as a belief in good versus evil transformed into something larger, more forceful. Some called them illuminati, today we call them ATOM, but they had a hundred names before that. They've always been the enemy of supernaturals, but it was fifty years ago that they took on the title we know them as today. And that name has brought us here. A place where the air tastes limited…perhaps confined?"

I stared with wide eyes at the story he'd weaved. I couldn't make heads or tails of it. For a moment I was reminded of Soren and the tales he would tell. I was at a loss for words.

Hendrik lowered his head, his voice a whisper. "In this moment, Mr. Lawson, I hope for us to speak without fear of repercussions."

I pondered. Hendrik didn't look like much, but he had an air of supremacy about him, one of which I'd seen but a glimpse. He felt intimidating, but in this moment seemed open and calm in a different way than usual. I looked at the darkness of the forest not far from us and pondered the future that might lie within. My stomach twisted with nerves. I didn't want to cross the invisible line I always felt lingered right in front of me, but something about the way Hendrik spoke made me feel like he was trapped too.

"You say the air inside these walls doesn't taste like freedom, yet you work for the people who keep us here," I said. "You run this place, but you have me out here after curfew, telling me about ATOM's past. You say they've always been our enemy. Our? It's your spells that keeps us from leaving. Forgive me for being blunt, but I'm not sure what to make of this."

Hendrik nodded as though he agreed with every word I said, yet his face remained blank. "Give me brutal honesty, Mr. Lawson. What do you think of the Academy? Do you feel it rehabilitates?"

Without a thought I laughed, but quickly cut it off. I expected some form of disapproval, but Hendrik gave me nothing. I debated my options, realizing that if Hendrik intended to punish me, or worse, nothing I could say right now would change that.

"The last thing this place does is rehabilitate," I admitted. "ATOM declared war on supernaturals because of what we are and because of what they want. This place has nothing to fix; there's no rehabilitation to be had. They want to control us. All ATOM does is plant seeds of fear. That's what the Academy is, a crop to sow. They're conditioning us to believe death and agony await us if we stand opposition. So you tell me, what is it you're trying to accomplish as headmaster besides helping plant that seed?"

Hendrik's lips quivered and he let out a gasp. A breath of relief?

"You're right. We don't rehabilitate; we recondition," he offered. "That's why the air tastes different. They're breaths that do not belong to us. They belong to ATOM." He shook his head and let his hands fall from behind his back. "You've been here a few months? Can you remember what freedom tastes like?"

I looked out at the distant wall that Tryst and I had repaired. I recalled the glimpse of freedom on the other side while rock simmered the skin along my fingers. I didn't remember the way the air tasted when I placed that last brick, or the breaths I'd taken before I came here. The only breath I remembered was my last, and it seemed stifled and short. My life before the Academy seemed a blur: a sinking boat, screams that raked across my chest, Colby Adams. I no longer remembered peaceful sleeps or the faces of those I'd helped. I tried to recall someone that I'd given a new life to or the feelings I'd felt when I received confirmation that they had made it to safety. I couldn't even recall a name.

"I should be able to but I can't," I said. "Everything that happened before here seems a lifetime ago."

"That's what the Tank does. It's what the Academy does," Hendrik agreed. "It takes what you loved, what you never knew you'd miss, and it steals it from your soul." Hendrik licked his lips and his fingers trembled as he ran them over his tie. "It's been so long since I tasted free air that I'm not sure I would recognize it if it came. Although, admittedly, I hope I'm wrong."

"You're suggesting you're as much a prisoner as we are?"

"I'm not suggesting; I'm stating a fact. Though I don't expect that you can understand."

We weaved through the grass, Blackwood growing closer. Anticipation grew as we neared, but with each step I noticed a change in the air. It felt heavier and somehow less fulfilling. The scent of pine needles and sap no longer filled my senses. Instead I tasted hints of sulfur at the back of my throat. My nostrils filled with the smell of fire freshly snuffed out, burned bark, and smoldering ash. My chest tightened and fear crept across my skin, the origins of which I didn't understand.

Hendrik seemed unfazed, though a look filled his eyes I couldn't decipher.

"I'm going to tell you something that few people know, Mr. Lawson." He looked at me the way long-lost friends looked at one another when they'd been reunited. "I've been involved in ATOM's program for longer than I care to scale. Imagine human lifetimes that seem an eternity. There are years I don't remember a thing, while others I can't forget no matter how hard I try. Microscopes, needles, and invasive exams were my life once upon a time. A terrible life."

His words were shaky, and the more he spoke the more his demeanor changed. His icy gaze melted and for a moment he appeared broken, a tamed lion that was once free but now existed in a cage.

"I could tell you of my years spent in stainless steel rooms, or my life pitted against other supernaturals in fights to the death," he said. "I could tell you how they broke and reassembled me over and over again. I could tell you, but you wouldn't understand. One's mind cannot grasp pain it has not felt. Just as no creature can understand what life truly is until it's felt one fade beneath its fingertips. The truth, Mr. Lawson, is that I became a part of this place to spare what remained of my soul. I birthed this Academy out of necessity. Most find it cruel. I cannot blame them, for they cannot understand what torture it has saved them. Even you."

His voice shook and he took a break, reaching down to run his fingers through the dewy grass. He licked it off the tip of his fingers, a cool wash of breath spilling from his lips. With a deep breath his trembling voice and shaking hands calmed. He offered me a smile, but I saw apology in his eyes. It was a strange vulnerability coming from a man I knew I should fear.

"That said, I am not the beast ATOM captured so long ago. I've been suppressed, so to speak. Nothing more than a neutered pet."

I felt a rainbow of emotions but I couldn't focus on any one of them. They bled together like a child's painting, dripping and sagging into one another until they were undecipherable.

"Why are you telling me this?"

Hendrik's eyebrows rose, deep lines creasing his forehead, and his eyes focused on the line of darkness that hung in the forest lingering only a few dozen feet away.

"I grow tired of this place. As do many, I suppose," he said. "After yesterday's events, I've no doubt that you are in search of a way out. You've been biding your time, and I do not blame you. This place *will* be the death of you. Wings or not, you are an angel. Angels were never born to be caged. You've kept your truths close to your heart on this peaceful eve. I respect that. If I were plotting an escape I wouldn't want to reveal it to anyone, which does bring into question my motives here today."

"Are you saying you're planning an escape?"

Hendrik sighed and nodded his head, staring into the woods. "Being the leader within a cage does not make a free man. Privilege does not harbor liberty. You see, I am unable to unlock the shackles placed upon me. You, on the other hand, may be the key."

"Are you suggesting that I can set you free?"

"I am, but such things do not come without a price. I know

this. In exchange for my freedom I am prepared to grant you your own."

My head began to spin and I felt disoriented. I wasn't sure if it was the strange stench that emanated from Blackwood, or the words I thought I'd heard Hendrik say.

"I help you get your freedom, you give me mine?" I questioned.

"Precisely."

"What's the catch?"

"The catch is that if you were to fail, it would be because you died in the process," he told me. "As I said, all things have a price. If you were to be caught, I could not protect you. As you can imagine, I have not spent lifetimes as a puppet to be caught cutting the strings. The risk falls upon you and you alone." Hendrik's demeanor had returned to normal. He smoothed out his jacket and buttoned it back up. "Not easy terms to accept, but life is not made of easy choices."

I felt nauseous, overwhelmed, and confused. First Gage, now Hendrik. My plan for escape seemed to be growing more complicated by the minute.

"So I either succeed or die. I have a lot to lose if it doesn't work out, whereas your hands are clean of all of it."

"I would not be standing here with you if I thought you would fail. Without your success, I too have lost my chance at freedom."

"No, if I fail you can send someone else," I reasoned. "It's not like I get a do-over. I think I'll pass."

"Perhaps I could entice you with something more than freedom. What if freedom came with something you wanted as much—if not more? What if I could return to you the gift in which you've lost, Mr. Lawson? What if there was a chance I could give you back your wings?"

I don't remember falling, yet the dew-soaked grass bled into the knees of my jeans. An ache filled my heart. Disbelief. For a moment I felt a breath of clouds roll over my face. When flying at night in pure darkness, you couldn't always see them, but you always felt them. I shivered. The world seemed quiet and slow. Crickets orchestrated a symphony that had yet to begin, and the stars started to twinkle across a darkening sky.

"They're gone," I whispered. I didn't want to admit it. I'd spent as much time as possible trying to ignore that truth, but I had to remind myself of what was real and what wasn't. "Nobody has the capacity to give them back. Not even you. Up until now I thought this was a legitimate offer." I laughed and shook my head, feeling angry and stupid. "Is this the part where Gareth steps out from the shadows and you call all the guests out to the yard to watch my demise? Was this all a tactic to breathe some air of hope into me before you took it away?"

Hendrik didn't flinch. If anything, he looked offended.

"I have shared my truths with you, yet you insult me as though I've tricked you," he said. "I may be a shell of what I once was, but I will not be assumed a liar. If I could return to my original state— what I was before ATOM captured me—I could do a great many things. Your wings are not out of that realm. I wouldn't ask you to risk your life for me alone. I am not a fool. I offer you the freedom you desire and a chance to be returned to your former self as well, but I can offer nothing more. Is this not enough?"

There was a sort of desperation in his eyes. A plea of hope that hadn't been there before, but I wasn't sure what to make of it.

"It's not possible."

"Are you certain?"

"Yes."

"And did you think a place such as the Tank was impossible before you came here?" Hendrik shook his head. "Of course you did. You can't understand the Tank because it is sorcery unknown to you. To most, in fact. Just like you could never understand the suffering ATOM has caused me. The Tank is a sample of what remains inside me, Mr. Lawson. It comes from an old world in which you are unfamiliar. I will not speak more of it. Not here. Should we come to an agreement I may be inclined to elaborate, but for now my offer stands. It comes with enormous risks, but I think it's fair to say it also holds equal reward."

He'd piqued my curiosity. The Tank was a place I'd never fathomed. It had dominance over its victims I couldn't explain. By that logic, perhaps he could hold up his end of the deal. Could there be such a thing capable of restoring what had been taken?

"If I agree, then Soren and Tryst come with me."

Hendrik sighed as if he'd expected it. "You must understand that the task at hand is not an easy feat. There are many factors—"

"They come with me and get their freedom or we'll take our chances on our own." I sounded confident but I was afraid. What would I do if he said no? Then I saw it in his eyes—he couldn't say no. He wouldn't. He wanted this too much.

"If you wish to be brash, so be it," he intoned. "I do not object to your request, but be certain you can trust them. If they were to expose our plan it would be a cruel fate for both of us."

"They won't," I said. "If I can trust anybody in this place, it's them."

CHAPTER 18

Tryst urged me for answers but I deterred them on the basis it was safer that way. She refused to accept that and I couldn't blame her, I wouldn't either, but I wasn't ready to tell. I felt nervous. The last thing I wanted was to place her and Soren in a position they couldn't come back from. Right now I didn't need to find a way out. Hendrik would give it to me. What came after that, however, remained a mystery. Until I knew it was safe, it felt best not to say anything.

I could see the scowl on her face as Tryst helped Soren lower himself into his chair. She accepted my evasion for now, but she wasn't happy about it. Soren's face scrunched and lines creased his forehead and eyes. I felt a pang in my heart. Soren lit up the room with his smile and sarcasm most days. Right now that wispy joy was gone, and I missed it. Much like my wings, I didn't realize how much I leaned on them until the crutch was no longer there. Soren and Tryst were that for me now, crutches I depended on. I relied on seeing them every day. Soren's wit and humor, as annoying as they could be, helped brighten each day, and Tryst kept me grounded and levelheaded. It was a bond I hadn't had in a long time. A friendship I wasn't prepared to lose. I could help them get the freedom they deserved, but the risk frightened me. I didn't want to be the reason anybody else got hurt.

Voices whispered and eyes followed me in the lunchroom. Most of it remained muffled, but I caught bits and pieces about how I was a walking death trap. People felt sorry that Soren and Tryst had to room with me, and the display of people going out of their way to avoid me had been made clear. I didn't give them the benefit of a reaction. I kept an even face and carried my tray toward my table when Gareth stepped out in front of me.

I stopped as he folded his arms and blocked my path. Bulging veins pulsed beneath his tanned skin and his white shirt had the sleeves torn off, exposing his strength.

"Problem, sir?" I asked, my voice plain and emotionless.

"You tell me. We've got work to do today. I want to make sure you're not going to be a problem."

Gage sat at the table behind him. His white shirt had strips of bloodstains along the back. He turned to watch, as did the rest of the room, but he gave me a strange expression, shaking his head before turning back to his food.

"I never am, sir. I'm ready to work."

Gareth scoffed. "After that stunt you pulled the other day, you damn well better be."

"That wasn't a stunt. I did what was right."

Gage shook his head in disappointment and closed his eyes. Gareth, on the other hand, became alight with rage, biting the inside of his cheek and flexing his jaw.

"You're an arrogant shit, you know that?" he said. "Angels. You stick your nose where it doesn't belong. You think you're better than everyone else, and that's the exact reason your kind is near extinction. You're nothing. And when I'm through with you—"

"When you're through with me what?" I interrupted. "You think you're the first to threaten me? I've seen—" I cut myself off. The last few days had been a whirlwind, and I wasn't myself. I took a quick breath, held it, and calmed myself. There was potential for me to get out of this place, no need to spoil things now. "I've seen a lot. I don't need threats, sir. With your guidance, I'm committed to finding the right path. For everybody. That includes Gage and Soren as well."

Gareth's rage flared. "You watch your tone, boy, or I'll make the Tank a holiday. Gage and Soren and every other guest in this place are none of your concern. You interject again and I'll string you up myself."

"Of course, sir." I gritted my teeth and met his gaze, enduring the moment with visions of all the terrible things I wanted to do to him. I smiled.

"You're cocky, Ash. It doesn't surprise me," Gareth said. "I knew it the moment I found out you were coming here you'd be trouble. You've got the same smart-ass remarks and arrogance that got most of your kind killed. Your parents were no exception."

A bulldozer crushed my ribs and the air vanished. My chest tightened and knees felt weak. The world fell silent. Everything moved in slow motion and a bulge formed in my throat.

Gareth leaned in, his voice a whisper. "To this day it's still the bloodiest fight I've ever been a part of. It was my pleasure to watch their lives fade at the hand of their own. A wrath unlike any other."

The world rushed back and my knuckles popped. The tray in my hand shook and the plastic warmed. Power flooded my hands and sparks formed between my fingers, burning into the tray. Wrath. I should've quelled it and hit him. I wanted to, but his words struck an unexpected chord. I froze up. Magic vibrated in my fingertips and the golden flash that sparked beneath the tray scared me. I didn't know how to respond. Rage on one side, fear on the other. I wasn't in control.

"Ash?" Tryst stood beside me, violet eyes not bringing their usual peace to my soul.

"Liar," I whispered.

"I never lie," Gareth said.

"They were good people. They have no business in your words!" The tray became hot, plastic folding inward. I lost control and dropped it to the ground. Without the plastic tray for cover, the blinding light in my hands was exposed. It spilled from my palm and I waved it violently as if I could shake it away. My skin burned.

Gareth's dark eyes were full with fury and pleasure. "Magic? Here? That's forbidden!" he screamed, but it was with a dark smile and a hint of laughter. "Your parents wasted their near-immortality. Cowards whose arrogance set their demise. They died quick. They deserved worse. They should've been made to suffer." The force I'd struggled to contain spiraled up from my soul. Gareth backed away, covering his eyes. "No control and an angel's ego. No doubt you'll meet the same fate as them. Perhaps by your own hand."

Rage pierced my insides. I keeled over, trying to regain control, but all I wanted to do was destroy the cruelty before me. I reached for Gareth but a pair of unseen hands held me back. I fought against them with every ounce of strength I had. Tables vacated, scattering across the room as people rushed out the doors. Gareth didn't move. His pearl-white teeth bared, a single hand blocking his eyes. I slid backward, unable to break the grips that restrained me. Heat burned my insides and the edges of my fingers. The realization that I was on the verge of losing control terrified me. I tried to deflect the rage and regain composure. The magic was wild, untamed, and craved release, but I couldn't let it go. I wouldn't. I struggled to draw it back, arcs of power crackling around my fingers. The harder I tried to make it recede, the stronger it became. I feared the relentless power on the brink of being unleashed and the damage it would do. I gritted my teeth and tried to focus. It was no use.

"Run," I screamed, as the room grew brighter.

Power expanded around me, circles of scorching light coiling up my arms. It burned me from the inside out, and the world became a wash of grey. I dropped to my hands and knees, trying to reel it back. It was out of my control. I felt it rising up from my soul, searing my insides as it crept into my hands. Without warning, an unexpected darkness overshadowed it. It crept over the light and weakened the wrath. It was a foreign energy, dark and not of my own creation. Sulfur burned my nostrils as the power inside retracted and fear rose in my throat. Bolts of terror swam around me, suffocating my uncontrolled power. It took hold of my magic and buried it somewhere deep inside. I was terrified and grateful all at once. The light that had amplified around me vanished like a flame beneath water. Smoke rose from my hands and my body trembled.

"You overstep yourself, Gareth!" Hendrik shouted. His hands gripped my shoulders and dragged me violently to my feet.

"Magic is forbidden. The Tank or death!" Gareth replied.

"That is not for you to decide,"

Gareth's eyes widened. "Sir, if I—"

"Silence!" Hendrik commanded, and the fear that filled the room spiked with vitality.

Gareth recoiled and lowered his eyes, shuddering beneath Hendrik's command. The headmaster squeezed my shoulders and guided me out of the room, shoving me through the door and into the hall. He gripped my arm and dragged me down the corridor to his office, throwing me over the threshold. I stumbled and rolled across the floor, crashing into the chairs in front of his desk. I didn't try to get up. His presence was overpowering my will to move. My breaths were ragged and sharp, anger and unexplained fear scalding my veins as adrenaline pumped through them.

"You fool!" Hendrik shouted, pacing across the room. His voice and face displayed emotions I'd never seen from him—anger and frustration. I blinked and he appeared in front of me, crouching down with a hand around my throat. He pinned me against the floor and magic warped around us. Fear forced itself into me and he lifted my body with ease, slamming me against a bookshelf. Books fell from the shelves and pages ruffled in the air. His eyes changed—the white vanished and a swirl of blue consumed everything. "You forget your place!" His words were ethereal, pressing into my soul. The breath I'd recuperated was stolen and fear flooded in. He came close to my face, eyes filling me with a terror I'd never known. "You. Forget. Your. Place."

Even Hendrik's breaths were staggered. His shoulders rose and fell, breath rolling over my skin. His eyes penetrated mine with colossal influence. I was swallowed by a wash of feelings I didn't want and couldn't articulate. Pain. Faces from my past haunted me, sending icy regret to cut through my core. Tears welled in my eyes. Death, regret, and sadness forced themselves over me like a rising tide. Soren, Tryst, the Tank. It was too much. Teardrops rolled over my cheeks and the room became a blur. Sorrow became all I knew. Heavy sobs fell from my lips and Hendrik released me. I tried to say I was sorry, but no words would come. I slid to the floor and buried my face in my knees. Heat seared my throat like a lit match, and fire scalded my shoulders. Gareth's words replayed through my mind.

"It isn't fair. He had no right to say those things. He doesn't know." The words weren't as defiant as I had hoped. Instead they were sullen and weak, my voice cracking. I was better than this. Better than vengeance and letting petty words hurt me. I felt stupid and weak curled up along the floor, tears streaking my face while I sputtered about fairness. I was a child again, stomping my feet against my uncle's arrogance.

Hendrik sat on the edge of his desk, arms crossed and his face still. There was no pity in his eyes.

"Gareth knows a great many things," Hendrik began. "He will use them to entice a reaction. Today he got precisely what he'd hoped for. If you give in to him, you will leave me no choice. It will force my hand and you'll be hanging by an iron-laced rope." His eyes were piercing, and he shook his head. "I made the wrong decision with you. Now look what you've done. You've risked everything!" He slipped into the chair behind his desk and took a calming breath. "In order to help one another, you must first help yourself. You cannot be baited by such trivialities. Forget the past. Look to the future. If you cannot do that for yourself, then do it for your friends."

Time stretched on as I sat in silence. It took me time to respond. Without screaming my voice was shaky, my lips trembling as though under independent control. I swallowed and it hurt.

"I'm sorry. It was foolish."

"Foolish does not begin to describe what that was." Hendrik sighed. "I apologize if I've hurt you. After our conversation last night, I realize how close I could be to tasting the free air again. I spent the night awake with excitement dancing through me, an emotion I felt certain had vacated every part of me long ago. Then I came to enjoy my breakfast and saw it all falling apart. It was a selfish reaction, perhaps, but a truth nonetheless. Perhaps I should have spent more time relaying the importance of this when we spoke." He leaned back and adjusted his tie. "We can have an arrangement, Mr. Lawson that we both stand to benefit from. However, this does not give you a free pass within the Academy. Our arrangement is private and until execution, you are a guest at this establishment. Nothing more."

Hendrik reviewed the rules of our arrangement once again. It wasn't necessary but he felt compelled to reiterate himself, especially when it came to the consequences of my actions should I step out of line. The more we talked, the more I wasn't sure how I felt about him. I liked the idea of having help getting out of this place, but I wanted it to be on my terms. He was firm that it would be on his, yet still it was my life on the line. When I asked about his plan, he was short, refusing any details until a later date. I didn't like that but he felt it necessary given my "outburst" today, as he put it. Before I could object, the door swung open and Gareth stormed in.

"Hendrik, we need to talk," Gareth said. He tried to look determined, but there was a glimmer of hesitation in his eyes. "Mr. Lawson has overstepped his bounds. Again. You cannot protect him forever. The Tank didn't work. It's time we rid ourselves of him in full."

"There were many lines crossed, Gareth. If punishment is to be delivered justly, then you too shall be held responsible for your actions."

Gareth's dark brows raised and the scarred skin of his face creased dramatically. "I beg your pardon? You're going to try and pull this again? I'm an advisor at this school. It is my job to ensure the guests stay in line and my responsibility to encourage rehabilitation in a measure I deem fit!"

"I've been reviewing your file Gareth, and there are many... shall I use the word 'episodes' to describe them?" Hendrik asked. "You challenge the ideals of the system with your own and although you never quite step over the boundary, you push yourself terribly close. As much as I can appreciate the success your methods have brought, I do not agree with them, nor does the system outline."

"This is the Academy, Hendrik. The outline does not exist."

"Oh, but it does," Hendrik interjected. "And antagonizing students in hopes of enticing a reaction is a boundary I do not believe should be neared for the mere sake of punishing them. If you wish to seek punishment for Ash's disrespect, then you will be held with equal accountability. As Gage was with Soren."

"They are to be trained, not respected." Gareth scowled. "Respect is earned. He and I are *not* equals."

"And by that logic, neither are you and I."

Gareth stepped back, betrayal in his eyes. "You old fool."

"I may be old, Gareth, but we both know I am not a fool. In fact, I have been in the business of rehabilitation for quite a bit longer than you and as such, my expertise on the subject is of higher value. After all, this is their last stop. There is no chance for redemption once their time at the Academy expires. I respect that chance. Your disrespect, as of late, however, will cease or I will see to it..." Hendrik's eyes flickered between Gareth and me. He took a breath. "This conversation will continue in private. Mr. Lawson, excuse us."

Even outside the office, the screaming was loud enough for anybody to hear.

Gareth didn't believe Hendrik was doing us a service, but setting us up for failure. He accused me of having something on

Hendrik, demanding answers as to why Hendrik protected me. Hendrik did not take kindly to the accusations, offering a swift reminder of who was in charge and what awaited Gareth should he lay down a challenge. Gareth backed off but didn't succumb entirely. Even he was afraid of what Hendrik could do, which opened up questions I hadn't considered, like what if there was a reason Hendrik no longer had whatever power he craved? If that power was really as old as he said, was it safe for him to have it? After all, I'd seen what he could do with the sliver of magic that remained. The thought of more made me nervous. Had I made a deal with the wrong person?

Hendrik's voice boomed over Gareth's, and I felt the effect ripple through the halls. I shuddered. "I will remind you that Mr. Lawson spent four days in the Tank—more than any student previous—and as such has not crossed a line since. Not one that you didn't push him over. I believe in second chances, Gareth. That is what this facility represents. The same kind of chance you once received. Since then you've become a respected advisor, and if you wish to remain so, I suggest you re-examine your position on the matter."

"I am not out of line on this, Hendrik. I got a second chance and I've made the most of it. More so than most, but you are harboring this boy."

"Or perhaps you have a vendetta against him," Hendrik suggested.

"What?"

"If you are unfit to lead him, I will assign him a new advisor or take him on myself," the headmaster said. "I'm beginning to feel that you are not in his best interest, or perhaps in the best interest of anyone at this facility."

Gareth laughed loud and deep. "Is that a threat?"

"Enough!" Hendrik's voice crackled like thunder and stormed through the Academy. "There are opportunities here for these guests. Opportunities I do not wish to see spoiled by a clash in personalities."

"So you, headmaster at this facility, who hasn't been in an advisory role in twenty years is conveniently taking on the mentorship of a single angel. Of him?" Gareth questioned.

"If you'd like to accuse me of something, Gareth, you're more than welcome to take it up with the office, or with me, if you care to go down that path. However, I see many things you do not. Which is why I am headmaster and have been since the inception of this fine structure," Hendrik reminded.

"And I'm questioning why a guest who has been here a few months seems to have more sway over you than a trusted advisor who has served with loyalty for a decade," Gareth continued. "It seems perhaps you have a personal interest invested in him."

"Perhaps I do. Angels are far and few between in this world. I will not be the reason they take another step closer to extinction. Not when they can add so much to our cause."

"Add what? Angels are a disgrace to supernaturals."

"And that, Gareth, is why I'm revoking your roll as advisor to Mr. Lawson, as well as Ms. Rivera and Mr. Kye," Hendrik concluded. "Should there be others you feel you are unfit to advise, I will happily take them as well."

"You're making a mistake."

"Then it is my mistake to make. Your advisement is noted and you may move along to the remaining guests under your command, unless I see fit to remove them from your supervision. This conversation is over."

I jumped to my feet and walked as fast as I could down the hall. I heard Gareth slam the door, and I kept my pace until I made it back to the lunchroom. All eyes were on me—even Gage's—upon my return.

As I passed his table he gripped my arm and pulled me aside. "You got a death wish, kid?"

"Get your hand off me. Now."

"Don't fool around. You want to get out of here, you stay in line and play your part," Gage muttered.

I ripped my arm from his grip and shoved him away. I leaned in so only he could hear. "Don't mistake me for one of the guards in your pocket. I don't take orders from you." I spat the words at him and Gage's anger flared, but I walked away before I could be on the receiving end of it.

"What was that about?" Tryst quizzed. Her eyes were wide and even Soren looked more alive than he had in days.

I shook my head, sliding back into my seat and eating from a new tray of food that waited for me. "Gage being Gage. Nothing to worry about."

"I don't mean that. Gage doesn't surprise me," she said.

"Hendrik and Gareth, on the other hand...what the hell is going on, Ash?"

"It's nothing."

"After everything that's happened, you're going to tell me it's nothing?" She didn't look impressed.

"Gareth said something to me and I let it get under my skin."

"No kidding. You'll be lucky if you get twice as many lashes as Soren, or more time in the Tank," she retorted.

"Can we not talk about that?" Soren cringed. "I'm trying to eat my rubber...whatever these are."

"Was that a hint at humor?" I asked. "Is the Soren we know still in there somewhere?"

"That's funny coming from the guy who got dragged out of here by the headmaster," he said. "I half expected to never see you again. At least not in one piece.

"I lost myself a little bit. I know. I got caught up in things and I let go. Gareth had it coming, but even still, it was stupid," I conceded.

Gareth had succeeded in making me look like an idiot, but he didn't understand how close he came to death. If it weren't for Hendrik, I would have lost control. The wrath inside me was dangerous. I knew that better than anybody. I reminded myself of the promise I'd made to myself. I needed to keep it all under control, especially if I wanted to escape. Though I still wasn't sure how I felt about Hendrik's deal. He was being too secretive. I didn't like that.

"In case you didn't learn from what happened with me, you know Gareth's going to have your head for this, right?" Soren asked.

"He's not going to have anything. At least not this time," I responded.

Tryst raised a brow and questioned me with her eyes.

"Gareth's not my advisor anymore. Or either of yours for that matter. Hendrik is."

Both of them glared at me, waiting for the punch line.

"Hendrik's the headmaster, not an advisor." Tryst paused, studying my face but somehow looking right through me. "Ash, you need to tell us what the hell is going on."

"I don't know. I'm still trying to figure it out, okay?"

"He doesn't look so good, Tryst," Soren said. "He did

something bad."

"I didn't," I said. "Maybe I did. I just need some time to process everything."

One of the guards escorted us back to our room while Gareth took his revised crew to the yard for work. A guard buzzed us in and once again we were on lockdown. I started to feel claustrophobic. I didn't like the attention this place garnered me. I was used to doing everything out of sight. Since I came to the Academy, I felt like I couldn't escape the spotlight.

Tryst and Soren grilled me with questions. Part of me wished Soren would go back to sleep. It'd be easier to avoid one of them. I didn't know how to explain myself. It seemed bizarre. First Gage, now Hendrik. What was it that drew them to me? I had hoped for time to sort things out, but I couldn't think with their stares burning into me.

Soren lay on his stomach, sprawled out on the bottom bunk. The bandages on his back were soaked brown. The first-aid kit had helped, but the copper had done a number on him. Even though the lacerations were covered, the bruising was evident around the bandages; purple and black sprawled across his skin. He tried to suppress the whimpers each time he moved, but he couldn't conceal them.

"Don't," Tryst ordered. "You need to rest. Another day off is a blessing; take it for what it is."

"I'm fine. Besides, Ash has something big to tell us. I'm not going to hide my face in a pillow while he does."

The attention fell back to me and I cursed Soren a little bit for it. Pressure mounted my shoulders and my heart palpitated, skipping across my chest.

"I don't know even know how to start," I said.

Soren winced as he propped himself up on his elbows. "By most standards, the beginning is a good place."

"Thanks." Sarcasm dripped off my lips and I sighed. I wasn't sure why I felt nervous. Maybe because I could only explain what had happened, but not why. I felt like I should know why.

"We'll get to Hendrik and Gage," Tryst said. "What the hell did Gareth do to make you risk tying a noose around our necks?"

Gareth's words replayed through my head. It was almost physical. My chest ached and breath caught in my throat. I felt the remnants of the wrath searing my fingertips. Even in memory he elicited as much rage now as he had in the lunchroom. I didn't want to talk about it, but at least I had an answer to that question.

"He said things about my parents. I shouldn't have reacted the way I did. I shouldn't have let it get to me. I lost control."

"I'll say! I've never seen someone cause as much of a ruckus in such a short amount of time as you have," Soren interjected. "At least not anybody who lived long enough to do it again. And your hands…what the hell was that?" I could feel Soren's eyes, but I didn't look back at him. Everything they wanted me to tell them were things I hadn't thought about in a long time. A past that I thought I'd put behind me. In reality, I'd never faced it. "Dude, after everything that's happened, this is not the time to hold back. This is the part where you share. You're among friends."

"I know that, but there's a lot going on and it's a long story."

"Good, I like stories," he insisted. "Besides, we aren't going anywhere. Lockdown, remember?" His eyes were wide, eager like a child anticipating a well-woven bedtime tale.

I glanced to Tryst, if anybody could steer this conversation elsewhere, it was her. She smirked and shook her head. "Don't look at me. I'm not going to save you. I want to hear this as much as he does. I think we deserve some answers."

Soren's face lit up with excitement. "I wish we had popcorn. This is going to be good. I can feel it."

My stomach churned. I didn't want to share, but I didn't want to shut them out either. If we were going to work together to get out of here, we had to trust one another. Soren was right, I was among friends. I knew that. They were all I had in this place; maybe all I had on the outside too.

With a deep breath, I revealed what Gareth had said to me. Revisiting it made me even more disappointed in myself. I'd let it hit me harder than I should have and I rode that emotion until it consumed me. It was stupid. Though my friends' reactions weren't quite as harsh. In fact, they seemed understanding. Even offering apologies for things they'd had no part in. I appreciated the kindness, but not the looks in their eyes. I didn't want pity. It wasn't shown to me the day I found out my parents died, and I didn't need it now.

Nostalgia of my childhood washed over me. I became lost in the story my memories created, wrapping them around me like the blankets I'd used to stay warm in the winter.

I could taste the morning air rolling off the snow-capped mountains. The pine scent rose from the woods. Flakes of snow fluttered to the earth from a grey, murky sky. Solitude. We'd lived in seclusion all my life and my parents sought to change that. They wanted the history of our kind as rulers of the underground to be our future, as the generations before them had wanted too. So far, not one had been successful. Between ATOM gaining more control and the typhons' fear-infused grasp on the underground, people were afraid to do anything but stay in hiding. My parents were on a mission to change that and make alliances.

"The enemy of my enemy is my friend," they said, and the typhons had plenty of enemies.

I remembered being sick to my stomach, worried about what fate they'd met. The elders had told them to remain in hiding, but they craved the world our storybooks had created for them: control, freedom, and an army of supernaturals to defend both. Our own camp had become divided: those who wanted our reign to return and our numbers to rise, and those who feared our extinction. My parents were supposed to meet with another group of supernaturals and create an alliance that would strengthen our numbers. It wouldn't be all that we needed, but it would be the first step.

They had left for that meeting, but they never returned. Nightmares had plagued me day and night, fearful for what might have happened. Weeks after they were supposed to return, I discovered they weren't just dreams.

My uncle had led a scouting party to retrieve them. A dozen left, but he returned alone. I still remembered the copper-brown that stained his once-silver armor. He smelled of blood and dirt, open wounds cut deep into his face and arms. His eyes were almost swollen shut. Dark veins spiraled across his chest like a black sun, a settling infection from an iron-based gunshot wound. Tears burned my eyes as he approached, but his piercing blue eyes were cold. His black-and-white beard didn't show sympathy or regret, only frustration. I had tried to ask about my parents, but I couldn't make words.

"Stand up," he demanded. His voice echoed around me.

It felt surreal. I tried to do as he said. If I'd learned anything growing up to be a boy of seven, it was that you listened to your elders and showed respect. I failed. He grabbed my shoulders and pushed them back.

"Stop crying." His voice was stone.

I stifled the sobs as best I could, but the tears continued to fall.

"You're a man now. Act like it."

He gripped my arm and my chin, forcing me to look at him. It wasn't gentle or consoling. He squeezed hard as I fought back more tears.

"Be strong, train hard, and if you're lucky, you'll be half the man your father was," he said.

There wasn't another word. He patted my back hard enough I nearly toppled over, and the next thing I remembered was the flap of the tent door opening. A beam of sunlight washed in, blinded me, and then it was gone. But so was he.

The pang I felt in my chest replicated the one I felt as a boy, trying to come to terms with the fact that my parents were gone. I had left the colony a few years after that and struggled through the world on my own. I hadn't thought about it in years and I wondered what had become of my old family.

"Do you think Gareth actually knows anything about them?" Soren asked.

I lifted my hands as if they had the answer, but they fell back into my lap. "I don't know. I wasn't told a thing about what had happened to them. You have to understand that angels are not loving and compassionate creatures by nature. They're cold, calculating. Come to think of it, they're a lot like the typhons. But it doesn't matter if he knows, the fact remains he used it against me and I let him. I played right into his hand, and if it wasn't for

Hendrik I'd be back in the Tank, or dead."

"And that's what I don't understand," she said. "Soren should've been sentenced to death for what he did. They've never tolerated violence among guests. Not ever, and especially not when there's a weapon involved. But Hendrik allowed it this time. Then he does the inspection of our room by himself and lets it all slide? Again, something isn't right there. And finally, he comes to the room and takes you away, and today he's protecting you from Gareth. What's going on?"

"Wait, what?" Soren said. "Hendrik came to our room?"

Tryst ignored him, her eyes were only for me in that moment. Her face fell still, her gaze curious but on edge. I suppose I would have been too. They'd been here for years and had never seen anything like this. She wanted to know why. Why now? Why me? But she didn't give me a chance to answer.

"They know we want to escape, don't they? How?"

"Escape?" Soren perked up.

"I don't know," I said.

"Are you sure they know? Maybe they were feeling you out. You didn't say anything to Hendrik, did you?" Her eyes were awash in panic. Her hands gripped the ragged blanket on the edge of the bunk and she began to fidget with the fabric.

"What is happening?" Soren's voice became background noise.

"Not exactly," I said.

Tryst shook her head and paced the room. "We are so dead."

"No, we're not."

"Are you kidding me?" she snapped. "Do you have any idea what will happen to us now that he knows?"

"Look..." I tried to find a smooth way to transition. There wasn't one. Tryst looked ripe with panic so I let it all go, the entire story, holding back only the part about Hendrik offering me my wings. I don't know why I did it, but part of me felt like if I told her it would change things. We needed to focus on what was important—getting out.

Soren's jaw dangled from his mouth, but he never said a word. He was shocked. I couldn't blame him. I wasn't even sure I believed it. Relaying it made it sound more ridiculous than I had realized. How could Hendrik sit idle under ATOM's control for so long? That took a level of focus and determination I couldn't comprehend. I'd been here close to four months and felt ready to snap. And if a person could lie in wait for that long—lifetimes—then what had changed now?

"And you believe all this?" Tryst asked.

"I don't know what to believe, but some of it makes sense: the glyphs at the gate, his magic, the Tank. That place is old," I answered. "An unknown enchantment? An ancient hex? I've never even heard of such a thing, but that isn't what has me concerned." Tryst raised a brow as if there couldn't be anything more bizarre than our enslaver asking us to set him free. "If it is true and he's only a piece of what he once was, what will he become?"

Tryst fell back on the bed. "And if he can make the Tank come alive the way it does already, imagine what he'll be able to do if we cut the chains that bind him to ATOM."

I leaned forward and ran my hands through my hair. It wasn't short like I was used to; it had grown long, and I gripped the blond strands. "I know, but does it matter? I can't stay here any longer, Tryst. I can't. Hendrik can get us out."

She sighed and leaned in, her panicked voice subsiding to a quieter version. "But at what price?"

CHAPTER 19

Hendrik sat across from me, silent since I'd arrive. I spent the quiet time between us pondering if I'd made a mistake. Tryst wasn't sure we could trust Hendrik. Neither was I. He had been the government's whipping horse for a long time. Had that changed? Could it after all this time? What if I wasn't rescuing us at all? What if I had sent us all to our graves?

The headmaster transcribed beautifully arched letters onto the parchment in his notebook. I couldn't read it upside down, but I admired the perfection in each character. For hands that looked aged, he remained steady and firm, each stroke a graceful mark of black against an off-white page.

Through the window of his office Gareth paced back and forth along rows of guests that pulled weeds from between the cracks of the cobblestone paths. He was a drill sergeant, and I read the obscenities from his lips as he scolded one girl and then a boy. Even Gage was on his hands and knees. Sweat ran down his face as he knelt in the hot sun. Gareth's gaze turned to me, eyes locking with mine even from a distance. A shiver ran through me as his hands clenched. He didn't turn away, and the fire in his eyes burned through the glass.

"Blackwood, Mr. Lawson." I jumped and turned my attention to Hendrik. He'd stopped writing. His notebook closed in front of him and hands clasped overtop of it. "That is the path you thought would be your salvation. And it shall be."

"You need me to go into the woods?"

"It was the one outlet you could have chosen as an escape," he confirmed. "The walls are too high, the barbed wire made of iron, copper, and silver, enough to hurt any beast that dares try to cross it. The stone is a maze of powdered metals, scalding any who touch it. The glyphs protect the gate. No supernatural in or out without the creator's consent. Mine. Blackwood is the logical route. It was where you would have gone on your own, is it not?"

I hesitated. I had already made the mistake of acknowledging the escape, I didn't care to elaborate. Then again, Hendrik didn't need to trick me into admitting anything. If he wanted to punish me, he could've done it after I stood up for Soren or earlier in the lunchroom with Gareth. He'd had ample opportunity to make an example of me and he hadn't. He needed me. The question of why still remained.

I nodded.

"Coincidently, Blackwood also happens to be the objective of what I need as well, but make no mistake, it is not a mere forest."

"So I keep hearing," I said.

"I'm sure you've heard a great many things, but the threat of what lies within is very real."

His blue eyes were intense and focused. After the wistfulness of remembering my childhood, they reminded me of my uncle. I shuddered.

"If freedom from ATOM is what you want, why not walk out the gates *with* us," I questioned. "Why do I need to risk anything?"

Hendrik's left eye twitched. "It is not only freedom I seek, Mr. Lawson. I wish to have returned to me that which was stolen. Much like you. You see, for me, freedom is nothing if I cannot be what I am."

"And so in order to have my freedom, I have to risk my life?" I asked.

"If you wish. Nobody is forcing your hand at this moment, but tell me, would you prefer to walk out of those gates a free man, or would you rather fly?" He didn't need me to respond to the question. He wouldn't have asked it if he didn't know the answer. "Then in order to obtain what we both want, a risk must be made. But you don't trust me." He pondered that last bit as if he found it confusing.

"Should I?" I asked. I ignored his startled reaction. "When I first arrived you put me in the Tank. A place I can only describe as deeply nestled somewhere between hell and whatever comes after. You put one my friend's lives at risk with a lashing that damn near killed him, and then you pardoned my own punishment and approached me with an offer to help me escape. All in all I'd say you've been a little inconsistent. And if we're still being honest, it's difficult to trust someone who serves the very establishment that persecutes us."

Hendrik unclasped his hands and acknowledged me with them. "All valid points. Although surely you can understand that I've done what is necessary to preserve myself. As have you. I did not know when you arrived that you would be the one I need. Had I, perhaps I'd have reacted differently. I have a role to play here, Mr. Lawson, as we all do. You yourself have played a role the past few months. We are all creatures of this fine world, and as such we share the instinct of survival."

"Let's say you're right. Say I believe all of that, it doesn't change the way I feel," I said. "You've given me a promise of freedom and flight. Nothing more. You want me to partake in this scheme of yours, but you refuse to share any details about it."

"Again, a means of survival, at least in part," he responded. "Perhaps the rest is habit. So you wish for a trust session with me. Okay, what would you like to know?"

A hundred questions raced through my mind all at once, too quickly for me to grab. I felt overwhelmed by the sudden opportunity. So much so I wasn't sure where to start. I tried to think small, something to get me started. The rest would come from there.

"Why don't we start with how old you are?" I replied.

Hendrik's lips twisted and his eye twitched again. "I am almost fifteen hundred years old."

"Fifteen…" I blinked and made him repeat himself. I couldn't have heard him right. His answer was the same. "How is that even—there are nothing but mysteries surrounding you. The Tank and the fear you can impose into somebody are abilities foreign to me. What *are* you?"

His lips parted to answer but he stopped, shifting in his seat. For the first time since I had arrived, I saw him hesitate. He seemed unsure of himself.

"An age-old question if there ever was one," he responded. "I am not a creature you are familiar with. At the moment I am not much more than a man with a few influences."

"That doesn't answer my question."

"That's because I am not finished." He lifted up a glass of water and took a drink, running his hands over the notebook in front of him. "Forgive me, it's been quite some time since I acknowledged my old self. Admitting such to someone now seems…"

"Risky?"

Hendrik smiled then, faint and not at all humorous, but a smile nonetheless.

"Indeed." He took a deep breath and seemed to contemplate his response. "I am known as a Genesis."

I didn't know what that was. At first I thought I'd misheard him. Had he meant genie? I shook the suggestion way. Even they were myths among supernaturals, and Hendrik articulated everything so well I couldn't have misheard. If he was as old as he'd said, there was a reason I hadn't heard of it before.

"Okay, and what the hell is that?"

His wrinkles creased as he considered the question. The lines around his eyes and lips deepened, jaw flexing in and out as his teeth ground together.

"I'm afraid I cannot share more detail than that," he said. "You want answers and I respect that, but I have not survived as long as I have by giving up my secrets in their entirety. I do hope you understand."

I did, but I hated him for it. Still, I didn't push the subject. I had other questions, and I didn't want the moment to be stolen from me.

"Okay, well that puts a stopper on things. I guess let's move on to the plan. What is it?"

"I appreciate your understanding," he replied. "The plan, as I'm sure you've been anticipating, is Blackwood."

"So it *is* the way out?"

He made a motion that resembled a shrug. "It is but it isn't. It is the first step of the staircase. What I need resides deep within the woods, and without it I cannot guarantee either of us anything. What I need from you is to enter the forest and retrieve this item for me. When you arrive back, I can grant you the return of what was lost to you. I will remove the glyphs from the entrance and you and your friends will be free to go."

"So Blackwood isn't the way out."

"There are many things in Blackwood, Mr. Lawson, but freedom is not one of them. Darkness resides in those woods. Evil that mythology couldn't even touch upon. Demons from the pits of misery shuffle in the shadows, cursed to the woods by the witches of Blackwood themselves."

"Witches? As in multiple?"

"Creatures of forgotten magic who've had stories spun about them for as long as stories have been shared. Every culture has a version all their own, but each nothing more than an inkling of truth. A sugarcoated tale wrapped in fine toffee, when the truth would reveal an apple rotted so deeply to its core that the maggots themselves flee the scent."

The imagery sent a chill down my spine. "And you're sending me in there to do what, kill them? I don't think so."

Hendrik laughed. It was amusing and genuine. "No, Mr. Lawson. I would never send a boy on such a mission. That would be suicide." He continued laughing, so much so it started to annoy me. "Oh, I'm sorry." He cleared his throat and tried to withdraw his humor, but lines of it remained upon his face. "The witches are not a threat to you, not directly. Their corporeal forms have long since been trapped within the confines of the woods, but their influence has not. Which is why I reiterate the dangers you will face: monsters, Mr. Lawson, beasts tainted by death, reborn in the shadows of torment. Souls reformed by anguish and suffering reside in that darkness. They're unlike anything you've encountered in your time on this earth. You cannot escape them. They move like the wind and strike like the fires of hell. When you face them, you will have no choice but to kill."

Hendrik's eyes gave off a haunted seriousness that looked deep into my soul. The air felt colder in the room and I fought back a shiver. I didn't like the idea of killing. There had been enough lives lost at my hands.

"There's always a choice," I said.

Hendrik frowned. "Perhaps you're right, but given the options of death or a long and prosperous life among the clouds, one would expect you'd choose the latter. If we had the time, I would educate you on all things Blackwood. Unfortunately, time is something neither of us have much of now. It seems we have found ourselves in a predicament that I did not anticipate. Your incident in the lunchroom started a fire I am unable to suppress."

I shifted in my chair, unease sliding over my shoulders like a skeleton's grip. The more questions I asked, the more tense I became. I wanted to know everything about everything, and once I did, I wished I'd never asked. I should've been excited to receive the answers I craved, but I wasn't. It continued to reveal how much my outburst had jeopardized things.

Although angels were disliked by many species of supernatural, banshees and typhons hated us the most. Since I'd arrived, Gareth saw an opportunity to take that hatred and make my life hell. Thus far I'd been on perfect behavior and Gareth wouldn't risk an uprising just to exact his rage. Instead he had waited for the right moment, and when it came, it was dashed by Hendrik's surprising interjection. Now Gareth had gone above his head and staged an intervention with his superiors at ATOM. He'd had his suspicions after what happened between Gage and Soren, but after Hendrik protected me in the lunchroom, he was certain we were up to something. It didn't help that he was right. Originally Hendrik had planned to spend months training with me, preparing for what lie inside the forest, but now we'd have only a few days. I cursed my shortsightedness.

"Does that mean we're leaving now?" I had wanted out of this place as soon as possible, no matter the risk, but the reality of it clasped around me like the shadowed hand of death herself. Tryst and Soren had been right; Blackwood wasn't an escape, it was a death trap. And if I wanted out of here, I had to walk into it and back again.

"I can see the change in your aura," Hendrik said. "It's cycled through a great many things since you entered this room. You are regretting this arrangement."

"I don't know if that's the right word, but I'd be lying if I said I wasn't nervous. You've built those woods up to be something I'm not sure I'm prepared to handle."

Hendrik smiled. "Surely you've spoken to Mr. Kye and Ms. Rivera about this. You will not be alone."

"Now that I know the truth of what's in there, I can't ask them to come with me."

"I'm afraid they do not have a choice."

I felt guilty. "Why is that?"

Hendrik frowned. "You forget that while at the Academy, the

two of you are connected. Linked. If you escape, Ms. Rivera is to suffer the reprimand for you actions. I will not be able to protect her. Not against Gareth and the superiors from ATOM. And unless I'm mistaken, wherever Ms. Rivera goes, so does Mr. Kye."

"What are you saing?" I questioned. "They didn't sign up for this. I told you I'd go and in exchange they'd get their freedom. It's not fair."

Hendrik shrugged. "Perhaps not, but you accepted responsibility for this arrangement without a full understanding of the risks. I tried to relay them to you, but you were being...I believe brash is the term I used. Your wings were more important than anybody's safety."

"That's not true!"

"Isn't it? Didn't you decline my initial offer for freedom? It wasn't until I sweetened the pot that you considered it. And even then, you demanded what you wanted without knowing the full circle of what we were getting into. Do not say I didn't try to warn you."

The words cut me down. He was right. This was my fault. "You can protect them. I've seen what you can do. You can keep them safe."

"Against ATOM? I am but one creature; I do not have it in me to overthrow their weapons and technology. I would crumble under the manpower alone."

"But I've seen what you can do," I insisted.

"If I were prepared to take on ATOM on my own, don't you think I'd have done so by now?"

"Then find another way. If I have to risk my life to get you out of here, then you can risk yours to keep them safe," I replied. "I won't have Tryst thrown in the Tank because of me. Not even for a chance at freedom."

"The Tank? Oh no, Mr. Lawson. The Tank is for those who might redeem themselves," Hendrik said. "If you were to escape, she would be subjected to the trial of threes. That is, first she would be lashed until she could no longer walk, then she would be wrapped in a copper wire—her metal of weakness—and set to hang while the wire cut and burned through her entire body. Finally, she would be radiated with a metal-dusted flame that would induce agony beyond either of our comprehension."

My face twisted in horror. "You actually do that to people?

What the hell is wrong with you?"

His face didn't move. His eyes were cold and if I didn't know better, I'd have thought lifeless. "The trials were put in place by ATOM. I did not create the rules here, I enforce them. We do what is necessary to ensure others learn from their peers' mistakes."

"Forget it. The deal is off," I snapped. "I'm not going to speak for her and volunteer her to enter Blackwood. I won't force her to risk her life, and I won't be the reason you string her up."

"I advised Gareth that I would be taking over as advisor to you, Mr. Kye, and Ms. Rivera," Hendrik began. "I hoped to have months to prepare you, but your actions have changed the course of things. I would postpone, but I fear once the officials arrive, they will kill you out of spite to set an example. You will work with me, Mr. Lawson, and have a chance at a new life outside these walls, or you will choose to stay and be subject to ATOM's wrath. If you consider the trials of three to be harsh and unconventional, then I advise you not to leave your fate to ATOM's creativity."

"So if I go, I choose between killing creatures of unknown horror and death, and if I stay, I die," I responded. "Regardless of my choice, you're sitting on top, aren't you? You let the dust settle and you find another to take my place. Lifetimes of planning have given you plenty of time to think this through. You've put yourself in a good spot." Hendrik frowned, but I didn't think it wasn't real. He'd feigned it all. The smiles, the laughter, the false hope there might be at freedom from this place. "You planned this. All of it."

"How dare you! You think I'd spoil my own chance at freedom?" He rose from his chair, anxiety choking the room before he repealed it. "I'm insulted, and I will not argue semantics. To survive, I have done as ATOM requires. If you were to use your eyes, you can clearly see I've tried heartily to remove myself from that role on my own terms. If it were to happen on theirs, I'd see a fate much worse than the trials of three."

"Then remove the glyphs and walk out the gates yourself. We can all go," I suggested.

The leather chair sighed as he leaned back in it. He looked defeated now. Exhausted. "We've been through this."

"It's a choice, Hendrik. Not one that you like, but a choice nonetheless. It's life over death.?"

"And I reiterate my stance. If I am to return to the world, I wish to do so as I was created. A life otherwise is meaningless to me. If choice is what you wish, I can place Soren and Tryst in the safety of the Tank. Although my ability to keep them protected by its reach is limited, which would mean you'd have to hurry your way through a place you cannot yet imagine."

"That's not a choice. That's torture."

Hendrik's eye twitched. "It may not be a choice you like, but it's a choice." He spit my own words back at me and they burned. "Had your actions in the lunchroom not occurred, we could negotiate. I could have prepared enough Soliloquy to guarantee their safety in the Tank. That isn't an option now, is it?"

"Then go into the woods yourself."

"You have all the answers, don't you, Ash?"

I shoved my chair aside and walked to the window, pointing at Gareth, who berated another youth.

"It's better than that, isn't it?" I questioned. "What have you been waiting for all this time if the answer is in the woods? You say you're a dog, neutered by the very people who put us in this hellhole. Why haven't you done anything about it then?"

"Because, Mr. Lawson. I cannot enter Blackwood physically. Contrary to what you may believe, I do have restrictions."

"Then why not someone else? Why'd you choose me?"

"Honestly?" he asked.

"Please."

"You're a fighter, Ash. I need a fighter for what's coming," he said. "I knew I could trust you because you won't conform. It doesn't matter how long you're here. Defiant until the end as your kind often are. But more than anything—and I'm sorry for this truth, but you asked for honesty..." He glanced at me with a frown upon his lips. "You're an angel. Nobody would miss you if you were gone."

CHAPTER 20

Truth. A painful reality. What you wanted to hear and what you *thought* you wanted to hear were never the same. Angels were a near extinct species. Most in my generation had never seen one and if they had, it was a Bigfoot sighting nobody believed; if only they'd gotten a clearer picture. For the many generations before mine, they remembered angels as being manipulative and harsh. They'd have been right. My family and the clan I came from were as cold and calculating as any. They were the typhons of yesteryear. One of the many reasons I didn't belong. Even taking away the fact that I stood alone from angel culture, and that I had tried to leave a positive impression on the world, I still managed only to blemish it. For many, I was simply the man who got their loved ones killed. Another painful truth. Maybe being cursed to the Academy had been a blessing in disguise. I didn't have to face the people who thought me a murderer. I didn't have to answer the whys of my failed mission. I didn't have to stumble over my words in an attempt to explain how I'd managed to offer them hope and instead wreak havoc. Hendrik was right, nobody would miss me.

My blood became acid that burned my insides in a way only a man writhing in guilt could understand. Not just for what I'd done before the Academy, but what I was doing now to Tryst. I'd set in motion a series of events I could not come back from. It was the ship all over again, and as before, it sank. I thought I'd learned from my mistakes, but the present situation showed otherwise. I'd put Tryst and Soren in jeopardy. I'd sentenced them to follow me down like a star destined to burn as it sailed through the night. Choose me and the risk of death, choose the Tank and risk death, or choose ATOM and face horrendous torture and then death.

The door buzzed and opened, but I remained in the hall. I wasn't ready to ask them to make that choice. I wasn't ready to look them in the eyes and tell them what I'd done. The guard, Mr. Calm, ordered me in with a handful of slurs. At least I think he did. His words were a wash of sounds. Everything moved in slow motion while reality bit away at me. I existed somewhere between life and oncoming death, nothing more than a wraith to those around me.

The guard's club struck the back of my knee and my leg gave out. My body sagged, but I recovered and stood firm once again. The sting resonated, returning a flare of life to me, but it didn't come in the form of stable thoughts or wise decisions. It came as a flicker of anger. He moved to hit me again, but I didn't let him. I caught the club in my hand, expecting only wood. It wasn't. My skin burned from the lines of metal embedded in the club. The guard's eyes widened when I didn't let go, smoke rose with the stench of burning flesh. Calm tried to hit me, balling his fingers into a fist and swinging up. I blocked it and without a thought reacted. My foot hit his chest with monster force. His body crunched beneath the impact and he crashed into the booth at the end of the hall. The Plexiglas warbled, the guard inside panicked and reached for his club. I threw the club I'd claimed as my own to the floor and stood idle. I didn't show any further sign of aggression. I stood quiet and lost in the dim hall awaiting what might come next. Both guards moved forward, fight burning in their eyes. I didn't move as they neared. Why should I? I didn't fear them. I had obeyed out of necessity. That necessity was gone. Death lurked at every corner. Even before I'd struck the guard, there was no decision I could make that wouldn't risk it. The world I existed in had become a shower of untruths, and I wouldn't live in the shadow of its façade any longer. I would own my life, but I would not live theirs.

The guard's club came up and I waited, wondering if he was as prepared as he thought for what would happen. He put everything into an attempted strike, but before I could dismantle him, something shoved me back and a blur moved past. Gage Daniels stormed through the hall and disarmed the guard, knocking him off his feet. Calm stepped back as if Hendrik himself had appeared from the shadows. He put his hands in the air and backed away. The other guard clambered to his feet and followed suit, apologizing profusely. Gage ordered them to stop and then whispered something. The world still swam around me in a trancelike fog. Both guards nodded at Gage before returning to their posts. Calm's eyes were daggers as he walked past me with a large dusty footprint embedded in the center of his pressed uniform.

"Wow, you do have a death wish, don't you?" Gage shoved me into the room and slammed the door.

"What the hell are you doing in here?" Tryst asked. "And what's going on out there?"

Soren sat up, his face wrenching at the movement. His eyes bright with fear as Gage walked farther into the room, and the deva slid to the back corner of the bunk.

"You're a cowboy. You're going to ruin everything!" Gage yelled.

"Will someone tell me what is going on?" Tryst snapped.

I shrugged Gage away and sat on the bottom bunk, staring at my hands. I should've seen clean fingers and neatly trimmed nails. Instead I saw lines of blood dripping off me and blue scratch marks from the woman I had tried to rescue in the harbor. It wasn't real, I knew that, but it stung just the same.

"What's wrong with him?" Soren asked.

"Get out of here, Gage," Tryst demanded.

"No. He's going to get us all killed."

"Us? Where exactly do you fit into anything?" she questioned.

"Hey, Flapper, shake it off!" Gage snapped his fingers in front of me. I didn't flinch. Sadness and regret overrode everything.

"What does it matter?" I asked. "This place will kill us all one way or another. Might as well go out fighting."

Tryst grabbed my shoulders and forced me to look at her. "Ash, what happened?"

I shook my head. How could I tell her that in the span of a day I'd condemned her? "I can't say. Not while he's here." I looked up at Gage. "Why are you here?"

Gage ran a hand over his shaved head. His sleeveless shirt

showed defined arms, dark red coursing beneath the surface through swollen veins. "I'm trying to keep you alive, but you're making it more difficult every day."

"What do you care?" I snapped.

"I care because you're wrecking everything I've worked toward for almost half my life," he responded.

"What is he talking about?" Tryst looked back and forth between us.

"It's above your head, little girl."

"Excuse me?" she said.

Before Gage could respond, Soren's voice crackled through the room with surprising vigor. "Shut up and don't you dare talk to her like that!" The room fell silent. With the spotlight on him, he turned sheepish and retracted into the bunk. "One person at a time. Can we please figure this out?"

The guilt and anger welled up inside me. I couldn't keep it in. There was no point. It all led down the same path.

"Not including Gage, we're all going to die and it's my fault. You should have never let me crawl out of the Tank, Tryst."

"Okay, elaborate please?" She didn't seem fazed by the fact that I had told her I was the reason we would die.

"He means he made a deal with Hendrik he can't go back on, and unfortunately for you, you're tied to him." Gage crossed his arms and shook his head.

"Ash?" Tryst watched with a wary gaze, backing away from me.

"How do you know that?" I asked.

"I told you, I've been working on this since I was a kid," Gage said. "Then you come along and everything goes to shit."

"Can we start at the beginning? I'm beyond confused." Tryst fell onto her bunk, skin paler than usual.

"Let me clear the air," Gage said. "You all hate me and you think I'm a dick."

"That clears up nothing. We know you're a dick." Tryst rolled her eyes.

"I wasn't finished." He sat next to me and the springs screeched in revolt. "I was never captured by ATOM. I *let* them bring me here when I was eleven so that I could do something. A mission I've been trying to complete ever since. It's required me to do things I haven't liked, be a person I didn't want to be, but it was a necessary evil." He turned to Soren and shrugged. "The things I've done to you have been horrible. I know that. But like everything I've done, it's for the good of supernatural-kind."

Soren didn't seem to think that was an acceptable apology and diverted his eyes to his fidgeting hands.

Gage sighed. "My mission has always been Hendrik. I was supposed to get close to him, become the golden child and his so-called *chosen one*. After six years, as you can see, that hasn't happened. I was never able to get close. I guess I wasn't what he was looking for. I had to settle and attach myself to the closest thing I could."

"Gareth," Tryst said.

"Yes. And Gareth takes joy from others' grief. He loves humiliation and hates anything he considers weak. A lot of banshees are like that. They have twisted minds in ways most can't comprehend. Did I like it? Hell no, but what I came here to do was more important than what I liked. Everything I've done has been to get as close to the top as possible. Gareth was that podium for me."

"So you're saying this is all a big show?" Tryst asked. Gage nodded but it only enticed laughter from her. "You expect us to believe that? You trapped Trace in the bathroom and tormented him when nobody was around. The things you've done to Soren are even worse. None of that was for show. Nobody was watching."

"You don't know Gareth like I do. He can smell a lie. Believe me," Gage answered. "Before you two got here, I tried to pull one over on him and caught the beating of a lifetime. It makes the lashing I received seem mild. You think what I did to Soren in the yard was bad? You have no idea what I've had to do."

"Because that's somehow convincing me you're a decent person," she said. "You're horrible and there is no explanation that will change that. So skip that part and tell us why you needed to get close to Hendrik."

"Because he's older than all of us combined. He's from a different world, an original supernatural. ATOM has tamed him somehow. They've found a way to control him because they can't kill him. Copper, iron, even silver, none of it hurts him. He's something different. And everything in this place is a ploy dreamed up by him. Hendrik's been playing ATOM since the beginning, biding his time. The Academy was Hendrik's idea in the first place.

Some last-ditch effort to get close to Blackwood. There's something inside he wants, but he can't get it himself. That's where Ash comes in, and a handful of others who failed before him. Like Trace."

The room fell quiet. I expected Soren to lash out in denial, but the shock in his eyes and the sadness that pulled at his lips could not be combated with rage.

"What?" Soren whispered.

"I didn't want to be the one to tell you, but there it is. You've always wondered what happened to him. It wasn't me," Gage insisted. "Hendrik happened. Like Ash, Trace thought he could get you two out of here. He couldn't."

Both my friends turned to me. Tryst didn't look upset or sad, she looked confused.

My breath caught in my throat and I swallowed a lump. "I don't know about Trace, but Hendrik does want me to go into Blackwood and get something. Don't ask me what; I don't know yet."

"And that's why you seem out of it?" she asked. "I thought Blackwood was what you wanted."

I turned away, focusing on the bloodstained floorboards. I didn't want to see her face when I told her. "After what happened in the lunchroom, Gareth has members of ATOM coming to inspect the Academy. Gareth knows Hendrik is up to something and he's trying to oust the headmaster. They'll be here in a few days, and if I'm here when they get here they're going to kill me to set an example. And anything that's linked to me."

I didn't need to look to see her stumble backward. She caught herself on the frame of the bed. "Oh."

"Nothing's set in stone," Gage said. "I can talk to Gareth."

"You pretending like you care is too weird for me." Tryst used the wall as a crutch to walk across the room and put distance between herself and Gage. "This whole thing is...a bit much."

"I understand you don't want to trust me, but I'm the only thing on your side right now without a vested interest."

"Bullshit," I said. "You *want* me to go into Blackwood and do the job you couldn't, and then god knows what you'd do with whatever I brought out. What the hell is in those woods?"

"You mean besides death traps, black magic, and demons? I'm not certain, but I think it's a trinity."

"What's that?" I asked.

"True power," Soren whispered. He stared through us as if we weren't even there. "A pyramid of energy created from three sources: light, darkness, and magic. One represents life, the other death, and magic—the one thing that exists in both. It's primeval. Impossibly rare and created only when the three aspects align in flawless measure. First, one must take life from another. Upon death, a spell must be cast at the exact moment the soul leaves the body, binding the two together. Finally, a piece of the living creature's soul must be joined to it, creating a trinity of life, death and power. A force unparalleled to anything this world could create on its own. When that is done, and blessed by the full moon's touch, a trinity is born. Whoever holds that trinity…"

"Holds immense power," Gage finished.

Soren nodded. "It is a deva legend told for generations. They say a trinity is how supernaturals were born."

"And Hendrik wants you to go get him one?" Tryst asked.

The room spun and I squeezed both sides of my head, trying to level everything out. Even with my eyes closed I felt my body warbling from left to right. "I don't know."

"I'll reach out to my contacts beyond the Academy and see what I can find out," Gage said. "But that sounds like something Hendrik would be looking for…and my father too."

"Your father?" I asked.

"Who do you think sent me on this mission? A man obsessed with dominance. He knew there was something in those woods. He has for decades, but without Hendrik as a guide, it can't be found."

"And who says you get to have it if we do find it?" Tryst snapped.

Gage rolled his eyes. "Let's worry about getting it first, shall we?"

CHAPTER 21

Gage left and awkward silence ensued. I was scared to make a sound, fearing reality might cave in around me. Then again, that might have been a good thing. I'd spent months trying to walk the line to keep Tryst safe, but in the end my actions brought the fate I'd fought to avoid. It was almost as if it were meant to be.

"I'm sorry." My voice seemed to startle both of them. I know it startled me. I had thought the words; I hadn't meant to say them.

"For what?" Soren asked.

I shook my head and uncurled my legs. They ached from being in the same position for such a long time.

"For everything," I said. "I thought I could get you out of here. I thought Blackwood was the key. I was wrong on both accounts and now you two have to pay the price."

"So don't go," Tryst said.

"You think I have a choice?"

"We *always* have a choice."

"Not this time. You don't understand. I have to go into Blackwood, because if I don't, I face ATOM. At least with the former I have a chance, no matter how small."

"You forget that I have to face ATOM too."

"No, I haven't forgotten. How could I?"

"If we face it and accept responsibility, there's a chance we can get off with a lesser punishment," she said. "We can show them what they want to see; that we want rehabilitation and it was a mistake. But if we go into Blackwood there is no coming back from that."

"They're not going to miss a chance to make an example. You said it yourself when I first got here. I'm..." I let my words trail off. I wanted to keep apologizing, but it didn't change the horrible position I'd put them in. "This wasn't the way it was supposed to happen."

Tryst stared out the window, eyes distant and cold. She pulled her bottom lip into her mouth and bit the edges. "It's fine. I told you I wanted out of this place. Now we have a way. We knew there would be risks involved. We knew there was a chance the stories were true. All that's changed is that we're no longer walking into a mystery. We know what awaits us."

"I can go into Blackwood alone. You two can have sanctuary in the Tank."

Tryst laughed. "Sanctuary? Is there such a thing in a place like that? Even if there were I'd still say no. You're not going alone." The defiance in her eyes told me it wasn't up for discussion. I didn't understand it. How could she care after all this? She nodded, as if a question had been answered. "This is life, right? If we don't die in here, we die out there. At least out there we have a chance for something more. Isn't that what you told me?"

"It is."

"Then it's settled."

"I'm coming too," Soren said.

"Not a chance," she replied. "You're not at risk right now, and we're not putting you in danger."

"She's right. If we come back with what Hendrik needs, he'll set all three of us free."

"No." Soren struggled to slide off the bed and forced himself to stand as upright as he could. "We lost our families together, we tried to find freedom together, we got caught and shipped off to this hellhole together, and together we've survived. All of it we did as a team. That doesn't change now. Not even if it means going into a damned forest filled with demons and god knows what else."

"Soren—"

"You heard me." His gaze hardened as he looked me in the eye. "I'm coming with you. You *know* you need me."

The moment he said it I knew he was right. Even if he wasn't, there was no talking him down. He would never let her go without him. He was a true friend and he'd stick by her to the end. That was hard to come by in any life, but especially this one. I closed my eyes and for a moment I wished things were different. I wished I'd handled things better. I wished Soren and Tryst had someone better looking out for them. These were good people. They didn't deserve this. They didn't deserve Blackwood. That forest would pit us against things we'd never faced: creatures and magic and monsters we didn't know could exist. Their lives were at stake; there wouldn't be any second chances. I did that to them, and they deserved better than me.

The guilt ate away at me until I could no longer bear it. I pushed it aside and buried it deep. I had to. Otherwise it would kill me long before anything else got the chance to. I needed to be ruthless and strong and face Blackwood head-on. It was up to me to keep my friends safe. I never had a chance to stop what happened on the docks, but this time I did. We could make it out alive, and I could give them what they deserved: a new life. A free life.

"I almost forgot." I reached into my pocket and pulled out a clear vial with dark blue liquid. "I guess in all the commotion I wasn't thinking. Hendrik wanted me to give this to you."

"What is it?" Soren asked.

"I don't know. He said it would help."

"You don't know? That's reassuring."

"Does it matter?" Tryst asked. "If Hendrik wanted to kill you— or any of us for that matter—poison would be the last way he'd do it."

"It's not going to kill you. It's going to heal you. We leave in a few days and if you're coming, you need to be ready."

Soren cringed. "If you think a drink is going to make me ready, you're delusional."

Tryst tore the bottle from my hand and shoved it into his. "Drink it."

"I guess the potential for death is around every corner now, isn't it?" Tryst and I glared at him. He gave a sheepish grin. "Too soon?"

"Yeah, too soon," Tryst replied.

He pulled out the cork and drank the liquid, and like clockwork the curfew buzzer sounded and the lights flickered out.

Soren let out a gassy burp. "Ugh. It tastes horrible."

"Get over it. It'll help," she said.

"I drank it, didn't I? And now I feel funny." His words became hard to understand, slurring more with each syllable.

"What kind of funny?"

"Creepy clown funny." Soren burped several more times and groaned. "Oh my…"

"What is it?" I asked.

"I have to tell you something," Soren whispered.

"Okay…"

"Screw this place!" He screamed and laughed.

Tryst shushed him. "Be quiet. That's all we need is for the guards to come banging at the door."

"All right, all right. Don't get your panties in a wad," he said.

"Do me a favor, don't talk about my panties."

Soren giggled. "Panties. What a silly word. You know what else is silly? Seeds. You literally plant this tiny baby thing in the ground, and in like ten years, it could be a huge tree or something. The world is so weird, huh? And you know what else is weird? Sand. It's like tiny baby rocks in a garden of—"

"Soren, what has gotten into you?" Tryst asked.

Soren burped. "Gross. That one didn't taste very good." He groaned a little, rocking back and forth and causing the bed to squeak. Then suddenly he stopped and stomped his feet on the ground. "You know what? Seriously, forget this place. Don't even be scared, guys. Demons and darkness? Oooooh! Pfft. I'm not even scared anymore." As my eyes adjusted, I watched Soren try to stand. He staggered and tripped over his feet, stumbling forward. I caught him and his body sagged into me. He laughed and wobbled, struggling to stand upright. His hands pawed over me until they found my face, and he squished my cheeks. "Dude, you have, like, the softest face ever."

"Okay then." I tried to help him to the bed but he pushed me away with a laugh and jumped onto my bunk. The mattress squealed in response.

"Are you okay?" Tryst asked.

His response began with a giggle that grew into laughter. "Hell yes! Blackwood ain't got nothing on us. We're going to mash those demons in the face!"

Tryst grabbed my arm and whispered. "Didn't Hendrik tell you what this was?"

"No, he said it would make him better."

She ran a hand through her blonde hair, pulling all the strands away from her face. "I think your information gathering skills need a little work."

"Guys!" Soren screamed.

"What?" we said together, voices laced with panic.

"I don't know. Nothing, I guess. I just love you guys."

He continued giggling, laughter growing with each breath. No amount of shushing could quiet him. The guards yelled from outside the hall. Tryst tried to cover his mouth but it made him laugh harder. He snorted as he struggled against her and mumbled something about a tickle fight before digging his fingers into her sides. She jerked away and a loud bang resounded from the other side of the door. A guard demanded silence, threatening a beating if we didn't obey. Soren's eyes opened wide as he feigned fear and mimicked the guard's voice. Tryst slapped him on the shoulder and finally he gave us silence. As if Tryst had knocked him out, Soren released a heavy sigh, followed by deep snoring. Just like that, he was asleep. Tryst covered him with a blanket and slid off the bunk, returning to her place by the window. She touched the glass and pulled away as it burned.

"You've spent an awful lot of time over here today," I said.

She shrugged. "I've been wondering what it's like beyond the walls. It's been a long time since I've seen it. I'm wondering if I ever will."

I watched the tops of trees sway in the breeze. It was all you could see beyond the wall. I chewed on the inside of my cheek. I didn't know what to say. I knew I couldn't promise her she'd see beyond it, but I wanted to

"I'm sorry for the way this all came about." I touched her shoulder. Her muscles tensed and I pulled away. "You must hate me."

She caught my hand in her own and pulled it back, sliding her fingers over mine. "I don't hate you." The response surprised me. I'd expected her to because I deserved as much. Instead she'd stood by me and refused to let me go alone. Her loyalty almost made me feel worse. "The truth is I wanted out of this place. I guess I thought it would be under different terms. That's all." She touched the glass again but this time she didn't pull away. Smoke slipped into the air from her fingers and she watched the skin burn. "A part of me hoped that one day I would walk out of here a free girl. I hoped to live out my life in a small house near a lake. Although I never knew *how* I would ever get there. I should've known better than to think I could leave this place without a fight. Stupid."

"It's not. We all have that dream. Although I think my house was actually in the trees. Somewhere inside of me there's a little kid who always wanted a tree house." I tried to smile, but the reality of our situation stripped it away. "Nobody deserves to be in this place. Not even Gage."

"I don't know if I would go that far. Although now that we know he has been playing a role this whole time and deep down he's a good old boy playing a psychopath, that changes things, doesn't it?" She rolled her eyes.

"You don't think he's telling the truth?"

"Is anybody in this place? Is Hendrik? My bet is he's leaving plenty out."

"I wouldn't doubt it." I turned as Soren shifted in the bed, making a playful growl sound in his sleep. "I'm sorry, I never meant to put either of you in harm's way. Is he going to be okay out there?"

"With all these apologies I'm starting to think you don't believe we'll make it."

"No, it's not that—"

Tryst smiled and patted my hand. "Soren's not a fighter, but if he can protect himself anywhere it's in the woods. To be honest, I'm more worried that we might make it."

"But that would be a good thing."

"Yes, but I wonder if we'll ever be truly free." She drew away from me and sat next to Soren. "Our parents lived off the grid. They believed they could live on their own terms. Freedom, they called it. They wanted to work their cause from the inside out without ever facing ATOM head-on. Using their abilities for good they thought they could change things." Tryst shook her head. "They were delusional."

"That's brave, Tryst, not delusional."

"The longest we managed to stay in one place was a year. Believe me, there's nothing brave about running. We spent our entire lives looking over our shoulders, and ATOM still caught us.

I remember SWAT teams pulling up in front of our house. My father led us away while my mother and Soren's parents caused a distraction. He told us to head north to Canada. We could find salvation and protection there. We could have a life. I cried and begged him to come. He said he would. He said he'd be right behind us and we'd be back together by nightfall."

"He never made it."

"Oh no, he made it. He stumbled into camp that night with a silver knife in his back. I tried to stop the bleeding but the silver had been in too long. The infection had moved into his bloodstream. With the right people and time...it doesn't matter. We had neither. ATOM had followed the trail. My father had led them straight to us. Karma, I suppose." She tucked a piece of hair behind her ear and shook her head, staring at the shadows as if they resembled an age-old riddle she had yet to solve. "I remember flashlights through the leaves and voices bouncing off the trees. The wet jaws of wolves snarled and snapped together—shifters converted to fight for ATOM. I didn't even get to see my dad turn to ash. He yelled at us to leave and we did, but we never made it north. Any time we got close something would derail our plan. We'd end up joining a cause we thought would earn us true freedom or a friend we'd made along the way would need help. I don't know. Maybe it was just us chasing a fairy tale. At fourteen we gave up on false hopes and tried to finish the journey we'd started. We were less than ten miles from the border when ATOM ambushed us with an undercover patrol. We were close, Ash. I think that's what's scary. Freedom isn't right outside those walls. Once we get out, that's only the beginning." Tryst took a breath. I expected to see tears in her eyes but there were none. This was something she'd relived too many times to be sad about anymore. Instead, she looked disappointed.

"But it's a *new* beginning, and we'll start it together. You need to have hope, even if that means fighting to keep it."

"And before that new beginning we have to survive Blackwood."

"It's not going to be easy, but we can make it. We *can* have freedom, but you have to..." I bit back the words. I'd said them before and it hadn't turned out well. Not for anybody.

"Have to what?"

"Nothing. I've spoiled that opportunity."

"Trust you? That's asking an awful lot considering we just met, isn't it?" The lines of sadness that creased her face faded and a faint smile appeared. "I do trust you, and so does Soren. You think you've painted us in a corner and that's why we're coming, but you're wrong. We're coming because we care about you. You're a part of us now, and with us, nobody gets left behind. Not ever."

I had a hard time looking at her then. I'd thought I'd lost any chance at trust and to hear those words didn't seem right. They were better than I deserved.

Tryst grabbed my chin and forced me to look at her. "We will get through this. Together."

My heart palpitated as she wrapped her arms around me and pulled me into a hug. It was the single greatest feeling up until she kissed my cheek. Her lips were soft and warm, lingering against my skin.

"Thank you," I whispered, tilting my head toward her. When the corner of my lips touched hers, I hesitated. A chill spiraled through me, but she didn't pull away. Her body pressed close and the edge of her lips touched mine again. Before I could close my eyes, the gentle touch had become something hard and slow. The room didn't exist. The floor vanished, the walls collapsed, and the ceiling was torn away by a storm of intensity I couldn't comprehend. A feral kiss that sent waves of vitality crashing through me. Her hands slid up my chest and around my neck; my fingers gripped the small of her back and pulled her against me. Our lips parted and her tongue rolled across mine. My pulse hammered, breath catching in my throat. I felt alive in a way I never had before, and a reverberation of energy intensified across my lips before the moment collapsed.

Tryst gasped and pulled away, eyes laced with fear. A drift of life force floated between us. A strand of white that twisted and turned like a dancer's ribbon. She covered her mouth as it dissipated, her fingers trembled over her lips. She tried to back away but I didn't let her. I wanted her to know that I didn't share her fear. Her kiss had lifted a weight off my shoulders that I'd let hold me down for too long, and the way she'd touched me ignited my soul with something I thought I'd lost—hope. I wanted her to have felt it too. By the way she'd touched me I thought she had, but fear was a force to be reckoned with, and this time it won. She pulled away and the moment was gone. The room had been reassembled and a single strand of life—nothing more than a breath—had broken apart whatever we had. She turned away, refusing to look at me. For her, it seemed the moment was ruined. For me, my world had forever changed. I became torn: a part of me hurt to see such fear on her face, but with the way she'd kissed me, another part of me felt I could fly, even without wings.

CHAPTER 22

Soren awoke a renewed version of himself. The wounds on his back had almost healed, and although they'd left behind a few terror-worthy scars, he seemed spritely. Tryst, on the other hand, seemed distant and not at all herself. I'd hoped a solid rest would help her realize that what happened wasn't a big deal, but to her it was.

"Everything okay?" I asked, hoping to break the ice.

"Yeah, why wouldn't it be?" she said.

"After last night things seem off."

"Do they? I hadn't noticed."

Her response seemed automatic, and she diverted eye contact at all costs. She paced the room and avoided me until the buzzer sounded and we were released from lock down. Breakfast was no different. The lunchroom was alive with chatter and the sound of forks scraping along plates, but our table seemed engulfed in a bubble of quiet tension. If it wasn't for Soren's occasional interjection, we wouldn't have said a word.

"Okay, last night was a little foggy, but it's all coming back to me now," he said. "I took the drink and...oh. I remember." He grimaced and leaned in, his voice a whisper. "First, I'm sorry that I touched your face; second, whatever I said about not being afraid was a lie; and third, your skin is unrealistically soft. I'm serious, Tryst, you should feel it. Reach over and—"

Tryst dropped her fork, ran her hands through her hair, and

pulled it back before excusing herself.

"Was it something I said?" he asked, but when Tryst didn't respond, he turned to me for answers. "Dude, what is going on?"

Tryst weaved through the tables and disappeared through the wall of doors. I dragged my fork through a pool of yellow liquid that swam around my eggs.

"I don't know, pick something: Hendrik, Gareth, the woods…actually, don't," I replied. "We shouldn't talk about any of that here. It's been a heavy few days; she might need some time to absorb it all."

"No, that's not it. I've known Tryst my whole life," Soren responded. "Something isn't right, and I think you know what it is. I have a nose for these things, you know." His eyes were penetrating; there was no avoiding them. Everywhere I turned I felt his inquisitive glare digging into me. Time seemed to stop and then he dropped his fork and gasped.

"What?" I asked, trying to hide the hesitation in my voice.

"You didn't."

"Didn't what? What are you talking about?"

He leaned in close, bright green eyes staring into mine. "You *kissed* her."

"What? No!"

"Yes, you did," he surmised. "You kissed her right on the lips." He studied my face as I tried to stammer a response, but I didn't stand a chance. "And she liked it; so did you. Oh boy, what have you gone and done?"

"Will you keep it down?"

Soren looked all too impressed with himself. "Admit it. Admit I'm right."

I tried to think of a different reason, something I could use to prove him wrong, but I came up empty.

"Fine, you're right," I relented. "It happened and it was great, and then all of a sudden it wasn't."

Soren's eyebrows rose. "Bad kisser, huh? That does have a way of ruining a moment. Believe me, I've been on the wrong end of a bad kiss before. Don't feel bad, at least you've got your looks going for you."

"It wasn't that. The kiss was fine. Her powers, on the other hand, caused a bit of an issue."

Soren cringed. "She freaked out again?"

"Of course she did. She's terrified of herself. The thing is, I'm not. I'm not afraid of what she can do, Soren. But she can't see that."

"That's because it's not about you. It has nothing to do with you at all."

"It doesn't?" I asked."

Soren shook his head. "Take a look around," he said, his eyes flitting across the room. "We're all damaged goods. Every person here. You don't mess with damaged goods, man. Not until they're ready, and Tryst definitely isn't ready."

"Damaged goods? Do you even hear yourself when you talk?"

He pursed his lips and tapped his temple. "A wise oak knows when the leaves are ready to change, and you, my friend, are a few seasons early."

"I give up. I can't even talk to you." I threw my napkin on the plate and stood up to leave.

"Wait, don't go. Sit down."

"Are you going to talk to me like a normal person?"

"I am what I am. Don't try to change me. Now try to keep up," he said. I rolled my eyes as he wagged his finger in my face and leaned across the table. "I don't usually share personal details—at least not about Tryst—but you're different than most. I tasted it in your aura when we first met, and I'm never wrong about stuff like that, so I'm only telling you this because you're an all right guy, okay?"

"Okay, but you haven't told me anything."

"Did you hear what I said? Try to keep up." He used his hand to acknowledge the room. "Everybody in here has a story, and it's probably not much different from the person next to them. Our generation got the crap end of the stick. It's never been safe for any of us. Nobody here has had it easy, and we're all messed up because of it. Tryst is no exception. A kiss, no matter how brief, is not nothing. In fact, if she let you get close enough to even consider it, that's *something*."

"Well, that something didn't end well."

"That's because Tryst's ability scares her," Soren said. "You've seen that first hand. What you don't see is that it rises and falls with her emotions. You didn't know that, but she did. That means even with that knowledge she let you get close. She *wanted* to try and control it. That's a huge step."

"So you think she needs time?"

"Look, I'm a deva, not an all-seeing eye. I don't know what's going to happen; all I'm saying is that for a brief moment, she was willing to try and take control. That's something I've been trying to get her to do for years."

"Then it's a good thing."

"It would be, yes. Having her want to control it because of you—or anybody for that matter—would be a great thing! Unfortunately, that opportunity shattered the moment you actually kissed her."

"Wait, what? What was I supposed to do, almost kiss her?"

"That actually would have been brilliant."

"You are literally no help at all, you realize that?""

"Relax, it wouldn't matter anyway. We wouldn't have the time to help her get past it. We'll be too busy getting flayed by whatever boogeymen lurk in the shadows of that godforsaken forest."

"You know how to put a damper on things, don't you?" I asked.

"News flash: reality sucks, dude."

"Wow, Soren, tell me how you really feel."

"You've been here a few months, but by Academy standards, you're still a baby, so let me take this moment to impart some of my infinite wisdom: good things don't happen. There are bad things, and then there are the things that come in between the bad things. That's it. In my experience, if something good comes along, it's best to get out of the damn way because it's not going to last. That's life."

His typical humor and sarcasm had fallen away. For the first time since we'd met, he was completely serious. There was an undecorated truth to the way he spoke, and the glimmer I usually saw in his eye was gone. For a moment, Soren pulled back the curtain and revealed how he truly felt.

"That's not life, Soren, that's being jaded. There's good out there. Sometimes you have to look damn hard for it, but it's there."

"Maybe for you, but for most of us that's reality. I keep things amusing because it helps me survive the day, but at the end of it, I know what I'm working toward. I'm not stupid. I know the only way I survive this world is to serve ATOM. Tryst knew that too, but then you came barging in throwing hope around like it's glitter at a unicorn's birthday. You don't realize it, but you're making a mistake."

"Am I? Is hope so bad?"

"It is when it's false hope."

"But it doesn't have to be," I said. "What if I could show you a life outside this place? What if I told you that you could have a home—a *real* home—and live without constant fear?"

"I'd say you were in need of medication." Soren laughed. "But I see why Tryst took a chance on you. You paint a pretty picture. You see the world in color; in reality it's grey. But I'm not so naïve. I know under all that paint it's still canvas. Strip away the color and it's just dirt."

"No, Soren. It's not. It never was. You've forgotten how to look at it." I shook my head and rose from the table. "Tell me, what scares you more? The fact that you might be wrong or that I might be right?"

"Neither. It all ends the same. I follow you and I follow false promise and die. I stay here, I live a life of servitude and die."

"You can't possibly feel this way. You're a deva—you see life and freedom in all living things. You can feel it. Taste it. You *know* the beauty that life has to offer."

"I do feel it, but I also know it's not for supernaturals. Not anymore."

"You're playing with me, right? I can't even believe you're the Soren I've spent months in the same room with."

"The masks we wear." Soren smiled.

"Are you really this cynical? Bad things happen, sure, but good things do too. After all the struggles she's faced, Tryst tried to take that step, can't you?"

Soren's smile faltered and he lowered his eyes. "I already took that step. His name was Trace. He inspired hope, love, and yes, even freedom. But that was before I saw the world for what it is. When he disappeared, I realized it was a lie. I'm not going to pretend that's changed. It hasn't."

"You tried and you got hurt. We've all been there. You think I'm not scared? Of course I am." I leaned across the table and looked him in the eye. "But I'll tell you what, I'm going to fight like hell for what I want, and if I die, at least I died trying."

"But you still died."

"So that's it? Life burned you once and you give up? Everything is a façade?"

"It's safer that way."

"Safer being a whipping boy? Safer being a rat behind glass, servicing the very people who took everything from you?" I asked.

"Don't act like it's the end of the world. I'm still coming with you. I would never let Tryst go without me. All I'm saying is I'm not setting any expectations."

We stared at one another for a moment, the roar of the lunchroom a background for the hopelessness on his face.

"I understand. I gave up once. I was ready for it to all be over," I admitted. "Luckily I had someone bring me back from that. I've got scars too, Soren, and they run deep. Some you can't even see. These people have taken everything from us, but they only win if we give up."

"You preach it, brother."

"No!" The word was a harsh whisper that caught him off guard. His eyes went wide and he tried to move away from me, but I grabbed his shirt and pulled him closer. "They can't have my hope, Soren, and they can't have yours. You don't have the fight left in you? That's fine. I've got enough for both of us."

I stared at him for a long time with so many things I wanted to say, but I couldn't find the words. I wanted to shake the despair out of him, but I knew that wouldn't work. He needed to see it for himself. I released him and backed away from the table, bumping into Gage as he walked past. He slipped something into my pocket, but when I reached for it he gripped my wrist.

"Not here," he said. His eyes held a warning, but behind that was a glimmer of something I never thought I'd see from him—vulnerability.

I didn't have a chance to respond. Gareth walked up and gripped Gage's arm, pulling him away from me.

"What the hell do you think you're doing? What did I tell you?" Gareth barked.

Gage didn't respond and Gareth turned to me, his eyes on fire with hate. He instructed me that Soren, Tryst, and I were expected in Hendrik's office at once. He stayed long enough to curse at me before dragging Gage from the room, scolding him the entire way.

I reached into my pocket and felt a small book when Soren grabbed my arm and turned me to face him. He had a fork in hand that he pointed at my face, but his hand trembled and his eyes had softened.

"You want me to fight? I'll fight. But not for me or you, it's for her. So hear this: you better not let her down. If you take us into that godforsaken forest, you damn well better get us out, because if I die, I will haunt your ass to the depths of hell."

CHAPTER 23

"Humans, supernaturals, demons." Hendrik stood before us and wrote the words on a whiteboard. "Three separate entities, yet all inhabiting the same world. You know humans, you are supernaturals, but demons are something else."

We sat in chairs as he paced the room and educated us. Superiors from ATOM would be here in three days. We had two to learn what we could before being set loose into Blackwood, which didn't leave us much time.

Humans and supernaturals we'd seen all our lives. We'd lived among them. Demons were darker creatures; cursed souls that had never passed to the other side. Beasts stronger than any supernatural could hope to be with abilities we had never known.

"I've never seen a demon," Soren said.

"Of course not. They do not roam freely as we do, so to speak," Hendrik replied. "Demons are restricted to the areas in which they were created, jailed by the boundaries of their curse. To understand demons, first you must understand the land you are about to enter."

Hendrik told us the curse of Blackwood went back two thousand years when the woods became home to a trio of witches, sisters who had emigrated from a far-off land. They had come to escape the first generation of hunters; humans who sought to destroy that which was not pure in their eyes. The witches were not malevolent women, but they had discovered a source of power lost to mankind. One that gave them gifts they wished to experience in a life of solace. They found that in Blackwood, a forest rich with life and beauty in a time before cursed lands and evil creatures ever existed. And within those woods they discovered a world of wonderment born of magic and tranquility, but power, no matter how innocent, eventually corrupts.

Hunters were not adept at giving up. They believed they were placed on this earth for one purpose—to cleanse it—and as such, their persistence led them to Blackwood. They attempted to eradicate the women, but the witches fought back with mythical abilities the hunters had never seen, forcing them into temporary retreat. However, the witches did not celebrate their victory. Instead, they collected the fallen hunters and used their newfound gifts to create a system of defense that would not be breached. Monsters contained in the shell of men who would become kings among beasts; an army not to be broken. But the witches did not yet understand the true nature of magic.

Over the decades, hunters from all parts of the world tried to destroy the witches, but succeeded only in enhancing their legend. The beasts dismantled their opponents with a breath of supremacy. A few were permitted escape to tell the tale, but those left behind perished, their souls twisted into something dark and foreign, doomed to eternity within the woods. Solitude and solace were no longer craved by the witches. They had decimated their opponents but knew as word spread of their dominance, stronger enemies would emerge. They desired power to strike those enemies down, but nature refused them, and they could no longer draw from the source. For the witches had created something unnatural in this world, and nature sought to balance it. The witches were enraged, but their thirst for more would not be quelled by nature's attempt at balance. Instead, the twisted souls that roamed the forest became sustenance for the witches; a fountain of youth that bled unnatural ability into their veins. The blood they consumed and the souls they devoured offered them new power. Power they used to enhance their beasts, granting them the ability to claim more souls for their masters. Those souls became a source they expected would never run dry, but as before, nature had a way of correcting imbalances. The souls the witches consumed brought a curse upon them—a spell that bound them to the woods, and the place that once gave them salvation would become their prison.

For a century no hunter dared enter the woods, fearing the beasts within. With the boundaries nature had set, this left the witches exposed and endangered. Their garden of souls had been harvested and the soil lay bare. As years passed, the witches grew weak and false immortality faded: skin sagged, wrinkles deepened, and hair greyed. Paranoia consumed their minds, but death's kiss would not embrace them, for nature would not allow it. Their souls had been corrupted, and they would not be given the peace death offered. Madness clung to every breath and with the rise of a blood moon, the witches merged everything they had left in a final attempt to evade nature's torturous wrath. Sparks rained over the earth as glass and gold, rubies and sapphires, and pieces of the witches' souls collided in the fire of moonlight. From the flames of undiscovered influence, a new era was born—enchanted collars that locked around the throats of their beasts and unleashed them upon the world. Their mission: any soul that crossed their path.

The beasts did as they were designed and served their masters, but the taste of freedom had touched their lips. Freedom they soon discovered was restricted. The enchantments within the collars could beckon the beasts at any moment, and they had no choice but to obey.

For the witches, youth returned, skin smoothed, and eyesight no longer waned. Beauty had been restored and they laughed in the face of nature. They thought they were gods that would not be ruled, but once again nature sang its song. No soul could be claimed in its entirety, freewill would not be broken by any force, and the taste for freedom would not be quelled.

Enoch, one of the witches' beasts, united his fellow creatures, and together they approached the witches, requesting their freedom. It was denied. The witches had no pity. The beasts were created as servants and nothing more, and in response to the foolish request, the witches became fierce and uncanny rulers. Fear and violence became the witches' tools, and the freedom the beasts gained to collect souls became their single reprieve. Regardless of their desire for independence, the collars forbade it. Time and nature, however, would work in their favor.

Every soul consumed corrupted the witches' minds further. Their hold on the beasts weakened and freewill sprouted roots, burying deep in their souls. The source called to them, influenced them, and Enoch began a collective to fight for what they sought, inspiring the beasts around him. They siphoned power from the witches' original source and grew stronger, facing their masters and demanding freedom. As expected, the witches refused and attempted to make an example of Enoch, thus began the revolt.

The war ended in the seventh hour of the seventh day of the seventh month, where the witches could fight no more. With no souls to harvest and no source to nourish them, they grew weak. The beasts overpowered the witches, but they could not reward them with death. It was not their gift to give. Instead, they granted the witches a life of servitude to the forest. One that would benefit the very force they'd betrayed time and time again—nature.

The beasts—a revolt of seven—cursed the witches in a mimic of nature's wrath. The women were swallowed by earth and wrapped in roots, buried deep within a tree of the beasts' own making, and sentenced to eternal comatose. The witches' powers would help the forest flourish, but their own freewill would be muted. In an act of finality, the source was embedded and sealed within the bark so that its potency might never be tasted again. Nature had won.

The creatures were proud of their victory. They used the magic they'd gained from the source to remove their collars, but like their masters, they did not understand nature's balance. They were not meant to exist and had obtained freedom that was not meant to be theirs. As such, nature was forced to respond not with man or beast, but one that was both—supernaturals.

"So in a way, the witches created supernaturals?" Soren asked.

"There are many things that contributed to their creation, but the witches were indeed one of them," Hendrik answered.

"And what about the souls? You said no soul could be claimed entirely. What happened to the pieces the witches couldn't consume?" I asked.

Hendrik frowned. "The remains became twisted fragments of what once were men. It was then that demons first touched the earth."

"And that's what we're going to face?" I asked.

"The demons are but a piece of a whole." Hendrik sat on the edge of his desk and sighed. "The situation we find ourselves in is not ideal. But we have been placed into a flawed system that sees us as slaves, as the beasts of Blackwood once were, and that will not do. This is a step for us to break the chains. As all things of importance, there is danger in that."

"Are we going to have to kill anything?" Soren asked. "I'm not keen on killing anything."

"The demons that inhabit the forest are not full of life in the way you think," Hendrik informed. "They have already passed, yet here they remain. They are stuck between worlds; darkness and time have tormented their souls into visceral things. You may not want to take a life. I respect that moral. However, once you step inside those woods, killing will be a necessity."

"Then what do we do?" I asked. "Copper, iron, silver? How do we destroy a demon?"

"Demons can take unconceivable damage and survive—if you can call it that. Those metals cannot hurt them. They were created with dark magic and as such, you must use something of equal fabrication."

Hendrik walked to the window and pulled the curtains shut. The darkness was broken by a few dim bulbs. He pulled on a canvas picture behind his desk and it opened like a doorway, revealing wood paneling like the rest of the room. After a few words, a blue field of energy appeared and collapsed, and the panelling vanished to reveal a safe. Hendrik opened it and stale air rushed from the metal chamber, carrying wisps of sulfur like a match that had been extinguished. He withdrew a long wooden box with golden latches and set it on his desk. Inside the wood casing were four daggers lying across purple silk fabric. The handles were encrusted in gold, shards of it spiraling around translucent blades. Each dagger was a different color: green, red, blue, and black. Beside them, an empty spot in the case creased the fabric. It looked as though one blade was missing.

"Glass, in all its fragility, is a powerful thing," Hendrik said, pulling out the black blade and eyeing it like a man reliving history. Each weapon had a stretch of gold in the center that reached from the handle to point. Glyphs I did not recognize had been engraved in the prized metal, and the black glass gleamed as if a fire lived within. "Each of these was made with precious stone: rubies, sapphires, and diamonds, melted in a fire of granite and coated in glass. There were few more than a handful created."

"Where did you get them?" Soren asked.

"I've been around a very long time, Mr. Kye. In those ages I've managed to collect a few things. These are among them."

"And these will kill a demon?" I asked.

"Mr. Lawson, this will kill anything with a soul and all things without." Hendrik smiled, dragging the glass along his fingers. "The symbols are identical on each, pieces of history from Blackwood. Each blade started as something less than it is now. The gold and glass and gems that made these fine weapons, were once encrusted in golden collars around the necks of beasts. Once the witches were bound to the Blackwood tree, the beasts removed their collars and created these. They were infused with power from the source and hexed as a means of balance. An oath was made on the eve of their release; should any try and claim more from the source than was rightfully theirs, the others were bound by oath to stop them."

"How do you know all this?" Tryst asked. She'd been silent the entire time, so hearing her voice felt good.

The headmaster returned the blades to the vault, but before he could respond, something startled him. Seemingly without cause, he moved in a blur across the room, wiping away the words he had written on the board. A commotion came from outside his office and the door burst open. Gareth stormed in with a small group of guards and a second ragtag crew following him. When they walked in, my chest tightened and my heart paused. A lump formed in my throat and my stomach turned into a pit of raging flames. It wasn't any ragtag crew, it was Colby Adams.

My hands vibrated, adrenaline, rage, and fear, all siphoning through the same veins. I gripped the arms of the chair in an attempt to restrain myself. I felt the wrath stirring within, adding to the cauldron of emotions that bubbled inside. I wanted to lunge across the room and sear his soul from the inside out. I wanted to watch his skin smolder as I devastated everything he thought he was. But there was another part of me that wanted to run from the room and never see him again. Seeing Colby again made me afraid.

"What is the meaning of this?" Hendrik stated, feigning surprise.

Gareth led the group with suspicious eyes. He walked into the room, checking each corner as if we'd hidden something. "With the allegations on the table, the officers coming down from ATOM thought it'd be wise to put some precautions in place before their arrival."

"And what are the allegations at hand?" Hendrik articulated each word as usual, not missing a beat. There was no inflection in his voice, no change in his demeanor. He seemed unfazed.

Gareth's scarred face crinkled. "That you and the angel are working together."

A hint of wispy laughter escaped Hendrik's lips. "Excuse me, but working together on what? Rehabilitation?"

Gareth's lips curled. "I may not know what you're up to yet, Hendrik, but I won't let you corrupt this institute. Colby here is going to keep watch and make sure nobody is out of line while we await inspection."

"I beg your pardon, but once again you forget your place." Hendrik's voice became quiet as he lowered his chin to meet Gareth's gaze. "This institute is built on the very fabric of what I am. I have kept us safe for over fifty years. I designed the curriculum. I facilitated the training. I am the reason there is an Academy. That means I am the reason you were granted a second chance. If not for me, you'd be a rat in a maze, bending over at the command of an orderly with a fresh supply of gloves." Hendrik stepped forward and leaned down toward the advisor, their noses almost touching. Dread engulfed the room and Gareth's shoulders slumped. He turned away, unable to remain strong in Hendrik's presence, but the headmaster gripped his face and forced him to meet his eyes. "You are not the only one with connections in the system, my friend. If you wish to see the arrival of our guests in three days, I am inclined to remind you of the respect I have earned. I am headmaster, and it is within my right to crush any who oppose my rule."

The air had been replaced by fear, and my heart no longer paused. It broke into a sprint. Soren and Tryst stepped back, moving behind Hendrik's desk. I fell against it, and I gripped the edge so I didn't drop to the floor. Colby jumped back toward the door, all too familiar with Hendrik's wrath, and the guards among the room funneled out into the hall.

"Have I made myself very clear?" Hendrik asked.

Gareth trembled, his words a scramble of sounds as he tried to retract his arrogance. "Yes, sir. Just trying to make my country proud."

"This is not about our country. It's about banshee pride and the entitlement your kind have always had," Hendrik said. "We've been through this before in your days at the Academy. Have you forgotten?"

"No."

"Then hear me: I will not sit idle while you blemish my name in hopes of obtaining my chair. That desk is reserved for me, built by me, and occupied by me, and until I am instructed otherwise, I will manage all that comes with that territory. Unless you're prepared to face me, I suggest you play your cards with care."

Hendrik withdrew the terror he'd submerged us in and oxygen returned to my lungs, but my hands did not settle. Seeing Colby had brought a wave of emotions crashing over me, but even more frightening was the idea I might give Hendrik even more power than this. A shiver ran through my body and goose bumps decorated my arms.

Gareth smoothed the wrinkles from his shirt and tried to wipe away the red finger marks on his face left by Hendrik's hand. He stood up straight and swallowed loudly, stumbling over his first few words before regaining his conceit.

"Using your unique gift to intimidate me is forbidden," Gareth accused. "It may be permitted against students, but not among faculty. You of all people know that, headmaster, since it was you who formed the rule." The more he spoke, the more his confidence returned, and before long he was pacing the room. "This is the reason I've requested an inspection. There was a time when the rules were firm and nonnegotiable, but as of late, you seem keen on bending them for your own will. I will not stand idle and watch this institution crumble…sir."

Hendrik's eye twitched. "Your associates will stay outside of the building at all times. We have a dress code to uphold, and they will abide by it. And there will be no smoking." He glanced to Colby, who chewed on his wet cigar. The bounty hunter tilted his cowboy hat with a grin and stuffed the butt into his jacket pocket. Hendrik stepped away from Gareth and took residence at his desk. "There is a guest suite on the south edge of the property. It should be adequate. Do leave it in the condition you found it. That is all, gentlemen."

It took a moment before they responded. Gareth and Hendrik were in a stare down. I half expected the headmaster to crush Gareth right then and there. Instead, Gareth grunted and ordered the others out. He closed the door behind him, but even after they were gone the tension remained. Nobody spoke. I think we were afraid to catch the other end of Hendrik's ire. His dark reach had overwhelmed the room and as before, it scared me. Not only because it enticed fear, but because no creature should have that kind of influence over others' emotions. It was terrifying, yet I'd agreed to get him more. Freedom? At what price? I'd made a deal with the devil himself.

CHAPTER 24

Anything we had been set to learn that day ground to a halt. The lesson was over. Regardless of the fact that we were on limited time, Gareth had managed to do something I didn't think possible—he got under Hendrik's skin. He'd wanted months to work with me, now he had days. For someone who'd waited this long to accomplish a task, he threw away half a day of preparation with surprising ease. That was easy when you weren't the one risking your life.

Frustrated and desperate for distraction, I took Gage's book from my pocket. I wasn't sure what I had expected to be in it, but a journal chronicling his time at the Academy was not it. The book was small and thick with hundreds of handwritten entries, easily only a portion of his time here. At first I thought he'd put it together as a ploy to convince me to trust him, but the shaky writing and crispy pages looked aged. This wasn't thrown together in a rush. This was legitimate. I flipped to an entry a few pages in.

July 27th, 2389

It's been eight months since I arrived and I've not succeeded. If anything, I've fallen in stature. For a brief time the other guests looked at me like a god. A defiant god, but a god nonetheless. Since then I've become nobody. This place is nothing like home. Father told me my mission was the most important, but this place is hell and I'm not sure I can make it much longer. There is a forest to the north. Blackwood. Whatever my mission is, it lies within those woods. Perhaps I could escape and find it myself...but Father would be disappointed with such a hasty reaction. He's counting on me. All the typhons are, as is the rest of supernatural-kind. I cannot let them down.

August 14th, 2389

The scars from the lashing have been here almost as long as I have, spare a month. The notoriety they earned me long expired. They still hurt and my back is a mess of scars. Twenty lashes. The price for striking an advisor. In hindsight a poor decision, even considering the brief stint of fame it garnered me, Hendrik was not pleased. I should be dead. Perhaps I should consider myself lucky. Having Gareth interject and suggest ulterior punishment was a blessing, albeit a painful one. He says he has faith in me to succeed. Whatever that means. I should not have faltered in my assignment. Youth and impatience got the best of me. I had been frustrated with my lack of progress. Father told me this would not happen overnight, but I did not expect to be here for almost a year. I will not make that mistake again. I will not let emotion rule me like it does most typhons. That is the downfall of my kind and if not corrected, it will be mine as well. Father taught me better than that. Instead, I will become a guest worthy of a trophy. Gareth will lift me on his shoulders and from there, I will be able to reach Hendrik and discover whatever secret it is he has buried in those woods. It is the key to bringing ATOM down once and forever. To obtain it, I will swallow everything that I am and become what I need to in order to succeed. The gashes in my back will become scars, reminders of my duty. It will ground me so I do not get lost, and it will reflect the price I am willing to pay for my people. Father will be proud. I will not let him down.

The emotion in the writing tugged at my chest. These entries were six years ago. I hadn't considered how long Gage had been here. He was nothing more than a child when he had arrived, and within a month he had been lashed near to death? Soren wasn't kidding, except this time the truth was more extreme than he had heard.

Each page was filled with entries top to bottom. Not a piece of empty space. I flipped through to the end of the book.

November 23rd, 2391

The guards delivered a letter to me in secret. If Hendrik or any advisor knew, they'd kill me. Little do they know the guards' loyalties come cheap. You do not decline an offer from the king of the underground. Although ATOM has pressed forward, the typhon council remains strong. The guards' treatment of me is proof of that. I suppose that is sign enough that Father is still out there, but I'd be lying if I said my faith hadn't wavered. I have privileges here that others don't. I am not wholly locked down as I should be. Still, this place and the lack of my father's voice have worn me.

Regardless, I have done well. I am no closer to Hendrik, but Gareth has taken a liking to me as I had hoped. He shares our vision. A white shirt may be in my future if I'm studious. Still, to earn his favor I must do things I do not like. Terrible things that make it hard to sleep at night. But I must. I cannot disappoint Father. Then again, perhaps I already have. Until today I thought he'd forgotten about me. It's been close to two years since his last letter. I try to have faith in him and our cause, but it angers me. Why did he send me to this godforsaken place? Does he despise me? Have I done something to displease him? Is it because I am not like my brothers? Perhaps it is none of these things and I am still here because I have not succeeded. I expected at some point he would come get me, but I should know better. Typhon until the end.

I have not opened the letter. I am scared to see what words he's scrawled within. Is it filled with hatred? Is he ashamed of my failure? Do I dare open it? It's been staring at me since the moon began to rise and I can't bring myself to open it…but it cannot be worse than what I've endured here, can it?

The letter is not what I expected. It is one of hope and promise, and support from my clan, but it also carries bad news. Two of my brothers have been killed. Another is comatose. ATOM has closed in and the council is on the move again, hence my father's silence. I should feel sadness for the loss of my kin; instead I feel a flutter of relief. I have never been admired by Father like they have. They always earned a level of attention I would have killed for. While they fought beside him, I am stuck here…still, they are family and I will mourn their loss as a typhon—tonight I bleed for them.

November 25th, 2391

My chest aches. Cords of silver are still embedded in the wounds, but Gareth has removed a few more. My blood has wept for our fallen.

After Father's letter, I've learned I have more allies here than I realized. Perhaps I have not paid Gareth the respect he deserves. I wonder if I've succeeded in my rising at all or if it was all Father's doing. I cannot be certain. I should not be here. I should be by Father's side. Things are not well on the outside and our family has been weakened. But here I must remain. My mission is more important now than ever. If I can discover what Hendrik is hiding, the guards will send word and he will come for me. Whatever it is, it could save supernaturals everywhere. It could give us the aptitude to deter ATOM once and for all. We should not have to leave this country to have freedom. It is as much our land as anyone's. I feel reinvigorated with my course of action. The fire is lit once again, and I must ensure I move forward. Too many people depend on me. I've learned there is an angel coming to us. An angel adept at evading ATOM. I've heard whispers that Hendrik is excited. It angers me, but I cannot be ruled by emotion. Perhaps there is a flicker of hope within the beating wings of a creature that was once our enemy.

I closed the book. I'd read enough. I didn't approve of the methods Gage had taken, but a part of me understood. That was why he gave me this book. It wasn't selected at random, there was purpose behind it. That didn't surprise me in the least. He wanted me to feel what he felt. I underestimated his intelligence. I stared at the stained bunk above me, pondering Gage's existence. What kind of father sends a boy here on a mission like this? A man who thought of you as a pawn rather than a person. A man like my uncle. I shuddered. I had never liked him. I had feared and respected him, but I never liked him. Gage's father sounded a lot like my uncle, and that made me almost pity him. Almost. The thought that I might have something in common with the typhon combated any pity I might've felt.

"What do you think, Ash?" Tryst asked.

"Huh?"

"You're not even listening? You've had your nose in that book for hours. What is it?"

I flipped through the pages, watching the scrawled writing become more refined. Even the words shifted as he aged through the pages, growing wiser than his years should have allowed. He had never been a child, only a soldier.

"Gage's journal."

I turned to a page and read through it. This installment was different than the rest. He was scared. It didn't sound like the voice in the other entries. It was somewhere in the middle. He hadn't heard from his father in so long he'd lost faith and wanted to leave.

I sighed. "I guess he wants to prove himself. We've got enough on our plate with Hendrik; adding more sticks to the fire is going to make it hard to control." I threw it aside and fell back on the bed. My eyes burned from staring at the words, and I rubbed my fingers hard against them.

"I hate to say it," Tryst added, "but having Gage might not be such a bad idea."

Soren scoffed. "You can't be serious."

"Putting the fact that he's a horrible individual aside, you two heard what Hendrik said—there are demons in Blackwood," Tryst reminded us. "Stronger and faster than any of us and with nothing to lose. We're not killers, Soren. It wouldn't hurt to have another person on our side who can fight."

I laughed, but it was more sarcastic than anything else. "Good luck running that past Hendrik. Remember, everything we know about Gage is a secret. Not even Hendrik knows. As far as he's concerned, Gage is Gareth's lap dog. After today, he'll never allow it."

"Then we don't tell him," she said. "He has the guards in his pocket, right? It's not like he needs Hendrik's help getting out."

I pondered it. I wasn't completely against the idea. Gage might be an asset to have out there, but could I trust him to watch my back? No. And he'd have expectations of the end result. Hendrik wasn't the only person who wanted what was in those woods.

"Okay, say we go along with that and Gage helps us through the woods. We survive and bring back what Hendrik wants. Then what? Gage is after the same thing."

"If it's a trinity, nobody should have it," Soren said. "It's buried for a reason."

"We don't know what it is yet."

"It's power," Soren said. "If it can restore Hendrik and if the king of the underground wants it, it's very, very powerful. That's a lot for one person, don't you think? Hendrik is already stronger than any of us and according to him, he's a shard of what he was. And Gage Daniels…he's the son of the typhon leader, who is king of the underground. Who is the lesser evil here?"

"To be honest, I don't know if I want it in either of their hands." I sighed. "Whatever *it* is. All I know is we can't stay here, and getting it is our way out."

"And don't forget Gareth and his group of bounty hunters," Tryst added.

I clenched my fists and rage bubbled in my soul at the thought of Colby. It made me long for the wings I didn't have so I might tear him up into the sky and watch him fall. If I did what Hendrik wanted, I could have that chance.

The thought sent guilt rippling across my skin. I shouldn't have thought that. It wasn't right. I wasn't doing this for my wings or revenge. I was going to do it for the freedom that the three of us deserved. I glanced up at my friends, who argued over Hendrik's power versus a typhon's notoriety for being cruel. I felt bad for them. If they knew I stood to gain something more than freedom, they might think that's why I put their lives on the line. It wasn't. I did this for them and for me. My wings were a windfall, weren't they? The longer I dwelled on it, the more I questioned my motives.

"Ash? What do you think?"

It took me a moment to respond, guilt had formed a lump in my throat that I had to force back down. "It doesn't matter who the lesser evil is. ATOM has had too much control for too long. It's time that changed."

"Trade one evil for another?" Soren sighed. "Getting out of this place is becoming more complicated by the minute."

CHAPTER 25

I had been summoned. Gage Daniels wanted to meet, and the two guards staring at me with clubs drawn let me know it wasn't a request. I didn't push back. I wanted to meet with him, and knowing it was coming was better than being ambushed in the shower. Still, bringing him on board was scary. A typhon was a wildcard in the best situation. Gage was as unpredictable as any. He knew things he shouldn't know. Things even Hendrik had thought were private. His journal might have humanized him in some form, but it didn't change the fact I didn't trust him. If anything it made them worse. Gage underwent drastic change to get close to Hendrik. But you could only pretend to be something for so long. Over time it would eat away at you and before long, you became the monster you were pretending to be. Tryst had been right, we needed him. Whatever demons Blackwood held were more than we were prepared to handle. Having a typhon would give us a better chance at survival and at this point, that's all anything was—survival.

A few months ago I had been trying to survive on the outside. I was a fighter and my life existed around breaking the rules and defying ATOM. Yet now, as I stepped into the hall, a clutch of tension held me. Fear at what would happen if I was caught. How my world had changed.

After holding my breath and wincing at every creak the floor made, I stood inside the typhon's room. It was larger than ours with a small, private bathroom. He sat on the edge of the queen-sized bed, a plush mattress beneath him. A small desk in the corner had papers sprawled across it and a chair tucked in the opening. He lived the high life at this end of the Academy. I was in the living quarters of a white shirt.

The guard pushed me in without warning and closed the door, leaving Gage and me to stare at one another. He walked toward me and took the book out of my hand.

"I'll take that." He seemed withdrawn yet somewhat brash. He tried to hide his embarrassment by flipping through the pages. He paused and read through an entry. His face shifted, relaxing at first, then hardening. "Nobody has ever seen this. If you tell anybody—"

"Aren't we beyond threats?" I asked. The man becomes the monster. My suspicions were cemented. Somewhere along the way the line between who he had been and who he pretended to be had become blurred.

"Listen, don't come in here and..." He turned away and took a deep breath. "I'm out of line."

"You are. It isn't easy to be one person inside and another out, is it?"

"What would you know about it?" he scoffed.

I shrugged, taking advantage of the extra square footage and pacing the room.

"When I first escaped the confines of my colony I didn't know who I was either," I offered. "I *thought* I was a nice guy, but the world was harsh. This place is worse. You tell yourself you're a decent person and sometimes you have to do bad things, but..."

He laughed. "Bad person? You got caught trying to offload a boatload of supernaturals to another country. Before that you'd rescued dozens of families, helping them emigrate from ATOM's grasp." He raised a brow at the surprised look I had failed to hide. "What? You think I don't know about you? There is no bad with you. You're a regular hero."

"I haven't always been that person. Maybe I never was in the first place," I said. "Regardless, is this why I'm here? To talk about regrets, misdeeds, and corrupt self-image?"

Gage's silver gaze flickered and he studied my face, searching for something. I tried to keep my eyes cold and still, taking a page from Hendrik's book. Leave nothing to be deciphered.

"You're here because Hendrik has something going down. Something in those woods. And with ATOM coming, my guess is it'll happen soon. You're here because I'm coming with you, and don't try to say I'm not. I won't—"

"I know." Now it was his turn to be surprised. He stumbled over his words. I think he'd expected a fight. He'd probably prepared a speech. I didn't need one. "There are things in that forest that I won't be able to handle alone. I'll need your help."

He processed that a moment and smirked, his other side shining through. "Damn straight you will."

"Don't get cocky. I'm not promising you the pot of gold at the end of the rainbow."

The arrogance vanished and he looked like he might be angry. "You mean to give it to Hendrik? That's a mistake."

"And that is my mistake to make. But I didn't say I was giving it to him either."

"You're going to keep it for yourself? You don't even know—"

"Stop. I haven't decided. In fact, I *still* don't know what *it* is. All I'm doing is giving you the chance to join us so you can get away from this place." I pointed to the journal. "You need to get out of here too. You don't deserve to be here. None of these people do."

"You want me to come with you to escape? Not a chance. I haven't given half my life to this place to walk away from the prize," he said. "I'm coming with you and whether you like it or not, whatever is in those woods is mine."

"If you come, it'll be on my terms, not yours."

Gage laughed. "I think you're mistaken, Flapper. I'm *letting* you escape. You think the guards follow Hendrik? He has less control over this place than he realizes. The only way your door opens after curfew is if I give the okay. If you want a chance at freedom, I'm the one who will give it to you."

He'd proven that the guards were in his pocket, but I tried not to flinch. I didn't want him to think he was in control, even if he was.

"If you're the all-knowing master, then what am I going to get, Gage? Since this is the typhon show, tell me what's beyond the shadows in the woods?"

"A trinity?"

"Are you telling me or asking me? I can't tell," I responded. His jaw flexed and he couldn't keep the frustration off his face. "You don't know what it is, and you don't know how to find it." I walked toward the door and knocked on it, waiting for the guard. "You have something I want—out of my room when the time is right. And I have something you've spent half your life trying to obtain—knowledge. If you don't work *with* me on this, then there's a good chance you're never getting out of here, and *if* you do, you can look Daddy in the eyes and see how you failed him."

Veins bulged within Gage's arms, glowing red like a storm of lava. His tanned skin turned to stone, rocks shingled down his arms and over his fingers. His eyes were swallowed by silver, arcs of fire flickering between his fingers.

I masked the panic that crashed through me. Gage was not a force to be taken carelessly, and I had no intentions of tempting the typhon, but I needed him to think I was in charge. I swallowed the fear, keeping my voice steady as I spoke.

"Or we can enter the woods together, take care of what needs taking care of, and decide what happens once we're out of harm's way. Neither of us has a chance without the other."

His shoulders rose and fell in sharp breaths. Hot air filled the room and molten fire rolled through the crevices of his rocky arms. His neck and face remained human, but his eyes were solid silver, flickering with passion.

"I *need* what's in those woods," he said. "It's nonnegotiable. You want out of this place, I can guarantee it. Hendrik can't."

Heat snaked around my body. Drops formed on my brow and ran along my cheek. I'd tried to make a point of staying honest. After what had happened on the ship, I didn't want to promise anything I couldn't deliver, but standing in the sweltering eye of a typhon's rage, I wasn't sure honesty was the best policy. A fight right now would destroy everything. Once again I stood between two evils. Did it matter who I promised it to? No. It wasn't about being honest, it was about getting what I wanted: freedom for Tryst and Soren. That came before anything. Even me. I put them in this position, and it was up to me to get them out. Being honest didn't matter. Being good didn't matter. Surviving did. It was a game of lives.

The realization that I would do *anything* to reach my goals seemed wrong. Evil even. It was probably those kinds of thoughts that brought ATOM to become what they had. Perhaps Hendrik too. Still, even knowing that, I accepted it. I had already done bad things. I had already been the reason people had died. If I had to tell a few lies and break a few promises to save my friends, it was as good a cause as any.

"You get us out and help us through the woods, and whatever it is, is yours."

He didn't respond right away. He examined me, studying me for a sign I was lying. I didn't give him anything. After a long moment, he reached out a scalding hand. The hard skin coating his fingertips receded to their softer counterparts, the fire dwindling to a spark and exposing a human hand with veins like any other.

"Give me your word," he demanded.

A Lawson never breaks his bond. A chill ran down my spine. My father's words ricocheted through my mind as I prepared to go against everything I had ever stood for. I felt a pang of guilt, but he was gone and had been for a long time. This world was a different place now. Once upon a time a handshake and my word were not trivialities. They were blood and soul and fire and heart infused in one. A bond unbreakable. That time was gone. Now I grinned and doled them out like the rubbish that rolled about my plate in the lunchroom.

"Agreed." I took Gage's hand and although it was skin, it felt like sandpaper and rock ground together.

A deal with the devil not once, but twice.

CHAPTER 26

Sun streaked the carpet in Hendrik's office. It was late afternoon but sleep still pulled at my eyes. I hadn't been paying attention. My mind had become a maze with no beginning or end. It unraveled into a knot of thoughts that collided with one another, ideas and fears intersecting in sporadic order. Who would I give the prize to now that it had been promised to both? Would we even make it far enough for my decision to matter? I'd thought Hendrik the key to our escape, but now I questioned it. Were either Gage or Hendrik a step toward freedom? The reality? There was no answer. The world was a labyrinth wrapped in questions with no answers and paths with no ends. Was I helping or sending us to an early grave? That was one of many fears that choked my focus.

Hendrik towered over me. He'd asked me something. What was it? I tried to avoid his gaze but it penetrated like a needle through the skin. I pushed away the negative thoughts that pressed against me. Feeding them would only help make them reality.

"Pardon?" I asked.

Hendrik disapproved with a tsk from his lips. "Demons, Mr. Lawson. An education you might want to obtain before facing them."

"You'll give us the tools to defend ourselves. That's all that matters, isn't it?" I asked.

"If weapons were all it took, perhaps, but they are not enough.

They will protect you physically, but will they defend you against a demon's heinous approach? Considering tonight marks your departure, I'd expect severe concentration from you. Have you listened to anything I've said today?"

"I..." I didn't put much effort into an excuse. He was right. I should've been paying attention. I put us all at risk by letting myself get lost in fear.

A demon's attack came in many forms. They were creatures not wholly dead or alive. They would find ways to seep into reality and manipulate us. According to Hendrik, a demon didn't need to hit you in order to kill. That was what made them so dangerous. Not unlike the Tank, a demon could deconstruct you piece by piece until you take your own life. As much as Hendrik stressed the importance of being prepared, I wasn't. He made it sound easy when he told us to recognize that just because we see or feel something does not make it so. The reality was so much different. I wondered if he had ever spent time in a place like that Tank. Did he have any idea what it could do to you? I shuddered at the memory. It had been months since I crawled over the dirt floor, shivering in my own urine and crying for it all to end. It felt like yesterday.

"So how do we know what's real and what's not?" Soren asked.

"That is an obstacle I cannot help overcome," Hendrik explained. "You must be instinctual in your quest. I will provide each of you with a vial of Soliloquy. It will aid you in an emergency, but will not help for the entirety of your journey. It is for you to keep your mind sharp. Doubt and insecurity will be your weakness. The demons will feed off it. If I could provide you with more, I would, but the potion is not so easily made, and we have run out of time. Together you must support one another to stay grounded."

"And since we're leaving tonight, I imagine at some point you'll tell us where we're going, how to get there, and what exactly you want us to bring back?" I questioned.

Hendrik slid into his chair and welcomed us around his desk. He opened the notebook in which he often wrote, wrinkled fingers running along the pages.

"The directions are unimportant," he began. "The woods are ever-changing, but the curse will draw you in. It will take you to a tree unlike any other. Roots will spill from the ground, power will drip from its leaves, and the witches' life forces will emanate all around you. The Blackwood tree." He closed the book and looked at each of us. "What I seek is not an item you can simply run away with. Without me, one might never know it exists. It is an unstable power that the witches themselves became lost in. A power that gave many of us our gifts—a trinity. It is energy and life in its oldest form—true magic. The beasts that rose up against the witches placed it within the Blackwood with a curse, and it's that curse that binds the witches to its roots. The curse allows for a limited withdraw. Under no circumstance do you take more than the tree is willing to give."

"What happens if we do?" Tryst asked.

"You do not!" His voice was sharp and quick. One of his eyes twitched and the intensity of his stare felt cold, even when it wasn't looking at me. "You. Do. Not."

"Okay." Tryst backed away.

He removed the case of glass weapons from his safe and pulled out the blue blade. It curved from handle to tip with jagged edges along the base and a sharp shingled design near the top. It reached longer than my forearm, and Hendrik spun it in his hand like an expert swordsman. He pointed it toward me, handle first, and urged me to take it.

It felt lighter than expected but carried an odd comfort. The glass glimmered like a gem, shades of blue shimmering from base to tip as it rolled in my hand. The golden handle felt strong yet soft, wrapped with a thin, ropelike grip. On the bottom of the blade a small shard of blue glass stood out like a spike. It thrummed with foreign vitality that swelled within the handle. It moved into my arms and startled me. If not for Hendrik's quick reflexes wrapping around my hand, I'd have dropped the blade.

"More than metal and glass, Mr. Lawson," he said. "These are weapons unlike any other. Welcome the enhancement it brings, for each blade offers a trait to its bearer unique to the individual. No two users shall ever have the same experience. Many would seek to relieve you of such a tool. I have kept these well hidden for hundreds of years. I do not relinquish them with ease."

"I understand."

"I do hope so, for without these blades you cannot retrieve what I desire. Keep them close and protect them at all times."

Hendrik handed a short green dagger to Soren, the edge serrated. A blade half the length of my own slid into Tryst's hand, glistening like a ruby polished in gold.

"This feels weird. I don't like having a weapon." Soren eagerly set the blade back in the case and wiped his hand along his shirt.

"When you see the dead eyes that haunt the forest, you may feel different, Mr. Kye." Hendrik ran his fingers over the emerald blade.

"Could you give us something to outrun them instead?" Soren's half smile looked more like a grimace. "I'm not a fan of blood or violence or haunted forests in general. As a rule, I avoid all things that cause discomfort."

"We are not all built for war, I respect that, but perhaps a chance at freedom and a life without fear could help you bear it," Hendrik responded.

"So what do we do with the tree?" Tryst asked, turning the weapon and examining the blade. She didn't seem comfortable with it either, but more so than Soren.

"When you find the Blackwood you will plunge one blade as deep into its bark as it will allow. The Blackwood's sap—its life, its blood—will run through the glass, allowing you to fill a small vial." Hendrik held up an empty glass container. "When the last drop falls, you have completed what you set out to do. You will then return to me."

"Blood?" Soren asked. "Didn't I say I don't do blood?"

Hendrik smiled. "A small discomfort for great reward. But be warned, upon its retrieval you must exit the forest with haste. I will know when the task has been completed and will await you at the forest's edge."

"How?" I asked.

Hendrik's eye twitched and he shifted in place. "I beg your pardon?"

I studied him a moment. I had never seen him look uncomfortable. Usually he knew the answer before I asked the question, or so it seemed, but this one seemed to surprise him.

"How will you know?"

He cleared his throat and adjusted his tie, closing the case on his desk. "The blood you extract will send out a very specific vibration. Once you've obtained it the demons that roam the forest will seek to claim it for their own, as well as any other familiar with its influence."

"So you're familiar with it?" I asked. He tried to ignore the question and pull the box of weapons away. I slammed my hand onto the wooden case and held it back. His eyes lit up with surprise. "The beasts of Blackwood. They had a name, didn't they? What was it?"

Hendrik jerked the box from my hand with immense strength. He held it tight under his arm, disapproving eyes staring into mine.

"I keep many things to myself. It is, after all, how I've stayed alive for as long as I have. You can respect that, can you not?"

"I think at this point it's within my right to demand answers. We're the ones risking our lives for you," I said. Hendrik's discomfort vanished beneath a mask of seriousness.

"You're risking your lives for freedom. A noble risk if there ever was one," he admitted. "Not to mention *other* things you stand to gain from this."

"Tell me their name. I want to see your face when you say it," I said. His lips tightened, eyes swirling with unease. Hendrik's darkness seeped into the room. I paced in an attempt to distract myself from it. "The curse of Blackwood was mere legend among supernaturals, but not you. You know details, history, and have woven a tale of intricacy around the witches and the creatures they once held. You know of their break for freedom, you know of these weapons, and in fact you have a collection of them. You're one of them."

His eyes fought a battle with mine, but it was he who wavered and turned away. He closed the safe with the weapons secured inside and fell into his leather chair. He let out a sigh that broke his perfect posture and caused him to slouch.

"Genesis," he whispered. "And yes, once upon a time, I was one of them."

The more he talked, the more his eyes came alive. He didn't talk of a forgotten land and strange creatures, he spoke about his home. When he told the tale of defying the witches and fighting for freedom, it wasn't a tale at all—it was a memory. That had been his fight. The Genesis's collars had been turned into blades, which begged the question that if there were seven of them, why did he have four?

"All these blades, pardon one, belonged to my fallen brethren. Some were taken by my hand, some by the hands of my siblings. The trinity is power and power is an addiction, Mr. Lawson. Even for those once held captive by it. Especially for them. The Genesis stood by their oath and destroyed any who tempted corruption by the trinity. Even if they were our brothers and sisters. It was not theirs for the taking. We would not have them walk the witches' path."

It hit me all at once, an epiphany that brought with it a funnel of emotions: fear, anger, surprise. I thought my legs might give out, and I leaned on the desk for support. It had never occurred to me that there could be more like Hendrik out there, and the moment I realized it, Hendrik knew. His eyes stared deep into mine and he offered a faint smile.

"That is enough for today, I think. Mr. Kye and Ms. Rivera, you may return to your room. Rest while you can. I will finish with Mr. Lawson and send final details soon."

"That's it?" Tryst asked. "But today is our last day. We don't have time—"

Hendrik raised his hand to silence her. "I assure you, Ms. Rivera, you'll have all that you require. Now, if you have a special request for dinner, please feel free to make it."

Soren and Tryst weren't fooled by the quick exclusion. Their faces revealed their suspicions, but they didn't put up more of a fight. Instead they left Hendrik and me alone, locked in a stare of frustration.

"You set us up," I said.

"I'm not certain I know what you mean."

"Yes, you do. You aren't unable to enter the forest, but if you go back it will break the oath." Hendrik's face remained still. His eyes swirled a darker blue than before, spiraling outward to consume the whites of his eyes. "If you go, the Genesis that remain will come for you."

He stepped back, putting distance between us. The swell of fear lingered at the edges of the room and a feral look came over him. His eye twitched and a part of me thought he might lunge forward and rip me to pieces. We both knew he was capable of as much. Instead, he remained statuesque.

"I served the witches of Blackwood for centuries," he informed me. "I took their beatings; I killed for them. I starved and suffered in ways you cannot fathom. And then I had freedom, lifetimes of it that ATOM snuffed out with the poke of a needle. And like my masters before them, I bled and killed and tortured and suffered, all so they would see me as weak. Weak enough to believe me on their side. Weak enough to trust me with a facility that trains their future prospects. Have you ever wondered how I managed to stay in a place like this for so long? It is not because I enjoy what I do, it is because I do what I must. It has given me the opportunity to get closer to Blackwood and closer to being what I once was. You will help get me there."

"And we're the cannon fodder, is that it?"

"ATOM is the monster, Mr. Lawson. Not I. Their genetic mutation has hidden what I am. They are the reason you no longer have your wings. They are the reason we are trapped in this prison. You long for what has been taken from you, but have lost only a piece. I have lost everything!"

"And I'm supposed to run into the dark forest and steal power that you swore never to touch again? Where does that leave me when the Genesis come calling?"

"It is true that when the Blackwood is opened and its life force released, my kin shall know. Will they come? I cannot say. They have been in hiding for ages. Should they come, they will see the reason for my actions and they will be forgiving. They would not wish enslavement upon our kind again. If they come, as I hope they will, we will be united as brothers and sisters. Once again the world will see the rise of Genesis."

"And what if they come and they don't want to unite? What if they want to keep true to their oath?" I asked.

"They won't."

"Well, if you're wrong, it's me and my friends on the line. If you're so certain, why don't you get the trinity yourself?"

"As I said, power is an addiction. Even for those once held captive by it." Hendrik's gaze faltered. His fingers fidgeted with one another and he looked lost. "I fear if I were to get too close, I would take too much. If I were to do that, the Genesis would not be so understanding. That is why I need you, Ash. I believe that the trinity is the key to restoring me, but I will not be tempted to relive the witches' history. Unlike some, I have learned from the past."

"Wait, you believe? You aren't sure?"

"Nothing is certain," he admitted.

"Well, you sounded pretty certain when we made this agreement. You're telling me we're risking our lives on a chance?"

"You're concerned about your wings," Hendrik said.

"You said you could give them back to me. If you have the

ability to do that, what are you waiting for? It would make Blackwood a hell of a lot easier to handle."

Hendrik's brows rose and he shook his head. "It is not in my repertoire at the moment, and if the Blackwood cannot fix me, then no, I cannot fix you either."

"So you made this deal on a whim to get me to agree?"

"I have very little doubt that this will not work, and your wings were nothing more than a sweetener. I thought freedom was more important than anything. Freedom for you and your comrades. Perhaps I misjudged you?"

"No." There was a tug of guilt. "Soren and Tryst are priority, but you promised me."

"Correction: I said what if there was a *chance* I could get you your wings back. I promised nothing."

"No, you said..." His finger came up to stop me and I paused, trying to remember his exact wording. The word *chance* echoed around every promise. I let myself be blinded by what I wanted to hear. "You played me."

"That was never my intention, though I'd be lying if I said I didn't use your desires against you. I apologize for that, but freedom alone is a gift worth dying for. You said so yourself."

It was as though my wings had been cut again. Their possible return faded like a feather drifting over the edge of canyon, rocking back and forth until it fell out of sight. I felt empty. Hendrik was right, I had been willing to die for freedom, but it was a lie to say I didn't dream of sailing through the skies again. The thought that I might have that chance had given me renewed hope. Maybe it was that hope that pushed me to attack Gage. Maybe what I wanted more than freedom was the chance to fly. Were they one in the same? At that moment, I wasn't sure.

"This doesn't bode well for trusting you."

"There is no choice but to trust. The evening is almost upon us. I seek to be returned to my former self; you seek freedom for your friends as redemption for the lives you've lost. That opportunity still stands before you. Take it, and perhaps your wings will find their way back to you as well."

I had been selfish. I knew that. It didn't make it hurt any less. I told myself the wings didn't matter. They were gone. But it didn't feel real. It felt like I was reeling in the loss for the first time all over again. I tried to shake it away. I wouldn't let it bring me down.

There was no time to dwell on the things I wanted that I could not have. Instead, I focused on what was within reach. Freedom. If not for me, than for Tryst and Soren.

"When do we leave?" I asked.

"Your room will be open at two in the morning. There will be no guard to escort you, but the path will be clear. Find your way to the east wing and exit through the garden. There you will find your supplies. Officials from ATOM will arrive here at six. That gives you a four-hour head start. With Colby and Gareth on separate patrols, we have limited opportunity, but I've formulated a distraction that will help."

"Then I better get some rest."

Hendrik sighed and placed a hand on my shoulder. I tensed at the sorcery that vibrated off his fingers. I knew the horror they could enforce.

"Animosity aside, I do believe Blackwood the answer to both our problems. I can protect you, Ash. You needn't worry," he assured.

I didn't believe him. How could I? But the truth was there were a lot of monsters in my way before I had to worry about Hendrik. As my father used to say, "Let's tackle one beast at a time, shall we?"

CHAPTER 27

Tonight. The word blitzed me with trepidation. Tryst and Soren felt it too. Both had nervous smiles and twinkles of fear in their eyes. We were really leaving.

Nine o'clock and the buzzer sounded. The door locked. A ghostly sound I'd hear for the last time. I lay on my bunk, staring at the rusted bars above. My stomach gurgled with delight. We'd had three trays of steaming food delivered. A parting gift from Hendrik, or a last meal. Meat had oozed juices onto the plate, mountains of potatoes swam in landslides of gravy that spilled over the edge. Salt and pepper had decorated long strands of green vegetables and swam in pads of butter. My senses had barely been able to handle the garlic and chives. The flavors rode me like electricity, and saliva still pooled in my mouth. It had been months since I'd had real food. It seemed a lifetime. In reality it was a blink compared to the time Soren and Tryst had been here. After the first bite they had laughed as though they didn't know how else to respond. Perhaps it was the only response fitting.

"Look at this, Tryst, look. I have a food baby!" Soren's belly looked swollen and he rubbed it back and forth.

Tryst laughed, and it made me smile. The food seemed to break down the walls she'd built around herself. "You're ridiculous."

A heavy sigh and his arms flopped on either side of him. "It doesn't even matter if we make it now. I thought I'd never taste real food again. I can die happy."

"That's not even a little funny."

"This is how I roll, Tryst. I keep it light and fluffy."

"Well, roll by yourself. I don't want to think about any of it right now."

"It's better than the paralyzing fear, isn't it?" I could hear the smile fall from his face. "Think about it: we're supposed to break out of the Academy, traverse a cursed forest, literally murder demonic beasts, all so we can get primordial tree blood to restore some ancient supernatural. I think I'll take light and fluffy right now."

"Well, it's a chance at freedom," Tryst whispered. "Better than the alternative."

"Yeah, well, I'm no killer." Soren shook the shaggy hair from his face. "What about you, Ash? You ever killed anyone?"

"Soren!" Tryst said.

"What? We're going into a demon-infested forest with real weapons and real monsters. I think we have a right to know if we stand a chance."

"You don't have to answer that, Ash," she said.

"It's fine," I said, but I didn't mean it. It wasn't fine. Thinking about it hurt. "Yes, Soren. Sadly, I have."

Tryst frowned. "What happened on the ship wasn't you're fault."

"You don't have to say that. It *was* my fault, but regardless, I wasn't talking about the boat.

Her face fell flat and Soren rolled onto his side, peering over the edge of the railing. "You mean?"

"I killed someone before that." I didn't know why I admitted it. I had spent half my life pretended it had never happened. There was a part of me, though, that craved honesty. A part of me that wanted them to know who they were working with. I stared at my hands and saw smears of red. "I was twelve. I'd left my colony and was on my own. I had no home, no food; I stole to survive. One night—" The words failed me. I swallowed hard and pushed past the discomfort. "A man—another supernatural—tried to take the food I'd stolen. It was for no other reason than the fact that I was an angel. For the most part, the world doesn't like us. They have reason enough, I suppose. But I wouldn't let him. He couldn't have it. He hit me, we fought, and then I killed him."

I hadn't just killed him; I'd destroyed him. He'd hit me in the face, and I dropped my loaf of bread into a puddle. I had lost control and beat him until my knuckles bled, but that wasn't the end of it. The wrath had thrummed through me and I unleashed it on the nearly incapacitated man. It had burned through his body and stole the color from his eyes. I could still smell the burned skin, and I'd never forget the black veins that rippled around his eyes. I shuddered. "But this time *will* be different." I repeated the words. If I said it enough times, could I make it true?

On the outside I helped people escape the country, and in return, I stood to gain a good amount of money. But it wasn't just the money. At least not at first. It was about helping people. As I sat on the bed, reliving the murder, I wondered if that was what I was doing now. Was I helping them or throwing their lives away in the hopes of getting something for myself?

"Ash? Are you okay?" Tryst knelt beside me, concern on her face. I was happy she was talking to me again, but I didn't deserve to be on the receiving end of her kindness.

I have to tell you something. I thought the words but I didn't say them. How could I? How could I tell her I agreed to Hendrik's offer once he'd sweetened the stakes and not a moment before? I had kept it from her and it ate away at me. The truth? I risked her life so that I might fly again. The reality swirled in my mind, even coming close to my lips, but I pressed them shut. I couldn't tell her. No. That wasn't true either. I *wouldn't* tell her.

"Yeah, fine." I offered the most sincere smile I could muster.

"Good." She smiled. "Don't beat yourself up about the past. We're going to get through this together. The future is where we need to be focused."

"She's right. Live together or die together. It'll be one or the other," Soren added.

"Soren! What happened to light and fluffy?" Tryst asked.

"What? It's true." He shrugged. "What does Hendrik think about our chances? He kept you behind today. What'd he say?"

The opportunity for truth rose again. I still couldn't give it to them. They were already scared. Hell, I was scared, but I needed them focused. If there was any chance that we could make it, they needed to believe in it. They didn't need to be bogged down with the details; they didn't need to know.

"He was just being Hendrik, you know? Making sure I knew how important this was to him. Reminding me of the stakes."

They were quiet. Tryst's eyes narrowed, questioning me. "You sure?"

"Uh, yeah? Why wouldn't I be?"

"I don't know. When you said that, I got a weird feeling. Like a shift in your aura."

Soren licked the air and raised a brow. "She's right. You do taste different."

I tried to keep my expression neutral, but whatever shift Tryst felt, she wasn't letting go.

"Ash, what is it?"

I cursed the both of them in my mind. Why couldn't they leave well enough alone? With that thought I realized how wrong I was. They'd done everything to keep me alive, and here I was throwing them in harm's way and lying to them about the reasons. They deserved truth.

"I..." The thought of coming clean made me queasy. My breaths came in rapid waves, chest tightening. "I wanted to escape so badly. I thought Blackwood was the door and all we had to do was open it. I didn't realize what we we'd be walking into. If I had I wouldn't have put you in this situation." I shook my head.

Tryst's hand touched my forearm. Her fingers wrapped around what they could and squeezed. "We all wanted—"

"Let me finish." I cut her off and pulled away. Her eyes saddened and it sent a pang through my chest. "When Hendrik first made the offer I said no. I wanted freedom, but not at the price he asked. I thought we'd stand a better chance on our own, but then he added something to it. Something I wanted—"

"What?" Soren asked.

"First, you have to understand that if I'd known how dangerous Blackwood really was, I never would have said yes." I sighed. "Maybe that's not true. I don't even know anymore."

"Ash, dude, spit it out. What did he offer you?" Soren asked. He looked sullen with fearful anticipation.

I shook my head, hoping it would clear my nerves. It didn't.

"He told me if I worked with him he'd grant me freedom, but also...he'd give me my wings back too." I waited for Soren to gasp or for Tryst to slap me across the face. Neither came. "It wasn't until after that I demanded your freedom too. I know it was stupid. I was only thinking about myself, not the danger you'd be in."

They still hadn't spoken. I stared at the floor like a coward. I couldn't look them in the eyes, not while I told them I risked their lives because I stood to benefit. My heart pounded like a bass drum, my temples throbbed, and when I could no longer stand the silence, I begged Tryst to say something.

"That was the real reason you made the deal. To help yourself," she said.

"No. I wanted freedom for us, I did! We'd been talking about escaping, but working with Hendrik seemed like more risk than it was worth. Then he said he could give me my wings back and it seemed like a bonus. Not only would he help us escape, I could fly again. I should have been straight with you from the start. I was afraid of how you'd react."

Tryst shook her head. "You disappoint me. Not because of what you did but because you kept it from us. Did you really think you couldn't tell us? It makes me wonder what else you're keeping."

"Nothing, I swear. You guys come first; you have to know that. I thought..." There was no justifying it. I made my decision and now I had to live with it. "I'm sorry. I didn't do it because I thought it was best for us, I did it because I wanted to fly again."

I finally looked at them, expecting beams of anger to shoot from their eyes. A lashing from Tryst's tongue to cut me to pieces, but they didn't look angry. Tryst had been telling the truth—she looked disappointed. Soren, on the other hand, didn't seem upset at all.

"Dude, you messed up," Soren said. "You kept the truth from us. That's not fair. We've been here for you every step of the way. I don't think it's too much to ask you do the same."

"I know, you're right. I—"

"But," he continued, "if I could have made a deal for freedom *and* a pair of badass wings, I would've too."

"What?" I looked up at him, confusion warping my features.

"Imagine it." He crouched to his knees and spread his arms, waving them up and down theatrically. "Soren Kye, deva extraordinaire and flying badass. Hell yeah. I'd rain leaves from the sky like a nature god! That'd be wicked."

"Are you kidding?" I asked. Tryst's lips were tight but Soren's animation had broken them into a grin. "I put you guys in this situation because of something I wanted. That wasn't fair. How can you not be pissed?"

"You put a lot on yourself, Ash," she said. "And a lot of it is unnecessary. You saw an opportunity to get us out. I told you that's what I wanted. It just so happened to come with a perk. Escaping through Blackwood on our own was a horrible idea. With Hendrik's help and knowledge we might make it. I think you made the right call working with him, but keeping this from us makes it hard to trust you. What if there's more we don't know?"

"There isn't, and I'll make this up to you. I promise."

"Okay, enough. You two are killing me!" Soren pretended to bang his head against the side of the bed. "We got it, Ash, you feel bad. And Tryst, you're disappointed. Time to get over it. Freedom isn't free. No matter how we planned to get outside of the gates, there was going to be a price to pay, and we're going to pay it tonight. Until then, I don't want to spend my last few hours dreading what's coming. If I'm going to die tonight, I'd like to at least spend some time fantasizing about what I'm dying for. Badass wings would be a great start. Do you think Hendrik can give me some too?"

In his own theatrical fashion Soren was right. Feeding the fear, the guilt, the anger—none of it made things better. We enhanced the beasts we nurtured. Instead, we distracted ourselves with what we might do on the outside and for a brief time I got lost in the fantasy. I could taste the steak and smell the smoke from the barbeque we dreamed about. Water clapped along the bank of the river not far from our potential home, and we joked about the jobs we might have. We relished the idea of having financial struggles or plumbing problems or shaking our fists at bad drivers, and then we enveloped ourselves in the idea of going off the grid. A cabin in the woods would be our home, fishing and hunting would provide our food. It was all a glorious dream.

All the talk must have exhausted Soren because somehow he managed to fall asleep, mouth gaping open and drool rolling along his chin. I admired how easily he found peace. I envied it. For Tryst and me there was none to be had. In a few hours the door would open and the rest of our lives would be waiting, or the end of them. My stomach tightened and I did my best to ignore the fear. I had to be strong like Tryst. She held it together through so much, and although she didn't deny being afraid, she didn't show it. She was strong in a way I wasn't; in a way most people weren't.

"Almost time. Want to get anything else off your chest before we plunge ourselves into darkness?" She smirked, but I could trace the apprehension in her eyes.

We watched the vampires assemble outside our window. Their advisor yelled orders and they dissipated into small groups, intent on doing their jobs as directed.

"In Hendrik's office today…" she said. "What was the real reason he told us to leave?"

I shrugged, trying to break the tension that mounted my shoulders. "It was about our deal. It's stupid."

"Ash, the three of us are leaving to enter a demonic forest and steal blood from a trio of ancient witches trapped in the earth and cursed to a tree. Ask me what sounds stupid right now?"

Her violet eyes pierced my soul and I shivered. She was fire, ferocious in a way most people couldn't be, yet the intelligence in her eyes examined me with a magnifying glass. I realized then that as much as I admired her strength, I hadn't given credit to her intellect. It made me wonder if she saw through me all the time. Was that why she wasn't angry? Did she know I had been keeping something? Did she know now? I didn't wait to find out.

I told her everything; explaining how I outed Hendrik for being a coward and sending us when he could go himself. I told her about the Genesis, and that taking blood from the Blackwood tree might beckon them to us. I also made it clear that I'd just learned this. I didn't want her to think I'd kept that a secret too.

"Wow," she said. "I can't believe you spoke to him like that. Not that it that matters, I suppose. It changes nothing. The *danger* remains the same."

"Of course it has. We have no idea what a true Genesis is even capable of. What if—"

"And it doesn't matter. Like Hendrik said, they might not even come. They've been in hiding. If they do, he'll reason with them. And if he can't, he'll be the one holding the bag. We're not keeping the blood for ourselves, remember? Hendrik wants it; he'll be the one dealing with the aftermath."

I sighed, tension gripping my shoulders. "I hope you're right."

"We're at risk no matter what: ATOM, Hendrik, Gareth, the guards, the demons of Blackwood, and whatever else might be in there. It's all a fight to get what we wanted—freedom. Soren was right, freedom isn't free, but neither is hope. You have to fight for that too. Right?"

I smiled. "Right."

"And so there's a chance the blood won't revitalize him. Who cares? That's not our problem." She paused, looking up at me. "But it is yours, isn't it?"

I nodded. "If it doesn't, I won't get my wings back."

"Oh…I'm sorry."

"No, it doesn't work like that. Not when I kept things from you. Freedom for you and Soren is more important than anything. You don't get to apologize to me."

"And why not? I understand why you did it, Ash. They're your wings. They're a part of you. It'd be the same if ATOM had cut off my arms or legs."

"It's not that simple."

"Isn't it? You act like we expect perfection," she said. "You act like you shouldn't have feelings and desires. News flash: none of us are perfect. If we were, life wouldn't be interesting; it would be grey and pointless. We make mistakes—all of us—I'm proof of that."

I laughed. "Mistakes? You always seem to have it all together."

"We all have our roles to play," she said, turning away from me. "Sometimes the hero, other times the villain."

"What does that mean?"

She shrugged. "Forget it. The point is I realized that you were right; I'd rather risk my life for a chance at freedom than die in here. You found a way to get us out, and it came with an opportunity to get something back that had been stolen from you. There's no harm in that."

"When you say it like that it sounds ridiculous."

Her hand touched my chest and she leaned in. "That's because it is ridiculous." She grinned.

Her touch lifted me like a cloud—effortlessly—and the stiffness in my shoulders broke away. A shiver moved across my chest; I wanted her closer. With the fear of what was to come and the possibility I'd never get to do it again, I wanted to wrap my arms around her in a tight hug and pull her against me, but after what had happened last time, I feared it would scare her. Regardless of my thoughts, the urge was too strong. My body betrayed me— acting on my desires—and I lost control. My hands gripped her hips and pulled her against me. When her body hit mine my pulse broke into a sprint. I froze, panicking at the action. Her shirt had slid up and the warmth of her skin touched the edges of my fingers. Adrenaline rushed through me and a ripple of cold shot through my veins, my nerves humming anticipation. I waited, fearful she'd pull away but wanting to give her the opportunity. Instead, she moved closer. The warmth of her breath moved across my arms and all the nerves that ricocheted inside me settled.

When I spoke, I whispered. I feared anything louder would break the moment. "Ever since the boat, I've felt like I can't do anything right, but you have a way of getting me out of my head. You saved me, Tryst. I didn't die in the Tank because of you, and everything you've made me feel since…I don't want to lose."

She laughed against me. "I think Soliloquy had more to do with that than me."

"No. It was before that—your voice, your words, the atmosphere around you. That's what made me pick up the vial. And when I got out, you were the reason I stayed straight. When I'm around you I feel…" My voice trailed off.

"What?"

"Stronger," I whispered. "I don't need my wings; you make me feel like I'm home."

I was certain she could feel the nervous tremor in my breath or the rampage of my heart, but her fingers circled my chest, calming me. I lifted her chin and her body tensed. She pulled away slightly.

"I…can't," she whispered.

"I'm not afraid, Tryst," I said.

"But I am," she said, studying my lips. When her eyes met mine, I could see the fear.

"Then let me be brave enough for both of us."

Our eyes were locked for a long moment. I feared I'd lose her. Feared that she'd pull away and a moment like this might never return. I was scared Soren was right. I'd almost given up hope, lessening my grip on her body, but then she nodded. She rose up slowly on the tips of her toes and hesitated, the edge of her lips brushing mine. Her breath trembled. So did mine. Her fingers pressed into my chest, crawling upwards toward my neck. She pulled me down toward her and if possible, I pulled her a little bit closer. Our lips touched and time stopped, but it was a kiss destined to be unfinished.

The latch on the door unlocked and the sound startled us. We pulled away. Our moment had been shattered. My pulse shifted from intense excitement to a fearful sprint. Red digits on the clock showed two o'clock and the door creaked inward, exposing an empty hall. Our moment was gone. Something bigger had arrived.

CHAPTER 28

As Hendrik promised, three bags awaited us along the brick-walled flower beds. A glass blade was sheathed into the side of each of them. They were heavier than expected, or maybe the fear of getting caught as we snuck through the Academy had weighted me more than I anticipated. Every creak in the floor, every whisper in the distance, all of it had sent my senses into overdrive. Now we were here awaiting a distraction to veil our escape, and all we were missing was Gage.

I paced the garden. Even with the walls providing cover, I felt exposed. Each minute that passed increased the chance that we'd be caught. My hands felt clammy and I stared at the door. Where was he? I checked my wrist several times for the watch that wasn't there. This was taking too long. Something wasn't right.

"You're making it worse," Tryst said

"He should have been here by now."

"Let's go without him," Soren suggested.

"We can't. We need him." I didn't like Gage, but he was a fighter. We wouldn't survive Blackwood without him.

"What if he had a change of heart?" Tryst asked.

"What if something went wrong?" I replied. "Whatever distraction we were supposed to get should've happened by now."

"We should go back." Soren sounded worried. His face looked even worse.

"We're not going back. I told you I'd get us out of here, and I will. Relax." Gage would be here. He had to be. He'd waited six years for this. He wouldn't let it slip away.

Another minute passed and my knees grew weak at the sound of Gareth's voice. We froze, panic circling like a tornado waiting to devour us. I ran back to the metal door that led to the gardens. Locked.

"Tell Colby to take soldiers around the east side and make sure it's clear. The officers will be here in four hours. I don't want anything to go wrong."

I felt the color drain from my face. We were too close. It couldn't fall apart now. I pushed Tryst and Soren against the wall, ordering them to get down as low as they could. They laid on the ground, using a flower bed as shelter. I pressed against the stone, ignoring the bites and burns of metal dust against my skin. I tried to gain cover from a small plant that sprouted leaves in erratic fashion. The leaves were thin, folding in gentle curves. It was like trying to hide an elephant behind a palm tree.

Gareth appeared in the opening. I hoped he'd keep walking but he stopped. His voice trailed and brow furrowed at the guard.

"Sir?" the guard asked.

Gareth silenced him with a finger and sniffed at the air. He turned toward the garden and for a moment, I swore he looked me right in the eye. Breath caught in my throat. I expected a roar of anger or a change in expression. He glanced at his watch, raised a brow, and then scanned the garden once again.

"Must be nothing," Gareth said, followed by a thunderous boom erupting in the distance.

The ground shook and my heart leaped in my throat as fire shot into the air on the other side of the yard. It lit the sky in a flare of orange, clouds of grey smoke smearing a perfectly black sky. Voices rang through the night, vampiric growls scattering in the darkness. Hues of orange and red and yellow danced alongside one another like an army of flaming soldiers who could hear a song that eluded the rest. Gareth bolted toward the explosion, screaming at the guards to stop the escape. My legs quivered as I inched my way toward the garden's entrance. Soren's hands clung to the back of my shirt like a child trying to stay close in a crowd.

Spurts of flame seared the Academy's barrier walls. A hole blasted not far from the one we'd repaired. Guards crowded together with weapons drawn as vampires fled to the outside world. Gareth screamed and guns fired. Vampiric growls roared in response, guards screaming with wild desperation as they were mauled.

"We need to go. Now," I said. There was no more waiting.

We broke into a sprint to the north. My legs felt weak with fear but weightless with adrenaline and I cut across the yard with unnatural speed. Soren and Tryst surprised me with their ability to keep up. We'd spent so much time as prisoners that I'd forgotten what we were: supernaturals. We moved in a blur like a blade through water, and the forest grew in front of us. Even in the darkness of night the wall of shadows inside the woods seemed black beyond compare. The closer we came, the more intimidating the woods seemed, but I didn't hesitate and I didn't look back. I feared the action alone would expose us. We wouldn't be deterred now. We couldn't. This was it.

A few hundred yards from the woods someone jumped from the shadows. My feet stopped, grinding into the earth and tearing up the grass. I withdrew my blade, fear lancing my chest. I tackled the invader to the ground. I expected Colby or a patrol guard. I wasn't ready to kill, but I was ready to make sure we got away. My blade pressed against their throat, a line of smoke rising from the skin. His eyes glistened silver and I cursed the arrogant smirk on Gage's face.

"What the hell are you doing?" I asked. "We were waiting for you!"

He laughed, which tempted me to hit him with the edge of the blade. "I've been out here waiting damn near an hour for you and your raggedy crew. I thought you chickened out."

Anger rose in my throat but I swallowed it down. Gage was being Gage. It shouldn't have surprised me.

"Come on, slowpokes," he said, shoving me off and jumping to his feet. He sprinted into the woods. He didn't hesitate or show an ounce of fear; his body vanished past the first line of trees and then he was gone. I waited for a sound: leaves rustling or branches cracking. I would've settled for the sound of dirt shuffling. Nothing.

Tryst and Soren looked at one another with glimmers of fear, holding hands as they followed the typhon into the trees. I shivered. The clutch of the forest wrapped around me, reminding me of the Tank's ability to coax hot and cold across my skin. More gunshots rang through the night and Gareth's voice ordered the guards to regroup, spread out, and search the property. I didn't wait to see what happened next. I held my breath and took the plunge, letting the cover of trees devour me.

The leaves were wet as they slapped against my skin. Then came darkness, tight and slithering around my body. I pressed onward. My legs felt slow and heavy like they were running through water. The skin on my scalp tightened and a shiver engulfed my body before I broke through the other side.

Through the black curtain, normalcy returned, but another world unfolded. Moss-covered stones sparkled and thickets of brush decorated in blue, red, and orange berries created a wall along the far edge of the woods. The ground felt hard and dry. It was desperate for moisture, yet somehow the trees remained strong and alive with trunks too large to reach around. Bushes were strewn about sporadically, branches covered in beautiful flowers and wild barbs that put a rose's thorns to shame. Croaks echoed, demonstrating life within the forest, but growls followed. I drew my blade as the noise reverberated, but it seemed impossible to decipher their origin. The sound bounced from tree to tree like rain off a stone, splashing in every direction.

"Got one of those for me, Flapper?" Gage eyed the blue glass blade in my hand.

"Hell no. You're dangerous enough without one."

Gage laughed. "On a scale of supernatural powers, it's not like you're lacking. If anything, I should get one of those and you should trudge forward empty handed."

"Ready?" I asked the others, ignoring Gage completely.

Soren's eyes were wide, his face pale with a hue of grey creeping in. He shook his head while frantic eyes scoured the shadows. Tryst grabbed his arm and coaxed him forward.

"As we'll ever be," she said. She drew her blade but looked awkward holding it. She wasn't comfortable with the weapon. Sometimes I forgot that not everyone was born with a blade in hand. It made me realize Gage and I were a different breed. I grimaced at the thought that we had anything in common.

The dirt heaved and sighed as we trampled forward on uneven ground. It seemed to move in waves, up and then down before a brief plateau. Water trickled in the background, and a low rumble hummed, vibrating the earth. We moved at a careful pace, each sound jerking us in a different direction. When I looked back at the path we'd walked, it had changed. The trees had moved on their own accord, the leaves' pigment faded, and the bark itself took on a different shade. At times I thought new trees had sprouted up altogether, while other times it seemed they'd disappeared. The forest felt alive. It moved as a living creature, a labyrinth of potent energy that attempted to force us in a single direction. We were without a golden path to lead our way, but the forest swept us up and took us where it wanted us to go.

"What did Hendrik tell you?" Gage asked. "What are we looking for?"

"He told me a lot of things, but right now you're on a need-to-know basis."

A strike of anger rippled across his face. "Don't think you're going to pull a fast one on me. We had a deal. Without me you aren't here right now. Don't forget that."

"I remember the deal, and giving you information wasn't part of it," I said. "You worry about keeping everybody alive and we'll all get what we want."

"Damn straight I will," he said, a silver fire burning in his eyes. "And if you need a reminder of what will happen if you play me, let me know."

I felt eyes burning into me. At first I thought it was the heat from Gage's anger, but as I fell back on the trail and let him get ahead, the sensation didn't leave. We were being watched. Eyes were everywhere but nowhere to be seen. They lingered in alleyways of shadows and decrepit trees. The branches themselves seemed to wane downward toward me, following my every movement. I ducked beneath their wooden grasps, tension riding my spine.

A canopy of leaves formed above us, branches swaying to block the moonlight. Darkness engulfed the woods, and our flashlights didn't help. The farther inward we went the thicker the darkness became. Trees and brush scraped along my arm and broke the skin, a tiny crack of blood filling the crevice. I brushed it off, expecting such a minor scuff to close, but when it didn't heal, I was reminded of the Tank. No sooner did I think it, the temperature shifted. One minute sweat clung to my neck, the next I shivered.

Hendrik's lesson came in a barrage of words that flooded my mind. I stopped, the earth still trembling beneath my feet. Shadows twisted and turned like black sheets in the wind. I stared into them, squinting as if I could penetrate the darkness. Icy breath caressed the back of my neck. I turned sharp and quick, blade drawn and glistening with a sapphire glow. Nothing. Sulfur clung to the air and an aftertaste of salt grated my tongue.

Soren and Tryst had stopped; everyone stared in a different direction. I felt a brush of cold in front of me. It bit at my skin and I stepped away, blade at the ready. My back pressed against the bark of a tree, but at least my rear was covered. The air continued to chill, clouds of breath spilling from my lips. We each monitored a section of the forest, yellow flashlights panning back and forth. When Tryst's beam shone over me, I squinted and covered my eyes, telling her to lower it.

"Ash?" The beam wavered and dots floundered in my vision. When I could finally see, I found Tryst's eyes wide with terror. Soren and Gage mimicked her expression and they all stumbled back.

The bark moved against my back. My heart made a heavy thud. The world seemed to slow. Blood coursed through my veins and cold sweat tickled the side of my neck. I inhaled deeply and turned to find a massive tree with black-and-brown-speckled bark creasing the wood. A cloud of darkness swirled a few feet above me, swallowing the top of the tree. All at once the bark seemed to move and two almond-shaped holes lifted. Empty white eyes without pupils stared back at me.

A blast of darkness ignited and pushed me back. It stole my breath and I stumbled, crawling back as a face pressed out of the bark: a nose first, then the curve of lips formed in the knotted wood. Black gnarled teeth parted and clanked together like a hammer on metal, dark goo oozing from between them. A body formed, stretching the bark outward with a loud creaking noise before it couldn't handle the force. The tree's outer layer shattered and shards of wood rained over the ground. A creature stood before us. A man. A cloth hung over his groin; the rest of him exposed with skin as black as the goo between his teeth, and white distended scars covering his body in intricate designs.

Gage's hand pulled me to my feet. "What the hell is that?" he asked.

"Demon," I said, squeezing the blade's handle. It responded with a will of its own: shimmering with a flash of blue that flickered inside. Strength and speed simmered together, vibrating outward from the handle and flowing through me.

The creature unleashed a primordial roar, dark fluid fluttering out of his mouth and over white lips. Clouds of breath pooled around him, contorted teeth hanging from his gums. His fingers were long, dark fingernails like the claws of a bear swiping at the open air in front of him. Adrenaline surged and the fight-or-flight instinct kicked into gear. I thought to turn everybody around and run, but the demon didn't give us a chance.

He lunged forward with incredible speed. Before I formed a reaction, heat and fire flared up beside me. Gage's skin hardened to stone and he plunged his fist into the earth, coming out with a handful of dirt and rock. His fingers squeezed around it, the lines of red that trickled through the crevices of his arm brightened. Flares of red spiraled around his fist and turned the earthy debris into a hardened ball of flame. He pitched it forward and the fireball became imbedded in the center of the demon's chest. The creature stopped. Streams of fire wrapped around him and seared his flesh. He glanced at the wound and then to us before releasing a shriek. Clawed hands peeled the rock from melted flesh. It made a wet sound when it broke free of the skin and he dropped it to the earth. The hole in his chest smoked, burned flesh filling the air. He growled and turned his sights to Soren who cowered behind Tryst. He gnashed his teeth and the sound of nails on a chalkboard screeched. He charged toward them and I ran forward, slamming into him from the side. My face became embedded in gooey flesh as we tumbled to the ground and broke apart. I rolled away, the black substance clinging to my face. I peeled it back like a wad of chewed gum, the residue burning.

I clambered to my feet, but the creature was already attacking. Claws tore through the air and I threw up my arm to protect my face. They cut into the skin like a hot knife through butter. A flash of warmth coated my arms and blood splattered the dull leaves at my feet. I swung the blade wildly, glass slashing into his belly. Black ooze ran from the wound. It was a good strike, but the demon didn't flinch. His claws came back down and I jumped back, a breath of sulphuric air brushing my face. The edge of my dagger cut across his thigh, and I pushed it hard against him. Muscles snapped and coiled beneath the skin. The demon dropped to his knees without making a sound. Pain was a figment of the mind, and the demon's mind had been twisted. He lived to serve the forest. To him, it seemed, there was no pain. My heart hammered inside me, chest hurting with panicked breaths. The demon was weakened, exposed, but what next? I knew how to fight. I didn't know how to kill.

Blood gushed from his wound, black liquid spilling down his leg. He grunted, almost unable to stand. He limped forward, his leg unable to withstand any weight. Animalistic growls reverberated in his throat and he swung to hit me, but I stepped away with ease, watching him struggle. He stumbled onto his hands and knees, pieces of bark embedded in his skin, interrupting the pattern of white scars that covered his torso. He wheezed for air, dark ooze pooling around him. A clawed hand swung out at my legs and I jumped away, adjusting my weapon.

"Kill him!" Gage's voice commanded.

I held the blade downward, prepared to strike. The demon crawled toward me, his injured leg dragging behind him. At first I thought to stab him through the back and penetrate his heart. Then I circled around and shifted my stance. I'd cut off his head. Quick and easy. I raised the blade and the creature looked up at me. I wondered if he knew his end had come. Perhaps he wished for it? Was this demonic prison hell for him? Was he thankful to have someone break his soul free? His colorless eyes met mine and a circle of sea green appeared, a dilated pupil in the center. My breath caught in my throat. For a moment I didn't see a monster that needed to be killed, but a tortured man from my past.

A man crawled forward, begging forgiveness. Cuts and bruises disfigured his face, blood rushing from his lips. One eye had swelled shut while the other—a murky green—pleaded with me. Profuse apologies fell from broken lips. I didn't listen. I hadn't cared. I'd been angry and nothing would stand in the way of my independence. He had begged me to stop—a jinn pleading forgiveness. I wouldn't hear it. He sought to take from me and failed. Now I would take from him. I unleashed the wrath, and left him nothing more than a smoking corpse awaiting a transformation to ash. But the sweet trickle of vengeance eluded me. Instead, I tasted anger and regret. I heard the gurgle in his throat as he choked on his own blood and watched life vanish from his eyes. It haunted me and I vomited over the pavement. Murderer.

"Do it!" Gage cheered.

The world rushed back and the demon had closed the gap between us. A clawed hand gripped my ankle and I stumbled back.

I kicked and struggled to break away, but even hurt the demon's strength was unmatched. If I hadn't killed the man in that alley so many years ago, he might have killed me. Now my hesitation could be the end.

Black goo covered my pants as the demon's hand wrapped around my leg. His grip was incredible. The tips of his claws dug into my flesh and I cried out, trying to kick him away. It was no use. My foot smashed into his face and his head jerked back, but he was relentless in his pursuit. He dragged me closer, my body jerking across the dirt. Gage ran down the hill, tore the blade from my hand, and brought it up and down in a single motion. A heavy thud and the demon's head hit the ground, rocking back and forth against the dirt. Blood squirted from his neck, muscles and tendons shriving inside the corpse as it collapsed to the ground.

Gage's eyes were wild. Blood dripped from the blade, and his eyes seared into me. "If you won't kill to survive, you'll never make it." He stabbed the blade into the ground and glared at me. "You're going to get us all killed." He trudged up the hill and vanished over the crest.

The demon's body lost all color. The black faded and only white remained. It began to crumble, flakes of skin peeling back and falling to the ground as it turned to ash. Crunchy bloodstained leaves swirled around it and the corpse shifted. It broke apart as the wind picked up and swept away the remains, carrying them to the forest's ceiling. When the wind died, the leaves fluttered like feathers back to the earth, cleansed of blood and revived. I picked up a bright green leaf. It felt soft and flexible in my hand. Out of death comes life.

Soren and Tryst stood at the top of the hill, their eyes were scarred with horror. We'd now seen firsthand what Blackwood had to offer. As much as we'd talked about it, none of us had been prepared. My heart hammered in my chest, my breaths came in ragged waves, and my hands quivered. After I had murdered the man in the alley, I'd made an oath to keep the wrath buried forever. The wrath meant death, and I would never kill again. Ironic now that if I wanted to survive, I would have no other choice.

CHAPTER 29

Part of me felt pity for the beast. The part of me that didn't feel pity felt weak like Uncle had always said I was. If he were here, he'd be furious. He had raised me after my parents died, or more accurately, he had trained me. I wanted a father; he wanted a soldier. If he knew I'd been such a coward, he'd have beaten me. I shuddered at the thought, unsure why he came to mind. The more I looked around these woods, the more I was reminded of home. I knew the demon was a monster but I hadn't prepared myself to kill. I wondered how that reality had eluded me. Perhaps it was because the way we thought things would be and the way they turned out were rarely the same.

The temperature had balanced. The air humid and heavy. My shirt clung to my back, broken leaves and smears of blood slipping out from beneath the bandage I'd wrapped around my arm. It was a flesh wound, but the demon's claws could have done a lot more damage if he'd gotten a hold of me. If I hadn't taken the severity of this place serious enough before, I did now. It was dangerous.

Gage took command, leading us through a quarry of trees and brush. I lingered at the back while he lectured us on the difference between life and death. We didn't need it, but he felt we did. After what had happened, I didn't blame him. If we weren't willing to kill, we'd be killed. Plain and simple. It was the logic of war. But we weren't at war; we were on a quest for liberty. Or were they one in the same?

"Right, Flapper?"

"What?" I had tuned him out. I doubted he had anything different to say now versus a few hours ago.

"You want to live, don't you? Or would you rather see your friends dead because you can't pull the trigger?" His silver eyes were arrogant and focused. I shook my head and tried to step past him but he grabbed my arm. "You think this is a joke?" He leaned in, attempting dominance.

I responded without words, grabbing his wrist and twisting it back. His grip broke but I didn't let up. I forced it back at an awkward angle and he dropped to a knee. I unsheathed the blade and pressed it against his throat. The skin didn't smoke, but I knew how sharp the edge was. I'd watched it slice through all the muscles and bone in that demon's neck.

"I know how to fight, don't worry about it." I whispered the words.

He didn't flinch, but he was careful not to move. "But can you pull the trigger?"

I looked at the blade against his neck. I had hesitated once, but I wouldn't make that mistake again. "You're a tagalong. You're here because I allowed it. In case you need a refresher, you've been at the Academy for six years and couldn't get done what I did in five months. Get over yourself."

He was on the brink, his wrist threatening to snap, but he gritted his teeth and put on his tough face. "You're a coward. All you angels are. It's your lack of finesse—"

I pushed his wrist until I felt it pop, careful not to break it. When he cried out, I smashed my fist into the side of his face and let him go. The force slammed him to the ground and I waited for him to get up. Instead, he rolled onto his back and kept his hands in the air.

"Hey, I *thought* we were on the same team! At least we were when I saved your ass back there."

"Same team? That's up to you." My face felt flushed and I regretted my actions. We *were* on the same team, but I had months of resentment built up toward him, and I felt embarrassed for what had happened with the demon. I let that control me. It wasn't his fault I'd been afraid. It was mine. I took a breath and collected myself. "I shouldn't have acted like that. You're right, we're in this together." I offered him a hand but he refused it.

"Are we?" he asked, narrowing his gaze. "Try to remember that the next time you want to attack somebody trying to teach you something."

I tried not to let his attitude get to me, taking a page out of Soren's light and fluffy book. "It's all right, Gage. I accept your apology. You were a douche and acted out of line."

"What? I never apol—" He squinted and shook his head. "Whatever, Angel Boy. Let's keep moving."

I felt a hint of amusement seeing his frustration. It was almost more satisfying than hitting him. As we walked, I wondered if Gage realized how much of a jerk he could be, or if he believed he was really just playing a role. The ever-changing expressions that came over his face made me think he wasn't sure either. Was it possible he felt as lost as I did?

We decided on keeping a formation as we walked: Tryst and Soren watched the left and right, Gage had the back, and I took the front. We had eyes in each direction. For a while it seemed to work, but then I noticed something else—the forest itself had shifted. The walls of brush that once lingered on the outside edges of the woods had moved in, and the farther we traversed, the more noticeable it became. Thorny limbs and bright-colored berries grew up on either side of us, and before long we found ourselves on a narrow trail. When we thought to turn back, the forest we'd left behind was gone. The trail we were on seemed an endless aisle in either direction. Frustrations grew, but I reminded myself that it wasn't up to us to find the way. The forest would take us where it wanted.

As we walked, the path became blocked with a massive tree that lay sideways across the ground. Roots gushed from the earth, slices of bark hung off its dead trunk, and a mist of dirt and dust floated around it, fabricating a haze that made it hard to see more than a few feet in any direction. Walls of brush hung on either side of us, wooden tendrils with sharp spikes woven together made it impossible to penetrate. There was no way to avoid the obstacle. We'd have to break formation and climb over the tree one at a time.

A twig snapped and we all turned, yellow beams cutting the darkness. Silence. My ears and eyes strained to pick up whatever lurked in the distance, but we were surrounded by heavy clouds of dust and a thicket of green plant life. The soft hum we'd felt when we entered the forest returned. It shook the ground like a quiet machine trekking across the earth.

"Here we go again, Flapper," Gage said. "You should decide now if you're going to fight or roll over and let whatever's coming gut us all."

He wasn't worthy of a response. I remained steadfast and drew my blade. I *was* ready.

The quiet felt heavy, enhancing the fear that swirled around it. Gage didn't admit it, but he felt it too—I saw it on his face. My pulse felt deep and slow and I kept my breaths long and quiet. A tickle moved over my skin as I swiped at an invisible spider that crawled along my arm. Even seeing there was nothing there, I still felt something moving.

"We can't just lie in wait, we need to keep moving," Tryst said. We all agreed. There was no use standing still and waiting for something to strike. We had to act.

The log's bark moved, shifted, and sighed as Tryst began to climb. It was too thick around to manage on her own, so I boosted her up first. Flakes of wood broke away and rained over my face. I coughed and tightened my lips, avoiding the shower of black that fell over me. Gage refused help. He took a few steps and leaped over it with vigor. He reached the top in an otherworldly bound, grinning before lunging over the other side. Soren wasn't as quick to trample the obstacle. He touched the moist, dead wood, and a look of sadness clung to his face.

"Someone did this," he whispered. His eyes held a gloss that didn't shed tears, but a wall of them built up in his eye. "The tree's spirit has not passed. It's still dying, but something won't let it go."

"I know you see this world different than the rest of us, Soren, but we don't have time for this. We *need* to go." I spoke softly. He wasn't the type to respond to urgency. He had to be handled a specific way.

His fingers traced the lines of bark before pressing his hand over the wood. I felt a pulse of energy shimmer around him. Bright green dots sparked between his fingers and spiraled around his palm. It filled the creases along the wood, running down like tiny green rivers. It felt cool like dew-covered leaves in early morning sun, but as Soren exhaled a breath laced with relief, a violent coughing fit started.

"Soren, you okay?"

He didn't answer, stumbling back with wide eyed panic. His voice rasped and he struggled to draw a breath. He hit his chest again and again as if he could dislodge whatever was stuck in his throat, but there was no change. He pawed at his neck and dropped to his knees. Saliva pooled from his mouth and his skin became ghostly. His body bucked before a wave of vomit spilled from his lips. It gushed out in unnatural volume, and he wheezed for air in between convulsions.

"Whoa, are you all right?" I gagged and covered my face, kneeling beside him. The vomit smelled acrid, like it had been sitting there for years and someone peeled back the layer of mold that had grown over the top to seal it.

Another wave of vomit came, this time followed by a very real breath. He gasped. "This place…it's sick." He wiped his mouth and drew in another breath. "The nature is corrupted." He looked suddenly exhausted, eyes fluttering like he might lose consciousness.

"Soren, what can I do?"

He stood up and stumbled back to the tree, pressing his hands and forehead against it. The tears that had threatened to fall now ran down his cheek. He pressed more magic against the bark, and then all at once drew it back. He shuddered, exhaling a long breath.

"It's gone now—the tree's spirit—to a better place. How anything can grow here is beyond my expertise. The soil, the air, the atmosphere—it's polluted with darkness, Ash. All of it."

"Soren?" Tryst sat perched at the top of the log, concern scrawled across her face. "Can you walk?"

His eyes wandered the path before finding her. He shrugged.

"We need to go," she said. "The sooner we get to the tree, the sooner we can get you out of here."

She tried to offer support but she didn't look well either. Bags had formed under her eyes, and her skin had paled. How long had we been here? It seemed like days. I yawned, suddenly feeling exhausted myself. Blackwood was gnawing away at all of us.

"Took you long enough," Gage said. He tapped his foot and stared at his wrist as if it held the time.

"Save it," Tryst said, helping Soren down the other side.

"Whoa! Take it easy, Nature Boy." Gage patted Soren hard on the back. "No need to cry. It's a tree. Look around, there are plenty."

Soren shoved Gage's hand away with an aggression I'd seen only once before. Lucky for Gage he didn't have a shovel this time.

"Screw you," he snapped. "You could never understand. It's beyond your realm of comprehension. Nature is not for the unintelligent."

Tryst smirked, helping Soren balance as he walked. The typhon's face ripened with anger. Gage stepped forward as if to assert some form of dominance, but I intercepted him, pushing him back.

"Leave it," I said.

He huffed liked a child, angry eyes flickering between us. He slapped my hand away and turned back toward the rotted tree. Heat engulfed his arm. Stone covered the skin, lines of lava coaxing their way through the crevices. He let out a growl and cocked back his fist, smashing fiery knuckles into the wood. The soft log broke inward with a moist thud. Strings of it clung to his arm as he pulled it out, smoke rising from the wet bark. He held out a handful of the tree's remains and threw them on the ground.

"It's. Just. A. Tree. Get over it." His gaze lingered, hoping to entice a reaction from Soren, who turned around with sadness still drawn upon his face.

A squeak came. Once. Twice. Then as a string of sounds like a cricket's song. It started faint, growing with each note, and the air grew cold. Mist spilled between my lips like a cloud. The sound came again and a skittering echoed from within the log. Gage backed away, pushing me toward it. His smoldering hand seared the fabric of my shirt.

"Go check it out, Flapper."

The skittering became loud, a stampede of scampering alongside an orchestra of squeals. An entourage of black and red spilled from the hole. Massive beetles the size of my hand swarmed the bark. Next came ants in a wave of red, followed by smaller beetles the size of my palm, but faster and more sporadic than their predecessors. They leaped from left to right, ranting in a choir of chitters as they trampled down the log and over the earth.

There was no need for a command. We all turned to run. Leaves slapped against us on either side of the path, there was only one way to go. The insects filled the path behind us, moving up along the thorny walls and covering the green with black and red. Flakes of wood filled the air as the insects devoured everything in their path like a mobile woodchipper. We moved at inhuman speeds. It wasn't enough. Every few steps they closed the distance.

Tree trunks began to fall through the wall of shrubs that encased us in the alley of pests. They were shredded by waves of scuttling legs that devoured them in a single surge. The flashlights became a hindrance, reflecting back on us as sawdust and debris clouded the air. A massive trunk landed in front of us, blocking us in for a second time. It was bigger than the first; there was no way we'd scale it in time.

Bugs hovered in front of us, an endless line of antennae, legs, and glowering eyes. Mandibles opened and closed like shears, metal on metal screeching. Fangs dripped green fluid as spiders inched forward. Their legs rubbed together and the tiny hairs that covered them fluttered into the air. My eyes watered and skin itched as they touched me. We had moved back as far as we could. The freshly fallen tree pressed against us and the vermin closed in.

The critters stopped their pursuit and united, merging together and defying gravity. They climbed upward in the air, building on top of one another. Black and red swirled together, spiraling up until they created a human-shaped figure. The gaps were filled until a dark body took form. At first it had been a silhouette of a person, but before long, defined features took shape: arms first, then shoulders, then legs that separated and walked toward us. Pieces of his body solidified as the bugs compounded. His cheeks became defined, his brow hanging drastically over his eyes. He was thinner than the last demon, but his eyes were as white as milk when they fluttered open. A pool of bugs spilled out around him, chanting their song like a god to be worshipped.

"What do we do?" Tryst shouted.

Soren reached out and unsheathed his blade, holding it awkwardly.

The beast growled and more bugs scaled his body. They gnawed at his flesh and slipped beneath his skin, settling in as his body absorbed them. His muscles became defined and his eyes glowed. A sinking feeling pressed against me as sulfur and rot filled the air.

Gage laughed, pushing Soren's blade down. "Right, like that's going to be enough. I'll take care of it." The sound of fire crackled along his arms as the rocky form took over. He scooped up a handful of dirt once again, but this time his entire arm ignited in flame. Magic and heat pulsed around him, and Soren shouted at him to stop, but the typhon didn't listen. I grabbed his wrist and jerked it back. The burn was instant and scalded my palm.

"What the hell are you doing?" he snapped.

"Fire isn't the answer," I said, waving my scorched palm in the air.

"It is when you have that coming toward you!"

"We're surrounded by wood, idiot," Tryst shouted. "We'll be trapped."

"You got a better idea, sweetheart?" he asked. "Or maybe our fearless leader will wave his blade in the air and then do *nothing*."

I scanned the area. There was no way out. Even if there were, we weren't going to outrun them. We'd already lost that fight.

"Ash?" Tryst pleaded.

Fear built in my chest as the chittering grew. The demon became a muscular beast with fangs that put a serpent's to shame. When he opened his mouth, a long forked tongue spilled out. It ran down his arms, slurping up the few stray critters that remained. They crunched between brown teeth, gloops of yellow liquid sputtering down his chin. His bones clicked and ground together. Black skin broke open and something thick and red slid out, covering parts of his arms and legs in bright red armor. His lips parted and the chittering sound that had haunted us screeched from his lips.

"Back up," I said.

Gage scoffed. "What are you going to do, try to talk him down?"

"I said back up!"

If I wanted us to survive, if I wanted *any* chance at freedom, I'd have to break the promises I made to myself. I made those promises to stay sane and alive, but right now, both of those were at risk. Stay and die, or fight for a chance to survive.

Magic rose from my soul. It had been a long time since I'd felt it fully, and like a floodgate that hadn't been opened in years, it broke through with unrelenting force. Heat thrust through my veins, forcing unease to ripen in my stomach. My hands trembled. Nervousness clenched my throat. Magic, no matter how long you tried to deny it, was never truly gone. You never forgot what it was like to wield it, but the longer you went, the less control you had, and I'd never had control of the wrath. It was one of the reasons

I'd sworn never to use it, but if we were going to die, it would be by my hand, not his.

The magic felt hot. It siphoned upward in a torrent, unfurling from my soul and stretching into my limbs. It filled me with a loose tension like an elastic being stretched for the first time. It swelled like a forgotten muscle and expanded into my hands. Only a spark at first; a knife against a stone. As it grew, light swelled and angelic command flourished between my fingers. The air moved, whipping the hair across my face. Sparks flickered over my skin, coils of otherworldly force snapping between my fingers. It cracked like electricity, biting at my flesh. I cringed. My jaw flexed so tight my teeth hurt.

The ground quaked as the beast broke into a run, roaring his embryonic thunder. Insects spilled out behind him like a pair of shadowed wings, charging ahead to weaken our defenses. Steaks of gold spilled from my palm. I screamed for everybody to get back as energy crackled up my arms. My body trembled, arms and legs threatening to give out. Attempting to contain it was like carrying a weight far too advanced for my ability. Relentless power washed over me and as it grew, it burned. It scalded my insides in untrained release. The demon was close; a few strides away. Control or not, I had no choice but to let go.

I held my breath and braced for impact. I screamed through gritted teeth and unleashed the angelic wrath I'd never trained. Spears of light thrust forward and sliced the darkness like a thousand white spears sailing through a shadow. The front line of insects was blown away, arachnids crashing backward like a rejected tide. A second pulse reached farther, slaughtering the ants and beetles that shielded the demon. The creature stumbled back, red armor melting and bleeding into his skin. Light spilled around me, a golden blaze swallowing the demon's form. The power stretched out in tendrils like a wraith's hand about to devour its enemy. Sulfuric darkness pooled off the beast, but as my magic penetrated through it, there was something else. A glimmer. A spark of life. A piece of humanity? I'd seen a flicker of it in the other demon, and here it was again. The thought distracted me and my power faded, but when the demon unleashed a fierce roar, the energy spiked. The wrath seared everything around me. My body trembled, heart jackhammering inside and ready to burst. Tears and magic singed my eyes as I felt the cry of his soul waning. I couldn't stop even if I wanted to. I'd lost control.

The wildness of the wrath frightened me. I tried to pull it back, but funnels spilled around me. Lances of gold jumped from my palms and snapped at the air. The walls of brush vanished in a radiated wave that left behind nothing but sticks. Smoke billowed everywhere, sulfur and ash burning my throat. A golden spike tore through my arm and ejected from my hand like a javelin, hammering into the demon. Dirt exploded like a grenade; beetles, ants, and spiders detonated at once. Green and yellow guts gushed while black and red shells disassembled and fell like rain. The darkness was gone, but so was whatever life had remained deep inside the creature.

I couldn't breathe. My body ached and I cried out, trying to pull the power back. The pain was too immense. The magic crested and decimated my insides. I screamed and dropped to my knees, and like somebody closed the door in the midst of a massive storm, it was gone. All the intensity siphoned back to the source and crashed through me. I hit the ground hard, body bouncing into the air and back again. The earth rumbled and broke apart, tiny cracks spreading all around me like a smashed windshield. I heard screams. I couldn't tell from whom. They could've been mine.

Smoke rose from my skin. I gasped for air, struggling to breathe and inhaling smoke. A stinging sensation covered my hands, the trickle of electricity snapping through me. I felt cold, my entire skeleton on fire and shaking at the same time. Blood coursed through my veins in icy waves. I felt exhausted. Regardless of the adrenaline that pushed my senses into Mach speeds, reality begged me to sleep. I shivered as the last remnants of magic echoed through me and dissipated. The tension in my shoulders tightened as a monsoon of insect carcasses fell around me. Some were intact while others melted into scorched earth like black wax on a dark canvas. The brittle ground was no longer brown but burned with a ring of black. The leafy walls that had encased us were gone, skeletons of their former selves. Between their branches, rows of trees could be seen marred with soot, smoldering in a haze of grey—a dead zone in the wake of supernatural rage. The wrath.

I gagged, my throat felt thick with ash but I couldn't eject it. I struggled to sit up. My body betrayed me, exhausted and thrumming like I'd put it through hell—I had. The earth around me was broken. I sat on an island of dirt, the crevices around me running deep into the ground. I felt eyes on me. They burned with questions, fear, and surprise at what I'd done. My kind was nearly extinct. Most supernaturals in the past few decades had never seen an angel, let alone felt the rarity of the wrath. Even unintentionally, it could have easily killed them all...or myself.

"Is everybody okay?" My voice sounded hoarse. Everything within me was exhausted. Using my abilities came at a price.

They responded with absent nods, their faces marred with soot and minor burns. Soren and Tryst looked shocked at what they'd witnessed. Gage looked at me like I was the monster. He knew about my kind, but to most, the wrath was a myth. In reality it was nothing more than an angel's curse, or gift, depending which side of it you were on.

"So my fire was dangerous?" Gage asked, staring at the destroyed woods around us. He had a point, but once the wrath was gone, it was gone. Fire had a tendency to linger and spread.

"We need to keep moving," I whispered. It hurt to speak.

I tried to hide the shaking in my legs and leaped over the gap toward my group. I stumbled and my knees gave out when I hit the other side. I rolled with the fall and tried to recuperate, but my legs were uncooperative.

"We should rest," Tryst said. "That was...intense?" The inflection in her voice changed and she drew her eyes away. I couldn't tell if she was surprised or scared. Maybe both.

"No. We can't." I fought through the ache and forced myself up. "We've come this far and we don't know what else is out here. Besides, by now, ATOM knows that we're missing."

"They might not even follow us into Blackwood," she said.

"But they might, and if they do, I'll be damned if I let them catch us now. Everybody up."

CHAPTER 30

We'd entered a new section of forest. There were no shrubs or flowering plants, only hundreds of trees perfectly spaced in symmetrical lines. To the west, a rocky cliff rose up into a blue sky, the tip of the mountain covered in cloud. I wasn't sure when night had become day. In fact, I wasn't sure how long we'd been here.

"I hate this place," Soren said. He limped along and picked at bits of vomit that stuck to his chin. He looked weary and tried.

"What's the problem, Nature Boy?" Gage asked. "Bugs, trees, earth. I thought this was right up your alley."

"I respect all living things until they try to eat me," Soren responded. "Which, thanks to you, almost became reality."

"Whatever that was didn't need me to have reason to attack. This whole place is a death trap. Besides, if your concerned with anything it should be Flapper. I could've killed all those things without almost blowing the rest of us to bits." He wiped a smear of soot off his face, exposing a line of burned skin. I didn't point it out, but something that minor should have healed by now. The more time we spent here, the more I realized where Hendrik got the idea for the Tank.

"We're surrounded by trees, moron." Tryst didn't hide the contempt. "If the smoke didn't get us, we'd have been trying to outrun a forest fire. It was the lesser of two evils."

Gage rolled his eyes. "You should be thanking me. When we're done here, you can remember I was the one who got you out of the Academy. As for these woods, they could use a good roasting. Take the whole lot of creepy-crawlies out of here."

I tuned out the bickering and drank from the canteen. Almost empty. We'd need to find water. The trembling in my legs had left me hours ago, but the warmth of magic simmered inside. It left me feeling stronger, but Gage's concern wasn't unwarranted. We were lucky; the wrath could've disintegrated all of us along with the demon. As much as it could protect you, it could hurt even more. I had barely managed to reel it in. Still, I stood by my original stance, I'd prefer to go by my hand than the demon's.

Rays from the sun slipped through the trees, streaks of warmth decorating the air.Occasionally it would touch the blade Soren refused to sheath, sending kaleidoscopes of greens shimmering across the ground. I walked beside him, in part to make sure he didn't fall over, but also because I needed to. With Blackwood around me and the wrath freshly summoned, I needed balance. Nature had a way of evening the scales, and being a deva, a vibration of calm emanated off Soren, although at the moment that part of him seemed lacking. The color had returned to his face, but the dark circles beneath his eyes were defined. More than anything, his will seemed broken. I didn't think it had been the bugs or the demons—although that was no picnic—it was the forest itself. Being here made him sick. Blackwood was his poison.

"What can I do?" I asked.

He didn't look up, instead watching his feet.

"You can't do anything now. You killed them."

I'd expected something along the lines of "I'm fine," or "Thank you for saving me from an army of legs and fangs that would have certainly gnawed the flesh from my bones." Instead he seemed angry and hurt.

"Not to use your own words against you, but they *were* going to eat us," I reminded him.

His black hair swung to the side and he looked at me beneath a furrowed brow. "I understand that and I'm thankful. I don't wish to see any life destroyed, but I understand it was for our own survival. It's not the bugs that bother me, it's all the trees, plants, and flowers caught in the crossfire. So much life lost. Is that how it had to be?"

My concern had been that I could've killed him and the others.

The trees didn't even make the list of things I'd considered.

"It was the best option at the time. Look, I know the world speaks to you in a different way, but it was that or fire."

He watched me for a moment, the creases around his eyes deepening. "I'm sorry, Ash. I'm criticizing you for saving us. That's not how I feel...or is it? This place makes me..."

"I know." I squeezed his shoulder.

"We need to stop soon. Tryst is growing weak. The forest is stealing from her. From all of us," Soren said. Tryst stood several paces back, offering a fragile smile. She looked more weathered than Soren. "I hate it here."

Soren wandered away, dragging his fingers along the healthy bark of each tree he passed. Drifts of green trailed his fingers as he absorbed bits and pieces of life around him. At this point I wasn't sure if it would help or hinder. I hoped for the former. He'd never be able to help Tryst in his current condition.

"Give him some space." Tryst appeared beside me. "It's all too real to him. He can't help it."

I nodded, trying to remain obscure as I examined her condition. She had paled over the past few hours and her forehead glistened with sweat. She shivered, rubbing her hands up and down her arms, but the air felt warm.

"He'll be okay." I hoped. This place was terrible. I never should have brought them.

"And how are you? That was something else back there." Typical of Tryst to be struggling, yet worried about everybody else. She probably wondered what the hell I had done. Still, she sounded apprehensive.

"Did I scare you?" I asked.

"No, it's...I didn't know angels could do that."

"They can't. Not really. For most angels, their reach is limited to touch. For a rare few, well, you saw what can happen."

"Your hands look sore."

She reached out to the blistered skin, but I pulled away. With the magic still churning inside, I was scared for her to touch me.

"I'll be okay."

"Is that what you call it? Seems to me like you're kind of shook up."

"Are succubi psychic too?"

"It's more or less a gut feeling. It's mild at best."

"Not mild enough if you ask me. I mean, it's hard to keep things from you."

"Why do you need to?" She was serious now. Possibly even offended. "I thought we were past that."

"I don't need to, and we are, it's—"

"Liar." She tried to take a drink from her canteen, but a single drop was all that remained. I offered her mine, but realized it too was empty. She sighed, looking weary, and drifted toward Soren.

I felt bad for letting her walk away. I should have stopped her. It had nothing to do with not trusting her. If she wanted to know about the wrath, I'd tell her, but not now. I wasn't ready yet. After all these years of keeping it contained, it brought back a life I thought I'd forgotten.

After my parents died my uncle became the head of our colony. The moment I showed signs of the wrath, he took me under his wing. I'd always admired my uncle. He was a war champion, a proven warrior, and what seemed like an all-around badass. I wanted to be him, and the wrath gave me the most attention I'd ever garnered from him. But it didn't take long to learn he wasn't interested in me. He wanted the wrath, something few angels ever obtained. We were all strong and fast, made of light and warmth. The light was what most called our gift, a close-range ability that could heal or hurt. The wrath was different. It took the light and intensified it, removing the ability to heal and destroying almost anything in its wake. Few had ever witnessed it, those who did almost never survived. My uncle was one of the few to survive it on multiple occasions. He refused to see its destruction. With me, he would harness it. Or so he thought. Any who'd attempted it before died trying. He was willing to risk it at my expense.

Uncle was a rough man, working me until my hands bled and my skin peeled back. He demanded I learn control no angel had ever managed, and no level I reached could satisfy him. Maybe it was my age. I was a boy. Maybe it was a beast never to be tamed. Regardless, it was a hardship I wouldn't bear. I told him I would stop using it. I told him it was too dangerous. He wouldn't listen. He said the wrath was a curse until I made it my gift. Not using it would be to disgrace the gods who gave it to me. I hated him for that.

The day I told him I planned to leave was a day like this. We stood in the woods near our home, cold air churning the leaves into swirls of reds and browns and oranges. His beard looked thick and full, covering a heavyset jaw. Icy blue eyes pierced through me, making me feel a cold that Mother Nature could never replicate. His white hair flapped in his face, the few strands of black that remained drifted across his eyes. He didn't brush them away. He was too angry. I was a boy of eleven and disobeying the direct command of the angel in charge—my superior. He gave me a chance to change my tone and go back to my tent. I didn't. I drew a line in the dirt when I denied him and he struck me as though I were a man. It stole my breath and sent me twenty feet through the air. I hit the dirt like an avalanche of limbs. I tasted bitter leaves and wet earth, blood spilling from my mouth. His knuckles and the white fabric of his robe were stained with it. Dots swam in my vision, my face sticky with blood. Hair clung to me in clumps, bruises, burns, and cuts ripe over my arms and face. Uncle towered above me, eyes ice-born daggers that thrust into my soul. I ran as fast I could. Fear and sadness propelling me. A heavy heart sagged into my stomach, blood clinging in my throat. I remembered the sound of his heavy feet stomping behind me. Hard breath flittered through a moustache that hung over his lip. Uncle was a man fixed on his prey. Old but never weary. He was a relentless soldier. Fear pushed me faster than I could manage on my own. Adrenaline overloaded my body in a rush and I ran until my legs grew weak, threatening to collapse and leave me to his fury. He had gained on me. The tips of his fingers scraped across my shirt sending lances of trepidation through me. I couldn't outrun him; I had no choice. His angry face was the last thing I saw. I leaped into the air and cut through the trees like I had become the wind. My wings were strong and quick, helping me vanish into the clouds. Uncle could outrun me, but nobody outflew me.

I shivered. The memory left an eerie feeling. My legs felt weak and although I was surrounded by friends—for the most part—I felt alone like I had at the colony. I shook it away. That wasn't my life anymore. Was it? Traipsing through the woods I realized it wasn't so different now. Different monsters preyed upon me, different rules oppressed me, and different losses haunted me, but I was afraid just the same. Still, I wasn't the same person who escaped those mountains. Anger no longer ruled me, and the man who once used his angelic talents to kill was gone. My power had been contained for nearly a decade, although I'd be lying if I said I hadn't been tempted. The day Colby captured me I'd come close to using. In hindsight, part of me thought I should have. If I'd been willing to pull the trigger as easily as Gage, I could have escaped. But then I'd have never met Tryst and Soren. That made me sad, but the reality was they'd have been safer.

"Thank god," Gage said, breaking into a run.

"What is it?" I asked.

"Water!"

Through the trees, whitecaps flickered up over a bank and Gage charged toward it. I said a silent prayer of thanks. My tongue felt like sandpaper shearing the skin off my lips as I licked them. I dropped to my knees and stared into the cold liquid. It ran downstream fresh off the hidden mountaintops. I splashed it on my face and my body screamed at the temperature change. If it were any colder it'd have been ice. I licked the drops off my lips, feeling revitalized.

Gage drank from his hands, steam rising from his fingertips. With water running down his face, he leaned back against a rock. Tryst and Soren filled their canteens, bubbles rippling across the surface, and with quenched thirst, they dropped to the ground, lying back and staring at the dwindling rays that stretched through the trees. The sun had coasted clear across the sky, and although refreshed, they looked unwell. My own body screamed exhaustion, but we had to keep going.

"Don't get too comfortable," I said.

"Ash, we need to rest," Tryst said.

"There isn't time. We'll take five, have a drink, and continue on."

"We've been walking all night and most of the day. Maybe it's been days. I've no idea. It feels like we've been here forever," Tryst said.

"She's right, dude" Soren added. "Even my aches have aches." He stretched out his leg and rubbed his calf.

"You don't understand. They'll have sent people after us by now. We can't afford to stop."

"And they might not have. You don't know how afraid of this place they are," Tryst argued.

"I hate to agree with the likes of these two, but they've got a point," Gage said. "Nobody is going to be of any use exhausted. A couple hours rest won't hurt. Even if they do come, we've got a good head start. Besides, after those demons, whatever they send is nothing we can't handle."

"You don't know Colby Adams like I do."

"The bounty hunter?" Gage laughed. "They won't be able to make up the ground we've covered. Even if they could, you can use your fancy golden glow to scare them off, or maybe rid yourself of them once and for all."

"I'm no killer."

"You could've fooled me the way you cooked that demon extra crispy, and damn near the rest of us too. And then there's the matter of the ship and all those—"

"You shut your mouth," I growled.

Gage put up his hands as if he were an innocent bystander. "Whoa, take it easy, Flapper. I'm just saying you're not some wingless fairy like I thought. We run into trouble and you can fry everybody in the way."

"That's not going to happen. You don't understand what it's like. It hurts and I can't control it. I won't use it again. Which is why we need to move. If they're coming after us, I want to be long gone when they get here."

"Relax, I've seen kids disappear into the woods before. Nobody ever goes after them," Gage said. "You know why? Because they know it's a lost cause, and we're nothing special."

"Great," Soren said. "That inspires a lot of confidence."

"Yeah, well, you have an advantage—me." Gage cracked his knuckles and leaned back, closing his eyes.

"We need to rest, okay?" Soren said. "No more argument." He pointed to Tryst. She leaned against a tree, head drooping. She tried to keep her eyes open, but it was a losing battle.

I felt a pang of guilt and nodded, helping Soren coax her down onto the ground. He slid his sweater under her head, but she didn't move. She was out. Her skin had shifted from pale to grey. The small lines beneath her eyes had become thick black circles. It was the worst I'd ever seen her. I hated this place.

Soren advised he had to wait to help Tryst until she was in a deep sleep. She didn't seem like she was waking up anytime soon, but he assured me he knew best. What he was really saying was that he didn't feel comfortable doing it in front of Gage. I understood. He wasn't a man I'd trust with a secret, but it didn't seem like he was moving any time soon either.

I paced as nightfall fell over the woods. Every moment we were still was a moment we increased our chances of danger. My stomach flopped, hunger and nervousness battling for dominance. I kicked at the leaves, trying to focus on patters along each one and distract myself, but every snap, buzz, or whistle had my eyes darting into the shadows.

"You know what your problem is, Flapper?"

I didn't want to ask but I knew he'd tell me anyway, so I glared at him and walked away, hoping to entice him to follow. "I'm sure you're going to tell me."

He jumped up and chased after me to the river's edge. I walked along it until we'd put a comfortable distance between us and Soren, but left me with a line of sight. This forest had a way of twisting itself around when you weren't looking. The last thing I wanted was to lose view of them.

"Your problem is that you're afraid. Fear is your weakness."

I laughed. "Given what you are, I imagine your kind sees everything as weakness."

"Forget I'm some big, bad typhon and listen. You were on the outside trying to be a good guy. I get it. But you messed up, got caught, and hundreds of people died because of it. Sad day; you feel guilty forever. It's not that you got caught, it's that you've forgotten who you are because of the outcome. That's weakness."

I rolled my eyes, bright green lights flickered in the distance. Soren was working. I had to keep this going.

"Educate me then. How *should* I be?"

"Nobody *wants* to be the reason innocent people die, but sometimes its unavoidable. It just so happens that you were there one time and saw it firsthand. You win some; you lose some. That's the price you pay when you try to screw over the man. Get over it. Sometimes sacrifices need to be made. You lost your wings? Tough break. You're alive. That's a small price to pay. Get over it."

"For a guy who claims he's not really an asshat, he just plays one at the Academy, you sure are acting the role more often than not, or is being a dick your way of giving a pep talk? If it is, it's missing the whole pep thing."

He reached into the river and brought up a handful of water, rubbing it over his face and the dark stubble that covered his scalp.

"Say what you will, but I get it done. You don't like that because you can't handle the reality that sacrifices must be made.

That's cool. This kind of life isn't for everyone. But for the sake of your friends, adopt that attitude until we're out of here."

"I'm being cautious to keep us alive. What's wrong with that?"

"It's wrong because I don't want to die," he said.

"So that's your point, I need to be more like you because *you're* afraid of losing?"

"No, you've *missed* the point. You and I aren't that different. We both want freedom from ATOM, and there's something in these woods that can help us get it."

"We're not the same," I disagreed. "I'm here to get freedom for my friends. You're here to steal ancient power and give it to a man who already has too much."

"This is what I'm talking about. You see what you want to see but reality escapes you. You're right, my father *is* powerful, but he's also one of the last few still fighting back."

"Is that what you call it? Fighting? He moves from city to city staying as far off ATOM's radar as he can, while still pretending he has a hold on the underground. Your father isn't a hero; he's a coward."

Gage gritted his teeth and clenched his fist. "Shut up."

"Am I wrong? You want reality? There it is."

"You don't know anything. My father—"

"I know your father handed his own son over to the people who've repressed us for decades. Where's the heroics in that?"

Heat flared around him and he smashed his rocky fist into the ground. Embers fluttered up like red fireflies floating through the air. His breath was heavy, eyes gleaming.

"Keep going. See what happens," he warned.

As much anger as he showed, there was vulnerability too. I saw the hesitation in his eyes and the way his face tensed and relaxed.

"You wanted to share truths. It goes both ways. I know why I'm here. Why are you here?"

His shoulders rose and fell, rock grinding together as he clenched and released his fists. He paced the ground, flares of red dancing around his fingers.

"Okay, let's do truths, but if I'm owning mine, you can be damn sure you're going to own yours," he said. The fire storm that rippled around him vanished, leaving a drift of smoke. "I don't know why I'm here anymore. My father *did* send me here on this mission. I wasn't alone though. He didn't throw me to the wolves."

He dipped his fingers into the river, splashing them in and out like he played an aquatic piano. "I believed in it at first—the mission— but as the years passed and I heard from him less and less, I started to doubt everything. My truth? My brothers were strong, relentless typhons like him. Respected. I was the runt of the litter and a screwup. I came into my abilities later than most and when I did, he wasn't impressed. A part of me thinks he sent me on this wild goose chase as a way to get me out of his way."

"So he gave you to ATOM?" I scoffed. "Don't you see something wrong with that picture? You've been at the Academy for six years. *Six years*. Every day your life was on the line."

"I know how long it's been!" he snapped, and withdrew his anger with a sigh. "He's a typhon. He's *the* typhon. King. He didn't get that title by letting his conscience get in the way. That's the truth you wanted, isn't it, Flapper? It's not pretty. It never is. It's cold and hard and it's real."

The helplessness on his face made me uncomfortable. He was a boy when he got here. Now he was something else. Not a man but something in between. As abrasive as he appeared, he'd been dealt a dud hand, but it didn't own him. There was something admirable about the way he played it; the way he didn't let his situation define him.

"So you think completing the task will impress him?" I asked.

"You think that's what this is about, Daddy's approval?" He stood up and laughed, brushing off his hands. "He abandoned me. Any hope of having a father in my life was extinguished long ago. The last six years have been hell, but I've survived. It's strengthened me, and I'll be damned if I let the shadows in the woods be the end of my story. If I can get this power, I can help stop ATOM. I'm not fighting for one or two people, I fighting for the freedom of all supernaturals. If I have to work with the man who left me to rot in prison to do that, so be it. Like I said, sacrifices have to be made. That goes for all of us." He nodded in affirmation as if he'd convinced himself of something. "Truth, right? Now it's time for yours."

All the vulnerability he'd shown dissipated. His lips tightened, jaw flexed, and his eyes narrowed. It was no longer arrogance that ripened on his face but determination. He had exposed something to me that he'd kept close to his heart. Maybe it was to prove a point, maybe it was the woods talking—Blackwood had a way of doing strange things to all of us—but regardless, for the first time since I'd met him, I felt like I'd seen a real part of Gage.

"Fair is fair," I said. "Let me have it."

He crossed his arms and studied my face, the final drifts of Soren's magic fluttering behind Gage. Soren waved at me to let me know he had finished. I felt a wave of relief knowing he was able to help Tryst, but the look on Gage's face left me uneasy for what was to come.

"You're not the only one struggling. It's hard. Life's hard," Gage began. "We're all fighting our own battle, but none of it matters if we don't make it out of here alive. The past only affects you if you let it. This, right now, this is real. You may not like it, but that means if you have to kill to survive, then you kill. If you have to use magic, use magic. Just give the rest of us a heads-up so we can get the hell out of the way. My point in all this? Don't get us all killed because you're too damn scared to make a mistake and have history repeat itself. Don't think about it. Don't hesitate. Get it done. I don't care how you do it, but pick yourself up. Fake it if you have to, but I'm not dying in here. You get me? *Whatever* you have to do. Get. It. Done."

CHAPTER 31

The smell of leaves and dirt were gone, replaced by smoke. The forest had grown cold and Gage started a fire. Soren and I moved Tryst close to help her stay warm. His magic had worked—she looked better already—but Soren looked terrible. Sickly green took over his skin, his eyes sagged with exhaustion. He could hardly sit up, opting to lay down with a backpack as a pillow. His breathing was shallow and every other breath came with a sharp wheeze. As much as we were surrounded by nature, it was of little use to him.

I stayed quiet and ignored bouts of Gage's arrogance. It had returned the moment anybody else was within earshot, but now that I knew the truth, it didn't bother me like it had. Gage had a level of intelligence I'd never appreciated before, mostly because he never let it show. He wasn't the brash supernatural I'd taken him for. There was more beneath the surface.

First watch fell on my shoulders while the others rested. As night took hold of the sky, the forest came alive: crickets sang, frogs croaked, and demonic entities growled in the shadows. None of them affected me the way Gage's words had. *If you have to kill. Kill.* A lump stuck in my chest. I had killed. It was true that it was a demon, but it was a life nonetheless. I had felt it suffocate beneath the golden grasp of the wrath, discovering that the humanity we thought destroyed had only been buried. Somewhere inside a spark had remained and I vanquished it. I swallowed hard and took a deep breath trying to calm my racing heartbeat. There had been truth to the typhon's words. Hesitation could get us killed. He wanted a relentless angel by his side. There was a time I had been. I'd fought for what I believed in without a second thought, but since the Tank I'd cowered behind it all, letting guilt and fear rule my life. I wouldn't do that now. I couldn't. I had to push past it for the sake of survival.

Other than the icy wind that cut through the trees, the night was eventless. I never woke Gage or Soren to relieve me. It was better that way. I wouldn't have managed any rest if I'd tried. A side effect of the wrath. It would last a day or two; the constant hum of potent magic moving through me. It forced me to stay awake, a true test of what was in control. As always when it came to the wrath, it wasn't me.

Soren mumbled in his sleep, his body jerking. He woke several times in the night, stumbling through ankle-high leaves the wind had blown in. Occasionally he'd try to pull life force from the woods. Wisps of green would flutter from his fingertips, and although it seemed to help for a while, he'd wake again hours later puking violently and leaving our camp with the lingering stench of bile.

My body ached with exhaustion, but my mind fired on all cylinders. Water rippled a few dozen yards from us. Like me, the river didn't sleep. It splashed against the bank and coasted downstream in an endless rush. The sound reminded me of the place I once called home, and the more I stared at the trees, the more this place resembled it. I paced the camp and stopped at the water's edge. This river moved faster than the one from my childhood. The one I remembered was calm. You could walk to the center and water wouldn't reach your knees. You didn't need a fishing rod, just a stick with a sharp point. This one seemed violent and unpredictable, water deeper than the eye could see.

"Is this where you're supposed to be?" His voice startled me, but not as much as it should have. I wasn't even sure I'd heard it. This place reminded me so much of home, it was like a memory had come to life.

"Hello, Uncle." I didn't turn to face him. I let the water wrap around my fingers like I would as a child. It felt cold like freshly melted snow.

"Look at me when I'm talking to you. You're a walking time

bomb. What the hell are you doing? Using the light, no, the wrath, with these people around? You're going to get yourself and every one of them killed."

I shuddered. Those were not words from a memory. The moon broke through a gap in the trees and sparkled over the river. I saw my reflection. It wasn't the young boy I'd expected. Instead, it was the man he'd become staring back at me. My pulse quickened and I glanced to the fire. My friends were still asleep. I touched the blade on my bag, the leather-wrapped handle felt soft. This wasn't a memory at all, yet it didn't feel strange that he was here.

I rose with caution, keeping my hand on the dagger. Uncle stood taller than me by half a foot. A white beard and moustache covered his face with thick white hair clumped together on either side. A few black strands struggled to keep what little color they had and flapped in the breeze. And his eyes. As blue and cold as anything I'd ever seen. They were the sky on a perfect summer day if you chiseled ice around the edges. His shoulders were broad. A thick man, my uncle. The strongest, most fierce and respected warrior of our colony after my father died. His chest swelled, making me feel childish in my own form. The veins in his arms bulged, wrapped in battle scars. His hands looked calloused, the skin dry and flaky. His lips were thin and chapped. It happened often from the cold where we lived. He stood with arms crossed, looking at me in disapproval.

"Even as a man—if you can call yourself that—you're still a scrawny mess," he ridiculed. "You call these arms?" He gripped my arm and his hand felt massive, hurting me as he squeezed. I pulled away and he laughed. "Skinny things. And your gift?" He stared so deeply into my eyes I shivered. "Uncontrolled still. I knew without me it would be. Though I was wrong in one aspect: you're still alive. I expected you dead soon after you left—if you didn't come crawling back."

"I'll never come back," I said. I didn't let his words cut me like he wanted them to. I'd spent a lifetime with them haunting me, but Gage had been right, the past had no control unless I let it. I couldn't fear it anymore. "Why are you here? How did you find me?"

"I'm here to make sure you don't go any farther. You're a thoughtless boy. You always were. But what you're doing now takes the cake as the dumbest thing you've ever done. Fetching ancient power for an old man? A fool's errand. You should've never let yourself get captured, and once you were, you should've fought your way to freedom or died trying. That's the angel's way. Making deals? Doing the devil's bidding? Pathetic."

"It was the only way I could keep them safe."

"That unkempt bunch?" He laughed. It was gristly and full, the way I imagined the barbarians of old might chuckle. "They're not your concern."

"They are my concern."

"They're not family. They're not our kind!"

"They don't have to be!" I shouted. The anger surprised me, but Uncle remained unfazed. "They're the closest thing I've had to it in a long time, maybe ever."

He moved so fast, I couldn't brace for it. The back of his hand hit me, knuckles rapping against my cheek. The force was unmatched, my head bouncing off the earth before I realized I'd fallen. The taste of dirt and leaves filled my taste buds. A wet leaf stuck to the side of my face and I peeled it off, spitting debris to the ground.

"You abandoned your family. Your cause. You were to be the avenger. The one who would change things for our kind. The one who would seek retribution for what they did to your parents. Instead, you frolic like a fairy, helping others in need instead of your own kin."

The moment I rolled onto my back his foot crushed my chest. It was hard and heavy like a Viking's hammer. I couldn't cry out. The air had been stolen from my lungs. When I finally drew a breath, he gripped my throat and lifted me to face him, fist driving into my face. Bones shifted in my cheek and my lip split, blood spilling from my mouth. His knuckles were rough like spiked hide, sharp and rough, cutting into me with each consecutive blow. A warrior's fist.

Black and white dots blinded me like burning stars on the darkest night. My brow swelled and sagged over my eye and blurred my vision. Upon release, I collapsed to my knees. It hurt to breathe. My pulse throbbed, each beat of my heart sending spikes of tenderness across my face.

"I should kill you." He drew his blade from a sheath on his back. For anybody else it required two hands, but for Uncle only one. The metal glistened, stretching out the length of my leg.

Streaks of iron, silver, and copper woven together in a glimmer of color. "Traitor."

All of this seemed too familiar. His words. The way he struck me was a reminder of the day I had left. A memory playing out in real time, but I was no longer a child. Blackwood did this.

He raised the weapon above his head. In the past, I would turn away and let it slice across my back. It would cut feathers from my wings, perhaps foreshadowing what my future held. This time, however, I could change things. I was no longer a boy, and I no longer had wings to cut.

I rolled to the side and the blade hit the ground. Sparks rose into the air as the metal hit stone. I kicked my leg out and caught the back of his knee. He hadn't anticipated it and his body drooped, but he was a seasoned warrior. He caught his balance and turned, but I was already gone. I sprinted through the woods, a blur in the shadows. I weaved left and right, refusing to let the woods slow me down. Nothing seemed strange. I knew where to go.

The ground rumbled, the heavy feet of an angelic giant traipsing behind me. I felt him gaining. His feet ate the distance between us with ease. A wheeze of breath spilled from his lips and whispered through his mustache. His hand grazed my back, calloused fingers scratching my neck. I took a hard left, leaving him to skid and recover, but within a few steps he was there again. I pushed as hard as I could but he was too fast. Like so many years ago, I couldn't outrun him. There was one way out.

I turned and dove into a gap beneath a thicket of brush. It cut along my back, thorns tearing through my shirt and into my skin as I crawled against the earth. As soon as I was able, I climbed to my feet and continued running. Uncle didn't wait. With two strikes of his sword, the bush collapsed into a pile of twigs. Water crashed like thunder and I ran toward it, leaping over stumps and deadfall like a doe through timberland. As before, the falls would be my savior. Uncle had made up the lost ground, fingers gripping my shoulder and ready to pull me back. I drew my blade and swung behind me, slicing into his stomach. A flesh wound, nothing more, but enough to have him retract his hand. He released a fierce growl. I'd angered the colossus of my nightmares. The sound of his blade warbled in the air as it left the sheath once again but he was too late. My freedom had arrived.

The earth ended where water cascaded over the edge of a mountain ledge, crashing into a pool of icy liquid that frothed below. I took a step and lunged out like a diver preparing to leave his mark, but I wouldn't go down. No. I would go up into the clouds where he could not follow. His wings would not take him to the speeds I could reach. I knew it. He knew it. And his vehement scream solidified it. I leaped forward, the thundering falls of my home and my uncle's abuse soon to be evicted from my life. They'd be nothing more than a memory once again.

"Ash!" Tryst's voice cut through the air, overriding the crash of water and the growls of Uncle's frenzy.

The world wavered. I soared through the air, waiting for my wings to stretch out, but they were gone. Somewhere along the way I'd forgotten Blackwood and fell into the memory. Shards cut across my shoulders like a hot knife, burning and slicing all at once as I tried to release a gift that was no longer mine. I twisted in the air, the muscles in my back tearing into scarred flesh. Unlike my memory, I couldn't fly away. There were no wings to carry me to the safety of the clouds. This time there was no escape.

Cold air slapped against my skin. I expected to tumble and spin out of control as gravity destroyed me and sent me crashing into the rocks and water below. But the realization that I couldn't fly changed the landscape—it changed everything.

The cliff was gone. The water was gone. Even Uncle was gone. I tumbled and hit solid ground. My body bounced and the impact knocked the wind from me. Panic gripped my lungs and when I could finally draw a breath, I sucked dirt and broken leaves into my mouth. I gagged and coughed up the debris, wheezing as I clambered for fresh air. I tasted blood, my lip still swollen and the lump above my eye as real as the dirt I'd ingested.

"Ash! Soren!" Tryst yelled again. Gage's voice followed, calling our names.

I pushed myself up, pulling my knees beneath me. Uncle's fist had left its mark, but so had the forest. Fresh blood trickled down my back and ran over my chin. I realized I was no longer on ground level. I sat in a hole, twice as wide as I was tall and twenty feet deep. Uncle was nowhere to be seen, but neither was the night.

Had I slept? Was it a dream? That didn't explain how I got here. I stared up at the brightened sky, pale blue with clouds coasting across it, and the air felt cold.

"Tryst?" I tried to shout, but it was a hoarse whisper. Trying to talk made me cough again, this time a lump of dirt coated in broken leaves shot out of my mouth. "Tryst?" I said again, louder this time. She never responded.

I tried to climb, but muddy walls collapsed beneath my weight. Roots dangled a few feet from the top; a tree's lifeline buried beneath the earth. I should've been able to jump high enough to reach them, but I couldn't make it more than a few feet off the ground. Everything that made me what I was, an angel, seemed dormant, and all energy reserves were depleted. I felt weaker than ever before, and when I punched dirt-lined wall in anger, it stung.

"Dammit!" I said, waving my hand in the air. The forest had humanized me in a way I didn't think possible.

I took a few steps back and tried running up the wall. The tips of my fingers slapped the roots, but I couldn't grab them. Tryst called my name, but my replies fell on deaf ears. I kicked at the wall, it hurt, but this time a piece of mud broke away and revealed a wooden shaft. I dug around it, my fingers caked in black. I uncovered a long branch that I tore from the muddy wall. I set it up along the side and used it as a ramp to get closer to the roots, but when my weight pressed against it, the branch snapped. I cursed and screamed, frustration boiling over. What the hell was this place?

An hour passed, though it could have been longer. I'd lost track of time. I sat with my knees pulled to my chest, eyeing the broken branch. I could feel Uncle's cold eyes sending spears of ice through me. Everything about this place confused me. Real, not real. Which was it? I replayed it all through my mind, wondering what the hell was happening. It was as though Blackwood had taken something from my memories and brought it to life, forcing me into a trap. That's exactly what it had done. This place was the Tank, but worse. Blackwood was hell on earth.

After sulking for as long as I could bear, I had an idea. This place might've been hell, but I wasn't going to let it take me. Not like this. I took the two pieces of branch and broke them into smaller pieces. Six of them, each almost a foot long. I jammed them into the earth as hard as I could, using the other pieces to hammer each one in farther. The first set was five feet off the ground, and I used them as a stepping stone to get closer to the top where I added another row. I pulled myself up again. The wood waned in the soft wall of mud and dirt. I felt them start to sag. I had to make quick work of the last row.

I hammered in the second last peg, but had nothing left to knock in the last. The others below me were out of reach, and the rungs of wood jutting from the wall were weakening. Tryst called my name again. She sounded closer this time. Excitement coasted through me.

"Tryst!" I screamed. "Tryst!" It was no use. She couldn't hear me.

The wood beneath my feet didn't last. The earth broke away and the rungs tumbled out beneath me. I groped at the air, catching the last peg I'd managed to bury in the wall. Wooden pegs bounced off the ground below, and my body strained to hold on to the last one. I was so close. I tried to use the wall as leverage and push myself upward, but more dirt broke away and I was left dangling by one hand, there wasn't enough room for both. My shoulder felt strained. The muscles ached from holding my bodyweight. I'd never felt so weak in my life. It was as if the hole had sucked all otherworldly strength away.

My mud-covered hand slid down the peg as it waned downward. I pawed at the earth, trying to scramble up the wall. It had no effect and I couldn't hold on. My fingers slipped and I screamed, bracing for impact with the bottom of the pit when Gage Daniel's silver eyes appeared over the edge. His hand shot out and grabbed my wrist. The momentum jerked my body to a stop and I crashed into the wall with a thud.

"Dammit." I cringed, dangling from the typhon's grip.

"You're welcome," he said, trying to pull me up. "Come on, work with me, Flapper."

He lay across the earth, shoulder hanging over the edge. The ground was slick, grass and dirt breaking away above him. My weight pulled at him and he slid forward, more of his body exposed over the edge. I felt myself drooping farther into the hole's grasp, but this time I was taking him with me.

"Pull!" My jaw flexed, feet scrambling against wet earth.

Gage screamed through a clenched jaw and his grip tightened. His skin turned to stone, the next level of his unnatural strength being summoned to the surface. The rocky surface made it easier to hold on, but the heat came with it automatically. The mud that coated my hands reduced the burn, but I still felt it, and with gritted teeth I pushed through. I wouldn't let go. One inch at a time my body rose and before long, the edge was in reach. I swung my legs over and rolled onto the grass above, steam rising from the bubbling mud in my hand.

The canopy of green that overshadowed most of our trek through the forest was gone and I stared up at cloudy skies. Any resemblance to home I'd seen around me before the fall had vanished. There were no waterfalls and no familiar trees. Instead, there were foreign oaks and evergreens stained with streaks of black that reminded me all too much of the demons we'd faced. My breath was heavy, muscles trembling and pulsing beneath the skin.

"You know," Gage gasped, "you're a lot heavier than you look."

"Scrawny, my ass," I said.

"What?"

"Nothing," I said. I could hardly push myself up, my hands felt hot and arms unsteady. "Where's Tryst?"

"I don't know. I woke up in the middle of the woods. Our camp was gone and so were the rest of you. I heard her calling, but when I followed her voice it led me to you." The last was said with clear disdain.

"How unfortunate for you."

I looked around, trying to figure out which direction I had come. "Tryst?" I yelled, but there was no answer.

"What the hell is going on, Flapper?"

"Blackwood. That's what."

CHAPTER 32

We followed the periodic shouts, but it led us in an endless loop back to camp. Sweat drenched our bodies as the temperature spiked. I fell to the ground, my shirt clinging to my body. The ashes of our fire long since snuffed out. It would be nightfall again soon and we were no closer to anything. I cursed and hit the dirt, smashing it with my fist.

"This is where he got it," Gage said, tearing off his shirt and throwing it to the ground. His voice was dry, lips chapped and flaking at the edges. "The idea for the Tank. Its darkness came from this place."

"Maybe." I hardly listened, scanning the woods for a hint of where the answers might lie. There had to be something to tell us where to go.

"No maybe about it," Gage countered. "I know about the witches and how Hendrik used to be a slave. His freedom was trapped somewhere in these woods with magic. And that same magic is now contained inside the blades the three of you carry. They belonged to his kin. Brothers and sisters that he hunted down and slaughtered."

I was surprised at how much he knew, but I hadn't considered what Hendrik told me to be slaughter. They broke the oath. "What makes you think that?"

"I told you. I have connections, Flapper. Hendrik doesn't spend all his time in his office, but his journals do. Years of information scrawled onto parchment."

I pulled out the blade and blue glass shimmered, looking fragile and decorative. It was hard to believe it could kill anything. I felt it would break if I dropped it.

"What else do you know?"

"Enough. Hendrik is a behemoth. He's spent lifetimes under the command of ATOM. Biding his time, I imagine. Long ago, before typhons took over the underground, and before the angels ruled it before them, there was his kind. Each of his brethren ruled a sector of the world, but one wasn't enough. Not for Hendrik. Like most generals, over time he wanted more and one by one he took it. Killing his own brothers when they wouldn't relinquish their land."

"But why? Why would he want so much?"

Gage laughed as if I should know the answer. When the laughter turned into a coughing fit, I threw my canteen toward him and he took a swig, thanking me in a wispy breath.

"Boredom? How should I know? Why does anybody do anything? Power, probably. I'm sure he gained something from their fall besides territory. I don't know. That's why we're here, isn't it? So you can get whatever it is we're searching for and bring it back to him? He wants you to restore the part that ATOM took, right?" When I didn't respond, he nodded his head like I had. "Of course it is. It's the same reason you don't know who you're going to give it to, him or me."

"I told you—"

"You told me what I wanted to hear. I'm a lot of things, but I'm not stupid. You haven't decided if you're going to hold up your end of our bargain. I know that, you know that, hell, even Soren and Tryst know that. You're biding your time—like him. You don't know who to trust but the truth is, you don't know anything about anything. You don't know the monster Hendrik was before ATOM tamed him. All you know is how dangerous ATOM can be, and you want out of this godforsaken place. God knows I do too." He coughed and it sounded sharp, phlegm flying from his mouth. "I don't blame you. I wouldn't want me to have it either. Not with what you've seen and heard of the underground. But you can't understand what it's like to be stuck in this place for so long. You don't know what it's like to do whatever you have to do to survive."

He was wrong. I did know. I had been desperate when I first left my colony. I had nothing and nobody. I scrounged, stealing whatever I needed: money, food…lives.

"Don't be so sure," I whispered.

"Don't pretend like you know. If you did, you'd understand I'm the lesser evil."

"Are you? Hendrik might be a monster, but your dad is the typhon leader. He's no better. If it were up to me, nobody would have it. Unfortunately, that isn't an option."

The typhon let out a strange laugh and shook his head. "What else can I do to convince you? Threaten you? Kill you? I could try and steal it from you once we find it. I could plead to your more intelligent side, if there was such a thing. Outside of that, I don't have many options either." He rubbed his hands along his arms as the wind picked up. The heat dissipated and the air cooled, a winter rush moved over us. Flakes of white fluttered from the thick clouds that churned overhead. "I'll tell you what though, before I get a chance to do any of those things, we need to find whatever we're looking for. Enough aimless wandering."

"Not without Tryst and Soren."

"Forget them. The longer we stay here, the worse off we'll be. Sacrifice. Whatever it takes, remember? I'm not dying in here."

"We're not leaving without them," I insisted.

Gage cringed as he struggled to his feet. If he felt at all like me, his muscles were binding, burning as if they'd been set on fire, even though my skin felt cold.

"If you think saving them is going to make what you did go away, you're wrong. There is no redemption for the things we do. Let's leave them. The world outside these walls is too harsh for them anyway. Even if they make it, they'll never—"

"That's enough!" I snapped. The air dropped a few more degrees and he shivered. "We're not leaving without them. I won't say it again. Now, what do you know of Soliloquy?"

"Whatever," he said. "It's Hendrik's brew. It's a potion that takes away the influence of the Tank. Why?"

"I have a dose in my bag. If we share it—"

"Then it will work for half the time," he said. A sort of desperation filled his eyes. He shuddered again at the cold breezed and licked his lips, eyeing my bag.

"Take it easy," I said, rising to my feet. "This place is messing with us. We can share the Soliloquy and then put together a plan.

Gage leaned down and dragged his fingers through the dirt. White frost had spread across the ground and it broke against his grip. Bits of it turned to water and melted in a circle around him. He scooped up a handful of dirt and squeezed it.

"Give me the Soliloquy and the blade," he demanded. His voice was soft, but he looked hungry. His eyes became distant as his pupils shrank to tiny pinpoints.

Nervousness clutched me. Blackwood's reach was immense yet subtle, a rat whose incessant chewing never ceased. With time it could sink any ship. By the look on Gage's face, he'd sunk beneath the surface.

"Gage, don't do this." I slid my arms into the straps of the backpack. "We have to work together."

"Give it to me!" He bit at his lip, splitting it open. Blood smeared across his teeth and trickled down his chin. The creases in his forehead deepened and the silver of his eyes leaked outward, filling it until his eyes were mirrors. Bulging veins along his neck turned bright red like hot coals after they'd been stoked.

An icy wind blasted through the trees, the river froze over in an instant, and ice crisped along my fingertips. It burned and bit, creeping upward along my arm. Gage stood on all fours and crawled forward like wolf cornering his prey. His veins were hot, steam radiating off his body. A rocky shell formed along his arms and across his neck, deflecting the cold. The rock didn't cover him entirely, but patches of it spread across his torso and shoulders like a stony fungus that wouldn't be contained. His eyebrows became frosted for a moment, but the icy hairs became wet and water dripped down his body, sizzling and screaming in revolt. The pile of dirt in his hand glowed bright red, dirt and rock melting together into a radiant missile. Magic vibrated around him and he growled, throwing it toward me. The rock burst into flames and I dodged it. A tail of heat zipped past my head and hit the tree behind me, embers of magic snapping against the bark. The wood smoldered and crackled with the rock embedded in the wood.

"Don't do this, Gage. Control yourself. Come back to me."

I drew the blade and energy thrummed through my fingertips. Gage's eyes lit up with hunger as power discharged from the sparkling glass and into my hand. Foreign might filled me. My muscles tightened and expanded, and something supernatural rejuvenated my body. In an instant I felt stronger than ever, the exhaustion that had beaten me down vanished beneath the blade's effect.

Gage trampled onward. He looked lethal and strong; ready to kill at a moment's notice. Rocks ground against one another as he clenched his fists. Fireworks of red rippled off his arms and sparked the air around them. His shoulders rose and fell, thick clouds of breath pouring from his lips.

He stalked forward and I stepped away, not out of fear, but caution. He wasn't in his right mind. I half expected him to break into a run and charge me. Instead, he stopped. His head snapped to the left and then right, his neck cracking. He dropped to his hands and knees again, a sudden scream breaking out from his clenched jaw. His arms trembled, the ground around him glowing red as heat spread into the earth. Steam rose from the layer of ice that covered the ground. It slowly melted and began to boil.

"Ash!" he screamed. His glare was a bright and fiery silver, but the anger he wore contorted into something I never expected—fear.

"Gage?" I asked. "Are you with me?"

"Ash, please." He reached out, begging for help. "Make it stop."

I was reminded of my time in the Tank and how painful it had been, but for a moment I enjoyed his fear. I had the thought to pull the blade across his throat while he was distracted. I could watch a waterfall of red spill down his chest and keep the Soliloquy to myself. I wanted to see the tears that filled his eyes begin to fall.

I shook the thoughts away. Realizing how much joy they had brought me made bile rise in my throat. These thoughts didn't belong to me. They couldn't. That wasn't who I was. These were mental intrusions from Blackwood. I stepped back and took a deep breath, trying to control the reality that had formed around me. Nothing changed. Everything felt foreign. Darkness, sickness, and despair swam around me, urging me to finish what the woods had started. I felt unexplained bouts of rage rising up. The wrath called to me. It told me Gage's blood would sate the fury and depression trying to embed itself in my soul. His life could rectify everything. It could make up for all the lives I had been responsible for.

"No!" I shouted. This wasn't real. I told myself over and over it was the forest's grasp that made me feel this way. I could beat this curse.

One must find harmony amidst his flaws, and then have the vision to realize that they are not flaws at all.

Those were the words Hendrik had shared. They were the key to unlocking our minds from this prison, but that kind of peace didn't come with a thought or realization. Peace could not be found in an instant. At least not in this one.

I collected myself long enough to form a thought. I pulled the Soliloquy out and popped the cork, drinking half of the purple liquid. Fruit and sweetness rode over my tongue, though the thirst I thought to quench was not immediate. It loitered on my buds, working its way through my body with flashes of the blood I could cover Gage's corpse in. I shuddered, the images lessening with each moment. With the next breath came release. The weight of destruction lifted from my mind and normalcy returned.

"Drink this, it will help." I dangled the vial on a string.

"Closer, I need it. You *have* to help me." He gasped for air, tears building in his eyes. I inched closer, putting the bottle in his hand.

"Take it."

"You *have* to help me!" he shouted.

"Take it!" I yelled.

"Help me get what's mine!" He snarled and launched himself forward, his shoulder smashing into my chest. The vial dropped from my hand and skidded across the frosty earth. He fought against me, jaws snapping like a rabid dog intent on tearing out my throat. Drool flung from his mouth, eyes crazed and teeth bared. "Give me the blade. I want what it's giving you!" He scratched at my arm and his fingers burned like an iron on flesh.

The more I pushed against him, the more it hurt. He was strong and savage, his actions sharp and ragged. I pushed his face away from me, my forearm against his throat. The bandage I'd wrapped around the skin seared and the heat slipped through, burning the open wound. I muffled a scream and struck back. My knuckles rapped against the side of his face once, then twice, bones cracking against one another. His head snapped to the side and back, unfazed by the impact.

"Again!" He laughed.

I pulled back my fist and let my elbow make impact. It was enough to knock him off kilter. He fell back and I planted both feet into his stomach with as much force as I could manage. It offered me enough space to escape and I jumped to my feet, both arms hot and aching. My movements were sluggish, the cold breath nature poured over us made it hard to move. My sweat-covered shirt had frozen shards of ice chaffing against my skin. The potion had cleared my mind, but it didn't change the potency of the woods. The bottle of Soliloquy lay on the other side of the fire pit. I made a run for it but Gage lunged again. I jumped back. Too slow. Sharp stone nails cut across my face and blood spilled into my eyes. It marred my vision and I stumbled over a rock.

Gage's voice was almost demonic as it echoed around us. "That blade should be mine."

I couldn't see, pawing at my eye to wipe it clean. I swung the weapon wildly, my depth perception thrown off. Gage laughed, but it was cut off by a heavy thud as something hit the back of his head. He crumpled to the ground and when he tried to stand, it hit him again. Tryst hovered over his body, a thick branch gripped in her hands.

"Were you planning on using that thing, or were you going to keep waving it at him? It doesn't matter, here." She dug through her bag and came up with a bandage.

"Thanks."

"You should drink the rest of this." She picked up the Soliloquy and threw it on my lap.

"I can't. He needs it more than I do."

Tryst stared at Gage's limp body. His typhon power was gone and his rocky skin receded. "You're more important to me than he is. Drink."

I shoved it away. "I had half. He and I will share it."

"Ash."

"Don't. We're all in this together...even him."

The fire crackled and smoked against wet wood. Gage lay almost lifelessly beside it, a large gash in the side of his head. It had stopped bleeding, but hadn't begun to heal. I had a feeling none of our wounds would until we were out of this place.

"I don't understand what happened," Tryst said. "When I went to sleep you were all here. Everybody was fine. But when I woke up—"

"We were gone." I stared at the flames, letting their heat warm my hands. Soliloquy had stolen the forest's clout, but I'd shared it with Gage, how long it would last was a mystery. "I'm surprised you woke up here. The forest didn't take you like it did us."

Reaching into her bag she pulled out an empty glass vial. "I drank mine before I went to sleep. I'll never forget the first time the Tank pulled me under. I won't ever go to that place again if I can help it."

She kneeled beside me and peeled back the bandage on my head. I met her hand with my own and held it tight. "We'll get out of here before that happens."

Gage stirred, rising from the bed of dirt. He rubbed his eyes and groaned. When his eyes met mine, he looked away, cringing as he examined the wound on his head.

"What the hell happened?" he whispered.

"I did." Tryst stood up, flipping her bag over her shoulders. "You're awake now. That's good. Let's get moving."

"Go? No, I need to rest for a bit."

"You've rested enough. We all have. Get up."

"It's nightfall. It'll be safer if we wait until morning."

"Look, Soren is lost out there somewhere and if you two are any example of what he might be dealing with, I intend to find him sooner than later. Now get your ass up or find your own way out."

Once Gage accepted that Tryst had taken the reins, we were on the move. She was relentless in her search, but after we'd circled back to camp for the third time, even she began to look defeated. Even with the Soliloquy in our system, the forest had a hold on us we couldn't break.

"Dammit." She pulled her bottom lip into her mouth and stopped at a circle of trees that looked all too familiar.

"We already went left," I said.

"And right," Gage added.

"Soren?" Tryst called out. Her voice echoed back to us. She hunched over with both hands on her knees. Sadness and worry creased her features.

"We'll find him." I squeezed her shoulder.

"Maybe," Gage said.

Tryst turned at once, pulling the red blade from her bag and pressing it against his throat. "I'm so sick of you. Don't you ever shut up?"

"Ouch, that hurts," he said, backing away. A drop of blood ran down his neck where the blade had cut him.

"Good." Her gaze narrowed. "I have to find Soren, and I won't give up until I do. You talk like that again and you'll lose something precious. Got it?"

He nodded. "I got it."

"Tryst?" I asked.

"What?" she snapped.

I pointed to her blade and the white sparks flickering within the glass. She turned toward me and they grew brighter. She moved to the left a little more, pointing it in the direction we'd come from, and it became solid white.

"What's it doing?" she asked.

"I don't know. Maybe it's telling us where to go."

"But we just came from there."

"This place is a maze. It messes with your head. What if going back is the only way to move forward."

"Soren?" she whispered. The blade flashed on and off like a switch and without a word she ran back toward the trail we'd traversed.

We ran for an hour, but this time we never returned to camp. The forest began to thin, trees becoming sparser. As they did, color faded from the woods. The thick brown bark that coated the trees became grey and thin. Leaves trickled to the ground in a crisp black rain, leaving the barky limbs barren. Tryst's blade brightened every few steps before starting to flicker and burning out, returning the glass to red.

"Soren?" She walked forward, tapping the blade like a flashlight whose batteries were dying. "Great, it's broken."

Gage grimaced. "I'm not so sure things like that get broken. Maybe we're here."

"And where's here? More forest, only this time it's dead. Wonderful."

A whisper came. Faint at first, then growing louder. The words were panicked and sharp and impossible to understand, but I recognized the voice. Soren.

"He's here," I said. "Somewhere. Who is he talking to?"

"Soren!" Tryst ran off, eager to find her friend. So was I, but after what happened to Gage and me, I didn't want to run charging into anything unprepared. I drew my blade and tried to keep up. Tryst didn't appear to feel the exhaustion that Gage and I did.

We came into a clearing of brown and yellow leaves but almost no trees. The glade was wide open with a rocky mountain face rising up on one side. Soren's voice was no longer a whisper. It led us along the base of the mountain and into a deep nook with a stony overhang. It was almost too dark to see, but the silhouette of Soren was in the back, pressed against the wall. I turned on my flashlight and Soren hissed, turning away. The sight of him caused me to drop it, plastic clanking against the ground.

Crouched in nothing but stained underwear, his feet were bare and covered in blood, thorns sticking out the sides of them. He shivered violently, sweat dripped from his hairline and streaked his face, revealing how dirty he was. His lips quivered, sputtering nonsense. Nothing coherent I could put together.

"Tryst," I said.

"What is it? Did you find him?" At first sight she covered her mouth; her eyes filled with tears. She dropped her bag and crawled toward him. "Oh my god, Soren. What's happened to you?" She brushed the hair from his eyes as he trembled.

"Tryst?" he asked. "No, it's not really you. Get away from me, demon!" He skittered across the ground on all fours and huddled in another corner.

"Soren, it's me. I promise it's me."

He turned and examined her, reaching out hesitantly as if she might bite him. His fingers were tattered with deep cuts and scuffs, each finger shaking. He touched the side of her face and almost began to cry. Blackwood had its hooks in deep.

She wrapped her arms around him and pulled him close. Hushing him with whispers. "It's me. I'm here."

He sobbed, all the tension from his body draining the moment she touched him.

"I can't...believe...it's you. It can't be. I saw what they did to you."

Tryst continued to soothe him with a calm and quiet voice. "Nobody did anything. I'm right here like always."

They sat in silence for a long moment before he looked up.

When he was certain it wasn't a trick, he pulled her into his own embrace.

"You'll never believe what I found, Tryst. He's here. He's always been here." His fingers dug into her cheeks as he grabbed her face and forced her to look at him. "Tryst, he's alive."

She pulled away, smears of dirt prints left on her cheeks. "Who is?"

His lips quivered and he tried to smile, but in the state he was in, it was almost a grimace. "Trace."

CHAPTER 33

Nobody spoke. Awkwardness filled the air; it was too much for any of us. Gage had cringed at the sight of Soren. After hearing Soren's words, Gage wandered away.

"Did you hear me?" Soren asked. "Trace!"

Tryst ran her fingers down the side of his face and tried to smile. Her voice was motherly. "Honey, no. Trace isn't here—" Her voice cracked and she stifled a sob. "Trace is gone."

Soren's happiness vanished and anger ripened. He acted like a child throwing a tantrum and screamed in her face, falling on the ground in a heap of sobs. "No. No. No. No. No! I saw him." He jumped up with surprising vigor and grabbed her shoulders. "I saw him and we spoke. He's coming back for me. For us. He's here, Tryst. You'll see. He's going to save us."

She looked at me for help but I had nothing to offer. Blackwood was a cruel mistress. There was only one thing that could help him right now.

"Where's your bag, Soren?" I asked. "You need Soliloquy."

"Here." Gage returned and held up Soren's backpack, but it was tattered and empty. Nothing remained but a ragged piece of fabric with the straps torn off and a hole in the bottom. It looked like an animal had destroyed it.

"Soren." Tryst held both sides of his face, trying to keep him focused.

"No. No. No. You'll see. You all will. He's here. He saved me from them."

"Soren look at me. Look. At. Me." She hushed him with her voice until he became very still. "Where are the things from your bag? Where's the blade? Where's the Soliloquy?"

He stared into her eyes as she repeated the question over and over. She was patient and calm.

"He took it."

"Who took it? Trace?"

Soren shook his head. "The bad man took it," Soren said. "The bad man took it, and he is coming for you." A single finger stretched out and pointed at me. A chill crossed my shoulders and rippled down my spine.

"Soren, can you tell me who the bad man is?" Tryst asked.

He nodded. "Trace saved me from him. From all of them. He led them away and he's going to get the blood we need."

"Blood?" Gage perked up.

"He'll come back for me," Soren said. "He told me so. Then you'll see he's real. They took my things but they won't take my Trace. He won't let them." He nodded his head in affirmation.

"Who, Soren?" I asked.

"Hello, Ash." Colby's redneck voice hit a chord like an out-of-tune banjo.

Soren shuddered, pressing himself into the wall as if he could hide within its confines. His voice whimpered. "Him," he whispered.

My body didn't know whether to be afraid or angry. Breath caught in my throat, and my face flushed. I couldn't see him, but his voice was clear. He was close.

"Long time no see," Colby said. "Come out here. Let's have a look at you."

Tryst saw the shift in my demeanor. Her eyes were wide, hands holding Soren's to keep him calm. She shook her head and told me not to go. I hesitated under the shelter of the nook, watching a damaged Soren shudder. There was no way out of this that didn't end in a fight. I knew that. Colby didn't come all this way to let me get away, and I wasn't about to let him take me back.

"Stay here," I said. "Keep him safe."

Tryst grabbed my hand and pulled me toward her. "Don't," she whispered, wrapping a single arm around my neck and pulling me toward her. "I can't lose you."

I let her hold me longer than I should have. Each second made it harder to push her away. There were no words I could offer to console her. Instead, I leaned in and kissed her cheek before pulling away and stepping into the glade.

Colby had Soren's green blade against Gage's throat and a bottle of Soliloquy dangling from his neck. His other hand had partially shifted, claws of a wolf stretching from his human digits and digging into the typhon's chest. The black cowboy hat adorned his head, tilted to cover one eye. The cigar in his mouth was lit, smoke drifting between his lips. Salt-and-pepper stubble was as present as ever, and he revealed a toothy yellow smile.

"Well, I've got to tell you, boy, I'm surprised you're here," he drawled. "I didn't expect you'd survive the Academy this long. Certainly didn't think you'd escape it. But then again, you didn't escape, did you?"

I stepped out of the shadows, sidestepping to an open area. "I'm not sure what you mean."

He laughed. "Sure you do. You and that Hendrik have become close, ain't ya? Working together on something big I hear."

"Not sure what Gareth has told you, but I'm not working for anybody but myself."

"Gareth?" Colby laughed. "Shows what you know, don't it? You're an errand boy for a fool, nothing less. But ATOM ain't going to stand for any of his hubbub, or yours."

"ATOM doesn't get a choice, but you do. Let Gage go," I said. "Turn around and disappear. Go back to the Academy, tell them we're dead or whatever the hell you want, but end it here, Colby. We don't have to be enemies. You don't know what they do to people at the Academy. It could as easily be you or someone you care about."

He lifted his clawed hand and wagged a finger at me. "No. You don't get to give me orders. You don't tell *me* how it's going to go. I spent eight years chasing you. You're a life mission for me, boy. The first time you showed up on our radar you were eleven. We found footage of you robbing that convenience store and flying into the night like some sort of bird or something. You've been trouble since the day we met. Ain't nothing changed now. There ain't no way in hell I'm walking away from this."

Gage's eyes were calm and locked on mine. He nodded to me,

the veins in his arms beginning to bulge, turning a hue of red. Seeing Colby now, all the fear I'd felt dissipated. A part of me had been scared to face the man who'd crippled me, but I couldn't afford that fear now. Everything in Blackwood was life or death, and I chose life. I chose to fight. I chose to keep my promise and save the people I brought with me.

"You took something from me. Something that wasn't yours to take. You're right; you won't be walking away from this." I dug my foot into the ground, letting rocks and dirt settle on top of my shoe.

"Oh, right, the wings. You still going on about that?" he asked. "Come now, you've hardly got use for them at the Academy. Besides, they're long gone. Shipped them off to Germany before we dropped your ass off. Highest bidder and all that, you know how it is. Those buyers get eager to see what their money bought them."

Colby grinned before he realized what was happening. I kicked a spray of rocks and dirt toward them. Gage's arms shifted to stone and magic pulled the assault closer. The debris ignited in flame and embers. Hot coals rained over them and Colby panicked, throwing Gage to the ground so he could cover his eyes. Glowing rocks burned through his hat and rolled beneath his pressed collar. He screamed and dropped the blade, tearing off his shirt and trying to shake the burning stones out of the fabric. They melted through the clothing and fell around him in a circle of bright red, smoldering against dry leaves.

"Damn you, Ash Lawson. Damn you to hell!" Colby screamed. He looked disheveled, his shirt steaming with holes peppered through it.

"Been there for months now," I said. "Thanks to you."

A calm fell over his face, but I recognized the look in his eyes and felt his demeanor change. He opened his mouth to speak but thought better of it, biting his lip. "You done gone and messed up now, boy. First my granddaddy's gun, and now his hat. I'm gonna have to make a mess out of you."

"No more threats. No more chasing me. This, whatever it is, ends here. You can decide how. Walk away, or don't. It's up to you. Either way, it's over."

He laughed. "You didn't have the gull to kill me two years ago when you had the chance, and I'm damn sure you don't have it in you today. And if you think that rocky giant is going to do it for you, well, you must think me stupid. You don't think I came here alone, do you?"

I heard the growl and the snap of teeth clamping together, but it was too little, too late. Gage screamed as a massive wolf's jaws latched around the back of his neck and pinned him to the ground. I didn't see where it came from, but without a thought I threw my boot into the wolf's side. Ribs cracked beneath the force and he flew back a dozen feet, skidding across the leaves. Gage cursed, blood pouring from the back of his neck. He jumped to his feet, picking up Soren's blade. The dagger burst into color, vibrant greens sparkling from the glass in Gage's grip.

Colby was partway into his shift: bones creaked and snapped, his face stretched outward, bones shifting and growing beneath the surface. His arms and legs buckled, unhinging themselves and bending backward into a crouch. The seams on his clothes ripped and clear fluid lubricated the transition, dripping down his arms as skin broke and fell away in strips, making way for a thick fur coat to push through the surface. Jet-black hair covered his body with streaks of white decorating his chest. Clawed paws dug into the earth, kicking dirt and leaves behind him. He opened his jaws, snapping at the air. Drool sagged from his jowls and fell to the earth as a low growl resonated in his throat. The glass vial still hung around his neck.

My blade enhanced everything. My muscles relaxed and expanded while fatigue faded beneath adrenaline. I was ready to face him, but Colby wasn't alone. A red wolf lunged from the rocks and tackled me. Huge paws pinned me to the earth, leaves crunching as I turned my head side to side to avoid its vicious bite. Saliva dripped like sticky rain, and raw flesh clung to its teeth.

Panic tasted thick at the back of my throat. I struggled with the wolf, using everything to keep his jaws from my throat. I tried to find a way to disable him. I couldn't. He was too strong, and Colby had closed the distance between us. An amarok: the shifter who could not be dominated by any alpha had taken a pack of his own and he'd let them do the dirty work. He'd move in only for the kill.

Adrenaline overrode my thoughts. That's what this was. Kill or be killed. No hesitation. I had to survive. I twirled the blade in my hand and pulled my arms away. Without any restrictions holding him back, the wolf's jaws snapped toward me, but he wasn't fast enough. I stuck the glass blade in the opening of his mouth, the sharpened point driving through the top of his gums. He yelped and pulled away, but I didn't let him escape. I gripped the fur and drove the weapon through his rib cage. He tried to jerk back but it made it worse. The blade slid deeper, driving the final few inches into his chest before hitting heart. He stopped fighting. Burned flesh seared the air and his body collapsed on top of me.

Inch by inch the body lost all color. The red coat turned grey and then white, growing hot until it started to smoke. His body deteriorated in a smolder that devoured him from the inside out. Before long there was nothing left but a wolf-shaped pile of soot. I rose from it, a shower of ash spilling off me in a cloud of white. Steam resonated around me, warmth from the deceased shifter rising in the air.

My heart rattled against my ribs. Adrenaline, rage, and fear danced alongside one another. The wolf's final ashes hit the ground and the tremble of nervousness that had clung to my chest vanished, replaced with remorse. The deed was done. I wanted to vomit. My insides felt cold and rotten, but I was alive. I did what I had to do. It was me or him. I thought telling myself would settle the unease. It didn't.

Colby didn't give me a chance to linger on the doubt. He leaped for my throat and I spun away. Claws dug into my back, tearing the scarred skin that once released my wings. I cried out and a flash of heat covered my back before the trickle of blood came. Colby's lips curled, baring fangs in what I could only imagine was a grand animalistic smile.

Another two wolves came out of the trees and rushed me. Colby's snarl snapped at the air and they stopped, backing away and turning their sights on Gage. I'd been claimed. He wanted to be the one who ended it.

He faked a lunge and I jerked the knife back, ready to strike. He examined the response, knowing full well today I intended to use it. We stepped around one another, a choir of jaws and teeth breaking in the air behind me. I told myself Gage would be okay. He had to be. I couldn't turn my back on Colby. I did that once, but never again.

He faked left and then right, watching my every reaction. He was aggressive, controlling the fight. Waiting for me to falter. I wouldn't. The wolf sprung forward in a full-frontal assault. I dodged left and planted my feet, both hands hitting his sides. The impact pushed him away, but I curled my fingers into his fur and held on tight. The skin stretched in my skin and I used the momentum against him, swinging his body around and throwing him into the rocky face of the mountain. Handfuls of fur fell from my hands. Bones crunched upon impact and he rolled off the rock. Colby shook and broken leaves flew off his body. I had thought he'd need a moment to recover, but he attacked immediately, this time catching me off guard.

He moved in a blur, a smear of black going left, right, left. His jaws clamped around my ankle, squeezing tight and breaking flesh. I felt the spill of blood and then he released me, running off. He'd vanished. Warmth trickled down my leg like boiling water over flesh. I limped, turning in a circle to find him. Gage had slain one wolf and faced another. It was smaller than the rest and moving in.

I heard the shuffle of leaves when claws cut across my back again, opening the previous wound wider. The attack dropped me to my knees and out of reaction I swung the blade wildly, catching the back side of Colby's hind leg. He yelped, hitting the ground and limping in a splatter of red.

My arm felt fuzzy and the blade became hard to hold. The muscles in my shoulders twitched and before I knew what was happening, Colby's claws cut the back of my leg. I dropped the blade into a pile of leaves and fell forward. The amarok circled in front of me.

Olive-colored eyes looked wild with the hunt. He lowered his head, stalking forward with methodical steps. I scrambled for the blade but it was lost in a maze of yellows and browns. Colby broke into a sprint and lunged. Massive paws hit my chest and hammered me back into the ground. Wet jaws clamped around my shoulder, fangs digging into my chest and back. Blood gushed over me, and I screamed. Flashes of white and black blurred my vision while angelic vitality pulsed. The wrath. I didn't need to summon it. It was coming whether I wanted it to or not. Gage was across the clearing, fiery fists searing into the last wolf. I feared for him, hoping he took cover with Tryst and Soren.

Blinding energy unfurled from my hands. The leaves were swept into the air, golden streaks crackling between the broken foliage. I pressed my fingers into Colby's body and the wrath collided with him like a train wreck. His body seized and he yelped, but it was muffled as golden beams gripped his soul. They cut through his body like lasers piercing flesh. Burned hair stung my nostrils while fear gripped my throat. The amarok, a king among wolves, had succumbed to an angelic curse. I only hoped I didn't go with him.

Colby's pulse slowed. His muscles gave way to the wrath that seized them. It engulfed everything that made him alive and burned it away from within. The heat became so intense I felt my skin split. Something spilled from my fingertips and spikes drilled through my hands. I cried out and the dots I'd almost surrendered to returned with a vengeance. The world waned in and out of focus. The blood that rushed from my wounds had left me weakened, and the wrath consumed me. My mind dimmed. Without consciousness, the wrath faded, dwindling inside. I felt myself falling and a bed of leaves crashed around me. My head bounced off the ground. Then there was nothing.

The world returned in a haze. Warmth simmered over my skin and my head throbbed with intensity. Colby lay a few feet away from me. His chest rose and fell with weak breaths, but otherwise he didn't move. His eyes stared at me, broken and defeated, but I didn't feel like a champion.

All the fur on the side of his body had been burned away. His skin had been torn open and blood gurgled from the wound. The skin was raw and burned, bubbles of swollen flesh popping as clear fluid spilled over his body. His breathing was ragged and wheezy, and power flourished around him. Bones crunched and his body shifted, the wolf fading to its human counterpart. As the leaves slid around him during the shift, a glimmer of blue revealed itself.

It hurt to move. My fingers were raw and blistered, the skin broken like a spiderweb that ran up to my elbows. I forced myself up and took the blade in hand. It hurt to hold, but as my fingers wrapped around the base, a jolt of revitalization shot through me. It didn't help with the damage that had been done, but it made me feel alive.

Colby lay before me, naked among a pile of bloodstained leaves. His left foot was lacerated, flesh curling back around exposed muscle and bone that had been cut. His chest and side were scarred with my handprints, the grey and white hairs that once decorated his chest were singed.

"That's a roll in the...leaves I never saw coming." His words were slow and wispy and when he laughed, it forced him to cough. His body spasmed and he cursed.

"I told you, Colby. It's over."

"Oh, it ain't over till I say it's over." He tried to grin but flinched. I knew he could still feel the scorch of my wrath. I could too. Lucky for me, it'd knocked me out before the full effect was unleashed.

I took the vial from his neck as Gage limped toward us. I handed it to the typhon who was covered in bites and scratches. He'd fared better than me. Most of them were superficial.

"Come now, Ash. You ain't no killer. Not really. You go your way and I'll go mine...or lay here until I can. We can call it even. I took from you, you took from me. Let's leave it at that, shall we?" He took a heavy breath and cringed. "You ain't no killer, Ash. Come one, Angel Boy. Be the man I know you can be." He was almost in tears. Was it the reality of what was about to happen or the pain? Maybe both. "I can help you, kid. Hendrik, Gareth, they're not what you think, and ATOM's at the Academy. They know something ain't right. They're waiting for you. I can help."

"It's too late for that. You know it is."

"It don't have to be like this. You ain't no killer, Angel Boy. We both know that. Don't be a killer. Please..."

"I wasn't a killer. At least I never meant to be. Now I have to. For them." I acknowledged Tryst and Soren as they crawled out from the mountain's nook, placing my hand on his chest. I wanted to turn away but I had to face my choice head-on. I put the tip of the blade against his chest. My hands shook, making it impossible to pinpoint the right position.

"Ash, please—"

I couldn't listen to him anymore. He gasped as the blade slid in and released a throaty gurgle. I felt resistance when it hit the ribs and I tilted the blade, forcing it the final few inches. My hand trembled as Colby's final breath left. It was short and weak. He didn't have any fight left to give. The color in his eyes faded, stolen by death. Stolen by me.

Colby Adams was dead. His body deteriorated and tiny flakes of ash lifted into the air as wind blew across the glade. I watched each of them flutter out of sight. Partly out of disbelief; partly out of respect. It was over. I should have felt a breath of relief. The man who took my wings and destroyed everything I had built was gone.

But I didn't feel relieved; I felt sad. I hadn't hesitated. I killed without pause. I took his life and the life of his allies because I had to, but there was nothing glamorous about it. I survived, as had my friends, but there was no victory, just more blood on my hands.

CHAPTER 34

We set up camp near the nook in which we'd found Soren. All was quiet. Even the beasts' rumbles we often heard had faded. Soren's head lay in Tryst's lap, and she ran fingers through his hair. We'd found his shirt strewn in the leaves, but the rest of his clothes had vanished. I gave him my spare jeans. They were too big, but better than the alternative of traversing in his underwear. My other shirt went to Gage. We'd used his tattered one to bandage ourselves.

"I remember the first time I killed," Gage said. I didn't have a response for him. How could I? He nudged me with his elbow. "Don't sweat it. The feeling goes away."

I shifted against the wall. I knew the feeling. It gripped my chest like a black hole, sucking everything inside. It felt cold and relentless, chilling my veins. Another grew in the pit of my stomach. Vomit stung the back of my throat. I'd thrown up twice. I'd keep this one down.

"Doubtful," I whispered.

"I don't understand what you're so upset about. If you didn't kill him, he'd have torn up you and your friends. You're practically a hero." The last was said with a shred of sarcasm.

"Whatever, I don't want to talk about it."

"*Whatever* is right. Get it done, right? Get over it. Bigger fish to fry. Like Hendrik."

Tryst perked up and stared at us over the fire. "Hendrik?

What's he talking about, Ash?"

"I have no idea. Go on, Gage. What tale will you weave for us today?"

His head rocked against the wall and he rolled his eyes. "You heard Colby. Hendrik can't be trusted. He's the ultimate survivor. He'll betray you to save himself. Survival at all costs."

"And you want the same thing he does, so isn't it convenient that this comes from you?"

"No, actually I find it rather inconvenient since you don't believe me."

"The man let us go," Tryst said. "How can you say we can't trust him?"

"Did he? He set you free in dense, cursed woods that he was too afraid to navigate himself, all so you could bring him an ancient gift to set *him* free. You three are puppets. As soon as you give him what he wants, he'll burn you at the stake." Gage settled in against the ground and stared up at the stars. "Believe what you want. Obviously I'm not going to convince you otherwise. But before you walk out of these woods and carelessly give him whatever he wants, you should make sure he's held up his end of the bargain."

"Or give it to you, right?" I interjected.

"Naturally, that's the option I prefer. It'd make my life a hell of a lot easier. But either way, I'm not going back to the Academy. Mission completed or not, I'm out of that hellhole and back to the real world."

"And how do you plan to do that?"

Gage shrugged. "I don't plan to do anything. I have connections, remember? King Typhon and all that."

He drifted off to sleep with an ease that made me jealous. We'd been in a fight for our lives and aside from a few injuries, he didn't seem fazed. While the same events ate away at me, burning like a hot ember. I hated him for that, yet a part of me remained grateful I wasn't that far gone.

I stoked the coals and threw a few branches on the flames. The fire grew, heat penetrating through the cold air that had befallen us. The fire cast a healthy glow around us, and I inched myself closer to it. I wasn't ready for darkness. Not yet.

"How is he?" I inspected Soren's feet. I'd removed the barbs, but the open wounds were wide and infected. He'd have trouble walking tomorrow. Thankfully we'd found his boots not far from camp. Though how much help they'd be with his feet in that condition I wasn't sure.

"Soliloquy is working. It's slow going, but I think he'll be okay." She brushed the hair from her face. "I think the realization that Trace isn't here will hurt most. He'll have to live through it all over again. It nearly broke him the first time."

"He and Trace were close, huh?"

"That's an understatement. Trace was special to him. To both of us." Her eyes fluttered shut for a moment and she took a deep breath. I took her hand in mine and squeezed. She smiled, but it didn't take the sadness from her eyes. "I hate this place, Ash. Even more than the Academy. Tell me we're going to make it."

I hated the doubt she felt. I wanted to take it all away, but I couldn't—I felt it too. The way Blackwood made me feel, the things we had to do, it was as nightmare. I shook my head, wishing I could chalk it up to a bad dream.

I'd made promises I couldn't keep before and I knew there was a chance I couldn't keep this one, but I couldn't bear the look in her eyes. If a few simple words could vanquish it, I'd speak them. After all, if I broke my promise, I wouldn't live to regret it.

"We will. I promise. We're close, I can feel it. Once we find the tree, we'll have the blood we'll escape this horrible place and start our new lives."

Her fingers interlocked with mine, her touch soft and warm regardless of the harshness she'd endured here.

"I hope so," she whispered. "Finding it is going to be the hard part."

"No, it's not." Soren's eyes didn't open but his lips moved. He shifted in Tryst's lap and rolled onto his side. "When the sun rises, I will show you."

Soren limped the entire way, but never once complained. He started with a stick as his crutch, but as the day passed he tossed it away and hobbled at an impressive pace. Whatever pain he felt was overridden by the chance to find his friend. It was more than I could say for Gage, who cursed and whimpered every step. I could relate. Spurs snapped around my ankle each time I put pressure on it. Barbs laced the muscles and shot up into my knee. It gave out on more than one occasion, but I did my best to remain strong. I tried to ignore the bite wound on my shoulder altogether. If Soren could fight through it, so could I.

Soren's navigational decisions were debatable. We weaved back and forth through the trees, and I was sure we'd passed the same landmarks multiple times, but none of us questioned him. We didn't have a better alternative. Additionally, he was struggling emotionally. The time we'd been apart remained a mystery. Nobody knew what he'd gone through and he wasn't quick to offer an explanation. He'd rediscovered a lost friend. A piece of himself he thought was gone. The realization that it was all a façade must have been unbearable.

We scaled an incline that steepened every few feet. By the time we crested the top, we were on our hands and knees, feet sliding against a slick slope of dirt. I rolled across the ground when I reached the top and discovered a shift in the air. It was no longer dry and scented with rotten pine. The air was thick, humid, and electric, the stench of decayed wildlife coming in waves that caused my eyes to water.

"God, what the hell is that smell?" Gage groaned.

"Blackwood," Soren said. "We're here."

Spikes of vitality prickled across my skin, slithering like a snake over sand. It pressed downward like a new force of gravity, measuring any who dared enter its realm. It had a life of its own, coming and going as it pleased and stealing my breath. The humidity alone made sweat form in my palms, but the fear enhanced it. It felt like Hendrik poured despair into my soul, but the headmaster wasn't here and whatever I felt was stronger and more subtle than anything I'd experienced.

"Where is he?" Soren sounded confused. "Trace should be here. He should be right here."

Gage scoffed. "Nobody else is going to say it, so I will. Trace is as gone now as he was a year ago. He was never here."

Soren cast a glare that could've turned the typhon to stone. "Shut up. You don't know. He saved me from those shifters. He wouldn't abandon me. Not now. Something is wrong."

"It's Blackwood," Tryst said. "Nothing feels right."

He shook his head, trudging forward and scanning the woods. We circled the area for half an hour and Soren didn't let up. He limped along, fighting to find the friend that didn't exist. Each time we found a new path, hope reignited on his face, only to dwindle away. Tryst was right; this would be hell for him.

Exhaustion wore us down, but Soren kept his pace. I lost sight of him somewhere around a bend in the woods, and began to worry. If the forest twisted while we were turning, we'd lose him again. I sprinted, calling out his name, but he never responded. Tryst and I kept running, but Gage refused to expend any more energy than necessary. He believed loss was like a band-aid—take it off fast and hard. Tryst and I felt Soren needed to be let down easy.

We turned the corner and found Soren on his knees at the bottom of a steep incline. A massive hill protruded from the ground, trees surrounding its base. Soren mumbled to himself, sobs destroying whatever words he tried to speak. We slowed our pace, hesitant to approach. I don't think either of us knew what to do or say to make him feel better. We lingered for a few minutes, watching his shoulders shake. I thought he'd broken and given up his quest for imaginary people, but then he fell back off his knees and a pair of legs that were not his own were revealed.

"Soren?"

Gage caught up, still complaining to himself. He pushed past us and stormed over to Soren. "You know what. I've had enough of this. Your friend is gone, Soren. Probably dead. We have a bigger goal here than searching for some long-lost boy—" Gage looked back at us, jaw hanging open. He shook his head in disbelief. "Trace?"

Bits of ashen flesh were revealed between clumps of mud and blood. Wounds covered his pale skin from tiny scratches to deep gouges. Most of them were red and swollen with infection. His clothes were tattered, hanging off a scrawny build. He looked starved. His eyes were open, golden orbs gleaming. The boy whose bed I'd slept under for months lay fatally wounded along a pit of dirt and broken twigs. Claw marks marred his chest and neck, while a vicious bite wound along his arm had scabbed over. The fatal wound, however, was a gouge in his side that hadn't stopped bleeding. Black veins rippled around the wound and expanded across his stomach.

"Demon." He breathed the word, his voice barely audible.

"No. No. No," Soren pleaded. "Stay with me! Don't do this." He gripped Trace's hand tight, tears falling in streams.

Tryst fell to her knees, taking Trace's other hand. "Wh-Wh-How?"

Trace smiled, head drooping. "For you two. I thought—" He cringed and began coughing. His face twisted and it took him a few dramatic gasps to catch his breath. "I thought we could be free."

"But how?"

"Hendrik," he said. Tryst looked at me as if I could answer the questions that raced through her mind. I couldn't. Trace touched her face, the movement looked heavy and difficult, but it was enough to regain her attention. "I made a deal to get us out. I thought I could. I almost did. Almost."

"You can come with us now," Soren said. "We can help you."

Trace shook his head. "The infection is too far. It's wrapping around my heart as we speak. I haven't much time, Soren."

"No." Soren's voice trembled and his face dropped into Trace's chest. Trace cupped the back of his head and stroked his hair the way I'd seen Tryst do so many times before. "Please don't do this. Please don't go."

"Be safe and know that I will watch over both of you," Trace said. Soren denied it, refusing anything he might suggest. Trace looked sad, holding his friend close before looking at the typhon. "Gage…"

Gage looked awkward and uncomfortable, but he stepped forward. "Yeah?"

"You have a chance that now eludes me—life. My time here is done, yours is not. Not yet. Take this." He handed him a blade much like our own, purple and gold shimmering in the glass. Gage reached for the blade and Trace moved with surprising speed, grabbing his wrist.

"What the hell are you doing?" Gage looked panicked.

Trace stared into his eyes, golden orbs glowing like a distant sun. "You have wronged many. Myself included. But I understand your mission, and I forgive you."

"I don't know what you're talking about."

"Gage?" Trace whispered, his eyes narrowed. "I forgive you."

The tension on Gage's face broke, and for a moment a look passed over him I didn't quite understand. He almost looked ashamed. After a moment of staring at one another, Gage nodded but didn't speak, moving away as soon as Trace released him.

The golden eyes wandered from face to face offering kind smiles until they met mine. He studied me to the point I felt uncomfortable. I shifted my weight from one foot to the other when Trace signaled me to come closer. I had never met the boy, only heard of him, yet his eyes found me as though they'd rediscovered an old friend.

Tryst and Soren backed away as per Trace's request, and I knelt down beside the boy. He looked like a ghost but somehow not defeated. He carried an air of calm and peace that emanated around him. It was as if he was satisfied with the end of his life and the way it came about. He stretched out his hand and I took it in mine. Regardless of how ragged he appeared, his grip remained firm and his skin soft. He pulled me close and I felt something I'd never felt before—tranquility. It seeped into my body, calming warmth that vanquished the despair that filled me. The regrets, the hate, the fear—it all drifted away from a simple touch.

"Finish what I could not," he whispered. "Take what you need and get my friends to safety. The forest will consume you the longer you're here. Keep them safe. Protect them. Love them. Be the angel your soul seeks. You do not need wings to fly." His grip began to falter, and his head fell against a bank of dirt. He coughed again, eyes glossing over and a tear running down his cheek.

Soren shoved me away and screamed Trace's name, but it was too late. There was enough time for Trace to meet his gaze and offer a brief smile. Black veins crawled up his chest and gripped his throat, spilling up over his jawline and across his face. A final breath drifted from his lips before his body sagged. Soren buried his face in Trace's neck, hugging his friend tight as the color vanished from his eyes. Pale skin turned grey and cracks formed as his skin broke. Black seeped out of the creases like oil across pavement before his skin turned to ash and flaked to the ground. It spread across his body until his entire form was nothing but an ash replica of their friend. It shattered in Soren's embrace. Once again, Trace was gone. This time for good.

CHAPTER 35

Soren lay on the ground, sobbing into a pile of ash. Pleas for Trace's return fell from his lips. He begged for it not to happen, but it was already done. The wind picked up and ash swirled into the air. Soren jumped to his feet, limping along and cursing the wind as it took pieces of Trace away. He swiped at the air in an attempt to grasp any flake of soot he could, but the only ash he retained was smeared across his skin. Tears fell down Tryst's face and I pulled her against me. As the final few flakes vanished over the trees, Soren dropped to his knees and unleashed a scream.

"What the hell is that?" Gage asked, breaking a silence.

A white orb lingered in the air where Trace's body had been, swirling with lines of gold spinning around it. It moved up and down and side to side before floating up the hill.

"His soul," Soren whispered, springing to his feet and chasing after it. "His soul! No. No, you can't have it!" he screamed.

The incline was steeper than it looked, and Soren trampled upward as if he felt no pain. The feeling of despair thickened, and cresting the peak we found an almost empty hilltop. A tree—if you could call it that—fifteen feet wide and at my best guess a hundred feet tall stood in the center. Its branches were as thick around as an oak, stretching like the goliath arms of a giant. There were no leaves, only large green bulbs spotted with white dots of mold, flowers that refused to bloom. Massive roots gushed from the earth, spindling above and plunging back down only to emerge again a few feet later. They were thick and covered in moss, not at all like the black bark that covered the tree. It looked like it had been scorched by flames and charred with destruction. Dark energy amplified off of it in tides of hopelessness. It became hard to breathe, as though the air at the top was thinner. Breath clung to my throat and my mouth went dry. My tongue became sandpaper, and my lips began to split. I reached for the canteen I'd filled an hour prior but found it empty. I hadn't had a drink.

The orb we'd followed flittered through the air, circling enormous branches and darting left and right. It drew closer to the tree before an arm of black smoke reached out and engulfed it. It pulled Trace's soul into the tree, and Soren lost his mind. He stomped across the ground, screaming as if the barky monstrosity could hear him. He demanded it return Trace's soul. He demanded it release him. It didn't.

Gage gasped. "This is it. This is why we're here, isn't it?"

Soren's eyes were almost evil. "How can you say that? How can you even care about this anymore? Trace, my Trace."

Tryst pulled Soren into a hug, but the deva's eyes were locked on Gage and ripe with rage. "Soren, he's gone," Tryst said.

The words pushed Soren away; he looked appalled. I expected him to scream and shout at her, instead he looked heartbroken and fell back into her.

"He's not. I can still feel him. His aura; his life force and the way it calmed each soul it touched. It's still here." He backed away and stared at the tree. "It took him away from me."

I could feel it too. Among the depression that drifted around the tree were flickers of light and hope like a life gone but not yet forgotten.

"He's still here." Soren reached out and closed his eyes, shades of green lustrous magic around his fingers. "He's in there among magic both dark and old. I can taste the sulfur and feel the death. It took Trace."

Fog seeped into the clearing from the base of the hill. Thick and heavy moisture filled the air, clouding everything around us. Tryst put her hand on Soren's shoulder and tried to pull him back but he wouldn't budge.

"We need to get you out of here. You're going to make yourself sick."

"No!" His voice was sharp. Streams of green zigzagged across the hilltop, wrapping around the tree like the stripes of a candy cane. "Its story unfolds before me." His skin turned a shade of green and his eyes widened. "It's full of violence and horrors that Hendrik never shared. A story similar to the one he told, but not the same."

"What does it show you?" Tryst asked.

The deva's green eyes expanded, glowing like a spark behind an emerald. His face fell void of emotion and his voice lost all emphasis. It was flat and empty, like a robot reciting a script.

"The witches came here as a final attempt at life, hidden from those that would hurt them. The Hunters were relentless, barreling through the woods with weapons drawn, trying to capture them." He walked forward, spreading his arms out wide. Spirals of iridescent greens spilled from his hands and wrapped around the tree. "Bodies fell here, here, and there. Dozens of them, deconstructed like toys. Blood everywhere. Nobody was a match for the witches and those that didn't die became enslaved. Men contorted into beasts, the humanity all but destroyed within them. With the trinity the witches gave them new life, but it confined them. Over time the witches realized the balance of nature had been broken, and nature's response was harsh. In seeking freedom, the witches found a self-made prison, feasting on souls in order to regain what they'd lost. But nature would not be cheated. They had broken the decree of balance, and in order to return things as they were, the witches needed to destroy that which they had created. But Enoch would not go easily. He would not allow the witches to appease nature at his expense, and so he started the revolt. The Genesis stole the trinity and everything it contained, cursing the witches themselves. They were bound with dark magic and banished to a life that would never know peace. A life among the very souls they'd consumed and any who died in the woods thereafter."

"Why didn't the Genesis kill them?" I asked.

Soren didn't hesitate in his response. Whatever connection he had with Blackwood right now provided all the answers he could seek.

"They could not, for killing their creators would be to destroy the power that made them, therefore destroying themselves." Soren turned to me, the brown in his eyes coming back to life.

Another riptide of gloom washed over us, this time stronger than the last. It came with a force that blew the hair from my face and caused me to stumble back.

"Hendrik is Enoch," I said.

Soren nodded. "He refuted nature's balance in a quest for power. The other Genesis did not share his dream. They wished for peace, and death, but they grew to fear Hendrik more than their masters. The witches mimic Gage's warning. Hendrik cannot be trusted."

"The witches?" Tryst said. "You're talking to them?"

"Their spirits are bound within the roots, their bodies not yet decayed. They wait to arise and for the curse to be broken. They're not happy we're here. They know what we're after and they know who sent us." He stumbled back and looked at the tree in horrors. "We are on the same mission as Trace, and the witches will kill us as they did him. They want us to leave."

"No," Gage said. "We came all this way. We're not leaving until we get what we need."

"This is their final warning," Soren said. "It's no joke, you guys. They're upset."

"We will leave," I said. "But Gage is right. First we need the blood. No more than what we're owed. Our freedom depends on it."

"Time's up," Soren said.

The power faded from his hands, and the lines of magic that wrapped the tree were devoured by black smoke that seeped from the bark. The ground trembled and a loud crack resounded. The bark on the Blackwood began to break and as the ground quaked, it ruptured. The tree split and bright green beams flashed outward. Mist drifted from the wood like a smoke machine while silhouettes appeared in the light. The shape of a head first, then shoulders. It stepped out of the opening and dark smoke wafted around it. The familiar face we'd thought lost to the Blackwood was revealed. Trace.

Ashen hair dangled to his shoulders, clumps of black goo dripping off the ends. Thick black scars had grown over each of his wounds and contrasted pale skin. His golden eyes had been replaced with milky orbs that looked everywhere and nowhere all at once. Black veins rippled about his chest and stomach, snaking up his neck and circling his eyes. Dark claws extended over broken fingernails, and a drop of sticky fluid ran off fanged teeth and dribbled over his chin. He hissed.

"Trace." Soren fell back, eyes wide with fear. Tryst guarded her friend, stepping in front of him and pulling out her blade. She knew the truth—that wasn't Trace. Trace was gone.

More bodies piled out of the tree behind Trace. First a demonic Colby Adams that stood next to the boy. His white eyes were almost glowing, jagged teeth stretching out over his bottom lips. Trace and Colby appeared the most composed, while the other five that followed seemed decrepit. Their skin flaked off in long strips, exposing the wet black flesh underneath. Their human teeth had been replaced with yellow and black bark, the edges of them curling like wood from a flame. They moved as a single unit toward us, unleashing an ancient sound of beasts forgotten from our world. With it came the stench of sulfur followed by decay and rotten meat.

"Leave!" They screamed in unison. Black spittle shot from their mouths, demonic tones swirling around us like a shadowed beast striking the daylight. They stopped, standing like statues in a single formation that watched our every move. It was as if they were allowing us a final chance to escape.

The air grew still. When we didn't concede to their demand, the demons charged like a herd of bulls. I drew my blade and lava scorched lines into Gage's arms. He scooped up a handful of dirt and flung it forward, bullets of magma peppering the creatures. Their skin sizzled, burned flesh stung the air and chunks fell from their bodies in ashy clumps, but they didn't slow. They roared in response, plunging onward in a wash of devil's breath.

All at once, the ground in front of us broke open. Thick vines swung out from the dry earth and rose like serpents. They snapped at the air like a whip, green waves dancing around them. Soren stepped in front of everyone, sadness filling his eyes while emerald magic snapped between his fingers. His hand moved left and the vines responded. Energy crackled and the roots lashed out at the demons. They fell like bowling pins, white bodies lined with black tumbling back toward the tree. A tear fell from Soren's eyes as Trace hit the ground, but the look on his face said he knew the friend he cared for was gone. Part of me wondered if that was motivation for him. The demon before him didn't deserve to look like his friend.

Gage ran into the mob of bodies that littered the forest floor and plunged a glass blade into one. I followed behind the typhon as a demon tried to sink jaded teeth into the back of his leg. I thrust the blade down and twisted it through his body. The demon screeched an ungodly sound, falling limp. I expected it to turn to ash, but it vanished in a mist of black smoke and seeped into the bark of the Blackwood.

More demons stepped out of the opening and trampled the earth. One woman ran at me. Half her hair was torn out, exposing a wet black scalp, the other half was dry and brittle, curling at the ends in thick knots and frays. She punched my chest, the impact like a hammer against a toothpick. My body folded backward, hit by the force of a thousand men. I rolled across the ground and down the hill we'd desperately climbed. The demon perched herself on the edge, her body a shadow in the thick fog that encased the forest. Her head canted to the side like a dog trying to understand what you were saying. She clamped her teeth together, biting at nothing before leaping into the air. She hit the ground with ease, earth exploding around her in fireworks of blacks and browns. The ground shook in response and she stalked forward, relentless in her pursuit. After a few steps, her body jerked and a red dagger poked through her chest. A gurgling sound came from her throat before she fell to the ground in a blast of smoke. Black blood dripped off Tryst's ruby blade, and she looked terrified at what she'd done.

Trace stood at the top of the hill and unleashed a blood-curdling sound that shot bullets through my head. He moved with unmatched speed—a blur of white and black—and crashed into Tryst, sending her flying back. I jumped to my feet, but it wasn't needed. A branch reached down from the tree above and coiled around his body. Soren stood partway down the hill, wisps of energy glowing around his fingers. He walked down to face his friend, looking broken and sad when he stared up at the demonic reincarnation.

"I'm sorry this happened to you," he whispered.

The demon responded with a mess of growls, unable to articulate a word.

"You deserved better," Soren said, driving the glass weapon into the demon's chest. Trace's face scrunched before his body exploded into a cloud of black. Then he was gone once again.

"Soren," I said.

"Don't." He held up a hand stained in black. "Get the blood and get us the hell out of here."

We ascended the hill to find Gage pinned to the ground by a demon. It's skin smoked with pebbles of hot coals embedded into pale flesh, but it didn't seem fazed. The purple glass blade lay stranded a few feet away in a stretch of dirt. Smoke swirled in the air like a time-lapse video of a storm rolling through. Three more demons entered the earthy arena and charged toward the typhon. Their teeth smashed together in a frenzy of hunger, but they wouldn't get a taste. Not with Soren there. He might not be able to feed off the forest, but his nature-born gifts flared without protest. This was his stadium.

Soren hobbled forward, vines wrapping around the demon's feet. With a wave of his hand, the demon's body snapped across the clearing, crumpling into a distant tree. He picked up the purple weapon in one hand and gripped green in the other, limping toward two more demons who'd fallen to the deva's wrath, bound by vines and branches. He drove blades into their backs, and in bursts of smoke they were gone, but it didn't seem to matter. As quickly as we could slay them, more entered the battlefield.

Fog and power shimmered in the air as more demons trampled into the clearing. Soren cried out and fell to the ground as claws raked across his chest. Blood seeped through his shirt and the demon's fist hammered him to the ground. Soren could hardly move. He was stronger in the woods, but he wasn't warrior. He curled onto his side and covered his face as if that could protect him. The demon's claws cut across his arm, tearing deep wounds into his flesh. He shrieked and it reminded me of the day he'd been lashed. Gage screamed and molten rock and fire pelleted the demon's back. It snarled and screamed but before it could move, Gage jump through the air in an otherworldly bound and crushed it beneath his foot. He reached down with rocky fingers and gripped the demons throat. Lava coursed through the crevices of his stony skin and intensified. His entire hand was aglow with red, smoke fluttering up around the creature's skin. In a few moments, the white of the demons eyes were glowing red, teardrops of lava spilling down and searing his flesh until all that remained was a drift of black smoke.

"Ash?" Gage screamed. "We can't keep this up. How about that fancy golden gift of yours."

"It could kill us all!" I said, dodging a set of talons that swiped toward me.

"Get it done!" he replied.

For each demon we killed, two more were unleashed. Each line of them slower than the last, but in time they would overwhelm us with sheer numbers. A dozen crept up the edges of the hill around us. I didn't even know where they were all coming from now, but Gage was right, we couldn't fight them. Not all of them. If we didn't get the blood we were dead anyway.

"Everybody get behind me!" I yelled.

Gage helped Soren and once they were out of the direct line of fire, I opened that special part of me that housed death. The wrath spiraled up with ease. I'd called it more in the past few days than I had in years, but as easily as it came, it wasn't tamed. The wild gift curated in my palms. As dangerous as it was, it made me feel strong. It infused me with unmatched energy, but above all, the more I used it the more it craved release.

A dozen demons moved toward us and a handful more came up the rear. Gold light sputtered and expanded across my hands. With each draw of energy I summoned, it flourished quicker than before, expanding in my palms. I screamed as it burned and threw it forward in a blast of electrifying force. It crackled in a wave and dark liquid rained over us, clumps of ashy skin rolling across the earth. Funnels of black swirled in a cyclone of smoke and more demons lurched from the tree. The wrath expanded in front of me, growing beyond my reach. Dots dotted my vision. I felt nauseated and my knees went weak. It spilled from my hands and the world shifted into a smear of grey. It was thunderous, moving around me, but it did so on its own accord. It was no longer under my influence. The earth shook, shifting beneath our feet. Dirt fired into the air like a cannon and the ground split open in front of me. The gap widened, swallowing demons in its wake. Heat nipped at my back and seared my shoulders. I panicked as the wrath moved around me. It wouldn't be long before it swallowed everything in its path. I tried to reel back it back but as expected, it would not be quelled. The strength and rage it ignited would not be ignored, and it refused any pull I might have.

Soren, Gage, and Tryst screamed my name. I couldn't respond. I had no control over anything. It burned my eyes and lips;

destroying me from the inside out. Streaks of gold spilled from my hands, mouth, and eyes. It devoured me, growing more expansive than ever. My body became the sun and scorched the earth. I smelled the dirt and forest burning, but I felt the skin on my hands bubbling. Demons squealed, the wind howled, and my friends' voices begged me to stop. I couldn't.

Gage yelled; Soren and Tryst's cries followed. My hands turned black and soot marred my skin, threatening to peel it back. Heat lanced the muscle in my arms; I screamed, unable to bear it. I shook my hands as if that could stop it. It couldn't. Streaks of it cut across the clearing like a laser searing lines into a tree. I was blinded, seeing nothing but smears of grey everywhere I turned. Fire rose in my chest, expanding in my throat. The air became hot, each breath drawing in heaves of smoke. I felt the lives of demons around me crushed to smoke while I seared myself alive. We wouldn't die at the hands of demons. We'd die by mine.

Through my friends' shouts, I screamed for it to stop, but it didn't retract. All I could do was try to deter its path. I fell forward, collapsing onto the ground and plunging power into the earth. For a moment, there was a reprieve. My sight returned, white dots flickering in front of me. Demonic bodies littered the ground, not all of them banished to smoke. They crawled forward, hardly able to move. The flesh on their bodies had burned away, their growls turned into weak snarls and wispy breaths. But the amnesty granted to us by earth was short lived. The ground ruptured and streaks of gold spilled from the broken earth. I half expected it to shoot straight up into the sky. Instead, it was erratic and beams shot in every direction like a disco ball. I'd sealed our fate.

The world became a blinding wash of white. My head throbbed, slices of heat slashing across my skull. My arms cracked open from palm to elbow, blood and golden light spilling out. I couldn't breathe. My pulse had gone from a racing sprint to a sluggish thud. My chest hurt, the lack of oxygen making me nauseated. Vomit rose in my throat, accelerating the burn that already lingered. Every drop of moisture had been zapped from my body. If it hadn't, I would have cried out in pain. As I fell weak, the wrath didn't subside as expected. If anything it grew. I tried to speak an apology. This wasn't the way I wanted it to be. But before I could utter the words, a heavy thud hit the back of my head. A spear of pain shot through my skull, the wrath vanished, and the world went black.

CHAPTER 36

Bodies littered the ground. Everywhere I looked was destruction. Trees smoldered, dozens of demons struggled along the ground like worms. Their skin smoked, staining the air with their stench. They growled and groaned, but I didn't panic. They couldn't hurt us at this rate. My head pounded. It felt like someone had pressed my skull into the ground with an anvil.

"Tryst?" I tried to talk, but it was barely a word.

I fought to get to my feet, electric heat snapping at the muscles. It ached through my body, crashing in waves of hot and hotter, leaving me dizzy. Steam rose off my arms, spots of skin blistered and red. My arms ached with crackling deep wounds that had scabbed over. It hurt to move my fingers almost as much as it hurt to hold the dagger, but I wasn't about to relinquish my weapon.

Massive crevices in the ground had split the hill apart. Smoke rose from them in grey waves while burned branches and vines lay strewn across the ground. The lines of trees that surrounded the hill were either damaged or gone, having been reduced to nothing but ash. My friends lay behind me, quiet and unmoving.

"Tryst? Soren?" I whispered. "Gage?" They didn't move. Their eyes were closed, skin marred with soot and parts horribly burned. "What have I done?" I reached for Tryst's neck to check her pulse. Her skin was hot to the touch, but her pulse steady. She coughed and rolled onto her side, gagging as dirt and soot were ejected from her mouth. Blood dripped from her nose, painting the ground while she tried to catch her breath.

When she had steadied her breathing, I wrapped my arms around her. "Thank god you're okay."

She hugged me back but it felt weak, and her hands trembled from the heat that had seared them. They were bright red like a vicious sunburn had left its mark.

"I'm okay." She cringed, letting me help her to her feet. "Soren?"

Gage and Soren began to stir. Soren had a wide burn across his forehead, and both arms were blistered. Blood dripped out of his ears, which were as red as Tryst's hands. He shook away his disorientation, but his eyes remained glossy. His chest hadn't stopped bleeding from where the demon's claws had cut him, and he struggled to get to his feet with Tryst's help. They shared a hug, but no words. What was there to say?

Gage got up by himself. He was unsteady at first, but it didn't take long for him to get his bearings. Blisters decorated his neck, his cheek had been cut, and his eye had swelled partway closed, but he still had the energy to stand.

"Is everybody okay?" I asked.

Gage coughed. "No thanks to you, Flapper. You nearly killed us."

"I told you I couldn't—I'm sorry."

"Enough of that," he snapped. "Get over it, right? Besides, that knock I gave you on the head seemed to do the trick. Though at a cost." He lifted his arms, revealing horrible burns that looked almost as bad as mine. The skin had split, and clear fluid trickled from the wounds. His shirt had been burned away, his chest badly seared, and his jeans were shredded. It looked like he had fallen into a pit of coals.

I felt the lump on the back of my head and remembered everything going black. I had wondered what stopped it. I'd hoped I'd done it myself.

"You hit me?"

"Don't get your panties in a bunch. We live to see another day, don't we?" The demons that had survived the attack were starting to recuperate. Their limbs healed, black scars stitching themselves back together. Their groans turned to growls and they began to rise. "Or not."

"The blood, Ash," Soren said. "It won't end until you get the blood."

I gave strict instructions that nobody was to kill any of the demons. That would only elicit a response for more from Blackwood. Instead, we let them crawl along the earth and I approached the tree, almost unable to keep the blade in my hand. Clear fluid ran over my arms, my body's attempt to repair itself, but the forest wouldn't allow it. Soren needed earth, Tryst needed the life force of others, but angels needed sunlight to replenish. Something I'd been deprived of in this shadow-strewn hell.

The Blackwood wasn't just a tree. It was a harbor of souls that the witches and the forest had consumed. Strands of hair and chunks of burned flesh were knitted over the shell of the tree. Soot marred everything. The stench of bile and sulfur flourished off the surface, stinging my nostrils, but worse than anything was the depression that leaked out. It made me feel sick and hopeless. Even without the hurt that resided all over me, I wasn't sure I could lift the blade. I didn't want to. What was the point? I took a deep breath and let my fingers touch the bark. Dots of red and black filled my vision. I felt dizzy, stumbling away. Drops of blood fell from my nose and mouth. Any lingering energy I felt from the wrath was siphoned away. I wanted to fall to my knees and let the tree have me. My soul belonged to it. It wanted me in a way nobody else ever could. There was a place for a horrible person like me inside. A place where I wouldn't have to feel the guilt and despair I'd caused in the world.

I lifted the blade, blue glass shimmering in the darkening forest. Any motivation I'd had the Blackwood sucked away. My desires evaporated. I didn't need freedom; I needed Blackwood. I thought to drag the blade across my throat and let the forest devour my soul. I craved the release and the warmth that would come from the blood. The blade touched my skin and I jerked away, steam rising as the glass burned my throat. The movement brought Tryst, Soren, and Gage into my sightline. They were being backed into a corner of burned trees by an onslaught of demons, and based on the sound there were more coming from the foggy shadows behind them. I shook my head. What was I doing?

The tree called out to me again. It demanded I finish what I'd started. It was enticing. A woman's voice singing and drawing me in like a siren on the water. I tried to shake it away but the voices wouldn't stop. It was old magic trying to devour me. My nose bled and drops fell onto the weapon. It stained the bright blue glass and a chill moved across my shoulders. The voice was right. I had to finish what I started.

I drew back my arm once again and plunged the blade into the wood. The glass should've shattered. Sparkles of blue should have littered the ground like tiny sapphires on a bed of dirt. Instead it slid into the tree as if it were flesh. Electric force snapped in the air. Each hair on my body rose with a static charge like lightning was about to strike. Day turned to night, and the moon came into full view above. Thunder crashed, though there wasn't a cloud in the sky. A gust of wind tore through the clearing and thousands of leaves clapped together like a wave whispering across the sand. Roars resounded on the air as several of the demons had repaired themselves. Black scars had stitched together their wounds and they started to crawl to their feet.

"Ash," Tryst yelled.

A pair of demons charged, and I twisted the blade as hard into the tree as I could. Each demon unleashed a primordial screech that echoed over the wind. Their cries were shrill, eerie sounds that crackled in the air, but the demons froze.

My blade ignited in a flash of blue that spilled from the tree. The wood creaked and shifted and the demonic doorway knitted itself back together. The obscurity and despair that pressed against me lifted, and a trickling sound filled the silence. The blade darkened as it filled with fluid and the small blade at the bottom of the handle opened. I pressed the vial against it and thick purple fluid filled it.

The remaining demons turned to smoke, the barky limbs of Blackwood absorbing them in their entirety. When the vial had filled, the blade sat empty in the tree. I corked the bottle and swung it around my neck, withdrawing the weapon with ease. Dead hair, wood, and pieces of flesh moved over the bark, weaving together until the wound I'd created had closed. Energy pulsed against my chest as the vial touched my skin. It was dark energy, vibrating against me but somehow contained within the glass. My weapon was laced with purple goo; I wiped it along my pants. With the blade sheathed, I hoped it was the last time I'd have to touch it. As strong as it made me feel, I didn't want to need it again.

"I've got it," I said. There was a relief in knowing we'd

accomplished what we set out to do, but with it the adrenaline that had carried me this far faded, and it allowed me to feel every bump and bruise on my body. Apparently there were a lot.

"It's done?" Gage asked. He looked defeated: burns and cuts littered his body, his clothing had become shreds of their former self, and his head was stained with black blood. He reached out for the vial around my neck and I backed away. The purple blade in his hand shifted. Each knuckle turned white as he gripped it. "Are you kidding? After all this, I want to see it at least." His eyes revealed a look that made me uncomfortable. I'd seen it before by the fire, and I took another step back.

"I'll hold on to it for now. The Soliloquy won't last forever. Once we get out of here you can have a look."

His brow furrowed and he threw the blade to the ground, purple glass cutting deep into the dirt. "I'm not going *crazy*, Ash. I killed a horde of demons for you. I deserve this much. After all this, you're still going to give it to Hendrik?" He smashed his fist into the tree.

"I don't know what I'm doing yet. My first priority is getting everybody out of here."

Gage cursed. "I thought after all this we were finally on the same page. I guess not. It doesn't matter anyway. Now that I know what it is, I realize I don't need you at all." He pulled the empty vial that once held Soliloquy out of his pocket and drew the purple blade from the earth. "I'll get my own."

"No!" I said. "We can't."

"Screw you, Ash. You're not calling the shots anymore." He tried to walk past me but I sidestepped, blocking his path and holding him back.

"Gage."

"Get your damn hand off me. Now. Or you're going to lose it." He summoned typhon rage that I wasn't prepared to match and the temperature spiked. I pulled away as his chest stung my already burned skin.

"Don't do this, please. Don't turn on us now."

Gage laughed. "Oh, you've got a sense of humor, do you? I'm turning on *you*?"

I held my hands up to show that I didn't want to fight. "Listen, we'll figure this out. I promise. But right now, we need to leave. Together."

"There is no *we*. The only people you care about are standing right beside you. I'm not one of them, Flapper, so don't tell me what I need to do. I *need* to get that vial, because you don't understand what will happen if I don't." He shook his head, fingers scraping his bloodstained scalp. The anger and determination that filled his eyes gave way to a flicker of fear when he said the last.

"What? But you said—"

"Forget what I said! It's been six years, Ash! Six years. You don't know what it's been like. To have a father abandon you with the enemy and give you some façade of a mission he thinks you'll never accomplish. He put me in that place to get rid of me. He never expected me to succeed. He expected me to die without having to pull the trigger himself."

"If that's true, then you know he doesn't expect you to come back with it," Tryst said.

"He doesn't expect me to come back at all!" Gage screamed. "I'm supposed to be dead. I'm an obstacle. An anchor holding back the typhon line. An embarrassment. He never expected me to become what I am, and if it wasn't for—you can't possibly understand. He knows how close I am now and if I fail...well, I can't fail."

"I'm sorry you've been dealt a crappy hand," I said. "I want to help you. I do. But I can't let you take another vial. We'll find another way."

"There is no other way. I'm taking that vial. So the question that remains is are you going to try and stop me?" The sadness in his eyes was gone, all that remained was determination.

"I don't want to, but if I have to, yes." I cursed the moment as I drew the blade from its sheath. I didn't want this.

Gage scoffed. "What, are you going to kill me? Talk about turning on someone. It's one more vial. One vial and everybody wins."

"That's not how it works," Soren said. "If we take more than is ours, the witches will—"

"Screw the witches. I want my life back!" Gage's foot swung out and caught my ankle, sending flares of pain from Colby's bite to shoot through my leg. I fell on my back and the blade flew out of my hand. He caught my weapon by the handle and with the grace of a dancer, spun it between his fingers and drove it back into the tree. Liquid filled the blade a second time, purple and glimmering as it filled his vial.

"No!" Soren screamed, running toward him.

Gage shoved him to the ground with ease, corked his vial and tore the blade out. The gash in the tree didn't close. More of the tree's blood ran over the bark, pooling on the ground.

The ground quaked and the three sets of massive roots that secured the tree to the earth began to shift. They slid from the dirt and disappeared into the trunk of the massive tree. Another layer of smaller roots beneath began to move. They unwound like a finely made rope, slithering into the trunk and exposing a final layer of thin spaghetti-like roots. They were white and covered in tiny black hairs, hissing as they unraveled and exposed the intricately wrapped prison that had been secured for millennia.

Three partially preserved corpses had been unearthed beneath the roots. Each had patches of bright green moss covering their skin. Their hands were folded over their chests, bodies draped in matching dresses: dark green, lined with white lace, and knitted at the chest like a corset. One had hair as black as midnight, the next a mousy brown, and the last was so white it seemed to glow. Their eyes were closed and sunken in, muscle tissue and bone jutting from a thin layer of nearly transparent skin.

"The witches of Blackwood." Soren crawled around the tree, stopping at each exposed grave and examining the women within. His fingers brushed the outer lining of the root bed and it responded, wrapping around his finger playfully. It drew itself up along his forearm, but he pulled away and crawled toward the woman with hair as white as snow.

"What did you do?" Tryst asked, but she didn't look at Gage. Her eyes were locked on the white witch.

Soren released a sigh and reached into the mossy coffin, brushing a strand of hair that clung to the witch's face. He ran the back of his hands across her cheek.

"Don't do that," I demanded.

"She's trapped," he whispered. "The door is open but she cannot walk through it."

"Good, that means we can get the hell out of here before the witches—"

"No," Soren said. "She is not a witch; she's a goddess. Stronger than the others, she's the queen of Blackwood. She has created so much for this world." His hand continued to stroke her cheek.

"Soren, stop!" Tryst said. "None of this is good."

He didn't respond, his eyes were lost in the mossy corpse, bright green sliding around his fingers. It trickled over her skin, and danced along the outer edges of her bed. Purple illuminations ignited around lines of Soren's power and he smiled. In moments, all the injuries that riddled his body faded and he appeared rejuvenated.

"Get away from her!" I said, grabbing his arm, but he would not be moved. Something grounded him to the earth, like his own legs were roots that reached deeper than I could pull.

An orb the size of a marble formed above the witch, purple on the outside with lines of green like a cat's eye within. It looked at each of us before beginning to turn. Frost formed at the edge of the witch's earthy coffin and slid along the roots. Tiny fireworks of green and purple spurted into the air as the frost moved over it. It danced like a silent orchestra inside the mossy bed until it had covered the witch's body.

"She wants to leave," he said. His voice was distant, his eyes dazed.

Tryst grabbed Soren but purple energy exploded between them and blew her back.

She wasn't hurt, but there was no getting close to him.

"What the hell is happening?" she asked.

"Nothing good," I said.

Gage's magic came to life and he reached toward Soren, grabbing his wrist and jerking it away from the woman.

Soren gasped and pulled his arm to his chest. "Ouch!" he said. Red lines wrapped around his wrist. "What is going—whoa..." He shook his head. "What happened?"

"What the hell are you thinking?" Gage snapped.

"Him? This is *your* fault!" Tryst shouted.

"My fault? All I wanted was to secure a future outside of the hellhole I've called home for the past six years."

"Yeah, well—"

"Enough!" I shouted. They both fell silent as I kneeled next to Soren. "What happened?"

"I...nothing. I can't explain it. She drew me in with her story. I couldn't help myself. I didn't want to stop. I wanted to touch her. She isn't a monster, Ash, not like the demons." He looked at Tryst, eyes still entranced and full of wonder. "She wanted to be left alone. Hendrik put her here, but she didn't deserve it. All she wanted was to appease nature."

In a single breath the air cooled several degrees and the skin tightened against my face. Pools of breath spilled from our lips and a melody came through the shadows. Its song was alluring, and the voice that sang it enticing. I felt a flash of happiness expand inside me.

"We need to leave," Tryst said, breath sputtering from her lips.

"But it feels so good," I replied, unable to contain my smile.

"Ash! Get with the program." Tryst shook me and snapped me out of the trance. I felt dazed, the happiness vanishing even quicker than it came.

The air became ice, the voice growing louder. Gage wasn't paying attention. He smiled, head drifting from side to side with the enchanting harmony.

"Gage!" Soren slapped him across the face and the typhon looked alarmed, shaking his head. "Time to go."

The remaining roots that bound the witch's ankles and wrists began to move. Like a dozen snakes, they unraveled and freed her body. A wall of ice and fog formed in the shadowed trees behind Blackwood and with it, the witch's song grew louder. It was hard not to listen. She demanded attention, and I wanted to give it to her. Upon Soren's command we covered our ears to muffle the sound. The fog began to seep over the clearing and when everybody turned to me, I mouthed the word *run*.

White mist crashed behind us like the thickest of fogs, masking anything that might be in pursuit. Trees crackled and shattered in shards of ice and bark as the frost devoured them in a single blast of winter's breathe. Nobody limped. Adrenaline was full force as we fought the pain in an attempt to survive. We came for a small piece of old magic and instead woke a colossal entity. We had no direction. We turned left, then right, any which way to slow the witch's breath that haunted us. It didn't falter.

"Out!" Tryst shouted. "Which direction is out?" She yelled into the air as if it had the answer, it didn't respond, but her blade did. White mist formed within the glass, a faint flicker following. We turned and it crackled, holding its color. More to the right and it radiated like a beacon of hope.

We moved like a flock, united and unwavering, but the forest had become thick once again. Thorny brush and rotted deadfall blocked our path. Some were cleared with ease while others we fought to scale, but regardless of our pace, winter's grasp didn't slow. It devoured everything: walls of brush shattered like a hammer through glass, trees exploded against the dirt, and the ground became slick. Shards of frozen bark shot past us like spears, and demonic roars rose among the icy haze. The terrain broke away and explosions of soil shot into the sky. Demons lurched from earthy graves, but not like the ones we'd faced. They looked almost human: hair intact, warm hues to their skin, but lips as white as the witch's hair. Their eyes glowed murky yellow, focused on the prey. Us.

They ran with speed and grace the others did not have. Their human teeth retracted in their mouths, replaced by long, skinny fangs. The tops and bottoms slid together like a jigsaw puzzle, the fury in their eyes unmatched by any beast. Claws tore through trees like a dozen saws, timber falling around us. The creatures didn't need to look where they were going. The forest existed within them as much as they existed within the forest. They hunted in pairs, moving from side to side and closing in around us. They were designed to ensure nobody escaped.

"You take right, we'll take left," I shouted to Gage.

He and Soren branched off, meeting a pair of demons head-on. Tryst and I turned left, ensuring the others stayed within our line of sight. If we lost sight of them, the forest could take them.

A wall of deadfall blocked our path. Dozens of thick stumps lined on top of one another. We didn't hesitate. We rushed forward and with supernatural ability, leaped into the air. We landed short, scrambling up the last few broken logs. Soft bark broke beneath our feet and Tryst screamed, losing her grip. Spiders, ants, and beetles screeched as they scurried out of the hole. I reached out and grabbed her arm, barely hanging on to a knot in the wood. She swung below, fingers sliding off my wrist. Smears of black whirled around us, demons moving in.

"Ash!" she cried out. Her fingers slipped down my arm, weakly grasping my wrist.

I squeezed as tight as I could and gritted my teeth, pulling her up. Her feet found a foothold that aided in her ascent. My shoulders burned and ached, damaged muscles screaming as I pulled her higher. I helped push her over the top and threw myself up after. I scouted the ground below, but the demons had vanished. One moment they ran around us, edging closer, the next they were gone. With bugs devouring the wood beneath us, we didn't wait for them to return. We jumped down, earth bursting around us as we made impact with the ground, and we ran as fast as our bodies would allow. Demonic screams echoed across the way and a pool of black smoke funneled into the air, vanishing above the forest's canopy. Gage shouted an obscenity of triumph, waving the purple blade in the air. Our path twisted and turned, dropping into a valley of trees, and I lost sight of my friends.

"Dammit," I said.

When we came up the other side, two demons lunged from behind a thorn-covered hedge. A woman and a man with claws drawn back and ready to strike. Talons tore across my chest, burning as they ripped through the skin. The impact was immense, sending me flying back through a wall of brush. Thorns and branches cut into me and I tumbled out the other side. Dozens of barbs jutted from my skin, but there was no time to remove them. Black smoke spiraled above me as a demon lunged from the top of a tree. He landed on my leg, pinning me to the ground and crushing my already injured ankle. I screamed, swinging my blade in response across his face. Smoke rose from the wound and black goo dripped out. He hissed, crawling up my body and pinning my wrists to the ground. His breath was hot, reeking of sulfur and decay. Fighting against my angelic strength he dominated me with ease. The beast's fingers coiled around my wrists. I felt the bone shudder, ready to crack. If I could have called the wrath again, I would have, but I didn't have anything left. My body had far surpassed exhaustion. I tried to roll out of his grasp, but his strength was unyielding. I thought this was it. I thought my last moments would be spent inhaling the breath of a Blackwood demon, but Tryst appeared and stabbed the demon through the back and vanquished it to smoke.

"Thanks," I whispered, trying to climb to my feet. As soon as my foot touched the ground, it gave out. I could hardly walk. I used a tree as a crutch to prevent myself from falling. "I can't."

"Come on, keep fighting," she said.

The snap of jaws resonated along our paths and an unknown beast growled. The ground began to rumble, the screech of demons singing alongside it.

"Go without me," I said. "I'll be fine." I hobbled down the

path, urging her to run.

"Forget it." She wrapped my arm around her neck and gripped my side, pushing me onward. The edge of the forest was a few hundred yards away. I yearned for the black curtain that hung in the distance. It seemed a lifetime ago that I passed through it the first time.

"There it is!" I shouted. "You can make it, Tryst, please."

Her eyes were fierce. She would not be deterred. "I'm *not* leaving you."

A flood of demons rose up behind us, destroying the obstacles we'd struggled with as if they didn't exist. They leaped higher and ran faster, crashing through the thorny brush. Shadows emerged from the icy fog. A dozen beasts like werewolf giants that walked on all fours. They stalked down the path, slow and steady, unfazed by the witch's winter breath that sought to deconstruct the forest.

Gage and Soren reappeared ahead of us, almost to the edge. Tryst and I moved as fast as we could. There was no fight left in us. Escape was all we had. My chest hurt, heart hammering against my ribs and breath caught in my throat. I put more pressure on my foot than I should have and daggers shot up my leg. It gave out and all my weight fell on Tryst, both of us stumbling to the ground with less than fifty yards to go.

We crawled forward. She screamed at me to get up, pulling at my arm. Hobbling on one foot was all I could manage. It wouldn't allow for any other pressure. I cursed Blackwood's hold on us. A wound so mild should never have affected me.

She took my hand and I hopped down the path. The demons closed in. They were only a few feet away, but in front of us was clear. We could make it to the wall of darkness. The Academy stood on the other side, and we'd be safe there. Strange that I sought the safety of the Academy now. How times had changed yet again.

The demons had narrowed the gap between us but we were too close. They couldn't have us. Not now. Leaves crunched beneath their feet, the witch's breath catching all of us. It folded around the demons as we neared the curtain, frosting their skin but not slowing them down. I saw their silhouettes as the icy vapor tried to claim us. I felt the cold bite my skin. It was ice and heat at the same time. It seared the back of my neck and arms, and I screamed through gritted teeth, trying to move faster. The demons were right behind us with claws drawn. They leaped into the air, and I knew then we'd never make it.

"Go!" Tryst screamed. She moved behind me and shoved me with a force I never knew she had. My limbs flailed and my feet left the ground. I sailed between two trees, the curtain of black wrapping itself around me. The darkness swallowed me whole and spit me out the other side. The air was cool and distinct. I knew the moment I felt it that Blackwood was behind me.

I hit the ditch and rolled. Lances of pain cut through me as the barbs embedded in my skin were jammed deeper. Fire scorched my leg from ankle to knee, stealing my breath. I came to a stop, winded, unable to tell one ache from another. Gage and Soren were a dozen feet to my left, crawling on their hands and knees away from the woods. To my right. Nothing.

"Tryst?" It came out in a shaky whisper. "Tryst!" My breath quickened, pooling from my lips. I shuddered. The witch's grasp had touched me, the cold still burning along the back of my neck and seeping into my bones. "Tryst!" I screamed. The word came loud and crisp; I didn't care who heard. I forced myself up on one leg, an electric sting resonated through the other. I tried to hop back toward the forest, stumbling to my knees. "Tryst!"

"You've returned." Hendrik's voice was cool and even. I froze and dewy grass seeped into what remained of my tattered clothes. Hendrik's blue suit was pressed; his silver tie glimmered beneath the moon.

"Hendrik! Tryst is in there. You have to save her."

He shook his head, both hands clasped behind his back. "I cannot enter the woods, Mr. Lawson. You know this."

Anger boiled inside me. Seconds were minutes. Minutes were lifetimes. Each breath lingering in my chest was another moment she couldn't survive.

I tried to run but I stumbled, crying out in pain. I crawled up the incline toward the woods. The branches snapped at the edge of the forest. I expected a swarm of demons with pale skin and yellow eyes to storm out. Instead, platinum hair stained with black goo and frosted shoulders stumbled forward. Tryst.

She looked confused; violet eyes distant and lost, body sagging with each step. She smiled when she reached me and collapsed. I tried to catch her but only succeeded in lessening the fall. I fell with her and she dropped into my lap.

"It's so beautiful," she whispered, staring at the sky. Exhaustion had beaten her into submission. Black blood covered her arms, and her clothes were tattered. The bottom half of her shirt had been torn away, the smooth pale skin marred by four claw marks. The edges veiny and black, pieces of goo stuck to her skin, and a bite mark on her shoulder revealed a dozen tiny holes. Lines of blood ran every which way over her body, and she shuddered.

"Tryst," I said. She didn't respond. Bags formed beneath her eyes all at once, deepening with each moment. "She needs to feed. She has to heal." I grabbed each side of her face. "Tryst, hear me. You need to feed. Feed from me."

She shook her head.

"You have to! You'll die."

She shook her head again.

"Soren!" I screamed.

He looked exhausted. He too had claw marks across his arm. Blood covered his limbs, and his face was marred with frostbite. Any of the rejuvenation he received from the witch seemed lost.

"I…" He gasped, falling to the ground. "I have no more to give."

Hendrik crouched beside me, his hand turning her head from left to right. "Demon bite. Interesting." He traced the wound along her neck. "You're out of the woods, which means the Blackwood's hold is no longer. Let her rest and she will recover on her own."

"No, she needs energy to heal. She won't get that from rest!"

"You will all be fine. Calm your mind, Mr. Lawson. There is nothing to fear."

Tryst's eyes closed and she was out. I slapped the sides of her face and called her name, but she didn't wake. Hendrik picked up the red glass blade beside her, examining the black fluid.

I jumped as demonic roars echoed from the other side of Blackwood forest. If it could, adrenaline would've pumped through me, but there was nothing left. Hendrik assured us we were safe, but the sound was enough to send ice through my veins.

"And your task?" Hendrik looked down at me with a still face. "Were you successful?"

"We just got out. We need to get inside," I said.

Hendrik looked over his shoulder and crouched beside me. "I apologize. You're so very right."

A dozen soldiers appeared at the edge of the hill. Their

weapons were drawn, red laser sights pointed at each of us.

"What the hell is this?" I asked.

Hendrik sighed. "Relax, Mr. Lawson, and do try to keep your voice down. The officials from ATOM are still with us, and as such we must take the utmost precautions. You and your friends will be taken somewhere secure for us to complete this transaction."

"Where?" I asked, but I already knew the answer.

"The only place you'll be safe," he said. "The Tank."

CHAPTER 37

The door slammed shut. If possible, the floor felt colder and harder than I remembered. Hendrik and the guards had left us locked in the cages while they attended to other matters. Whatever that meant. Something about being locked up didn't make me feel very safe.

"Ash," Gage said. "What did I tell you?"

I didn't respond. I wasn't about to play the I-told-you-so game.

The air felt cold. I wondered if we'd already fallen within the Tank's embrace. Had the Soliloquy worn off? Part of me didn't care. I felt more exhausted than ever before. My aches had aches, my eyes burned, and there were parts of my body that they'd gone numb. I fell against the floor and let my body sag. Hendrik had been right. Being away from Blackwood, I felt my body beginning to heal. It wasn't perfect, but I thought I might be able to stand soon. All of that was for naught if we didn't get out of the Tank.

"Ash?" Soren's voice came from the cage across from me. It was too dark to see, but if his voice was any indicator, he felt as defeated as I did. "Are we going to be okay?"

I wanted to tell him yes and grant him peace of mind, but part of me wanted to be truthful and tell him no. I didn't have a clue. I had envisioned we'd walk out of Blackwood in one piece, and Hendrik would be waiting with the gates wide open. I'd hand him the vial and we'd walk through without consequence. I tried to formulate a response. Truth or lie? Was there a difference at this point or was it all a guessing game?

"No, we are far from fine." Gareth's voice cut through the shadows. It was the last thing I'd expected to hear in the Tank.

"What are you doing in here?" I asked.

"Receiving punishment, like you, *angel*." He said angel like the word alone could hurt me.

"We're not being punished. Hendrik said—"

"You really are that dumb, aren't you?" Gareth laughed, his deep voice bouncing off the concrete walls. He was in the cage with Tryst.

"Tryst? Are you in there? Are you okay?"

She didn't respond at first. I heard shuffling along the dirt and she groaned. "Yeah, I'm here."

The moment she spoke, my entire body felt at ease.

"Lovely, the succubus is awake." Gareth sighed.

"Gareth," Gage said. "What happened?"

"I did something stupid," he snapped.

"What are you talking about? What'd you do?"

Gareth snarled. "I helped four stupid guests escape into Blackwood and the officials from ATOM found out."

"What are you talking about? You didn't help us. Hendrik did," I said.

"Whatever you say, Wingless. You think I didn't see you in that garden? Hendrik's little distraction wasn't enough to save you, and you weren't fast enough either. I saw you running across the yard clear as day. I wasn't the only one either. I had to kill two guards to keep your secret, but it still wasn't enough."

"I thought Gage owned all the guards?"

"Gage doesn't own anything, his father does, and even his reach has limits. There are supernaturals out there who believe in ATOM's cause. They feel they're the answer to putting our country back on the map at any cost. I'm one of the few trying to stop that, and I was close too. If it wasn't for you, I'd have accomplished my mission."

"Here we go," Gage said.

"Shut your mouth, boy!"

"You can't talk to me like that anymore."

"I can talk to you any way I like. I built everything here for us," Gareth said. "I've been working for over a decade to bring down Hendrik and the Academy. I was this close to finishing it. The officials would come down, I'd dethrone Hendrik and take over, and we'd have control of this entire facility."

"And then I came along, huh?" Gage asked. "Father's need to get rid of distractions messed everything up for you."

"You were a scrawny, disobedient child who could do nothing right. I was a loose end he wasn't quite ready to cut. You and I both thought we could prove him wrong and regain his good graces, and we almost did. Look at what we accomplished," Gareth said. "You were a thorn in my side but you became my spear. We didn't die; we thrived, and I turned you into the typhon your father never could."

"A lot of good it did. Now look at us. If ATOM doesn't kill us, Hendrik will. We're all as good as dead."

"No," I said. "Hendrik and I had a deal.

"Don't be a fool, Ash. Not after everything we've been through. It makes you look weak," Gage said.

"You think he's lying?"

"Of course he is!" Gareth snapped. "The man only knows self-preservation. You're nothing more than an errand boy. I tried to tell Gage that but he wouldn't have it. At least if he'd listened, the two of us might have survived."

"Is that what you call what we've been doing?" Gage said. "I couldn't stay another day in this place without scratching my eyes out. If only I'd gotten word to Father."

"Your father doesn't give a piss about us. We're ants on the hill. He sent us here to die because we didn't belong in his grand scheme."

"But if he'd known I had succeeded, he would have come."

"Did you?" Gareth asked. "It doesn't matter. I tried to reach him before my capture. There was no response. I didn't expect one. He anticipated you'd die within your first month here. He was almost right. Don't waste your energy thinking he cares now."

"What about the guards?" Gage asked. "We don't have all of them, but we have enough."

"ATOM has deeper pockets than King Typhon. Any that remain cooperate with them out of fear."

"We can entice them with more," Gage suggested.

Gareth sighed. "You don't get it, do you? You still hope that one day your father might see you for what you are and come back. He's not coming back. He never was."

"Shut up."

"No! Face your truths, boy. Your father hates you! I've been more of a father to you than that man ever has. And unlike him, I risked my life for you. Now it seems I'll die for you too."

Gage had no response. I sat along the floor listening to my own breaths and running hands up and down my arms. The cold had begun.

"I thought Hendrik wanted out," I said. "That's why he sent us there."

"I did." Hendrik's voice entered the fray with a hint of humor. The strike of a match snapped and golden flame appeared in the center of the room. Hendrik lit the wick of several candles on the wall, casting a glow through the room. I covered my eyes and realized the burns on my hands had partially healed. My arm remained damaged and my ankle still throbbed, but I managed to stand on it. The Tank hadn't taken hold of my injuries yet. I was getting better. The Soliloquy must've still been working. "Now let me see what success you've brought."

"Don't do it," Gareth said.

"Silence!" Hendrik snapped. Fear rose in the Tank and devoured the room. Cold quaked along my skin, heart racing and threatening to explode. The moment lasted a few seconds, but it felt an eternity. The blue that filled Hendrik's eyes faded to their human counterpart. He sighed, adjusting a disheveled tie and withdrawing his power. "Tell me, Gareth, did you believe you'd outsmart me? I've been on to you for years, but I overlooked your behavior because of the results you earned for our guests. It garnered me respect among ATOM. But when you infiltrated my office with an outsourced bounty hunter and threatened my reputation among ATOM officials, I could stand by no longer. And for what? To protect a boy? Your weakness for the typhon almost cost me centuries worth of work!" His voice was monstrous, shaking the walls of the Tank. "You could have been a part of this with me; the right hand to a god who would devastate those who held us captive. Instead you chose loyalty to a fool, all the while pretending to be his child's father. You will die a fool's death while I revolutionize the supernatural world." Hendrik moved in a blur, standing outside my cage. He reached in, eyes locked on me. "I can feel it—the vitality of the Blackwood. Being within its vicinity helps return a portion of what I was."

He opened his hand, veins crackling with flashes of black running through them. I hadn't planned on giving it to him. I didn't know what I'd planned. All I wanted was for us to be on the other side of the gate, walking away from here, but now it seemed I wouldn't have a choice.

Darkness pressed against me stronger than the Tank alone. Hendrik suffocated my thoughts and a chill embedded itself in my bones. I felt terrified. Any thoughts of freedom vanquished themselves from my mind. He controlled me with fear. I knew I could bear it—I was strong enough—but there was something new. Something dark and enticing about his hold on me. I wasn't just afraid, I *wanted* to help him. His influence left me pining for his approval.

"Ash, don't," Tryst said.

Hendrik's terror expanded, filling the room. Everybody dropped to their knees, shaking from the intimidation he forced upon them. I took the rope necklace off. Purple liquid spun in the vial. I tried to fight him. I tried to hold onto the rope, but he compelled me further with a simple squint of his eyes. I relinquished it into his palm.

The headmaster's eyes lit up like fireworks. The whites of his eyes were gone, swallowed by blue, and his vicious embrace amplified. I fell onto my hands and knees, the muscles in my body shaking like I'd endured an intense workout. My pulse was quick, my breaths sharp. I shivered. I felt violated and controlled, like he'd been inside my mind in a way even I couldn't manage.

Hendrik held the vial inches from his face, breathing in the scent that emanated off it. He smiled more widely than I'd ever seen, his eyes blazing with joy. "Centuries of planning and lifetimes of torment have led me to this." He uncorked the vial and brought it to his nose, sniffing the blood. "This moment is euphoric." He shuddered, lips trembling at the edge of the glass. His hands shook as he tilted it back. One gulp, two gulps, and the blood was gone. The vial smashed into pieces when it hit the floor. Hendrik dropped to his knees. His breathing became ragged. Shoulder blades rose and fell with violent breaths. Bones cracked and joints snapped. Wisps of shadow jumped from the walls and swirled around him. A breeze pushed through the Tank with the rotten scent of Blackwood. A circle of black swirled around him, throwing each of us to the back of our cages. I squirmed against the concrete wall as it bit into my skin. "The power of the trinity becomes me. The Genesis shall rise!" he screamed.

Lines of purple flickered around him. Hendrik groaned and dropped on all fours as another wave of magic burst through the room. Dark veins rippled beneath his aged skin, smoothing the wrinkles. His flesh tightened and grey hair thickened into a rich brown. The icy blue in his eyes deepened. The fabric seams of his suit were no match for the body growing within. They tore and fell to the ground, the buttons on his shirt popping in every direction. His body jerked upright and Hendrik's arms stretched out. Spurs of shadows slammed into him. He cried out as his body shifted and cracked, muscles growing within. All at once the room fell silent and Hendrik collapsed to the ground.

It was hard to breathe. The candles still flickered but the wind had swept the dirt floor into the air, creating a mist of black dust that took several minutes to settle. Hendrik's skin was speckled with it, his back rising and falling with steady breaths. He groaned, attempting to stand, and then laughter spilled from his lips. He pushed himself to his hands and knees, body convulsing with laughter. It worked.

He rose with ease, the creaks and groans of aged movements faded somewhere beneath the youthful man before us. His face was the same. It was the Hendrik we knew, only now the lines that creased his mouth and eyes were gone. He was youthful once more. His vibrant blue eyes shone with vitality, and his body had turned back time by three decades. He pulled his shirt closed, buttoning it with the three buttons that remained.

"And the Genesis has risen." He grinned. Even his voice sounded more youthful. "You, Mr. Lawson, are not nearly the failure your record represents." He tilted his head, each bone cracking like a row of dominoes. "I am a new man, and as such, my first order of business is to rectify my own failures."

Hendrik moved to the cage holding Tryst and Gareth. He didn't use a key. Instead, he gripped the metal door and ripped it from its hinges, tossing it to the ground. He gripped Gareth by the back of the neck and lifted him with ease, dragging him to the center of the room.

"Tell me, Gareth. Who is king now?"

Gareth couldn't speak. His eyes darted to me in a plea for help. After all I'd seen the advisor do, I thought seeing his fear would make me happy. Instead I felt helpless.

"Do not look to him. Look to me!" Hendrik screamed, forcing Gareth to meet his gaze.

"Yo—yo—you are, sir." Gareth cringed and turned away.

"And what are you?" he whispered.

"I—am—nothing."

"You're a coward," Gage said.

Hendrik's head snapped toward Gage with glowing blue eyes. I expected rage and fear to be delivered, instead he sighed. "I survive, Mr. Daniels, which is more than I can say for you and the rest of this lot. I am master in my world. You are but a mosquito I have yet to swat."

"Surviving is all you do, and barely at that," Gage retorted. "If you were so powerful, you wouldn't have needed us."

He smiled. "You have your father's arrogance," Hendrik said. "If you weren't a typhon, I might like that. Your father is king of all insects, but still nothing more than a bug. You are no better." He lowered Gareth and ordered him to stand. Influence filled the air around him and the banshee struggled to stay upright. He kept his head down, shuddering beneath Hendrik's demeanor. "I will show you what a king can do."

He pulled out the black glass blade I'd seen in his office and pointed it at Gage. Arms of black spun around the blade and shot through the cell. It swirled around the typhon and his eyes went wide with terror. He screamed, crying for help. He tried to find safety among his cell, but the anguish didn't waver. Tears filled the typhon's eyes and he pawed at the cage. His skin smoked against the metal, but he didn't flinch or pull away. Instead he stared up at nothing, begging for help. I imagined that was what I looked like at the end of my time in the Tank.

"Please, stop," Gareth whispered. He tried to move but he couldn't. Hendrik had ordered him only to stand, and it seemed he was forced to obey.

"What's that?"

"Please, sir. No more."

Hendrik grinned and sheathed the blade behind his belt. He extended his hand and the darkness amplified. Gage hit the ground, writhing against the dirt.

"Father, no!" Gage shouted. "I'm sorry." He sobbed, tears spilling from his eyes. He pawed at the earth, cowering at the air.

Hendrik's power lifted his body and threw him into the wall. Bits of concrete fell around him.

"Stop!" I screamed. "We had a deal!"

Hendrik appeared in front of me in a blink. His eyes were sapphires, beaming through me. "Not for him we didn't!" The youthful voice had been replaced with something gruff and darker.

"But you knew he was coming."

Hendrik raised a brow. "I did."

"And I did what you asked. I'm asking only for leniency. *We.* We did what you asked. If it wasn't for Gage, we never would have made it back."

The black streams that surrounded Gage lessened, fading to a light mist that drifted above. He squirmed with sadness, crying into the dirt. Hendrik studied me, tapping a finger along his chin.

"Fine." He rolled his eyes and snapped his fingers. The darkness around Gage coiled in the air and drifted into Hendrik's palm. "Happy?"

Gage didn't rise. He lay curled on his side, urine spilling out around him. Wounds we hadn't seen made bled from his chest and his body shuddered. Shadows swirled in Hendrik's palm like a snake twisting over skin. He pet it with his finger, coaxing it higher into the air while he circled Gareth. The banshee trembled, tears streaking his face. If he could, I thought he might fall to his knees. Hendrik wouldn't permit it.

"It's been so long since I had you back." Hendrik spoke to the shadow like a boy might talk to a pet. The blackness responded and swelled. "Let's show them what happens when they disobey."

Hendrik stopped in front of Gareth and stretched out his hand. The magic leaped from his palm and hammered into his chest. Gareth screamed, his legs buckling, but he did not fall. His voice curdled and the candles dimmed. Hendrik didn't let up. The darkness expanded and the scent of sulfur obscured my nostrils.

"No!" Gage cried out, lifting his head from the floor. "Please, stop!"

"Bow!" Hendrik commanded.

The power twisted around Gareth's body and he dropped to his hands and knees. Blood ran from his ears, eyes, nose, and chest. It drizzled along the floor. I screamed for Hendrik to stop but it was nothing over Gareth's pain. He squirmed and a few moments later fell still. Silence. Hendrik kicked him onto his back and the darkness peeled itself out of his chest, leaving a gaping hole in the banshee's body. It slithered into the air with a white orb dangling behind it. Hendrik smiled as it fell into his palm, the obscure power dissipating around it.

"For your betrayal, it costs you one soul," he said, bringing the orb to his mouth.

Gage was helpless on his knees, staring at the body outside his cell. "No, don't take him."

"He is mine to take!" Hendrik snapped. He rolled the orb across his fingers. "For his betrayal, I devour his soul, thus rejecting his chance to pass to the other side. He will live forever inside me, adding to my gain, but never knowing peace." He brought Gareth's soul to his lips and sucked it down in a single breath. With eyes closed he shuddered. "Oh, it has been too long."

Black lines filled Gareth's veins and the color drained from his body. From the center of his chest outward, he turned to an ash replica.

"That's horrible," Tryst whispered. She covered her mouth. I don't think she had meant to say it out loud.

"Is it?" Hendrik raised a brow. "Your kind devours life force just the same."

"No, it's not the same," she said. "We don't steal people's souls."

"Apples and oranges." He smiled. "You see, disrespect is one thing, but betrayal is another. Betrayal is a loose end that never gets cleaned up. You of all people, Ms. Rivera, know that loose ends have a way of coming back to haunt us. After all, it was your own loose end that resulted in the death of both your and Soren's parents, wasn't it?"

Tryst's face paled. Soren had spent most of his time in the cell with his head buried in his knees. At the mention of his parents, he unfurled.

"What do you mean?" Soren asked.

"Don't," she whispered, eyes begging Hendrik not to go on. "Please."

"Oh my." Hendrik coyly covered his mouth. "You mean he doesn't know?"

"I said shut up!" she screamed, charging out of open door toward Hendrik. A shadow spilled from his hand and Tryst flew back into the cell, liquid darkness pinning her to the wall.

"Don't be shy, Ms. Rivera. This is a safe zone. Tell him."

Tryst stared at Soren, tears streaking down her face. She shook her head. "I'm sorry."

"Tell dear Soren how your hunger killed them. How an ATOM guard found you hovered over a dead body, crying at all you'd done. Tell him the fear you felt as you sucked the life from the guard that discovered your secret. Tell him how badly you wanted to devour every piece of his life, and how you pulled back at the last moment to let him live. Tell Soren how the guard later returned with an army to slaughter your families while you two fled."

The black restraints dissolved and Tryst fell to the ground. "It was an accident! I didn't know how to control it. I didn't mean—" Sobs caught her throat.

Hendrik broke the latch on Soren's cage and the door screeched open. "She's bearing her heart to you, Soren. Don't you have anything to say?"

Soren looked up in fear and crawled back to the corner. "It isn't true. Tryst?"

She couldn't respond. She was in a mess of tears and heartbreak.

"Loose ends, Ms. Rivera. Tell me again how horrible I am." Hendrik sighed. "Don't feel too bad. We all have our secrets. Ash less so. Since his arrival he's been rather forward with his deceptions: taking money from innocent people and offering them freedom, childhood murders, and let's not forget how he threw your lives in jeopardy for a pair of new shiny wings." He winked at me and grinned. "But Soren has a secret of his own, don't you, Mr. Kye?"

"I—" Soren cut himself off.

"Oh, don't spoil it!" Hendrik snapped. "Secrets are everywhere. They fuel our society. Don't they? Tell me, Tryst, have you fed since you spared the life of that guard?"

Tryst looked up at him with contempt and sorrow. "No."

"No, not once? Are you sure?"

"Of course I am!"

"Mr. Kye, can you confirm this truth? Has Ms. Rivera indeed been *clean* so to speak?" Soren's sadness flashed to fear. "No, you can't. You see, Tryst, while you think you're feeding like a deva and letting nature soothe your soul, Mr. Kye is sneaking you bits of life force in your sleep."

The last of Tryst's tears fell and she looked across the Tank. "What?"

Hendrik laughed. "How could you believe that a succubus could survive off the land? It's an unnatural thing. You were born to feast on souls—like me—yet you're riddled with guilt because of the nutrients you must consume. It's pitiful. You're weak with *humanity*."

Watching the exchange sent a storm of emotions through me. Anger rose up and I clenched my fists, hitting the cage door that contained me. The metal stung my hands but I succeeded in drawing his attention.

"So that's it?" I asked. "You're free from all things human?"

"Exactly, Mr. Lawson. It's how I survive the Tank."

"And Trace? How did he survive it?"

Hendrik frowned. "Trace was...different. At peace in a way that most weren't. For most, the Tank's key lies in their ability to accept themselves fully. Human emotion is weakness," he said.

"And you think that makes you better than us? You've been cooped up from the rest of the world for far too long."

"I agree!" He grinned. "With the cooped-up part, at least. You three each strong creatures in your own right, but the humanity inside you prevents you from reaching your full potential. It's a shame. I could have had use for a man like you by my side, Ash."

"Could have?"

"Yes, *could* have. To think otherwise is...well, I think the human term is naïve. You can't possibly think after all this I can let you go."

"Of course you can. Blood from the Blackwood in exchange for our freedom. That was the agreement."

"Indeed, but it seems you've missed the point I've been leading up to—loose ends, Mr. Lawson. You, Ms. Rivera, Mr. Kye, and Mr. Daniels are potential future problems for me. It is important that nobody knows what has happened here. Which—since you're a little slow—means your freedom and wings will not be had."

"What problem? All we want is to be left alone," I said.

Hendrik walked toward me, breaking the statuesque remains of Gareth as he stepped through them. He stopped outside the cage, dragging his fingers across the bars. "I have not sacrificed centuries to let it go to waste. I will not follow Ms. Rivera's example and have any of your mistakes come back to haunt me. I appreciate you, Ash, and all that you've done for me, but it's time for our adventure together to come to an end. Now the big decision; where do I start?"

"You're a weak, traitorous fool," Gage said.

Hendrik shrugged without looking at me, his eyes wandering from cell to cell. "I am a survivor, Mr. Daniels. That is why I will walk out of here and you will not. We'll start with the typhon." He walked toward Gage's cage, wrapping his hand around the cell.

My mind raced, and I smashed into the cage in an attempt to break through. The metal burned but rage whitewashed the pain. I shouted and cursed at Hendrik while the hinges squealed, but they wouldn't break.

"Speaking of loose ends," Soren said. "Tell me, *Enoch*, what about the witches?" Hendrik's body went still. "You're the one that turned the Genesis against them, aren't you? Never mind, I'm sure you're not worried. Now that they're free, I'm certain they'll be forgiving."

Hendrik licked his lips and turned to Soren. One of his eyes twitched, icy gaze studying the deva, no doubt searching for truth among lies. I applauded Soren's quick thinking. I wished I'd thought of it earlier. If I had, Gareth might still be alive.

"The witches are trapped, Mr. Kye. Buried in the Blackwood with the curse we placed upon them."

"But what if I set them free?"

"You couldn't."

"Couldn't, or weren't supposed to?" Soren quizzed. "You can feel Blackwood. Surely if there were another vial in this room, you'd know?"

Hendrik turned in a circle, sniffing at the air. "Lies. It's my own power that vibrates around me."

"Are you sure?" I asked. Hendrik's eyes darted between Soren and me. He looked panicked.

"Or is it the second vial we took that released the witches?" Soren asked.

Hendrik smashed through the metal gate and drew the black blade. Blood seeped from Soren's throat as he pressed it into the skin.

"Lies!"

"Maybe." Soren squirmed. "Maybe it wasn't the second vial at all. Maybe it took the magic of nature to awaken them." Green and purple light flickered around his fingertips.

"You didn't!" Hendrik whispered.

"He did," Gage said, raising the vial of blood he'd stolen.

Hendrik licked his lips, eyes flickering with excitement. Frost formed on the outer edges of the walls, seeping inward from the bricks. The air cooled, ice spreading across the ground. My heart raced, this was not the time for the Tank to take over.

"Release me," Soren said, but it wasn't entirely his own voice. It seemed airy and soft, almost methodical. "Now." Ice formed around his body, outlining him against the wall. Hendrik looked suddenly surprised and backed away. The wound on Soren's neck sealed shut, the only evidence of an injury the blood that stained his skin. He pushed off the wall, skin smoking and the edges of his bare shoulders covered in ice.

"No…" Hendrik stumbled back. "Guards!" Hendrik called. Light shone from the stairwell and a trio of armed guards shuffled down the stairs with weapons drawn. "Shoot them. Kill them all!" Hendrik shouted.

The guards lifted their rifles and adjusted their sights, pulling the triggers without hesitation. No response. Ice scattered across the metal, spiraling along the barrels and devouring them. The weapons shattered into icy shards, and the guards fled. Ice crept further over the room. This power wasn't the Tank at all.

Soren stalked forward, eyes glowing white. Hendrik stumbled back, mumbling to himself and crawling away from the deva. Ice ate away at the walls, spreading along the metal of each cage. As Soren's hands moved, the ice followed. White frost crisped over the metal, shattering the hinges on the remaining cells.

"She's angry with you, Enoch," Soren said, strange magic riding the air around him in wisps of green and purple. "You lost what was once yours and now you've taken that which does not belong to you. You betrayed the oath of your kin, but more so, you betrayed the curse you placed over your masters. Masters that have suffered eternity at your hand."

Hendrik scampered to his feet. "Even if they're free from the curse, they're still bound within the confines of the forest." He sounded confident, but still he backed away. "We were not so foolish as to rely on a single spell. Loose ends and all."

"They are trapped, and although her sisters are still in slumber, she is awake. But she watches you. The white witch watches from the blanket of darkness that binds her," Soren informed. "I, however, am one with the forest, and I am not bound by nature's curse." Soren's body moved in a strange manner, as if it wasn't his. The movements were fluid and smooth, a level of grace in each step he didn't normally carry. "We may have broken the chains, but it was I who warmed her soul. Here I am, Hendrik, with our lady's force guiding me." His wrist snapped and Hendrik's body was thrown across the room. He hit the wall and collapsed to the ground.

"Soren, don't do this," Hendrik pleaded. "We can make an arrangement. One that works for both of us. You're bespelled. I can fix you." The darkness swirled into his palm, but Soren snapped his fingers and ice formed around it. Hendrik pulled away and it shattered on the ground.

"Your abilities are nothing to my lady's. You fear it, but you mustn't. She believes you can be rehabilitated."

Hendrik looked confused. "She won't kill me?"

"No," Soren whispered. "Death is not a gift you shall collect by her hand. You will suffer as your masters have suffered and beg nature herself to do it." White breath spilled from Soren's lips and a sheet of ice formed beneath Hendrik. His legs slipped out from under him and his knees hit with a crunch. The ice cracked and the headmaster cowered as it crept up over his legs. "The cycle must be complete. Only then will nature see the correction in balance and lift the curse that binds my lady. Only then can she know peace."

Cold wind shot through the room and cut against my skin. Frost crackled along the ceiling and like a thousand spiders scurried down along the walls. Webs of ice spread from every direction, covering Hendrik. Green and purple streams twisted around him and he cowered beneath it. Soren shook, arms trembling from the immense power. Ice crisped over his hands and up his arms. He cringed, muffling a whimper. His skin bruised, blackness forming beneath the ice. He wasn't strong enough to contain it. It was the wrath all over again.

Hendrik witnessed the hesitation in Soren's power. He took the opening to break free of the icy prison and shards of ice shot around the room. Shadows swirled around the headmaster and he cut the black blade across Soren's leg. The deva stumbled back and Hendrik's fist cracked against his chest. The ice covering Soren collapsed and a blast of darkness burst between them. Soren's body folded at the force and he crumpled against the wall.

"Soren!" Tryst ran toward him, but he was unconscious. Flakes of ice clung to his fingers, his arms marred in frostbite.

"Enough of this!" Hendrik's voice filled the room. Fear flooded us, intimidation infused the air. "I will not be commanded by such weakness!" His voice became thunder, shaking the room and piercing my ears. "I am a Genesis. I am slave to nothing!"

Tendrils of despair distorted around him. His front teeth retracted and a pair of long, narrow fangs ejected from his gums. Drops of green venom clung to the tips, waiting to be injected into their prey. His shadow grew behind him, massive wings spreading across the wall. They were unseen by the eye, held only by darkness, but as they flapped, sulfuric wind stung my face. His fingers became talons, black and sharp as the grizzly's paw. He swung them against the cell, cutting through the bars as sparks shot around him.

"The witch may be free of the Genesis' spell, but the curse of Blackwood remains, and as long as we live, so shall it!" He laughed. "Even through possession she fails to destroy me. Fools. You think you've unleashed an ancient force to rival me? Nature herself bound the witches because she could not contain the rise of the Genesis. Her power evades us." His tongue slipped out between his lips, forked like a snake. His eyes were swallowed by an icy blue, white slit pupils flickering to each of us. Genesis, a chimera created by the hands of the witches of Blackwood, and built to destroy any who oppose it.

Hendrik stalked across the Tank, kicking Tryst away and exposing Soren's unconscious body. Hendrik's terror filled the room, rivaling what the witch had displayed. Instead of ice, fear swept over us.

"I had thought only to kill you," he said. "Now, I'll devour your souls and force you to live eternally within my darkness! You shall never know peace."

The wrath sparked inside me, but I hadn't had the time to recharge. It filled me with angelic strength. I wasn't sure I had enough energy to release it, but I wouldn't stand idle. The power combated my fear, encouraging trembling legs to stand. I gripped it tight and let it fill me with warmth. I would protect my friends at any cost.

I hit Hendrik in the back as hard as I could manage, pinning him against the wall and releasing the wrath. It sizzled through my body, jumping from limb to limb, but I didn't have it in me to release. The power faded to nothing more but a hum beneath the surface.

Hendrik's elbow flew back into my face. The force was more intense than anything I'd felt. I skidded across the floor and crashed into a cowering Gage, who did little more than whimper in the wake of Hendrik's presence. He held the vial of blood in his hand, and I pulled it away as Hendrik's power flourished.

"I will consume your soul, and you will experience your nightmares for eternity."

Fear bit and clawed its way through me as his power rose. Faces from my past reemerged. The dirt floor became black water splashing around me. Screams wailed in the distance. Waterlogged corpses clawed at my flesh, fingernails tearing at my skin. Tara's voice rippled through the night, screaming for her daughter. Samantha and Jasper floated past me. They held hands, and Jasper clutched Braven Guardlink to his chest.

"Why?" he asked. "Why did you kill us?"

"Jasper, I'm sorry," I pleaded. "I didn't mean—"

"Murderer!" Samantha screamed.

Frustration welled up inside me, anger rising in my chest. I pushed the wet corpses away from me. "No!" I yelled back. "That's not true." A wave crashed over us and their bodies vanished. I was alone in a sea of darkness. There was no sound. No bodies. Only me. "It wasn't my fault," I whispered.

"Damn right!" Harry's voice echoed through my mind. I turned to find him floating behind me, treading water beside his wife's still body. "When you think you can't push any more, you give it a little extra sauce for me, you hear?"

I nodded. "I will."

His face flushed and his brow furrowed. "Not like that. Say it like a man!" he demanded.

"I will!" I screamed.

"That's it, young fella." He wrapped his arms around Dorothy and kissed her forehead. They both drifted beneath the surface of the water.

Another wave rose and crashed over me. Saltwater filled my lungs and I gagged, churning in the water. My body spun beneath the surface and then I hit something hard. The ocean vanished.

I found myself on the dirt floor of the Tank, wet and shaking. Hendrik approached the cell, shadows dancing around him. The wrath was gone, but I didn't need it. I climbed to my feet and uncorked the vial. Hendrik stopped.

"Such power would kill you," he said.

"Then you wouldn't mind me drinking it." I tilted it with trembling hands. My hair dripped and I smelled like saltwater, but Harry's voice still ran through my mind. Hendrik was an imposing force. Even after telling myself I wasn't afraid his power still infiltrated my body. I felt scared. Scared of him, scared of the blood, scared of death. But I didn't have room for fear. Not anymore.

"You don't know what you're holding. Give it to me!"

"I'm holding restoration and a chance at freedom. Everything you promised and failed to deliver."

He shook his head, stepping closer. "You know I couldn't risk being sought out. I've spent too long under their command. Freedom is at my fingertips. Imagine what you feel and amplify that. What would you do? I wanted what had been taken from me."

"And we gave it to you! All we wanted was what you promised us in return."

"Take it. Take your freedom and your lives, but give me the blood."

"I tried that already; it didn't work out. You know, loose ends and all that," I repeated.

I put the bottle to my lips and Hendrik rushed forward. Gage jumped between us, hands emblazoned in fire and rock. He punched Hendrik in the face, the Genesis' head snapping to the side and smashing against the cell wall. He bounced back fluidly and Gage dove behind him, pulling the blade from Hendrik's sheath and burying it in his back.

Hendrik stumbled forward and I backed away, pulling the vial back from my mouth. The dagger jutted from his back, dark goo oozing from the wound. Hendrik's shoulders popped as his body distorted, reaching back and pulling the weapon out and tossing it to the ground.

"Fools."

He lunged at Gage, claws tearing into the typhon. I corked the vial and dove for the blade. Gage and Hendrik rolled over one another, black and red streams crackling out from between them.

Hendrik ended up on top, smashing his elbow into Gage's face. Tendrils slithered out from Hendriks fingers and gripped the typhon's throat. He gagged, pawing at the power as it tightened.

Blood had soaked into Hendrik's dress shirt, his brown hair no longer perfectly placed but erratic. Black veins crackled around his eyes. He licked a drop of venom from his fangs, his eyes swirling like a whirlpool. His power fluxed with each breath, fear rising and falling like the tide. Gage trembled beneath.

"Enough!" I shouted.

Hendrik's head tilted around slowly, eyeing me. I held the blade in one hand and the vial in the other. He lunged for the blood and I hit him with the dagger, a thick slice opening across his chest. Blackness ran out like liquid shadows, but he didn't falter. He hissed, a deep rumble reverberating from this throat.

"I am a god compared to your filth." Hendrik snarled, baring his fangs. "I seek to save supernatural-kind yet you seek to destroy me."

I dodged each of his strikes and parried, cutting him again and again. His skin split like a peapod, but he didn't hesitate. Shadows filled his palms and magic pinned me to the wall.

"I will devour your soul and siphon away your wrath," he shouted. "I will take the Blackwood blood from your ashen hands and crush your remains."

He pressed his palm against my chest and I screamed. Arms of smoke drilled into me. It tore through my skin and pressure threatened to crack my ribs. It swam inside me like a foreign entity, infecting my torso. Dots swarmed like a hive of angry wasps, biting and stinging at my body. The room went in and out of focus. I screamed, struggling against the malevolent power binding me to the wall, but it wouldn't break. Flashes of darkness came, each lasting a few moments longer than the last. Sulfur stung my nostrils; my head swelled as my body went numb. A blaze of white seared my eyes. Black again. Something hit my face. I couldn't tell if it hurt. A blink of violet filled my vision, warming me with a glimmer of hope, but then nothing.

CHAPTER 38

Gravity pulled me to the earth. My body bounced and movement ceased. I felt numb, breathing in dirt and exhaling sulfur and bile. Darkness clung in my eyes, pulses of foreign energy splitting through my skull. Eternity passed.

My eyes fluttered open; the room was a blur. Voices. Screaming. The numbness faded and my heart thudded with failed aggression. Each breath stung like I inhaled needles. Magic lingered in the room. It wasn't dark nor light, but there was something familiar about it. My fingers moved and flakes of dirt clung to my skin. The cold floor seeped through me, ice soaking into my bones. I groaned as reality returned with vengeance. My body revolted when I tried to push myself up. A blast of white flashed in the room. Voices screamed and the room came into focus.

Gage was hardly conscious. Red lines burned into his neck from where Hendrik's dark grip had held him. Blood streaked his face, bruises and cuts marring his body. Soren was awake, crawling toward Tryst. He looked defeated and broken, but a survivor of war. His face was stained with blood, his lips split, screaming Tryst's name, and yelling for her to stop. It was too late.

Tryst lay over Hendrik's body. Her eyes had been consumed by violet. Her shoulders rose and fell with intensity, the pale skin that covered her face whiter than ever. The claw marks on her stomach were gone, as was the bite on her shoulder. Hendrik lay lifeless beneath her. His icy gaze had greyed, the color of his skin shifting to match. A drift of life force lingered from his lips to hers. It was white and black twisted together. She devoured it in a single breath and fell back.

"The cost of freedom," she whispered.

Her violet eyes were wide and afraid. She looked both terrified and ravenous. Her eyes darted to each of us.

"Tryst?" I asked. My voice echoed as if I lived in a haze. Icy hot waves washed over me. I found the wound in my chest, blood running down my body.

She stared at Hendrik's body and screamed, covering her mouth and scurrying back. When she hit the wall and couldn't move anymore, she climbed to her feet and ran for the stairs.

In an attempt to stand, I stumbled forward. Soren and Gage caught me. My legs were weak, flickers of pain moving outward from my chest and spreading through my body. The wound was the size of a quarter, black goo crusted the edges. I touched it, but I couldn't feel the pain I expected. A wash of black fell over me and the room came back. I felt dizzy.

"We need to go," Soren said. "Before the Tank's power returns."

Gage agreed, each of them wrapping one of my arms around their necks and dragging me forward.

"Tryst," I whispered.

"She's outside, Flapper. She'll be fine. Give her a few minutes. She just saved all of our asses."

The door creaked open and morning seared my eyes. I cringed as its warmth beat down over us. It took a moment for my eyes to adjust, and when they opened I saw a blue sky. Thick clouds bubbled overhead, and I drew in a massive breath, regardless of the discomfort it caused.

"What the hell?" Gage said.

He and Soren let go and I fell to the ground. The sun beat down, pouring over me the energy I craved. I ignored the curses that spilled from Gage's mouth, and the cries of disbelief from Soren. I needed this. I let the sun warm me to my core, revitalizing me enough to at least lift my head. Once I could, I saw the horror.

Bodies littered the yard and the grass had been painted red. Ashen corpses and bodies dressed in fine suits had been decimated. There were no guests, no guards, only death.

The fountain in front of the Academy had been reduced to

rubble, water spilling out over the cobblestones. It merged with the splatter of blood and a river of red seeped down the path to the entrance. The copper-, silver-, and iron-laced gate that once held us captive had been destroyed. The stones glyphs that retained power over us shattered. Windows throughout the Academy had been broken, and the stone pillars that held up the awning were all but crumbled.

"What the hell happened?" I asked.

"Your girlfriend happened," Gage replied.

I glanced up at him, expecting a sarcastic expression. It seemed his thing to do in a situation like this. But his face was serious.

"Tryst?" I asked. "Soren, is that even possible?"

He stood wide-eyed in shock, shaking his head. "After she feeds things can get a little dicey. She's unbelievably strong and erratic, but she isn't capable of something like this."

Gage scoffed. "Maybe not normally, but she just devoured every bit of life Hendrik had in him. He's a Genesis, the first supernatural, and he was just restored to his original power. There's no saying what kind of rush she'd get from a life force like that."

I hoped Soren would have an argument for that, but he nodded his head absently. "You're right."

I stumbled forward, checking the pulse of the few bodies I could find. Nothing, but they hadn't turned to stone because they were human. ATOM officials? I called out, not sure if I could expect a reply, but there was no response.

We wandered into the Academy, it had been decimated. The polished wood was cracked and broken, the chandelier had fallen and broken to pieces, and blood laced the walls. Ash littered the entire floor like a heavy winter snowfall. We found a change of clothes in the bedrooms and food to take, but there were no signs of life.

"Tryst!" I called out from the Academy steps. Nothing. "Where the hell is she?"

"Do you hear that?" Soren asked.

Gage and I both strained to listen but shook our heads. There was nothing. Soren ran around the side of the building.

"There!" He pointed.

We still didn't hear anything, but after a few minutes we saw it. A black dot on the horizon, a helicopter coming toward us.

"We should run," Soren said. "It has to be ATOM."

"No," Gage replied. "You see that red-and-brown emblem on the side? That's not ATOM. That's typhon. It's my father."

In a few minutes the helicopter was upon us and the closer it came, the more surprised I was at the size. As it lowered, wind cut across the grounds, grass waving in forceful winds, whirling a hundred ashen corpses into the air. A brown-and-red emblem was painted over the front and side of the chopper. The typhon family crest.

"You can come with us," I said.

"Thanks, Flapper. But it's not that time. Not yet." Gage offered me a genuine smile. "Here, take this."

I curled my fingers and found the vial of Blackwood blood. "No. We had a deal and I never held up my end," I said. "Now's my chance." I tried to hand it back but he pushed me away.

"No, it could give you your wings back. You deserve it."

"Or turn me into a monster."

"That too, but my father is monster enough already," Gage replied. The helicopter door slid open and armed guards jumped out. "That's my cue. Good luck, Flapper. Go find your friend." Gage ran toward the helicopter and the guards helped him inside. Once secured, the machine rose into the air. I hung the vial back around my neck.

"Now what?" Soren asked.

"We find Tryst."

"And how do you suggest we do that?"

"Easy," I said, walking along the stained cobblestone path toward the gate. "We follow the bodies."

To Samantha, the little girl whose blue-green eyes changed in the sunlight, I'm sorry. To Jasper, the boy with the hand-carved spaceship piloted by Braven Guardlink, sent here from another world to save his family and destroy ATOM, I'm sorry. To Harry, Dorothy, and every other soul claimed by the ocean of ice and fire, I'm sorry. When I close my eyes I hear your pleas. You ask me why. I do not know. Your screams ripple through my darkness. Your lives and pain forever haunt me and any solace I might seek. I thought myself a beacon leading you to safety. I realized too late that I was the reaper's scythe.

The End

ABOUT THE AUTHOR

M.R. Merrick is a Canadian writer and author of The Protector Series, and The Rise of Genesis. Having never traveled, he adventures to far off lands through his imagination and in between cups of coffee. As a music lover and proud breakfast enthusiast, he's usually found at the computer between a pair of headphones and a large bowl of cereal.